Mountain
Of
Fear

Cynthia Hickey

DEDICATION

Thank you God for the idea and
creativity to write.

PROLOGUE

The sound of the hammer
echoed over the small Ozark
mountain. He struck the nail
once, twice, three times,
securing the paper to the
doorframe of the new camp store.
He stood back and read the
printed words.

WARNING
By order of the Righteous
Survivalist Group,
under Command of General Duane
Watkins,
any trespassers on this mountain
will be shot.
This land is being reclaimed by
its rightful owner.

The breeze whistled through
the trees, ruffling the paper's
edges. The wind teased it some
more—pulled it free and let it
drift to the ground. The young
man bent to grab it when the

wind snatched it from beneath his fingers.

He watched it skitter away. The wind gently lifted the warning, let it dance upon the dirt-packed surface in front of the store, then carried the paper, wafting and twirling, into the forest.

Taking a few steps to retrieve the paper, he changed his mind. He looked out over the campground. The lake shone black and smooth in the falling dusk. Fire pits were clean, swings hung silent. The windows of the store were freshly cleaned and invisible.

He whirled in the opposite direction. He'd done what he'd been sent to do. It wasn't his fault the freak breeze had sprung up. The boy looked again for the paper. The scrap of white shone from the top of an evergreen tree. He shrugged. It'd blow down tomorrow.

After walking several miles, he entered a campsite. Ten men huddled in silence around the dying embers of a fire. Several of them, clothed in camouflage, sat assembling automatic weapons. The rest cleaned an assortment of rifles and handguns. One man drew a knife across a whetstone, the sound rasping in the still air.

One man sat alone, head bowed with no weapon at his feet. The weight of the world appeared to be on his massive shoulders. "Is it done?"

"It's done." The young man swallowed past the lump in his throat.

Without looking up, the man said, "Go on home, boy. Your work here is done."

"But, I want to stay."

The man's head jerked up. His eyes hard. "Do what you're told. Your granny is waiting."

The young man released his breath with a huff and turned, walking away. "Still don't know why I can't stay."

"Cause I'm the boss here, and I said for you to go." The big man stood. "It ain't safe for you here. I don't want you messed up in this."

"Too late for that." The boy muttered other words under his breath and stomped to a waiting trunk.

The words "Find me a hostage," drifted to him on the early afternoon breeze and his eyes shifted to where the big man barked orders to a smaller man wearing fatigues.

1

"Well, that's it then."

Rachel Kent stood back and shut the door on the rented U-Haul, closing the door on the last fifteen years of her life.

All that was left of her material possessions she'd packed into the U-haul with the panoramic picture of the Grand Canyon painted on its side. Her two whining offspring sat in the cab of the truck, their Cairn Terrier between them.

She rested her forehead against the closed door of the trailer. The coolness of the metal soothed her aching head. A lone tear escaped Rachel's eyes and trailed down her cheek. Sniffing, she rubbed her hand roughly across her face before the other tears welling in her eyes, could follow their leader.

Squaring her shoulders, not looking back, she strode to the driver's side of the truck. Yanking the door open, she climbed into the front seat. Her daughter, Melanie, fifteen going on twenty-one, sat staring straight ahead, her long, blue-striped hair hanging flat down her back. Rachel cringed, noticing the faded jeans Mel wore were ripped at the knees. The cropped tee shirt wasn't much better. Once a bright, fluorescent pink, it had faded to a dull orange-pink. It was a direct contrast to the stripes in her hair.

Rachel's twelve-year-old son, Dustin, bobbed his head to the music on his headset. He jerked his chin up, acknowledging his mother's presence, and continued to pet the small wheat-colored dog lying beside him. The dog raised its head to greet Rachel, then rested on the young master's knee.

"Tell me again *why* we're doing this," her daughter demanded before Rachel had taken her seat.

"Mel, we've gone over this until I'm sick to death of talking about it." Rachel slammed the heavy door, turned the key in the ignition, and started the truck. "I can't find any work here. Not something that will pay the bills anyway. Your father's life insurance is almost gone. We need to move. We're going to stay with my parents for a while. They're very excited about getting to spend time with you and Dusty."

"Right." Mel folded her arms across her chest.

Rachel turned her head to look at her daughter. "Melanie, please. Try to understand. I'm doing what I think is best for us. I'm not excited about leaving behind my home, either. It hasn't been easy since your father died."

"Oh, and you think it's been easy for Dusty and me" Mel stared out the passenger window.

"Don't be so dramatic. You'll make new friends. You're a very likeable person." *Except to your brother and me*. Rachel backed the truck carefully down the driveway, watching the car she towed through the rearview mirror. She frowned as she backed through one of the flower beds. "Besides, this is at least a three-day drive. It'll give us a chance to spend quality time together. I miss the time we use to spend together as a family."

"Dad died. We're not a family anymore." Mel's words hung heavy in the air of the truck cab.

Rachel opened her mouth to speak. No words issued forth and she clamped her lips closed. Ignoring the pain her daughter's words caused, she put the truck in drive. A horn blared as she merged onto the highway. Smiling an apology, Rachel met the gaze of the outraged driver and waved. She steered the truck back into her own lane.

It wasn't long before Dusty and Mel fell asleep. Rachel listened to the music of the droning tires and passing cars. Occasionally, she'd find herself drifting into the next lane, her heart stopping each time a car horn blared.

I shouldn't be doing this. You should be driving this truck, Dennis. She sniffed against the tears stinging her eyelids. *What were you thinking?*

Dusty interrupted her melancholy reminiscing. "Mom?"

She glanced over and smiled, pleased to have someone to talk to. "Yes, Sweetie? Did you have a nice nap?"

"I have to pee."

Rachel sighed. "Don't use that language, Dusty. You know I don't like it."

"Well, I do. Have to go, I mean."

"Now?"

"Of course now," Mel cut in. "He wouldn't have told you otherwise." She ran her fingers through the striped tresses, smoothing them against her head.

"Mel..." Rachel narrowed her eyes.

"Yeah, I know. Watch my mouth. Be respectful." The girl turned to stare out the window.

Rachel patted Dusty's knee. "I'll pull over at the first rest stop we come to. Will that be okay?"

Dusty replaced the headphones on his head, and nodded.

Rachel glared at her daughter, hazel

4

eyes clashing with blue. Mel rolled her eyes and turned away.

It's going to be a long trip. Rachel turned her attention back to the road. *Am I doing the right thing?*

A short time later they pulled into the parking lot of a rest stop. The towed car bounced over the curb as Rachel took the corner too sharply. "Sorry," she muttered.

Mel opened the door and climbed out before the truck came to a complete stop. She slammed the door behind her, not leaving it open for her brother to follow, and headed alone to the restroom.

Rachel pulled on the door handle and shoved the door open. "Melanie Elizabeth Kent! You almost shut your brother's fingers in the door." Rachel struggled with the clasp to her seat belt. Releasing it, she slid from the truck, wincing as her short-clad legs stuck to the vinyl seat. Mutt bounded past and Rachel grabbed his leash.

She reached over and plucked the headphones from Dusty's head. "You go first. You can hold Mutt's leash when I go."

"Sure, Mom." He flashed a quick grin and sprinted toward the restroom.

Rachel followed at a more sedate pace, allowing the dog freedom to nose around and lift his leg on every bush they passed. She glanced several times toward the restrooms. As time passed, she worried, shifting from foot to foot, and gnawed her lower lip. She breathed a sigh of relief when Dusty appeared and took the dog from her.

"Stay close." She put her hands on Dusty's shoulders and turned him to look at her. "There are a lot of strange people hanging around here. Transients stay in these places all the time. I'm always hearing things on the news. You yell loud if someone bothers you, and I'll come running."

"Okay, Mom." He flashed another of the face-splitting grins she loved so much, the ones where his eyes disappeared and his face lit up. He sprinted back to the truck, tugging on Mutt's leash.

Rachel watched him until her full bladder screamed for release. She pushed open the restroom door.

Mel stood at a cracked and dirty mirror running her fingers through her hair. She didn't acknowledge her mother. The girl withdrew a stick of eyeliner from her pocket and lined the already heavily lined lids.

Rachel peered under the three stall doors and, not seeing anyone, chose the closest to the exit door. She glanced around for toilet seat liners, grimaced when she saw the dispenser was empty, and lined the seat with toilet paper.

"You did line the seat, right, Mel?"

Her daughter's heavy sigh hung in the air between them. *Were all teenage girls this trying, or did I just get lucky? Yes, it is definitely going to be a long trip.*

"Mother?" Mel whined, her voice reverberating through the tiled room. "I'm ready to go now. What's taking you so long?"

"May I please use the restroom in peace? Since when are you so worried about me being with you?"

Mel sighed again, louder, and Rachel heard her stomp out of the restroom.

Rachel shook her head. "It all has to be on her terms." She read the names and phone numbers on the walls, frowning at some of the crude language.

Someone posted a warning about the coming Armageddon. Another scratched in a No Trespassing, Violators will be Prosecuted. Rachel squinted, trying to make out the rest of the words, but someone had scratched through them, writing Ha Ha in black marker.

She flushed the toilet with her foot and backed into the swinging stall door to push it open. Turning on the faucet, Rachel glanced into the mirror and frowned. Where had that tired-looking woman come from? Reaching up, she pushed her bangs to the side, out of her eyes. Hazel eyes shone back at her.

"Mother!" Mel's voice rang with impatience through the door.

"I'm coming, Mel." She used a paper towel to open the door, careful of the germs that might be lurking there. Wadding up the towel, she tossed it in the trashcan and let the door slam behind her. "I thought you weren't in a hurry, Mel."

"I don't want to just stand here. People are staring."

Rachel laughed and strolled past her. "It's probably the bright blue stripes in your hair, or the several pairs of earrings you're wearing. Maybe, it's the holes in your jeans."

"Okay, Mom. I get the picture."

"You could've waited in the truck if you didn't want people staring at you." She glanced toward the U-Haul. She couldn't see Dusty. Rachel whipped her head around. "Where's Dusty? He's supposed to be in the truck."

"How should I know? Am I my brother's keeper?"

"Yes. As a matter of fact, you are." Rachel scanned the playground, her heartbeat accelerating.

Several people walked dogs in the pet area. More supervised young children on the play equipment. A few men stood around trashcans smoking cigarettes. Smoked butts littered the ground around their feet. One met Rachel's gaze and winked. She frowned and continued to scan the area.

A woman stood, bent slightly, scolding

her child. The woman's shrill voice rose above the surrounding noise. An elderly couple walked a small dog, saying hello to everyone they passed.

There he was. Over by the slide. Rachel released the breath she held. She called his name and waited to make sure he'd heard her before walking back to the truck. She turned the key and switched on the air conditioner while she waited for Dusty and Mel to join her.

Leaning forward, Rachel rested her forehead on the steering wheel and waited for her racing heart to slow to normal. *Why do I worry so much*? A tap on the window startled her, and she bolted up.

The man who'd winked at her stood there, teeth stained with nicotine showing as he smiled through a scruffy beard.

Rachel took quick note of her children approaching the truck and waved to them to stay where they were. She cracked her window, just enough to speak through. Turning to the man, she asked, "Can I help you?"

"Howdy, little lady. My name's Rupert. Your boy told me y'all were going camping. Which campground? Maybe I can show you the way." He placed another cigarette between his lips and flicked open a lighter. Cigarette smoke invaded Rachel's space, tickling her nostrils.

Her heart thudded. "That's our business."

The passenger door opened and Dusty and Mel climbed in. *Don't they ever listen?* Rachel hit the automatic lock button, causing the man to laugh.

"Looks like you're headed across country."

"Maybe." Rachel locked eyes with the man's blood shot ones.

He winked again. "Bet I'll be seeing you again, real soon."

Rachel's eyes followed him as he strolled away and she raised her window. She threw the gear shift into reverse and backed out. A horn blared. Rachel yelped, slamming her foot on the brake. She glanced into the rearview mirror as another driver leaned on his horn again and sped passed them.

"Mom, be careful."

"I'll see what I can do, Mel." Her hands tightened on the wheel, knuckles turning white, as her heartbeat returned to normal. Seven o'clock that evening, she steered the truck into the parking lot of a cheap hotel close to the freeway. The garish neon sign flashed a red vacancy.

"They probably don't even have cable here. Or a pool." Mel's eyes widened like saucers.

"We don't have time for you to swim anyway." Rachel turned off the truck. "We're just staying the night."

10

"There's a Denny's restaurant across the street." Dusty unhooked his seatbelt. "You can eat whatever you want."

"I'm not a bottomless pit, you know. Like you."

"Stop fighting, please." Rachel opened her door. "Stay here while I get the key to a room."

A bell tinkled as she pushed open the glass door. The woman behind the counter barely acknowledged Rachel, not turning from the game show on her small television. She waved a hand toward a peg board, telling Rachel to go ahead and pick a room. "One bed or two?"

"One, please."

"Bottom floor or second?"

"Bottom."

"Room four, eight or ten."

Rachel glanced outside, noted the room closest to their U-Haul and took the key to number four. "Thank you." She handed the woman her credit card.

The woman nodded, temporarily diverted from her show, and slid the card through the credit machine, making a carbon copy of Rachel's card. She passed the paper and a pen across the counter.

Signing her name, Rachel carefully tore off her copy and stuffed it into the pocket of her jeans. "Thank you, again."

"Welcome." The woman switched her attention back to the television.

Mel and Dusty were still arguing when Rachel popped the trunk on the small car they towed. "Both of you stop fighting and give me a hand with these suitcases."

"Tomorrow night we're camping. Right, Mom?" Dusty took the larger suitcase from her hand.

"Day after tomorrow. I'm excited about the KOA I've chosen." Her mind drifted to the man in the baseball cap, and she shuddered. "It's new and built right by a lake. The brochure is really lovely. We'll arrive there by early afternoon. That'll give us time for a short hike." She handed the other suitcase to Mel. "I want to stick to our schedule. Grandma and Grandpa are expecting us on a certain day and I don't want to worry them."

"Mom, isn't that the man from the rest stop?" Mel stopped, looking over Rachel's shoulder.

Rachel turned, her heart in her throat. Standing at the end of the row of rooms, was the man from the rest-stop. He tipped the brim of the faded baseball cap he wore.

She ushered her children toward their room. "I'm sure it's a coincidence. There aren't many motels around here."

The glow of the man's cigarette burned brighter as he took a drag. He lifted a hand to wave and Rachel slammed the door closed. Her heart thudded painfully in her chest. *Is he following them?* She struggled to remain calm and fisted her trembling hands at her sides.

Mel stopped just inside the room. "Green and orange bedspread. Who decorates these places." She gasped, turning to Rachel. "One bed, Mother? You have got to be kidding me. I have to share a bed with you and Dusty? That's sick. If my friends ever found out I shared a bed with my brother they'd…"

"I'll sleep in the middle, Mel. I couldn't afford a room with two beds. Our money has to last until I find a job."

"This trip just gets better and better." Mel dropped the suitcase by the door and flopped across the bed. "Where's the remote?"

Dusty looked around the room. "I don't think there is one. Oh, yeah. Here it is. It's chained to the TV." He went to hand it to her, the chain stopping just short of Mel's outstretched hand.

"I give up. Let's go eat."

Rachel stopped her. "I was hoping to have sandwiches."

"Again? Please, Mom. Denny's isn't that expensive."

Rachel looked from Mel to Dusty, who smiled, hope shining in his blue eyes. She nodded. "Fine. But let's make it quick. It's getting late and I have another day of driving tomorrow."

"Do we have to walk?"

"It's across the street, Mel." Rachel grabbed her purse from the dresser.

She ushered the kids out of the room, taking care not to leave the key behind.

They were almost across the parking lot when Rachel saw the man again.

He stood in the shadows, turned in their direction

Her heart stopped. She faltered, catching her foot in a pothole.

Mel shot her a look and shook her head. "Geez, Mom. What's wrong with you?"

"Nothing." Rachel quickened her pace to catch up with Mel and Dusty. She grabbed them each by the elbow and dragged them across the street, glancing back over her shoulder. The man was gone.

They slid into a corner booth at the she diverted her attention to the menu. She scanned the salads, made her choice and waved to the waitress to let her know they were ready to order.

She rolled her eyes as Dusty and Mel ordered hamburgers and fries. What did they think a hamburger was, if not a sandwich? She shrugged. Pick your battles, her mother always told her. Problem was...Rachel allowed Mel to spur her into a lot of them.

Rachel returned their menus to the

waiting server and leaned against the back of the booth, watching the waitress walk back to the kitchen. *Didn't she know those black slacks were too tight on her? And that hair. How did anyone get it teased up that high?*

Leaning forward, Rachel propped her chin in her palm. At a nearby booth, another mother sat with three small children, one of them a squalling infant.

Mel stuck her fingers in her ears to drown out the baby's cries.

Rachel rubbed her temple, willing the dull pounding to go away. The waitress plopped their food on the table, shot them a quick smile, and spun around to wait on another customer. Rachel picked at her salad, half-way listening to the sibling squabble going on around her. At least it wasn't her two this time. They were both totally involved in their burgers.

A gust of cool air blew across their table and Rachel glanced up to see the capped man enter the restaurant. Her fork suspended in mid-air as he took a seat at a nearby table. Yellowed teeth flashed a smile in her direction.

"We're finished." She grabbed her purse and jumped up from the table.

"Mom," Mel clutched her Rachel's arm. "It's him again."

"Him who?" Dusty spun around.

Rachel grabbed her children by an arm and pushed them through the door ahead of her.

The man's laughter followed them out the door and into the street.

"I get the shower first." Mel slammed the hotel room door behind her, the force shaking the picture on the wall.

"Fine," Dusty retorted. "I pick what's on TV."

"Whatever!"

"Don't use all the hot water!" Dusty yelled back

Head pounding, Rachel rummaged in her purse for aspirin. She glanced around the room for a glass. There wasn't one. She tossed the pills in her mouth and swallowed, grimacing against the bitter taste.

How easily it seemed to be for her children to push aside the fact that the stranger in the ball cap may be following them. Rachel sat on the side of the bed. They might be in the middle of nowhere, but his showing up everywhere they went was too much of a coincidence for her to feel comfortable.

Later that night, Rachel lay squeezed between Dusty and Mel. She listened to her son's quiet snores and the low murmurs of her daughter. With tears rolling down her cheeks and dampening the pillow beneath her head, she cursed her dead husband.

*

Wesley Ward placed a plastic mug of

water into the tiny microwave and pushed the start button. Leaning against the counter, he ran both hands through his hair as he waited for the timer to buzz. He removed the mug from the microwave and stirred in two teaspoons of instant coffee. Taking the cup of hot coffee to the wooden table in the center of the room, he sat.

A manila folder lay before him. He picked it up and scanned the contents for the second time. *Ex-military, huh? Yep. This is one bad dude*. Wesley raised his head and peered out the small window into the deepening dusk. *And this is one solitary cabin. No wonder the other forest service ranger quit*. He lifted the mug by its handle, grabbed his rifle from over the fireplace, and carried them with him outside.

The clearing around the ranger cabin sprouted green with scattered wildflowers. A cottontail rabbit bounded across the ground.

The crisp mountain air felt wonderful as he breathed in a huge lung full. *How long until they discover I'm here? Will they try to ambush me or meet me head on? Will they even care?* Wesley shook his head.

A hawk soared above him, capturing his attention. He watched as the bird floated on the breeze, dipping and gliding.

Wesley propped the rifle against the door jamb and sat on the top step, continuing to watch until the hawk disappeared from sight. He ran the contents of the file through his mind. He knew Moe was on this mountain; the question was where.

He sipped the now-warm coffee. *What is the man up to?* Wesley shrugged and emptied the mug into a nearby bush. "I'll see what I can find out tomorrow." He laughed at himself talking out loud with no one to hear. "Just the way I want it."

He heard a squawk from the radio inside the cabin and pushed himself reluctantly to his feet. Wesley opened the door, stepped inside, turned, shook his head, and grabbed the rifle. "Can't leave you out here." Placing the rifle and mug on the table, he answered the radio.

"Ward here."

A man's voice came through the line. "We got nothing."

Wesley set his jaw firmly. "Nothing? At all? You don't have others working on this?"

"Nope. Just you. Doesn't warrant the man-power, but I'll see if I can get someone up there to help you."

Wesley shook his head. With his free hand, he swung the small wooden chair around and straddled it. "How can one man disappear, much less one man with a group of followers?"

"You tell me." The man's voice held a hint of humor. "That's what I'm paying you for."

Rolling his head, Wesley worked the kinks from his neck. "I'll go scouting tomorrow. The last ranger said he kept receiving threats. Somebody wanted him to leave this mountain. Pronto."

Wesley rose from the chair and paced the small room. "I'm fine alone. Don't send anyone else. It's easier for one man to remain inconspicuous. I want the element of surprise."

"Is that your final answer?"

He laughed. "Yes, Sam, that's my final answer."

"You shouldn't be alone now, Ward. You need to focus on something other than what happened."

"I am focusing on something. Moe."

Sam snorted.

"You're like an old mother hen, Sam. I've got plenty of supplies. This assignment is mild compared to what I'm used to. You know that. Man, you were there!"

"You got to work through it, Ward."

Wesley squared his shoulders. "I'm fine. I'm dealing with it."

"You're alone too much," Sam insisted.

"Yep. I like being alone. Nobody nags you. Besides, I have a partner..."

"God."

"Yes, I'm talking about God."

"Okay. Anyway, I don't nag."

Wesley laughed again and leaned his

back against the counter. "You do too nag me. You're the only one I let get away with it." He grabbed his mug from the table and refilled it. "Gotta go, man. Don't worry. I'll find Moe." *Or he'll find me*. He hung up the phone and smiling, lifted the mug to his lips.

2

Rachel glanced at the schedule she held in her hand and smiled at their punctuality. They'd arrived at the new KOA campsite on the banks of a beautiful lake. She pulled up in front of the camp office, left the truck running and hurried inside to rent their space. Within minutes she was back.

Mel and Dusty hadn't moved. *Maybe they'd been frozen permanently into postures of stupor.* She shot them a look of pure exasperation and put the truck into drive. She drove around the site, looking for their space. There it is.

Their assigned site was situated almost directly in the center of the grounds. Rachel frowned at all the campers crowding around them. Already she felt claustrophobic, and they hadn't even left the truck.

The view of the lake took her breath away. She climbed from the truck and rushed to the water's edge. It was mid-day and the sun shot diamonds across the blue glass of the water, causing her to squint against the brilliance. The last few days of worries slipped from her shoulders. "Dusty. Mel. Come look at this."

They stared at her as if she'd sprouted horns, and remained seated.

"Fine." She walked back toward the truck. "If you want to go hiking, then we need to set up camp and pack the backpacks with food for a picnic." Without moving, they continued to stare at her. "Now."

She unlocked the towed car and pulled the camping equipment from the back seat, leaving it in a pile beside the car. Rachel grabbed a broom and swept away the small rocks and leaves from their camping spot. She worked at a furious pace sending clouds of dust and debris into the air around her. She sneezed and slowed her broom's sweep.

Once she made the site as smooth as she could, Rachel dragged the tent from beside the car. Unhooking the cords, she jumped back as it unfurled. The faded tent wore many patches. Although Dusty had used it several times with his father, this was the first time Rachel had the opportunity to do so. She located the set-up instructions and perched on a camp stool to read them.

Dusty set up camp without complaint,

his headphones still in place over his ears. Mel grumbled and complained when Rachel asked for her help.

"Come on, Mel. It'll be fun. We'll stay the night here and be at Grandma's and Grandpa's the day after tomorrow."

"Why can't we just go now? I don't see why we have to waste time camping in some bug-infested campground." Mel waved her arms. "Look around, Mom. There's *people* everywhere. Strange, weird looking people." She wiggled her eyebrows. "You know how freaked out you get around strangers."

Rachel watched as Mel became more animated, waving her arms around to emphasize her point.

Dusty removed his headphones and left them hanging around his neck. He took the tent instructions from Rachel and shoved them back in the tent bag. "I know how to set up the tent, Mom." He turned to his sister. "You're the only weird looking person here."

His sister snarled.

"I don't know when there'll be another chance for something like this, Mel. Once I get a job, I won't have vacation time for at least a year. Try to be accommodating, won't you? You might actually have fun. I know *I* will." Rachel hammered a tent stake into the ground, the force of the hammer reverberating up her arm.

"I doubt it." Mel's hammer struck

another stake.

"You might surprise yourself." *Thud*. Rachel pounded in another, releasing her frustration.

"Mom?" Dusty yelled from the other side of the truck. "Can we go into the camp store and buy things for the hike? We don't have to eat the same stuff we've been eating for two days, do we?"

"We ate out last night."

"Mom!"

Rachel sighed and straightened, popping the kinks out of her back. "I believe I must have the two most ungrateful kids on the face of this planet."

"Please?"

"Fine. Get some money out of my purse and buy what you want." She turned to Mel. "Go with your brother. Be responsible, Mel. Make sure he doesn't go crazy—and don't forget to buy water. Remember, we're on a budget." Rachel tossed Mel a backpack and grabbed the other two. "Tie up the dog. He can't go into the store with you."

She shoved heavier jackets into the packs and a small first aid kit. "I must be insane."

Rachel looked around the site for anything else they should take. A definite chill lingered in the mountain air and ripples spread across the pond. She rifled through her purse, eventually shoving the entire purse into the pack. She tossed in a bag of dog bones and zipped the bag closed.

She pushed the lock button on the car door and, spotting the roadside assistance pack in the back seat, grabbed it. She decided to make sandwiches, and lifted the lid on the small ice chest. *Dusty and Mel will probably come back loaded down with junk food. I'm not in the mood to deal with headaches and upset stomachs from eating only sugar. They need to eat something of substance.*

Rachel laid out slices of bread, slapping mayonnaise on them with a plastic knife. *What is taking them so long? Dusty eats a lot. I'll make two each.* She placed slices of ham and cheese on the bread and slid the sandwiches into small Ziploc bags. *There, finished.* She tossed the baggies into her pack.

Setting the packs next to the tent, Rachel waited for her children to return.

Several people strolled by, welcoming her to the camp and passing a few minutes in idle chit chat. One elderly lady came by with three small, yapping dogs.

"This is Roy, Fred and Barney," she introduced. "We love it here. Don't we, my little dears? We're going to come back every year. The foliage is so lovely and the lake water so clear. I told myself it's just like looking into a mirror. Why, just the other…"

Rachel vaguely listened to the woman drone on. She peered over the woman's shoulder, hoping for Dusty and Mel to come rescue her.

"...so I told my dear Harold that I would just have to..." the woman didn't seem to notice Rachel's lack of involvement in the conversation.

Rachel sighed in relief when Mel and Dusty joined her and she politely excused herself from the talkative woman.

"Gee whiz, Mom." Dusty bent to pick up one of the packs. "What's in these bags? We're only taking a hike. They weigh a ton."

"Just the essentials. Things for emergencies." Rachel noticed Mel already wore the pack with what they'd purchased from the store. "What did you buy?"

"Cookies, chips, things like that." Mel hoisted the pack more securely on her back. "Let's get this over with."

Dusty grabbed Mutt's leash and smiled as his mother grunted under the weight of her pack. "Maybe I did pack a little too much for a short hike."

"You shouldn't be so paranoid." Mel frowned.

"Let's not fight. It's a beautiful day." Rachel locked the truck and car. She glanced at the tent and supplies. Dusty groaned when she asked him to leave his headphones. "Listen to the music of nature, Dusty."

She lifted her head in appreciation, taking in the singing of the birds and the whisper of the wind through the branches over their heads. A mockingbird serenaded them and she let out a laugh of joy. The stresses of life since her husband's death kept her feeling oppressed and, as she walked, Rachel could feel the burdens slide from her shoulders. She laughed again, louder, and threw back her head. She held her arms out from her sides.

"Dance with me," she sang.

Mel rolled her eyes and walked faster, putting herself in front of the line.

Rachel laughed again, slowing her walk. She looked up and admired the changing foliage of the trees. A gentle breeze blew, showering them with a rainfall of red and gold leaves. She flung her arms wide again and twirled. Several small leaves caught in her hair. "Isn't this glorious?"

"Mother, please. You're embarrassing me." Mel quickened her pace.

"In front of who?" Rachel stopped and looked around. "There's no one else here."

Dusty reached up and pulled a leaf from Rachel's hair. "Just ignore her, Mom. It's nice to hear you laugh."

Rachel gave Dusty a hug and kept her arm across his shoulders. He pulled away. "It's too heavy."

27

Small twigs and dried leaves crunched under their feet as they walked. Momentarily free of his leash, Mutt ran in, out and around their legs, threatening to trip them.

"Stop." Rachel held up her hand. "I said stop, Mel. Listen." They stopped and stood still. Far off in the distance, Rachel could hear a faint popping sound.

"What is it?" Dusty snapped the leash back on Mutt's collar.

"Hunters...maybe." Rachel turned, trying to determine from which direction the sound came from.

"No, Mom." Mel looked back down the trail. "Listen. That's not a rifle. That sounds like automatic gunfire." Instead of single pops, the sound resembled the frantic popping of popcorn.

Rachel frowned, her brows lowering. "This is government land. You can't hunt here. Besides, hunters don't use automatic weapons, do they? Dusty?"

"Dad and I never did. Illegal hunters might, I guess." He scowled. "There's no sport in that."

They stood huddled together. For several minutes, Rachel kept them there and listened to the shooting. She fully expected to be shot where they stood and drew her children closer to her. Every pop caused her to jump. Head pounding from tension and nerves frazzled, Rachel resisted the urge to scream.

"Let's go back," Rachel advised. "It's not safe for us to be hiking out here if stupid people are being reckless and target shooting."

"I don't think they would use automatic weapons," Mel scoffed. She drew away from her mother and hitched her backpack to a more comfortable position. She started back down the trail toward camp. "Sometimes you're so naïve. They're probably poachers and miles away from here."

After a short while, the popping sounds quieted and they stopped to rest. Rachel let out a sigh of relief and opened one of the water bottles, passing it around. "Anyone hungry? Sandwiches?"

"Not really." Dusty took a swig from the bottle and passed it to his sister.

"I just want a candy bar." Mel opened her pack and took out three chocolate bars, handing one to each of them.

"Is that toilet paper?" Rachel asked in surprise. She bent forward and peered into the open pack.

"Yeah. So?" Mel glared at her.

"But that's something I would do, Mel. Even I didn't think about bringing toilet paper." Rachel laughed. "You must have some of my paranoid tendencies after all."

"As if." Mel rolled her eyes and zipped the pack closed. "I'm not using leaves to wipe my behind." She stood. "Let's go."

Close to camp, Rachel stopped them again. "Listen."

"To what?" Mel asked.

"To nothing." Rachel turned to them. "Shouldn't we be hearing sounds from the campground by now?" She took a few steps closer to camp. *Where are the barking dogs and laughing children? When we left, the sounds of camp followed us into the trees.* "You two wait here."

Dusty and Mel followed her to the edge of the woods and stopped. The three of them looked across the campground. Things were scattered and debris littered the ground. Tents were collapsed, stools overturned and the smell of something burning drifted to them on the breeze.

"It looks like a strong wind blew through here," Rachel observed.

"Maybe a microburst," Dusty guessed.

"It's not the season, dummy," Mel corrected. "Besides, we would have felt something. There's barely a breeze at all. Nothing that could do this, anyway."

"Shhh!" Rachel hissed, looking at the dog. Mutt's hair bristled along his back. "Dusty, hold tight to Mutt's leash." She ventured a few more steps into the open. "You two stay here. I mean it. Something doesn't feel right."

Rachel's flesh broke into goose pimples

and her heart-rate accelerated. The images before her spun in a dizzying circle. Car doors were left open and one automobile idled in front of the camp store. The shattered front store window lay in shards, sprinkled like glitter across the sidewalk. She took a few more steps.

"Mom?" Dusty and Mel joined her.

"I told you to wait back there."

"Why are we whispering?" Mel's voice cracked. She tugged on her mother's arm. "Look. There're bodies everywhere." She pointed to the open door of the store.

Rachel looked again and gasped. Her hand rose to cover her mouth. Upon closer inspection, she noticed a jean clad leg hanging from an open car door. A woman's arm stuck out from beneath a tent. To her right, she saw the body of a child hanging over a swing, one shoe missing. The more she looked, the more bodies she saw. A man sat slumped in a camp chair, a woman huddled at his feet.

"Oh, my God." She turned. There was the woman and her three dogs. Blood pooled beneath the woman. One of the dogs feebly lifted its head and whimpered. "Get out of here! Now!"

"Mom?" Mel's voice rose even higher. "Look through the store window. It's the man from the rest stop. He has a gun, Mom. He's looking at us."

Dusty started to cry. "There's another

man by the bathroom. He has a gun, too."

Rachel whirled and her eyes met those of the man from the rest stop. His dark eyes crinkled at the corners as he smiled and he lifted his gun to take aim.

"Run!" Rachel shoved her children, causing Mel to stumble. "Back to the trees. Don't look back. No matter what happens. No matter what you hear. You keep running."

Mel regained her footing and, with Rachel still pushing against her back, turned and fled.

Voices called out behind them. Gunfire followed them into the woods. The men's laughter and crude jokes chased her and the children. A bullet slammed into a nearby tree trunk, showering her with leaves.

"Come on, lady. Let's play!" One of the men laughed and sent a volley of gunshots over her head. "We promise not to hurt you."

"Dusty! Mel!" Rachel's panic rose, threatening to choke her. Tears spilled down her cheeks. She crawled through the bushes, slapping branches away from her face. "Speak to me. Where are you?"

"I'm here." Mel stood from where she'd dived into the bushes. She bent to brush off her knees.

"I can't find Mutt." Dusty scrambled through the bushes toward Rachel.

Rachel shoved them again. She could

hear leaves crunching under the men's feet as they searched. "Keep running. As fast as you can. I'm right behind you."

"What about Mutt?"

"Don't worry about Mutt. He'll find us." Rachel whirled as she heard crashing through the underbrush. "Run!"

Instead of following the trail, Rachel veered them away from it. Tree branches whipped at their faces and tangled in their hair. Once they'd left the trail behind, Rachel fell back, keeping her children in front of her where she could see them. She kept them moving, shoving at their backs when they slowed.

When she could no longer hear sounds of pursuit, Rachel allowed them to stop. She bent over, hands balanced on her knees as she gasped for breath.

"What happened?" Mel's eyes were wide in her pale face.

Rachel shook her head. "I...don't...know." She stood and looked around. "We can't stay here. It's almost dark and those men have got to be behind us. They didn't seem to be in a hurry to catch us, though. Come on." She led them further into the woods. The trees grew thicker as they walked. The branches overhead blocked out the sunlight, casting them into near darkness.

The three stopped as they reached a bluff. A few feet below them, Rachel could make out a slight overhang.

"Dusty, can you make it down there?"

He peered through the gloom. "Sure. I've climbed worse than that before. I'll go first."

Rachel gnawed her lower lip as Dusty climbed over the top of the bluff. Occasionally, he dislodged rocks, sending them rolling down the hill. Rachel clasped her hands together. After several anxious minutes, she breathed a sigh of relief to see him safely out of sight under the overhang.

"You next, Mel. Be careful."

Mel sat on her behind and slid her way down.

"Don't slide, Mel," Dusty called up. "You're leaving a trail."

Rachel followed suit, careful to climb, rather than slide. At the bottom, she looked up trying to determine whether they had left any signs. She spotted dislodged rocks and broken branches. Nothing she deemed glaringly obvious about where they'd gone. She turned and ducked to join her children.

Dusty piled fallen twigs and constructed an effective cover for their small cave.

"You're a genius, Dusty," Rachel told him, her voice shaking. The cover, although effective at hiding them, shut out what light was left in the day and plunging them into a thick darkness.

"Cub Scouts."

"Did anyone think to bring a flashlight?" Mel peered further into the cave. "It's dark in here."

Rachel patted her backpack. "I did." She gave a shaky laugh. "I brought the emergency kit from the car. Just in case."

"Turn it on, Mom. Please. I'm really scared."

"I can't, sweetheart. What if they see the light?"

"You think they're still following us?" Mel scooted as far back in the shelter as she could.

"I'm sure of it. We're witnesses." *And that one man has followed us for over 300 miles.*

"You shouldn't have canceled the cell phone." Mel folded her arms across her chest. "We could've called the police."

"We couldn't afford it, Mel." Rachel let her pack fall to the ground. "It was an unnecessary expense. At the time, anyway."

"Don't worry, Mel." Dusty let his pack fall to join Rachel's. "We're well hidden here." He looked up as pebbles rattled over their heads. "I thought."

Rachel moved to put her arms around them and pulled them close. "Be quiet," she whispered. "Maybe they'll pass us by." She waited, scarcely breathing. The scrambling noises came closer and they heard whining.

"That's Mutt." Dusty pulled free from Rachel's arms and poked his head from the shelter. "Mutt. Here boy." The dog rocketed down the slope, launching his sturdy body into the boy's arms.

Dusty buried his face in the dog's fur. "Boy, am I glad to see you."

The sight of the dog cheered Rachel and she smiled at the pleasure on Dusty's face. Pressing back against the cave wall, she drew Dusty and Mel close to her. She put her head back, and closed her eyes. The forest sounds which had earlier brought her so much pleasure, now filled her with dread. *Which sounds are natural and which are made by those men?*

"Can we pray, Mom?" Dusty burrowed closer to her.

"You can. I don't pray, Dusty. You know that. I quit a long time ago. If it makes you feel better, go ahead. It can't hurt."

*

Wesley searched the ground around his feet for signs. *Any sign would be good, Lord.* He rose, allowing his eyes to scan the forest. He'd been walking for an hour, not finding so much as a foot print that wasn't his own. A jaybird scolded him from a nearby tree.

Wesley smiled and whistled a response. Taking the rifle he'd propped against a tree, he set off in long strides to further his search. *The previous ranger reported suspicious characters, but darn if I can find any sign of them.*

Stopping to take a swig from the canteen hanging around his neck, Wesley pulled a bandana from his jean pocket and mopped his brow.

He stopped and sat in the springy moss at the base of a tree and pulled an energy bar from his shirt pocket. He took a bite and laid his head back against the tree. Closing his eyes, he listened.

The silence was eerie, yet soothing. Very little moved in the bushes around him. Wesley opened his eyes. A spot of red against the green. He rose and walked to the low-lying bush. Reaching out, he plucked the piece of flannel from the branch. *Someone's been here. Since it rained, too. Could be hikers, and yet...*

He shoved the fabric into his pocket.

Retrieving his rifle from the ground, Wesley continued his search.

Dusk fell as he returned to his cabin. Wesley prepared another cup of his favorite brew and twisted the dial on his radio.

"Sam? Ward. I found something." The microwave buzzer timed and he reached to take the mug. "A piece of flannel." Wesley straddled the chair and sipped the hot liquid. It burned his lip and he set the mug on the table.

"A piece of flannel." Sam laughed.

"I know it's not much. Might not be anything, but it's the most I've found since I've been here. I'll widen my perimeter tomorrow." He leaned back in the chair, ignoring the wood's shrieks of protest and fingered the scrap of fabric.

His mouth opened and his eyes widened as he felt himself going over. "Whoa!"

Wesley grabbed for the radio he'd dropped.

"Fall out of your chair, buddy?" Wesley held the radio away from his ear as Sam's laughter burst through.

"Nothing...stubbed my toe..." He grinned. "Yeah, the chair fell over. I never could lie to you."

"That's right and don't start now."

"All right. I'll call the same time tomorrow."

Wesley hung up and righted the chair. He'd spilt the coffee, sloshing it on the floor. Looking at the spreading stain on the wood, he shrugged and started a fresh mug. Taking the mug with him, he headed outside in what was quickly becoming his nightly ritual.

Standing on the stoop of his log cabin, he stared into the falling dusk. He smiled and scanned the small clearing, watching a rabbit hop from sight. He hadn't known at first why he'd accepted this assignment, but now he did. It was for the solitude.

Content with only his company and those of the woodland animals, he lowered himself, groaning, until he sat on the steps. He'd twisted his back falling from the chair. Wesley chuckled. Served him right.

He leaned against the door and lifted the mug of coffee he held to his lips. *Oh, yeah. Thank you, God, for solitude.*

He sat without a sound and watched the sun fall behind the trees. He shivered in the night air, but didn't go inside. Dusk was his favorite time of day. Things slowed down and grew quieter. *Nothing better, Lord than a cup of good coffee, a beautiful view and being surrounded by Your creation.*

It bothered him that he hadn't found more signs of Moe or his men. He laid his head back against the rough wood of the cabin door. All leads pointed to this mountain. That man's group had to be here somewhere.

"We'll find him." Wesley listened to his voice fade across the clearing. "It's just a matter of time."

Birds burst from a nearby bush as he spoke, causing him to chuckle again. His eyes followed them as they disappeared over the rim of trees.

*

The hefty man called General, looked up from the papers scattered across the table in front of him, and acknowledged the man who'd entered his tent.

"General." The man saluted.

"Rupert." The General nodded, his eyes running over the overalls and faded shirt the other man wore. "Everything go as planned?"

"Well, um, not exactly, sir." Rupert's foot rasped across the floor of the tent as he dragged it back and forth.

"Explain." The General folded his hands over his ample stomach and leaned back in his chair, the wood creaking beneath his weight.

Rupert took a deep breath. "Some campers escaped."

The General's chair banged back to the ground and he slammed his massive fist on the table, scattering papers. "Are you going to tell me what happened, or do I have to drag it out of you bit by bit?"

"We went in as you said. Guns loaded. The campers didn't know what hit them. We'd just finished when this woman, a fine looking woman, General, and ..."

"I don't care what she looks like!"

"Yes, sir. And a couple of kids came upon us. They ran off into the woods. We lost them."

"Lost them?"

Rupert's eyes lowered to the floor. "Yes, sir. We followed them into the woods. Tracked them quite a ways. But, yes, we lost them."

The General rose from his chair and walked around the table to stand before Rupert. "Trained trackers like you all and you can't find a woman and a couple of kids?" His voice rose.

Rupert's voice dropped to a whisper. "No, sir."

The General stared at the man before him. "Do you think this is a game, soldier? Isn't that what you were doing? Playing at some game?" Not waiting for an answer, he paced the tent. "This is my mountain! Do you understand that? Been in my family for generations, until the government took it. Stole it right from under our noses. Right from my granddaddy." He paused and turned back to Rupert. "I served in this country's army, soldier. Gave them twenty years, and they won't give me back my land." He pounded his right fist into his left hand. "Now, I'm going to take it back. By force. I'm going to earn my title as General, soldier. The title I deserve. It's mine."

"We'll find the woman, sir. We'll find her and kill her. Just like the others." Rupert raised wide eyes to meet the General's.

"Well, wait just a minute now." The General stopped and stroked the heavy beard he wore. "A fine looking woman and two kids. Infants?"

"No, sir. Older. Teenagers, maybe."

"Bring them to me alive. Hostages

41

might be useful. I assume you can pick up their trail?"

"Yes, sir."

"What about the ranger's cabin? Anyone living there?"

Rupert shrugged. "We haven't checked."

"You haven't checked. What kind of army am I running? Are y'all a bunch of bumbling idiots?" He swiped his hand across the table, knocking the papers to the floor. "Pick those up. When you're finished, sweep this tent. You're lucky I don't whip the stupidity right out of you."

Rushing across the tent, Rupert dropped to his knees and scooped the papers into a pile. Once he'd retrieved the papers, he held the bundle out to his boss.

The General knocked them to the floor. "I don't want them! Put them back on the table where they belong." He shook his head. "I'm surrounded by fools." He turned sharply and exited the tent.

His eyes roamed the small clearing dotted with tents. Men sitting around a low burning fire looked up as he passed. The General glared at them as he stalked past, his combat boots kicking up dust and leaves. He stooped before a small tent, and pushed aside the flap.

Boxes sat piled around the edges. A

small gas powered generator clunked away beside a refrigerator. He headed toward a chest in the corner. Kneeling beside it, he opened it, pulling out cigar boxes and manila folders. Locating the box he searched for, the big man clutched it to his chest. *This is it. This is the deed that proves I'm the rightful owner of this mountain. I don't care what taxes weren't paid. This land is mine. No one has the right to take away a family's land.* He laughed. *They'll sit up and take notice now. Fools should have paid attention to the posted signs. Serves them all right. All them trespassers deserved exactly what they got.*

He was interrupted by Rupert poking his head inside the tent. "Sir, we'll pick up their trail at first light."

"You'll pick it up now. I don't care if night is falling." He placed the folder back inside the chest. "Check out that ranger cabin while you're at it." His body creaked as he rose to his feet. "Remember, I want the woman and kids alive. They'll come in handy."

3

Darkness fell with the speed of a falling curtain. Before they had time to register that night had crept up on them, they found themselves thrust into inky blackness. Rachel kept her children huddled close to her body and listened to their breathing as they slept. She smoothed back the hair from their faces and rubbed their arms. She couldn't see them, but she could reassure herself they were all right by running her hands over them. Rachel placed a hand on each of their chests, relishing each rise and fall of their breathing.

Okay, we'll get through this. Yes, we will. It's dark outside. Can't see a thing. That means they can't see anything either, right? Rachel's thoughts spun through her mind, tumbling over themselves as she sat. Her eyes strained to see through the blackness. Her head pounded in rhythm with her heart. Rachel's ears strained for the slightest sound outside.

What was that? An animal? One of the killers? God, help us! You will, won't you? Dusty believes you will. Don't let us die out here. Why don't you hear me anymore? My parents are waiting for us. They're going to be worried. Crack. *There! Surely that was an animal. Okay, I've got to stop this.* Rachel shook her head. *I'll go through our supplies in my mind. Yes, that's what I'll do. That'll keep me occupied. Sure. That's what I'll do. See what we've got. Okay. Toilet paper, flashlight, matches. Do we have matches? I'm not sure. There might be some in my purse. No—I quit smoking. Wait. I stuck a lighter in there...just in case.*

We have a flare gun. A flare gun! Could that be considered a weapon? It's a gun. She gave a small laugh. Maybe *if the guy was caught on fire first. I'm so glad I brought our warmer jackets. We've some food. Mostly junk food, and there's water. We'll be okay for a couple of days. Oh, God!* Rachel's eyes widened.

Not a couple of days, surely. *We can't stay here. I don't know my way around this mountain. What if we get lost? What if we get killed?* She bit down on her lip. *We won't get killed. I won't think that way. We'll find help somewhere, somehow. I've got to pull myself together. I have...*A sob caught in her throat. *I have to—for Dusty and Mel.*

Rachel's rambling thoughts slowed as minutes passed and she found herself drifting to sleep. She fought to keep her eyes open, but with the darkness closing in on her, giving her nothing to focus on, she gave up.

Mutt woke them the next morning, whining at the entrance to their cave. He stood, neck hairs bristling, and stared up the precipice over their heads. Rachel crawled to him and pulled the dog back inside. She clamped her hand around his muzzle, silencing him.

Turning her head, she heard Dusty and Mel rustling behind her. Squinting through the gloom, Rachel watched them crawl to her side. She put a finger to her lips.

Twigs snapped above their heads and men's voices drifted on the early morning breeze. The men discussed which direction they should go. One man laughed and another mentioned the "young" girl and the woman. One complained about someone called the general and something about having some fun.

Mel gasped and drew closer to her mother. Rachel held up her finger again and shook her head. She handed the dog to Dusty and put her arms around the shoulders of her children. Together, they sat—not moving—until the men above passed.

"Let's go, Mom," Mel whispered. "Please. I don't want to stay here." The young girl's face was streaked with dirt and makeup. The mascara and dark eye liner she'd worn the day before lay in dry lines on her cheeks. There were leaves stuck in her striped hair. Rachel thought they must all look, and feel, as if they'd been living in the rough for longer than one night. She knew she did.

Rachel reached up and touched Mel's face. "We can't go now. We've got to let them get past us. Get some distance between us and them."

She drew back into the cave. Turning to Dusty, Rachel whispered, "Son, could you hand me the backpack with the food? And a water bottle? We'll eat something. Afterwards, I'll check and see if the coast is clear, okay?"

Dusty tossed her pack. Rachel rummaged through it, finding apples.

She tossed one to Dusty.

"Is this it?" His smooth forehead wrinkled and he plopped backwards, off his knees.

"I'm afraid so. We don't know how long we'll be out here. The food and water have to last as long as possible."

"We need to make a plan." Dusty took a bite. "People always have a plan in situations like this."

"You are so stupid." Mel threw her pack at him, bouncing it off his shoulder. It landed with a dull thud. "What do you know? You're just a kid."

As Mel raised her voice, Rachel glanced at the ground above them. *Can they hear her?*

47

"I know things." Dusty rubbed his shoulder. "I watch TV."

"TV! Dusty, you're a moron." Mel wiped her apple against her thigh.

Rachel grimaced. Mel's jeans had to be dirtier than the apple.

"Mom, Mel needs to stop being so mean."

"The truth hurts, don't it?" Mel took a big bite from her apple.

Their munching sounded abnormally loud in the small cave. Rachel glanced repeatedly over their heads, doing her best to chew the crisp apple without sound.

When finished, Mel threw her core at Dusty.

"Come on, you two. Now's not the time to fight. We need to stick together." Rachel picked up her daughter's apple core. "We should probably bury these. What if those men find this place after we're gone? They'll know for sure we were here."

"Great idea, Mom." Dusty dug his hands into the moist soil. "Come on, Mutt. You can help me."

Crawling back to the cave opening and peering outside, Rachel listened. Birds chirped. Small animals rustled through the brush. Not hearing anything that appeared out of the ordinary, she crawled out further and stood just outside the entrance to the cave. Tilting her

head, she peered back up the way they'd
climbed down.

She turned and glanced down the
mountainside. They were close to the bottom of
the cliff. The rest of the way looked too steep
and unsafe for them to attempt going down.
Huge boulders jutted out of the sides of the
small mountain and visions of broken bones ran
through Rachel's mind. She shuddered. She
decided the wisest way would be to go back up.
She whispered for Dusty and Mel to stay with
the dog and remain quiet.

Rachel crawled as she climbed, using
bushes and roots to pull herself. The rocks dug
into her knees through her jeans. The higher
she climbed, the more she expected to be
spotted. Her breathing quickened. She prayed
she wouldn't hyperventilate.

Perspiration beaded on her brow and
she tensed in anticipation of a bullet with every
snap of a twig or rustle of a bush. The loud
whispers of Dusty and Mel drifted upwards and
Rachel hoped no one stood at the top of the
cliff where they could also hear.

Peering over the edge of the cliff and
not seeing anyone, Rachel breathed a sigh of
relief and pulled herself over the top, scraping
her stomach. She lay there a moment to catch
her breath. The muscles in her arms quivered
from the effort. Standing, she dusted off her
hands. With hands on her hips, she looked in

both directions.

She thought they'd wandered farther from the trail yesterday and was surprised to see they were only about fifty feet from it. They'd been running in a panic the day before, not paying attention to their surroundings.

Today, she took note of how the thick foliage blocked out most of the light from the sun and how the trail seemed to disappear at the edge of the precipice. On closer inspection she saw she stood at a scenic overlook. The trail continued a few feet further on, branching sharply away from the cliff.

She took in the view before her. A small mountain valley spread beneath them, the green of the trees startling bright. Some of them were beginning to change into their fall foliage. The view was beautiful. Rachel sighed and switched her attention back to the trail.

The forest came alive around her. Birds flitted and twittered from the branches overhead and a rabbit bounded across the trail. The wind rustled through the trees.

Okay. Animal sounds meant no one was around, didn't it? She'd heard that somewhere. Okay, it was safe. All they had to do was find the freeway and they'd be all right. They could hitchhike their way out. No...hitchhiking was dangerous. Stop it, Rachel. Do what has to be done. She stood there for a moment more before climbing back down to the cave.

Dusty and Mel launched themselves at her as soon as she entered the cave.

"Mel was worried about you, Mom." He buried his face in her shoulder. Rachel could feel the wetness of his tears soaking her shirt.

"Mel was worried, huh?" Rachel hugged him back, hard. "I have a plan. We need to get out of here and find the freeway. We'll head back the way we came. See if our car is still at the campsite. If it's not, we'll hitch a ride to the nearest police station."

"What about the killers?" Mel peeked over her shoulder. "They're still out there."

"They're ahead of us. I heard them pass."

"Yeah, but they could've doubled back." Dusty lifted his head from her shoulder. "It happens all the time in the movies."

"That's just the movies, son."

"Well—the movies are based on fact."

"No, they're not!" Mel had quit whispering. "You're just trying to scare us. Mom, make him stop."

"Mom, we can't go back to the campsite." The wide-eyed look on her son's face gave her pause.

Rachel set them both at an arm's length from her. She stared into their eyes. "All right, you two. Listen to me *very* carefully. We have got to stop this bickering. Seriously. We're leaving this cave and we will have to be quiet.

I'm going to try to lead us to the road. I'm not sure which way is safest and we'll have to guess. I've decided we're not going to follow the trail back. Dusty made a good point. I think that is what the killers would expect us to do. I'm going to need you to cooperate. If I have to listen to your fighting while trying to keep us alive, I will lose my mind. Got it? Am I making myself clear?"

They nodded.

"Good. Let's quietly gather up our things and you two follow me. I'll take Mutt's leash." Rachel took it from Dusty, hoisted up her backpack and led them out of the cave.

Outside, she again felt vulnerable. More so than when she'd climbed up alone. Three made a bigger target. At the thought of a bullet ripping through one of her children, an iron fist clenched Rachel's heart. With a deep breath, she went first, keeping the dog close to her side.

When she reached the top, she froze, looking in all directions, and listened. Hearing nothing that concerned her, she waved for Dusty and Mel to continue. Rachel waited, bouncing on the balls of her feet. She started at every twig snap or bird call. When Dusty and Mel arrived next to her, she sighed and pulled them close. They stood together, looking down the trail.

"Well," Rachel pointed. "This is the way

we came. Do we go back that way, staying off the trail and look for the road, or do we turn left and hope it comes out somewhere else by the road? Let's vote."

"You're letting us have a say?" Mel whipped her head around.

"We're all in this together." Rachel met her daughter's gaze. "I'll be honest with you, honey. I haven't a clue which way to go. There are dangers both ways."

"I say we turn left." Dusty pointed.

"Me, too. Those killers are back there." Mel tossed her head to the right.

"Are y'all sure? We don't know what's that way. We could get lost. We could go in circles."

"We're sure," they told her in unison.

Rachel nodded and turned left. The farther they got from the overlook, the darker the woods. The light was as faint as dusk and Rachel's throat tightened. She shivered as a slight breeze blew over her.

A bird flew close overhead and cawed. She stifled a scream and jumped. Rachel glanced back at her children, cheeks flaming. Dusty grinned and Mel rolled her eyes. Rachel expected a smart reply and was surprised when Mel remained silent.

They walked for half the day before Rachel felt comfortable letting them stop and rest. They shared some cookies and a water bottle. Mel seemed to take great pains in wiping off the mouth of the bottle after Dusty drank.

Mutt startled Rachel by letting out one solitary bark. Dusty grabbed the dog and clamped his hand over its muzzle.

Rachel motioned for them to move back into the security of the bushes. Over the pounding of her own heart she could hear the rapid breathing of her daughter. Rachel glanced at Mel and gave a quick shake of her head, pleading with the young girl to be silent.

They hunkered down in the bushes to wait. Dusty trembled against Rachel's side. She heard the crunching of leaves and the men talking. *Why, they don't care if we hear them. They're not worried about secrecy at all*. She stretched her neck until she could see them through the foliage.

There were three of them. One appeared to be not much more than a boy— close to Mel's age with long, shaggy blond hair. The other two appeared older than Rachel and they both sported long hair and full beards. One of the men's beard was peppered with gray. All three were dressed in camouflage fatigues and they carried automatic guns. Strapped around their waists were belts holding an assortment of items from knives to canteens.

They laughed as they walked, joking about the carnage left behind at camp. The one who'd spoken to them at the rest stop, recounted how they'd caught everyone unaware and how easy it had been to gun them all down.

Rachel was shocked at the easy manner in which they spoke of killing. She drew her brows together and pulled air sharply through her nose. Not one of the men seemed to show remorse. Not even for the murder of the children. They appeared to feel the campers deserved their grisly deaths.

Spotting the tears running down her children's faces, Rachel's heart tightened in her chest. Her hands trembled. She couldn't be brave for all three of them. She was too much of a coward herself.

Rachel stiffened as the men passed within an arm's reach of where she hid. She wrinkled her nose at the odor emanating from them. Obviously bathing didn't appear to be a major concern.

"They can't have gone far. I heard a dog bark." The older of the men stopped, his narrowed eyes peering through the surrounding bushes.

Her heart beat so hard and loud, Rachel was sure he'd hear her.

"They ain't here," the blond young man pointed out. "I hate this stuff. Tracking ain't for me. I like the action."

The older man clapped the boy on the

back. "You and me both. But we'll have some fun once we catch 'em."

Once the men were gone, Rachel grabbed her pack, motioned for Dusty and Mel to do the same, and led them across the path the men had taken. She hoped, with any luck, they could circle around and find themselves back on the trail.

Two hours later she again let them stop to rest and kneaded the flesh of her thighs. She was too out of shape to hike continuously as they'd been doing, with a heavy pack on her back. Dusty and Mel seemed to be faring better. Mutt sat at his young master's feet, panting.

Rachel watched as Dusty absent-mindedly petted the dog. Mel sat staring into the bushes. Weariness and despair settled over them and her heart plummeted. Dusty was the optimistic one in the family. He'd always found the good in things. Mel was the fighter. Every day with her was a battle proving how strong-willed she was. Where would Rachel be if her children gave up?

"Dusty," Rachel spoke up. "Tell me something good about what we're going through."

Mel's head shot up.

Dusty grinned, wiping his tears on his sleeve. "Well...we're together. You said you wanted this trip to be a bonding time. Something we would always remember."

Rachel smiled. "I did, didn't I?"

"I think we could have spent time together without crazy people wanting to kill us." Mel folded her arms across her chest, and sulked.

Rachel nodded. "Yes, but would you have been as willing to be with us? Right now you don't have a choice. There's no one else around, but us—and them."

"What's so wrong with spending time with my friends? You always have a problem with that."

"Not always. I just enjoy spending time with you, that's all."

"Well, you got your wish." Mel turned away from her.

Dusty glanced at his mother, and shrugged.

Rachel's voice shook. "If we should die today, I'll die happy. I'm with the two people who are most important to me in this world."

"I don't want to die. I'm afraid." Mel's mouth quivered.

"I'm not." Dusty sat up straighter. "I'm going to heaven. I got saved last summer when I went to VBS with Joey."

Rachel patted his shoulder. "That's nice, honey, but I'm just talking. Just passing the time while we rest. We're not going to die." She picked up her pack and stood. "Let's go."

Mel punched her brother in the arm as

she passed him. "Way to go, dork. You know that kind of talk bothers her. What is *wrong* with you? You always have to bring up that church stuff."

"Look who's talking." Dusty rubbed his arm. "You're the one who's always upsetting her."

Rachel glanced back as Mel glared at him. The girl shrugged before following her. Dusty hitched up his own pack and set off with them.

"I'm sorry, Mom."

Rachel's steps faltered. "For what, Dusty?"

"I'm the man of the family. I should be protecting you, not crying like a little baby."

"Oh, sweetheart." She stopped and dropped her pack. "Come here." She held her arms wide to hug him. "Just your being here makes me stronger. You're so brave. Tears are okay."

"I'm going to be sick." Mel dropped her pack and collapsed to the ground. "We're lost." She lay back against a moss-covered log, her gaze covering the area around them.

"Oh, look, huckleberries." Rachel picked a small black berry from a low growing bush.

"Can we eat them?" Dusty peered at the berry in his mother's hand.

"Sure. They're actually kind of sweet. I use to eat them all the time when I was growing up." Rachel handed the berry to Dusty and bent to pick another for Mel.

Mel popped the berry into her mouth. "They are sweet."

"Good." Dusty picked a handful and stuffed them into his mouth. "That apple at breakfast and cookies at lunch didn't last long. I'm starved."

Rachel let them rest and eat for the next half hour. She sat and ate as many of the berries as she could pick but wasn't able to relax. Her body jerked at each sound from the surrounding forest. Her eyes refused to remain still, flitting from shadow to shadow like a butterfly.

Mel grumbled about walking more when she was told to get up. When something rustled the bushes close by, Dusty pointed out how much bears loved huckleberries. Mel grabbed her pack and rushed to join her brother and mother.

"We're lost."

Rachel's shoulders slumped. "Mel, we've been lost from the moment we left camp." She stopped and turned. "The only alternative to walking is to wait for those men to find us. Which would you prefer?"

"To keep walking." She lowered her head.

"Good." Rachel put her hands on her hips. "I'm tired, too. I'm tired and hungry and my feet hurt. Dusty, how about you? You doing all right?"

He nodded. "I'm fine, Mom. I can keep going."

"That's my man." She beamed at him. "Melanie, let's keep moving."

It wasn't long before Rachel noticed they were moving farther up the mountain rather than down. She turned and looked behind them. They were definitely climbing. She noted the gradual slope of the trees and took a deep breath. It was cooler, too. The air grew thinner.

Rachel looked forward. The trees seemed to get sparser as they approached the top of the mountain. *Less places to hide*. She looked to the east, saw the mountain appeared to be thicker with trees in that direction, and changed course. She had no idea where they were going, only that they needed to keep moving and find a place to hide for the night.

*

Gunshots. Screams. Wesley followed Sam into the mansion built into the South American hills. His breath rasped through the gas mask he wore, sounding more robotic than human. They'd chosen to break in the backdoor, sending other troops in through the front.

Sam turned left and Wesley stayed right behind him as they tread down a long hall, bordered on both sides by large terracotta pots and tall, ornate posts.

Wesley raised his weapon, letting loose a volley of shots as a man dove across a hallway. Another scream burst from a room ahead of them. Sam turned back and, using his right hand, motioned Wesley forward.

A movement to his right attracted Wesley's attention and he dove, narrowly being missed by the grenade thrown in his direction. Plaster rained down upon his helmeted head as the grenade exploded. He glanced around, frantic for sight of Sam.

The other man waved at him from across the hall, motioning he was moving forward. Wesley nodded and rose to his feet. He winced as his right leg threatened to give way beneath him.

Glancing down, he saw the piece of six-inch wood protruding from his thigh. Blood soaked his fatigues. With a grunt, he pulled the shard free and tossed it aside. Ignoring the pain, he continued after Sam.

Another volley of shots and he roared, joining his own weapon's fire into the chaos. When it ended, only smoke and silence remained. Wesley trod softly, peering into each room as he passed.

He stopped before one, his heart a cold stone in his chest. A little girl lay covered in blood, looking up at him. Dropping his weapon, he fell to his knees beside her, drawing her limp body into his arms. "It's all right, honey. We'll get you help." He tilted her face to meet his and smoothed the ebony hair back from her pale face. "Stay with me, okay?"

He searched, trying to locate a wound. Three bullet holes riddled her body, one just above her heart. Wesley plastered his hand against the bubbling hole, trying desperately to staunch the bleeding.

The girl shuddered. Still brown eyes stared into Wesley's and he groaned, his insides turning to ice.

Wesley woke sweating from the nightmare and tossed aside his blankets. He reached down and rubbed his thigh, feeling the pain.

Tossing his legs over the side of the bed, he buried his head in his hands. *Even up here, I can't get away from the images. God, help me.*

He forced himself from the bed and went to stare out the window into the night. *Why'd I take this case? All I want is to be left alone. I don't want to search the woods for this maniac.*

4

Dusk fell as they came upon the small log cabin. Rachel and the children sat huddled behind thick foliage. Chewing the inside of her mouth, Rachel pondered what to do. She bit too hard and tasted blood.

Mutt whimpered beside her and she pulled him close. Although his body quivered with tension, Rachel took comfort from his solid warmth.

She studied the clearing in front of her. Low-lying bushes held the woods at bay. A split rail fence lay fallen in pieces, bordering the property. The cabin appeared uninhabited, yet her heart beat heavy and unsteady in her breast.

The moon, unobstructed by trees, lit the clearing, offering them no protection should she decide to cross the small clearing. No smoke rose from the small rock chimney. The windows and doors were closed tight against the coming night. The only sounds she heard were those of her and the children's breathing.

"Okay." Rachel kept her voice low. "I'm going in. Stay here and keep Mutt quiet. Under no circumstances are you to follow me, understand? I'll be back for you. If I'm not back in fifteen minutes, keep searching for the road, all right?"

A tear shimmered down Mel's cheek. "I don't have a watch. How will we know when fifteen minutes is up?"

Dusty elbowed her. "We don't need a watch. Mom will be back. Right, Mom?" He raised a tear-streaked face to her.

Rachel placed a quick kiss on his forehead and slid off her backpack. "Of course I will. Watch the pack and hold on to the dog." She winked at Mel and stepped into the clearing.

Standing as still as possible, she listened before proceeding toward the cabin. She walked slow, stopping every few steps. As she got closer, Rachel noticed the cabin was indeed occupied, the stoop swept clean of dirt and debris, the windows clean.

Rachel stepped on the small stoop and lifted her hand to knock. She hesitated and chose instead to turn the latch. The door swung open and she winced when it creaked. She stopped at the threshold. "Hello? Anyone home?"

Hearing no answer, she walked inside.

The small cabin appeared to be two small rooms including a loft with a ladder. Two doors were on the back wall. A stove and small refrigerator were placed along the wall to her left. On the counter sat a microwave. The rest of the room contained a small table, sofa and chair.

On the back wall between the two doors stood a fireplace. She eyed the rifle hanging on a pair of deer antlers. A man's jacket lay slung across the back of the sofa. There were no photos or artwork. No other personal belongings, other than a plastic mug, and a few dirty plates.

Rachel left the door open and strolled around the room, being careful to touch nothing. She stopped before the refrigerator and contemplated opening it. Her stomach growled, making the decision for her and she stretched her hand forward.

The creak of a door stopped her. She whirled. A strange man wearing only a towel walked out. She screamed. He yelped and jumped back.

Rachel bolted for the door, glancing over her shoulder. The man stood there with a towel tied low on his hips. His wet hair lay smoothed back against his head, dripping water onto his shoulders.

He held up a hand. "Whoa. Stop."

Rachel turned, her breath coming hard

and fast. "Who are you?"

"Wesley Ward. I'm the new ranger. Who are you?"

She saw him clutch the towel as it threatened to slip, and he ducked back into the room he'd exited. He popped his head back out. "Don't go anywhere."

Turning and screaming again as her children burst through the door, Rachel stumbled backwards. The children barreled into her. Dusty held her pack in his hand, banging it into her leg. She lost her balance and fell onto the table, sending a metal box crashing to the floor. "Don't you two ever do what you're told?"

"We heard you scream." Dusty's eyes searched her face. "Are you all right?"

Rachel saw Mel's open mouth and turned to see Wesley standing a few feet from them. She took in the solid, muscled chest and tanned skin. Way too much tanned skin. She frowned and tapped Mel's shoulder. "Close your mouth, Mel."

Holding a tee-shirt in his hands, Wesley entered the room wearing a pair of jeans. "If I'd known I was having company, I would've been dressed."

He didn't look pleased and Rachel fidgeted, stammering. "Oh...well...we..."

"Would anyone like to explain to me what's going on?" Wesley took a step closer.

"Why are the three of you in my house?"

Rachel stepped back and closed the door behind her children. "We need a safe place to stay—and a radio."

He glanced at the metal box. "Well, I did have a radio." He held up a hand. "I can tell this is going to take more than a minute. Let me finish getting dressed and then you'll have my undivided attention."

"Do you have anything to eat?" Dusty asked. "Mom is being really stingy with our packed food."

"Dusty!"

Rachel flushed and turned to Wesley. He lifted an eyebrow and nodded toward the refrigerator. "Help yourselves. There's not much. There's also some instant coffee in the cupboard. I'll be right back." He disappeared, closing the door.

While Dusty and Mel attacked the contents of the man's refrigerator, Rachel hurried to the cupboard and retrieved the coffee and another mug. Using an old-fashioned pump over the small stainless steel sink, she filled the mugs with water and slid them into the microwave. The buzzer went off and she grabbed the mugs, burning herself in her haste.

"Ow!" She shook her hand. Stirring in the coffee, Rachel sniffed in appreciation, watching Dusty and Mel attack the remains of a frozen pizza. Dusty tossed Mutt a hotdog as he bit into a slice of pepperoni pizza.

"That pizza's old. You must be hungry." Wesley rejoined them dressed in a white tee shirt, jeans, and worn cowboy boots. A gold cross hung around his neck. His dark brown hair, although still damp, curled around his shirt collar. Blue eyes, framed in thick lashes, contrasted with his tanned face. His rugged features just kept him from crossing over the line into being a pretty boy.

Mel stared. Rachel elbowed her, distracting the girl, and flushed as Wesley raised his eyebrows. She bent her head, blowing on her coffee. Remembering his, she reached for it and handed it to him. "I made you some."

The corner of his mouth twitched as he accepted the offered cup. "Thanks." He leaned against the counter and waved her to a chair. "Okay, I'm listening."

They all spoke at once.

"They killed everyone!"

"They shot at us!"

"We really need to get to a radio."

Wesley sat his cup on the table. "Slow down." He pointed at Rachel. "You. Name first."

She took a deep breath. "I'm Rachel Kent. These are my children, Melanie and Dustin. We camped at the KOA, you know the new campground, and went on a hike." Her voice shook. "When we returned—everyone was dead. We saw two men. There are actually three…we saw the third one later. They have automatic weapons. When they spotted us, they started shooting. We ran into the woods, spent the night in a cave and, well, now we're here." She squared her shoulders, daring him to not believe her. "Now, can we use your radio?"

Wesley stared at her, his eyes roaming over her face. Rachel squirmed, not looking away.

He crossed his arms across his chest. His jaw set. "You can't use the radio."

"Why not?"

"You broke it." He motioned his head toward the metal box lying in pieces on the floor.

"Oh!" Rachel leapt from the chair and rushed to pick up the radio. "Can you fix it?"

Wesley shrugged. "Don't know. I'll have to look at it."

"I'm sorry." Rachel set the radio on the table.

He waved her comment away. "This was yesterday?"

"Maybe the day before." Rachel's lower lip trembled. "It seems like we've been in the woods for a week. I know it hasn't been a week, but…"

Wesley held up a hand to stop her. "Are you sure they had automatic weapons?"

"We're positive." Dusty spoke around a mouthful of hotdog. "When we were hiking, we heard the shooting. It sounded like popcorn."

"Popcorn, huh?" Wesley scratched his head. "Well, you can stay here tonight. Tomorrow, I'll try to make contact on the radio. You three can sleep in the loft."

It wasn't until he spoke that Rachel realized how tired she was. Her legs trembled, threatening to give way beneath her weight and she leaned against the table for support.

Mel stood staring at Wesley as Dusty climbed into the loft. Rachel pressed her lips together and pushed herself upright. Putting her hands on Mel's shoulders, she turned her daughter around. "Bed, Mel." She watched as the girl headed up the ladder after Dusty.

Mel tossed one more glance at Wesley before disappearing.

"Don't worry."

Rachel turned to Wesley. "About what?"

"About your daughter. Don't worry. I'm not interested in little girls." His mouth twitched again, deepening the cleft in his chin and revealing a dimple.

Lifting her eyes to his, Rachel crossed her arms across her chest. "What if they're interested in you?"

*

Well, God. This wasn't exactly the sign I was looking for. Wesley watched as Rachel finished her coffee. *The woman hadn't eaten anything. Probably nothing left to eat after those two kids finished raiding the fridge.*

Wesley smiled. She looked uncomfortable, squirming in the hard wooden chair. She'd hardly met his eyes since they barged in on him. He shrugged. Let her squirm. He turned his attention to the radio.

Opening the back, he saw it in pieces. *Well, it was old.*

"No luck?"

Wesley raised his eyes and looked into Rachel's face. He shook his head. "Nope."

"I really am sorry. The kids and I have…"

He raised his arms and folded them behind his head, leaning back in his chair. "There's a shower. You're welcome to it."

Rachel smirked. "That bad, am I?"

He nodded. "Pretty dirty."

"Okay." She rose from the table, left her mug where it sat, and disappeared into the bathroom.

Wesley shook his head. *Okay, Lord. What are You doing?* He stood and paced the room. *Why are You tossing these three in my lap? They've already run into Moe, he knows they're here, and the radio's busted. I don't want this kind of responsibility.* He huffed. *Sam will come checking when he can't reach me. He can take them out of here.*

He glanced down at the dog sitting at his feet. He bent to scratch behind its ears.

71

"You're a cute little thing, aren't you? All wiry hair and stubby legs. You could use a bath, too."

The dog whined, jumping up on him.

"Fearsome beast." Wesley laughed and moved to the sofa. He bunched his jacket beneath his head and waited for the woman to get out of his shower.

He turned his head when she appeared, clean and wearing the same dirty clothes. "No other clothes?"

"We only went for a hike." She looked defensive, hazel eyes shooting sparks.

Wesley looked at the three backpacks. "I thought with three…"

"I have a tendency to over-prepare."

Laughter welled up in him. Rachel's eyes flashed and he lost control. "I'm sorry." He sat up. "Bet you didn't prepare for this."

"Excuse me?"

He laughed harder. "Sorry. Really, I am. I've been up here searching for these men and you three fall from the sky."

Rachel put her hands on her hips. "What are we going to do, Mr. Ward?"

"Do?" He fought to squelch his laughter.

"Apparently our stumbling upon your cabin has put you out. Surely you have a plan for getting rid of us."

"My boss will be calling here tomorrow. When he doesn't reach me, he'll come looking.

Then, we'll fly you three out of here."

"Fine." She turned. "Good night, Mr. Ward."

"Wesley, please." A snort escaped him.

Rachel's back stiffened. "You are a rude man." She kept her back ramrod straight as she climbed the ladder to the loft.

Rising from the couch, Wesley walked over and blew out the gas lantern on the table. He shook his head, still smiling. *Really not what I expected today. Life is full of surprises.*

He opened the front door and stepped outside into cool darkness. *How far behind them is Moe?* Ducking back inside, he grabbed his rifle and sprinted out the door and across the clearing.

Using every scout technique he'd been trained on, Wesley searched a wide perimeter around his cabin. *Well, here's where she and the kids hid.* The grass lay trampled beneath an old oak and he picked up an empty candy wrapper. He raised his eyes, peering through the night. *No sound now but the birds and insects..*

He trod on, searching the ground around his feet, not wanting to step on any tracks. Two hours later, he headed back to the cabin none the wiser as to Moe's whereabouts.

Hanging his rifle back over the fireplace, he was taken aback to discover Rachel sitting on the couch.

"I couldn't sleep." She shrugged in

answer to his silent question. "Where'd you go?"

"Looking around." Wesley swung a chair around and straddled it.

"Looking around." She took a deep breath. "Should I be scared, Wesley. Of you? Are you one of them?"

"If I were, do you think I would tell you?"

"Why not? We're here and not likely to go anywhere. Maybe you're holding on to us until these men get here."

He shook his head. "No. I'm just a ranger."

"I don't believe that."

"Believe what you want, Rachel."

She plucked at a snag on the worn couch. "I've taken your bed. I'm sorry." She rose and walked to the cupboard. "Mind if I have another cup of coffee?"

"Go ahead but you should probably eat something."

"I couldn't. Would you like a cup?"

"No, thanks." He studied her as she poured the water into the mug she'd used earlier and placed it in the microwave. Her auburn hair was tousled. *So, she did try to sleep.* Her figure was slim, not too slim, and rounded where it should be. *She doesn't look very strong, Lord, but I think there's more to Rachel Kent than meets the eye.*

She turned and caught him staring. Squaring her shoulders, Rachel met his gaze. Her lips trembled.

Wesley smiled, one corner of his mouth tilting up. *Okay, so she's not a s brave as she wants me to believe.* "It's good coffee. Imported. My one indulgence."

She dropped her gaze and sniffed the mug. "It is good."

Sighing, Wesley rose from the chair. "I'm going to bed. Keep the light off, will you?"

He threw himself on the couch and stretched out as far as he could. He tossed and turned, ending up on his left side, facing the back of the couch, knees bent. Wesley grabbed his jacket from beneath his head, and rose. Without looking at the woman still sitting at his table, he laid across the rug spread in front of the fireplace and closed his eyes.

5

Wesley's eyes shot opened, and he sniffed in appreciation. Smells of frying bacon drifted across the room. He rolled over, stiff from his night on the floor. Sitting up, he stretched and saw Rachel standing by the small stove.

"Want some breakfast? I've cooked eggs and bacon."

"Yeah." He scratched his head with both hands, leaving his hair pointing in all directions. "Smells good. Did you sleep?"

She smiled. "A little. On the sofa you abandoned. It's a good fit for me."

Dusty and Mel climbed down the ladder. Upon reaching the bottom, Mel shoved her brother aside.

Dusty yawned. "Yum, real food." He ran

to the table and plopped himself in one of the chairs. Mel took the other.

"Dusty, Mel. Let Wesley sit down. It's his house."

"They're all right. I've eaten standing before." He took the plate she held out to him, her fingers brushing against his. Their eyes met and he smiled, seeing a flush spread across Rachel's face.

He watched as Rachel served the children and fed herself from the pan. She giggled when she caught him looking. "If you can eat standing up, so can I?"

Wesley raised his eyebrows and picked up a slice of bacon.

The front window of the cabin exploded in gunfire, showering them in glass. Wesley dove, dragging Mel to the floor with him. Rachel and Dusty ducked beneath the table.

Mel screamed. A long, shrill, continuous scream.

Wesley cringed from the sound.

*

Mel's screams bounced off Rachel's eardrums. Wesley clamped his hand over her daughter's mouth, effectively silencing her. The girl struggled against him, clawing at the hand covering her nose and mouth. Rachel released her breath as Wesley shifted his hand, freeing Mel's nose.

Mutt yelped as the shooting continued

and joined them under the table.

Rachel closed her eyes. Bullets dug chunks from the wood floor. Immediately she snapped them back open. "Oh, God. Oh, God, Oh, God." Her fingers dug into the flesh of Dusty's arm.

He pulled free of her and clamped his hands over his ears.

"Rachel."

She turned to see Wesley motion his head toward the back door.

Rachel nodded and grabbed the nearest pack. "Get the packs!" She stood to grab the rifle and shrieked as bullets slammed into the fireplace.

Wesley grabbed the tail of her shirt and pulled her back to the floor. "Go. There isn't time for the rifle."

Dusty and Mel each grabbed a pack and Wesley shoved them toward the door. The four of them crawled, crunching, through the glass and out the back.

Once outside, with the cabin between them and the shooters, they darted headlong into the woods.

Rachel struggled to push aside the dense branches and briar bushes behind the cabin. Wesley led them over a mile before stopping. Rachel leaned against a tree trunk, her breath coming in gasps.

Wesley took the pack from her and

slung it over his shoulders, grunting. "What in the world is in here?"

"Essentials," she wheezed.

Mel bent at the waist, hands balanced on her knees. "Mom suffers from paranoia."

Rachel gazed around her at the others. Mel's mascara had left dried lines upon her face. Now, her hair lay plastered to her face and neck with sweat. Dirt streaked Dusty's face, except for a tear track down each side. His tee shirt was ripped at the shoulder.

The boy picked small pieces of glass from the palms of his hands.

Sliding to the ground, Rachel put her head on her bent knees. Her short hair stuck to her neck with perspiration. "Well? Care to tell me why I couldn't grab the rifle?"

Wesley shook his head. "Were you asking to get shot? I was too busy getting you guys out of there to grab it. Do you have another weapon?"

She raised her head. "We have a flare gun. And some junk food, water bottles, one flashlight, no matches, but we do have a lighter. There's three jackets and six sandwiches, probably smashed. Oh, and very little medical supplies. Whatever is in the car emergency kit. I did manage to take that." Rachel plucked a piece of glass from the knee of her jeans. "I don't suppose you're like McGyver and can make a weapon out of string?"

He shook his head. Leaning against a tree trunk, arms and ankles crossed, he stared at her. "Sorry. But I am impressed with what you do have."

"Mom is never unprepared. She usually over-does it." Mel joined her mother on the ground.

"I'm glad she didn't choose this time to be under-prepared."

Rachel's mouth twitched remembering last night's comments. "You said you knew who these men are?"

"I have an idea." Wesley slid to the ground. "A pretty definite idea. The forest service received notification a man escaped from prison. He's a very mean and vicious person. He has a group of men with him who live somewhere in these hills. They pride themselves on being some kind of a survivalist group. They believe God has given them this mountain. Evidently, all others are trespassers." His mouth twisted.

"Before this man was sent to prison, they'd done something similar to what happened yesterday. Only then, it was a single family of campers. I don't think anyone would have imagined they'd wipe out an entire public campground." He shrugged. "The campground is bound to have been discovered by now. We just need to keep a low profile until help comes."

"And stay alive," Mel pointed out. "Don't forget that minor detail."

Wesley glanced at Mel, then smiled at Rachel.

"Yeah. Mel's a piece of work. What about your boss? What time is he supposed to radio you?"

"Two o'clock."

"That's a while."

"Yep."

Rachel sighed. "Do you know the way to the highway? We're lost."

"Can't go by the highway. This man, Duane Watkins, goes by the name of Moe, will have all the main roads watched. He knows you've gotten away and now he knows I'm with you."

"Why hasn't he come after you before?" Rachel tried combing her hair with her fingers. "I mean, if he's killing everyone who spends time on this mountain."

"I haven't been here that long. I'm actually here to locate Moe." He grinned. "Lucky guy, ain't I? You three drop him right in my lap." He stood up. "Break's over. We can't stay in one place too long. I guarantee you, they *will* be looking for us."

"Why aren't you winded?" Rachel muttered under her breath.

"I keep in shape by running. I'll go as easy as I can on you, but those guys won't stop and we can't either."

Mel huffed.

"You can stay here if you want. I'm sure those men following us will take good care of a pretty little thing like you."

Rachel observed the widening of Mel's eyes. Her daughter wasn't use to someone speaking so bluntly to her. *Well, I've tried to shelter my children. Probably not a good thing.* She flashed Mel a quick smile. *Maybe she'll learn to appreciate me more.*

She sighed and picked up her pack. Wesley reached over and took it from her. "You and the kids take turns with the other two. I'll carry the heavy one."

Giving him a quick smile of relief, Rachel wrapped the dog's leash securely around her wrist.

Wesley led them further into the trees until he found a small stream. They took a moment to wash their faces and drink. He turned, leading them across the creek and followed it north. Occasionally he would have them enter the creek, walk a ways, then exit. He kept them always heading north.

Rachel hated the squelching of wet shoes and worried over foot disease. She cast a quick eye over her children's feet, looking for any sign of limping or soreness.

"Wesley's trying to throw the killers off our trail." Her son stepped closer to her.

Mel rolled her eyes. "You're such a know-it-all, Dusty."

Flinging her arm around Dusty's shoulders, Rachel gave him a quick squeeze. "You're doing great. I'm proud you know so much."

Wesley stopped, neck craned, looking up a steep incline.

"What is it?" Rachel stepped next to him.

"There's a cave up there. I'm trying to figure out how we can get up there without leaving any trace behind." He dropped the pack to the ground and walked a few feet around the steep hill. "Over here. It's not as steep and it's fairly hidden."

Rachel dragged the pack behind her and dropped it at his feet. The side of the hill rose vertically, with nothing to grab a hold of but a few bushes. "We're supposed to climb up there?"

"Yep. You three start climbing while I wipe out our tracks." He pointed out the path she'd left. "Don't drag the packs, Rachel. Carry them, or leave them."

Dusty scurried up the rock face like a monkey, Mel close behind.

Rachel hugged her way up. She grabbed at a weed to assist her and slid a few feet as it pulled out of the ground. She fought to get a hold, scraping her hands. She held them in front of her. The rocks had dug in, cutting furrows into the tender skin of her palms. Tears welled in her eyes. Alarmed, she felt Wesley prop his shoulder against her bottom and push.

"Pardon me."

Peering down to see him grinning up at her, Rachel blushed and pulled herself onward. Once at the top, she collapsed. Mutt whined and licked her face. She half-heartedly pushed him away. "That was the easy way up?"

"Easier." Wesley peered into the cave. "Did you say you had a flashlight? I need to check and make sure this cave is unoccupied."

Mel bolted up. "Unoccupied? As in animal?"

"Exactly as in animal." Wesley took the flashlight from Rachel. He tossed the light to his left hand, opening his right. Blood smeared across his palm. He grabbed Rachel's hands and turned them over. She pulled away, uncomfortable under his scrutiny.

Wesley met her eyes for a second and patted her shoulder.

He wiped his hands and the handle of the flashlight on his jeans before shining the light into the shallow cave. "All clear. Dusty, help me pull up some of these fallen branches to hide the entrance. Mel, go through the packs for the first aid kit. Give it to your mother."

Rachel sat there, holding her bleeding hands in front of her. She also had several cuts and scraps from the climb on other parts of her body. They stung badly. She accepted the first aid kit gratefully from her daughter and set it on the ground.

Mel then handed out their jackets and crawled over to the corner of the cave to sleep. Within moments, Dusty and the dog curled up next to her.

Sighing, Rachel glanced at her daughter. She'd expected Mel to help her. She fumbled with the latch on the plastic box, leaving blood smears. Once she'd opened it, she pulled out gauze and medical tape, holding one item in each hand.

When she grunted in frustration, Wesley crawled over to her. He took the supplies away from her. Rachel groaned and pulled away in embarrassment.

"No. Let me." He sat cross-legged on the ground and placed the gauze and tape in his lap. Retrieving the antibiotic cream, he rubbed it gently into the palms of her hands.

Rachel drew in a sharp breath as the cream stung. As Wesley continued to massage the cream. Butterflies took root in her stomach and her face heated. Her breath hitched as the stinging stopped. Her hands grew warm under his touch and she closed her eyes.

"So?"

Rachel opened her eyes to see him glance at her left ring finger. She could barely make out the faded tan line of where her wedding ring had once rested. She'd worn it until a few months ago, mostly to discourage any eager suitors.

"Where's your husband? Where are you guys headed?"

"Headed?"

"Most people who stop at a KOA are passing through to somewhere." He tore the gauze with his teeth and wrapped her hand.

"My husband died two years ago. The kids and I are headed to my parents." Rachel tried to pull her hand away as he taped it tightly. "I'd promised Dusty we'd have some fun along the way." She smiled, lifting one corner of her lips in a smirk. "Some fun, huh?"

"Things happen." Wesley secured the tape and started on her other hand. "Good example of wrong place at the wrong time." He finished wrapping her injured hands, placed everything back into the box, and scooted against the cave wall, folding his arms across his chest.

"Thank you." Rachel squinted through the growing gloom to where Dusty and Mel slept. "I don't think I could've taken the stress alone anymore. I am sorry to have dragged you into this, though." She wasn't sure whether it was the stress of single parenting she talked about or the stress of running for their lives. Either way she was glad of the man's company, stranger or not.

Wesley shivered. "You're welcome. For the hands and the company." His lips twitched. "I didn't have anything else going on."

Rachel shot him a quick smile. "You're cold." She took her jacket from the ground and held it to him.

He shook his head. "I'm fine. You keep it." He leaned across and draped the jacket across her shoulders. "You should try to sleep. You look done in. I'll keep watch."

"You sure?"

"I'm sure."

Sitting propped against the wall opposite Wesley, she watched him shiver. *Who is this man who's willing to risk his life for us? Was he what he appeared to be? Just a good man, who seemed a bit put out about being thrust into someone else's problems?* She shifted against the dirt floor, trying to get comfortable. The thought he might be one of them luring her and the children closer to those who wanted to kill them, crossed her mind. She shrugged. She had no choice but to trust him.

She saw him squirm again. He caught her watching and stared. Rachel grew uncomfortable under his gaze. "What?"

Wesley tucked his hands under his arms. "I'm wondering what God let me get myself into."

Frowning, Rache burrowed deeper into

her coat. "I don't believe in God."

"Really?" Wesley sounded amazed. "Kind of hard not to. Believe I mean, living out here. His creation surrounds us."

"It's not that I don't believe in Him. It's more like I don't have much use for Him."

"I'm hoping Moe won't know about this old logging road I'm leading you to." Wesley's voice cut through the darkness. "But I am wondering whether you and the kids can handle the distance." Rachel saw his head turn as Mel whimpered in her sleep. She could barely hear his next sentence. "And I'm praying for our safety."

Rachel peered at him, disregarding his words on prayer. She had to trust him. He seemed to know these woods and she didn't. If praying made him feel better, then so be it. Let him pray.

She swung the jacket around so she could put her arms through the sleeves. Zipping it up, she lay on her side in the dirt, using one of the packs as a pillow. Secure in the knowledge Wesley would watch over them, she closed her eyes and fell asleep, her exhaustion stronger than her worry.

*

Moe hooked the straps on his overalls as he stepped out of his tent. The walkie talkie on his hip crackled. He pulled up the antennae and pushed the button. "Tell me you got them,

Rupert."

His face heated as he listened.

"We blew that cabin apart, General. Riddled it with bullets and they still got away."

"Again? You lost them again?" He asked through clenched teeth.

"The new ranger is with them."

"How...did...they...get...out...of the cabin?" Moe's jaws hurt from the pressure he exerted on them. He paced the camp, knocking men aside as he stormed past them. One man jumped out of Moe's way, his foot landing in the fire. He howled and hopped, slapping at the burning embers clinging to his boots.

"Out the back, sir."

"Out the back." Moe swore again. "Didn't it occur to you, Rupert, to station someone in the back? Do I need to replace you? Demote you from a position of leadership?"

"No, sir."

"Don't come back without them. Do I make myself clear?"

"Yes, sir."

Moe released the button and slammed the antennae back into place. One of his men walked too close and Moe sent him reeling with a doubled fist to the side of the man's head. He kicked at a rock and stalked into his tent.

The radio beeped again. He yanked the antennae with his teeth. "What?"

His body tensed, insides churning. "I'm

sorry. I thought it was someone else...They got away." His voice was low, apologetic. "I'm doing the best I can with the men I have," he whined. "They're a bunch of bumbling idiots."

Feet dragging, Moe walked to his chair and plopped into it. "Yes. I'll do better."

He slid the antennae down slowly, then laid the radio on top of the table. Massive shoulders hunched, Moe placed his face in his hands.

6

Rachel woke the next morning, just as the sun peeked over the mountain. The rays slipped through the branches across the mouth of the cave, painting those inside with golden stripes. She peered around, locating her still sleeping children.

Wesley hunched near the cave's opening. He turned and held a finger to his lips when she sat up. Her eyes widened, and she nodded. He waved her over and Rachel waddled in a crouch, careful of her hands.

For several minutes they sat, frozen. Rachel heard the quiet murmurings of more than one man passing below their cave. She leaned forward, peering over the outcrop.

The men kicked at fallen rocks and overturned logs. One pointed out a broken branch. The group stopped, looking around them. Wesley grabbed Rachel's waistband and pulled her into the cave. She scooted as far back as possible, leaving Wesley to eavesdrop on their pursuers.

Rachel couldn't make out everything they were saying, but it was obvious they were looking for her and the kids. Did they know Wesley was with them?

One of the men cursed.

"Be quiet, fool. Want them to hear you? Moe'll have our hides if we let them get away again."

Rachel sat, her back plastered against the dirt wall, for several tense minutes. She raised a trembling hand to run fingers through sleep-mussed hair. She fought to control her breathing.

"They've passed us," Wesley joined her against the back wall. "I don't think they know this cave is here. I think they spend most of their time higher up the mountain. I'm counting on that." He pulled one of the packs to him. "Let's take an inventory of food and see what we can spare for breakfast. At least pull something out for the kids."

Rachel nodded and, opening the pack containing the emergency essentials, set aside the first aid kit. She also set aside the flashlight. Opening the pack further, she spotted extra batteries, the flare gun, a bar of soap, a glow stick, road flares and four water bottles.

Withdrawing her purse, she dumped the contents on the ground. She grunted in disgust. A metal pill box, tube of lipstick, ink pen and other items suited to a woman's vanity. Rachel scooped up the items and stashed them and her purse back in the pack.

Wesley grabbed the second pack and pulled out a package of donuts, three more water bottles, a pack of gum, a bag of chips and a package of peanut butter crackers. He looked up at her, one eyebrow raised.

Rachel shrugged. "I sent them into the store alone." She examined their small stockpile. "Can we sneak back to your cabin and wait for your friend?"

Shaking his head, Wesley told her to look out the cave and to her left. Rachel crawled forward. A plume of dark smoke rose above the trees. "They set fire to your cabin?" She turned to him, eyes wide, shaking her head. "Why would anyone do that?" She stood on her knees and stared at him, temper rising.

"Don't know. Had their reasons, I expect." Wesley repacked their supplies, leaving out the donuts and one water bottle.

"Won't someone see the smoke and come?"

"Probably."

"Then we'll be rescued." She sat up straighter.

"Don't get excited. No one knows where we are."

Rachel's shoulders slumped under the

weight of her disappointment. She sat, legs crossed in front of her. "You don't talk much, do you?"

"No, Rachel. I'm a man of few words. That's why I enjoy being a forest ranger. It's solitary, quiet work."

Dusty and Mel stirred from their slumber in slow, lethargic movements, rubbing sleep from their eyes and yawning. Mel gathered up the jackets and stuffed them into the pack. Rachel's eyes widened in surprise at her daughter's unprompted action. She opened her mouth to comment and clamped it shut at Mel's closed expression.

"It's donuts for breakfast. Go easy on the water. It's got to last us." Rachel tossed the package of donuts to Dusty and a bottle of water to her daughter.

"Donuts! Yeah, Mom!" Dusty grabbed a handful of the small, white powdered rings.

Mel sighed heavily, her shoulders slumped.

"Mel?" Rachel scooted next to her.

The girl burst into tears and buried her face in her mother's shoulder. "I hoped it was all just a bad dream." She sniffed. "This is our third night out here. We should be at Grandma's and Grandpa's by now."

Rachel hugged her daughter to her chest. "We'll be fine, Mel. People are bound to be looking for us by now."

"Sure." Dusty spoke around the donuts in his mouth, his lips ringed by white powder. "They'll have found our car and not our bodies, Mel. They're probably swarming all over these woods right now. Right, Mr. Ward?"

"Call me Wesley. You're right. I'm sure they're searching for us."

Rachel met his eyes over Mel's head. There was little emotion on his face as he watched Mel's emotional outburst. Rachel arched a brow at him and he turned away.

The girl sat up. "Then we can use the flare gun. That way they'll be able to find us."

"Right along with the bad guys." Wesley pushed aside the branches covering the cave. "Who do you want to bet is closest?"

Mel slumped again, her bottom lip protruding.

"Smart idea." Wesley commented as Dusty dug a hole and buried the donut wrapper.

Dusty grinned, eyes shining. Rachel smiled at the pride on her son's face. "We did this the other night, too. Just in case the bad guys found out where we'd been. Now, maybe they won't know for sure where to start looking for us." Dusty saved one donut and fed it to Mutt.

"Don't waste food on the dog, Dusty."

"It's not wasting, Mom. Mutt's part of the family."

"Can't argue with that." Wesley moved

next to Rachel, his mouth inches from her ear. His breath tickled her neck. "The dog is good for your son's morale. Let it be." He stood and grabbed the heavier pack. "Let's go."

"Can't we stay here?" Mel didn't move. "Until we're found?"

"By who? They've already been by once this morning." Wesley slid his arms into the pack straps. "Do you want to take the chance they won't be back?"

The girl shook her head, hair flying around her face and grabbed her pack. Hoisting it across one shoulder, Mel hurried to Wesley's side.

Rachel noticed how Mel made a point of staying close to Wesley. Her head barely reached the man's shoulder. Wesley glanced at the girl in amusement as her closeness caused her to bump into him. Rachel frowned and he stepped away, putting more distance between himself and Mel. Rachel bit the inside of her lip. *What could he do? Mel was Mel.*

They slid down the cliff, Wesley hissing orders for them not to leave a trail. Their descent, although easier than their ascent, left Mel crying out in anger as she ripped the leg of her jeans. Rachel shushed her, pointing out the knees were already ripped.

"That's the way they're supposed to be, Mom. *This* rip isn't supposed to be here."

Sighing, Rachel began her own awkward

slide down. She went quicker than she'd planned, her injured hands not allowing her to grasp anything to slow herself down, and landed in an undignified heap at Wesley's feet. Face flaming, she allowed him to take her arm and help her to her feet.

"You all right?" Wesley stared frowning at the path they'd left down the side of the hill.

"Nothing hurt but my pride."

He shook his head, turned and headed off, leaving them to follow.

Rachel attempted to wipe off the back of her jeans. The ground was damp. Instead of dust, she was caked with mud. She groaned inwardly and hurried to keep up with the others.

Again staying close to Wesley's side, Mel's hair with the bright blue stripes contrasted with the green foliage around them. Rachel occupied her mind, trying to come up with ways to disguise her daughter's hair. Then she noticed Wesley's white tee shirt, Dusty's yellow and red striped one and her own black shirt. She was the only one not shouting color amidst the green and gold of the autumn leaves.

At least I'll blend in. She sighed, her breath catching. *We're never going to survive this. We're wandering the woods with a stranger. A handsome stranger. Mel won't leave his side. My daughter hates me. We have very little food or clean water*...Rachel's breath quickened. *We*...She dropped the dog's leash and stopped.

She held her hands out in front of her. They shook violently. She stuffed them into her armpits and tried to ignore the rising pain in her chest. Rachel counted to ten, concentrating on taking deep breaths. *Oh, no. Not now*. She bent over and balanced herself with her hands on her knees. She whimpered at the pain from her palms, and shifted to her elbows.

"Rachel?" Wesley's voice drifted to her.

"She's having an anxiety attack," Mel explained. "It used to happen a lot right after Dad died, but it hasn't happened in a while."

"You two get in there and stay down." Wesley pointed to a thick clump of bushes. "I'll take care of your mom."

Dusty grabbed Mutt's lease and followed his sister.

Wesley knelt on the ground and pulled Rachel down beside him. "Listen to me, Rachel." His voice dropped to a calming octave. "Put your head back down and concentrate on your breathing. You'll be fine."

Lowering her head, she closed her eyes. *One, two, three*...

"Would you like me to pray for you?"

Her head snapped up. "What?"

Smiling at her, he repeated, "Would you like me to pray for you?"

Shaking her head, Rachel took a deep breath. "No. God deserted me a long time ago. He doesn't listen to prayers on my behalf."

"Sure He does."

Rachel stood, squaring her shoulders and stared down her nose at Wesley who continued to kneel at her feet. "He doesn't."

"Feel better?" Wesley shrugged and rose to his feet.

"Yes. I do. I've never gotten over an anxiety attack that quickly before."

He laughed. "I prayed—before I asked your permission."

Rachel glared at him. "Don't do it again." She stalked to join her children.

"Can't promise."

Hearing the laughter in his voice, she quickened her pace.

Two hours later, they stopped next to another small stream. Wesley fished three snack bags of chips from the pack and tossed them to Rachel and the kids.

"You've got to eat, too." She held the bag out to him. "We won't survive out here if something happens to you."

"I'm fine. I've gone on one meal a day before."

"But you haven't eaten anything today. At least share mine." She offered the bag to him again.

He waved an empty water bottle at her.

"Drinking." Wesley stopped and refilled the bottle from the stream. "I had a couple of those little powdered things at breakfast and a person can go quite a while on just water.

Rachel's mouth opened and grimaced in disgust as he guzzled the creek water. "That water isn't purified."

"Really?' Wesley stared at the bottle in his hand. "Been drinking it for years. It's a wonder I'm still here."

"You could get dysentery, or cholera."

"Rachel, you'll be drinking from these creeks before we get out of here, I guarantee you." He grinned. "There's nothing sweeter than cold creek water."

"I have to use the restroom." Dusty shifted from foot to foot.

"Me, too." Mel cocked a hip.

Wesley capped his bottle. "Rachel, you take Mel. Dusty, come with me. Under no circumstances do you walk to where you can't at least see my head. Understand?"

"We need privacy. If we can see you, you can see us."

"Privacy will get you killed, Rachel. There's no room for modesty here."

"Fine." She turned to leave, back straight. Rachel stuck her nose in the air, took two steps, and tripped over Mel's backpack.

She lay sprawled in the decaying leaves and dirt, hands throbbing. Her face grew hot as the blood rushed to her head. With as much dignity as Rachel could muster, she put her battered hands beneath her, pushed up and regained her footing.

Despite her resolve not to, she looked. Wesley's shoulders shook with his silent laughter. Rachel glanced at Dusty who sported a huge grin. A loud guffaw burst from Wesley, despite his efforts to hold it in, sending startled birds into flight from the trees. Rachel's back stiffened more. Wesley put his arm around Dusty's shoulders and led him in the opposite direction from the females.

Rachel glanced around them in alarm. What if their pursuers heard him? What if they saw the birds fly into the air?

"You are so embarrassing, Mom." Mel turned away from her and unzipped her jeans. "I mean, really. How mortifying to fall like that. In front of Wesley."

"It was an accident, Mel."

"I know, but he laughed at you." Mel turned, scorn on her young face. "He laughed really hard."

"So." Rachel unzipped her jeans. "It wasn't the first time, and it won't be the last time I've been laughed at."

"Don't you ever lose control?" Mel's secured her jeans, her voice rising. "Do you always have to have the last word? It's killing you, isn't it? Having Wesley in control?"

Rachel stood, zipping her jeans. "Don't be ridiculous, Mel. And you should call him Mr. Ward. I don't want to be in control. I don't know where we're going or what we should do."

"If we hadn't stopped to go on this stupid hike, we wouldn't be here! This is all your fault. You never take into consideration what I want. It's always about you—or Dusty. I didn't even want to go hiking." Tears fell down the girl's cheeks, mixing with the dirt on her face. Her voice broke. "It's all your fault."

Gathering her daughter into her arms, Rachel patted her back. "Oh, baby. I'm sorry. You have to believe I wouldn't have intentionally stopped at that campsite if I had known. I would never endanger you. Not on purpose."

Mel sniffed and pulled away. "I know, Mom. I was just dumping on you. Really. I'm cool with the hike and camping. Sort of. I'm just really scared."

"So am I." Rachel spun when she heard the crack of a snapping twig. Leaves rustled. She looked for Wesley and Dusty, finally spotting Wesley's back too far away for her to have heard him step on anything. "Follow me," she whispered. Ducking, she led her daughter away from the sound and over to the ranger.

"There's something over there." Rachel grabbed Wesley's arm

He stared for a moment, his dark blue eyes sweeping the area. "Come on." Tossing a pack to her, he handed the dog to Dusty and, without a backward glance, led them off at a run.

Popping sounds followed them. Bullets kicked up the dirt and leaves and Rachel squeezed the bridge of her nose to ward off a sneeze. Each bullet seemed to hit closer to her pounding feet.

Rachel's eyes widened in horror as a slug hit Wesley, and he hit the ground rolling. She paused and turned toward him.

"Keep running!" He struggled to his feet, holding his arm tight against his side. "Go!"

"You're…"

"Run. Now." Wesley grabbed Rachel's arm with his free hand and dragged her with him.

Mutt barked. The hair stood straight on the terrier's neck.

"Mutt, here!" Rachel tossed over her shoulder. "Come, boy."

A bullet slammed into the ground near the dog, sending it yelping after the others. Rachel felt Wesley falter as a bullet slammed into a tree beside him. He lost his grip on her arm.

"Wesley." She held back, waiting for him to catch up. She slid under his good arm, offering her shoulder for support. Rachel shrieked and ducked as a bullet zipped past her head.

Wesley pushed her away. "Leave me. Take your children and go. I'll catch up."

"Stop it. We won't leave you." She urged him on, following his instructions as he directed her. Her body ached from exhaustion by the time he called a halt. Her every breath a burning agony.

"Stop." Wesley slid his arm from her shoulder and sagged against a tree.

Rachel stopped and listened. Not hearing anyone pursuing them, she helped Wesley slide to the ground. She moved his arm away from his side.

"They're playing with us."

"Playing? They shot you."

"Just winged me. They could have killed me if they wanted to." Wesley held his arm out from his side.

Across his ribcage, under his right arm, Rachel could see a deep, bleeding furrow through the torn tee shirt. "Can we stop here? I need to clean that."

"Just give me a minute to catch my breath. You can clean it later."

"Wesley, we…"

"Later. We need to find a place to hide."

Rachel glared at him. "Stop acting like a

man for one minute and..."

He looked up at her, brows drawn together in puzzlement. "What would you like me to act like? A woman?"

"Oh, for Pete's...You know what I mean." She motioned Mel over and, with her daughter's help, they got him to his feet.

"Not much farther. There's an overhang down by the creek. We can stay there."

"Won't they find us?" Dusty was in front, holding tight to Mutt's leash.

"If they look hard enough they will. There'll only be one way down and we'll keep an eye on it. We'll keep the flare gun handy, okay? We can use it as a weapon if we have to." His answer seemed to satisfy the boy and Dusty turned around, ready to lead them in the direction the ranger directed them to go.

Seeing Wesley grit his teeth and hold his arm tight to his side, Rachel moved closer. He shrugged off Rachel's offer of help. With a defiant tilt of her head, she hefted the heavy pack on her shoulders. He frowned.

"This really bothers you, doesn't it?" She smirked.

"What?"

"Me carrying this pack." She held aside a low hanging branch. "Goes against your grain, doesn't it?"

"Yes, Rachel. It does."

"Well, swallow your pride. You're

wounded. You can't shoulder this heavy pack and that's final." She stepped back for Wesley to walk in front of her.

"Oh, no, you don't. I can still take up the rear."

Rachel stopped, hands loosely on her hips. "You're as white as a sheet, Wesley Ward. You're sweating and breathing hard. I'll take up the rear so I can see you when you fall." She pursed her lips together and raised both eyebrows.

"You'd hear me fall."

She continued to stare at him.

Shaking his head, Wesley turned ahead of her and walked away. "Well, we can't stand here and argue about it."

Rachel smiled over at Mel who watched them. She looked worried and Rachel kept the smile on her face until her daughter followed Dusty.

Wesley held back a branch for her to duck under.

"Thank you." She waved him on. He sighed and shuffled forward. The red stain on Wesley's shirt continued to spread. His steps slowed, and he stumbled.

She moved forward and pushed her shoulder under his arm, taking some of his weight. When he protested, she hushed him, not relinquishing her hold around his waist.

Sunset kissed the sky by the time they

reached the creek. Rachel looked down and sighed. Another muddy hill to slide down. She sighed again, louder, and tightened her pack, before releasing her hold on Wesley.

7

As Wesley stumbled, heading down the hill, Rachel stepped once more beneath his arm. Her feet threatened to slip out from underneath her as she worked her way down the steep creek bank. Wesley's weight caused her feet to sink in the red clay mud, covering her shoes.

Wesley instructed them to head under a shallow overhang next to the muddy creek. His breath came in short gasps. Relief eased the lines in his face as she helped him sit, propped against the dirt bank.

"Dusty, I need you to be look-out for a while. Can you do that?"

"Sure, Wesley."

Dusty's pleased smile warmed Rachel's heart. With the dog beside him, the boy stationed himself at the foot of the path.

Wesley raised his arm, and twisted his uninjured arm around to feel his side.

"Here let me." Rachel lifted Wesley's arm. The blood dried, leaving the cotton tee-shirt stuck against the wound. "This is going to hurt. I'll try to be quick." She took the torn part of the shirt in her hand, struggling to keep a hold of it, despite her bandaged hands. Once she'd obtained a solid grip on the shirt, she yanked it away.

Wesley drew in a sharp breath.

"Sorry." She raised her eyes to his.

Taking one of the bottles, Rachel poured the water over his wound. The flow and the ripping away of the shirt caused the wound to bleed profusely, soaking the waistband of Wesley's jeans. She used more of their precious gauze and bound his wound.

"Ow!" Wesley glared at her as she pulled the gauze tight and tied it off.

"You want to bleed to death?"

She dug through her purse until she found the small tin of Tylenol. Shaking three of them into her hand, she handed them to Wesley, along with the remaining water in the bottle. "I'm sorry. Tylenol is all I have for the pain."

"Thank you. It's better than nothing. I've been injured worse than this before." He tossed the pills into his mouth and raised the bottle, downing the pills. "I'll be fine in a while." He closed his eyes, leaning his head against the dirt embankment. "You need to cover our trail."

"How?"

Wesley opened one eye. "The path's pretty muddy. Take the bottle, fill it at the creek and try to wash away our tracks."

Nodding, Rachel hurried off to do what he'd asked.

The cold creek water numbed her sore hands. As the water filled the bottle, the gauze from her hands floated in the ripples. Blood from Wesley's wound had soaked them clean through. Now only mud stains remained.

She lifted the bottle and headed back up the muddy incline. Sloshing the water over their tracks smeared them, not obliterating them and she headed back for more. By the time she'd finished, Rachel trembled with exhaustion and her hands were once more covered in red clay. She grimaced and held them out to Mel to unwrap.

"Mom?" Mel's eyes were wide with fright. "Is he going to die?" She held the muddy gauze away from her, using her fingertips and nodded at Wesley.

"No, Mel. He's not going to die. He'll be fine after he rests." Rachel glanced at Wesley and he shivered. She hurried to where they'd tossed their packs and dug out her heavier jacket. She placed it across his chest and shoulders.

Wesley smiled without opening his eyes. "Thank you."

"Your welcome." She turned back to Mel. "The bullet just crazed him, sweetie."

"Well, how long are we going to sit here?" Mel grew edgy. The girl sat on the ground, legs crossed Indian style, bloody gauze on the ground beside her. She bounced her legs up and down.

"Relax, Mel." Rachel reached across and placed a hand on her daughter's knee.

Mel jumped up, grabbing her mother's arm. She pulled Rachel a few feet away. "We *need* him, Mother," she hissed.

Rachel eyed her daughter's hand until Mel removed it. "I know that, Mel. What is wrong with you? The man's injured. He needs to rest." She looked around the ground for a stick. "I need to bury this gauze. Help me, will you?"

Locating a stick, Rachel squatted next to the creek and scraped the wood across the clay surface.

"People are shooting at us, Mom!"

"Lower your voice." She glanced over to where Wesley rested. "Wesley said they were only playing with us. They could have killed us at any time. They didn't. I think we're all right for now."

Mel hugged her arms around her chest. "This isn't real. I should be back at home. At school--in math class."

"And your twelve-year old brother

shouldn't be sitting guard, watching for killers." Rachel stood and glanced over to where Dusty sat. His silhouette appeared very small to her as he sat, back ramrod straight, one arm draped around the dog. Mel was right. They shouldn't be here, and neither should that man sitting injured against a damp dirt wall. "We would all rather be doing something else, Melanie, but we're not. We're sitting here next to a muddy creek, with an injured man, and crazy people with guns chasing us."

She turned her head, Wesley's eyes on her. She rushed to his side. "How are you feeling? Can I do anything?"

"I'll be fine." He shook off the jacket and sat up straighter. "Your daughter's right. We should be moving on."

"I'm sorry you heard that. Mel can be selfish."

He got to his feet, using Rachel's shoulder for support. "No, she's just a teenager. They only see what directly impacts them." He handed her a jacket and walked over to whisper something in Dusty's ear.

Dusty smiled up at the man. Rachel smirked and stuffed her jacket back into the pack. Her son missed having a man in his life. He'd often gone camping and fishing with his father. Those were the few times Dennis had kept his drinking to a minimum.

She sighed, and shrugged. *I failed*

somewhere as a wife, but I'm not going to fail in my role as a mother. Rachel shook her head to chase away the depressing thoughts. *I can't keep dwelling on the past. My children need me now more than ever.*

Wesley moved to her side and reached out to take the pack from her.

"No. You're wounded. Now is not the time to be a gentleman. We went through this already."

"I'm fine, Rachel. The rest did me good." His eyes lowered to her hands. "I know your hands are hurting you. Where're the bandages?"

"Covered with clay and buried. I can handle the pack. Besides, every time we stop, it gets lighter.

He laughed. "Yes, it does." Wesley pressed his arm against his side and turned away.

*

Wesley led them across the creek and into the denser foliage on the other side. He did his best trying to steer their way through the thick bushes. Dusty tried helping, but most of the time, the boy didn't have the upper body strength needed to clear a path. It didn't take long for them all to be bathed in perspiration.

Keeping his arm tight against his wound, Wesley concentrated on blocking out the pain. He stopped to catch his breath and looked over the others.

Rachel sported a long scratch down one side of her face where she'd neglected to duck fast enough from a springing branch. Mel worked on untangling her long hair from a low hanging limb, her eyes swimming in tears. Even the usually optimistic Dusty seemed to be lagging.

Wish I had a machete. Even a knife. Our progress through these thick briar bushes is too slow. He shook his head and turned to lead on. He led them through the woods in a zigzag pattern, trying to avoid the thickest foliage. Even with careful navigating, they were all scratched, bleeding and wearing torn clothing by the time they passed through.

A rapidly flowing creek waited for them, gurgling over rocks and fallen trees. Rachel stood at the edge, staring down into the water rushing and bubbling over boulders of all sizes. She raised wide eyes to Wesley's face. "You've got to be kidding! We're going to cross that? I can't see the bottom. The creek water's brown."

"Can you swim, Rachel? Can the kids?" His eyes ran over her face. Her eyes were huge in a pale face covered with dirt and scratches. Her short hair stuck up in weird angles where it wasn't plastered to her neck. Under different circumstances, he might have laughed.

She nodded.

"Good. It won't be over your head, but it is running swift. I'll lead. Each of you grab a firm hold on the waistband of the person in front of you, and try to keep your balance. One goes down, we all go down." He ran his eyes over their faces, meeting each one's eyes in turn. "Dusty, you're right behind me, followed by Mel, then Rachel."

He heard their sharp intakes of breath as they stepped into the frigid water. He glanced over his shoulder and saw Rachel's chest heave with quickened breaths as the creek rose. First to her thighs, then waist, chest, finally coming to a stop right under her chin. She clamped her lips together and raised her nose high in the air.

Mel was the same height as her mother, but Dusty's feet were soon swept from beneath him. He held tight to Wesley's belt and allowed himself to be pulled along.

"The pack is too heavy," Rachel called above the roar of the creek. "It's filling with water."

Wesley glanced back again just as Rachel lost her footing and went under. His stomach plummeted right along with her.

Her head broke the surface of the water and she gasped, coming up coughing. She sucked in water as she submerged again. The more she fought to regain her footing on the slippery rocks, the more she failed and would again submerge herself, dragging the others with her.

Fighting to regain his own footing, Wesley yelled. "Stop fighting it." He struggled to pull the others with him, trying to use the larger boulders as leverage. "Be still, Rachel."

He slipped, banging into one of the boulders. Pain flooded his body and he groaned, falling. Icy water closed over his head. Blood from the freshly opened wound flowed in crimson swirls around him. The others tugged, trying to get him to his feet.

Planting his feet against the rocky bottom of the creek bed, he pushed up, breaking the surface and regained his footing. He fought against the current, every muscle in his body screaming as he dragged Rachel and the children behind him.

They were all breathing hard by the time they reached the opposite bank and they flopped to the ground like stranded fish. Rachel groaned as Dusty and Mel collapsed on her, shivering, trying to catch their breath.

Lying flat on his back, arms thrown wide beside him, Wesley turned his head toward Rachel. "Are you hurt?"

"No. I'm just thinking of all the ruined supplies in my backpack."

Wesley stared at her and burst into laughter, rolling into a ball to protect his side. "Ow! Rachel, you are something else. We're lying here in wet clothes, with night approaching fast, no way to get warm, and you're worried about a couple bags of chips."

Mel bolted up—and screamed.

Whipping around, Wesley grit his teeth. Four men with guns stared at them from the opposite bank. The younger one waved, then ducked when the man standing next to him took a swipe at the back of the boy's head.

Wesley leaped to his feet, grabbed Dusty by the shirt and flung the boy into the bushes. Rachel and Mel scrambled ahead. Their pursuers laughter rang out, following.

An hour later, Wesley allowed them to stop. He leaned against a tree and watched as the other three crumbled to the ground. Listening for sounds of pursuit and, not hearing any, Wesley commanded the others to stay put. He stalked away and scanned the area.

He hated to leave Rachel and the kids alone. Fatigue showed in their faces and slumped postures. Defeat threatened them, etching lines deep in their faces. They couldn't spend the night where they were.

He walked a circle around the area, looking up the side of hills for caves and down into the creek bed for an overhang to hide under. He found nothing that looked remotely safe or secure. This close to the top of the mountain, there wasn't much above them to provide access to caves.

Following the creek, taking care not to leave footprints in the muddy soil next to the water, Wesley turned his attention to the treetops. Several times he startled a forest animal and his heartbeat quickened when it bolted into the woods, crashing through the bushes. Sometimes the rustling caused him to squat quickly, ears straining. When he'd gone as far as he deemed safe, Wesley turned and headed back.

Rachel bolted to her feet when he emerged from the woods.

He shook his head. "Nothing. No cave or overhang."

"Where will we stay? We can't stay here."

Looking at the trampled ground around their feet, Wesley agreed. "You're right. We can't. Follow me." He led them down the creek, making them walk in the rocks at the shallow edge. "Here." He pointed up into the branches of a large tree with an incredibly twisting and gnarly trunk. "We're sleeping in the trees tonight."

"You have got to be kidding!" Mel stared up into the tree, a look of total disbelief on her face. "You are kidding, right?" She looked so much like Rachel when she was astounded that Wesley found himself laughing—again. He hadn't laughed this much in years. And here they were, running for their lives. It's as if all his survival training went flying with the birds.

"Cool." Dusty grabbed the lowest branch and swung himself up. With the agility of a monkey, he climbed. Stopping halfway up the tree, he looked down. "What about Mutt? He can't climb trees."

"Mutt will have to stay on the ground." Wesley held out his hand. "Come on, Mel. I'll help you." The girl placed her smaller hand in his strong one. Telling her step by step, Wesley guided Mel up the tree, one branch at a time.

"Dusty stood balanced precariously on one of the thicker branches. "Wesley, don't forget about Mutt."

Wesley took Mutt's leash and led the dog into the bushes. Finding a thick group of low-lying bushes, he tied Mutt's leash securely and commanded the dog to stay. Then he went back for Rachel.

"I can't, Wesley. I'm afraid of heights." She turned and gave him a shaky smile.

"You have to. I'll help you." He held out his hand. "Trust me, Rachel."

She stared down at his offered hand. She looked back up, meeting his eyes, and shook her head.

He kept his hand extended. "Come on, Rachel. There isn't much time."

"Come on, Mom," Dusty called down to encourage her. "If Mel can do it, you can, too."

"Those bad guys are still out there." Mel held tight to the branches around her. "They're probably coming right now." She lowered her voice. "You're going to get yourself and Wesley killed."

"But my hands." Her breath caught. "I can't climb."

"I'll help you." Wesley kept his eyes focused on Rachel's.

Taking a deep breath, Rachel placed her hand in Wesley's. He helped her up the tree, climbing with her, keeping her body between his and the tree trunk. His heart flipped as she leaned back against him. Her hair smelled of the creek and reminded him of just how long it's been since he'd been this close to a woman.

Taking her right hand in his, Wesley guided it to the next branch. He smiled as she found her perch in a wide junction between two heavy branches.

"It's such a long way down," she whispered, teetering. Wesley put a steadying hand on her shoulder and pulled her back until she sat, straddling the branch.

He took their packs and hung them from stout limbs before crawling over and sitting beside Rachel, his shoulder touching hers.

"The jackets are wet. We'll all have to sit close together to keep warm." Wesley waved the children over. "This branch should support us. Lean against the trunk." He pulled Dusty between his legs, placing the boy's back against his chest and instructed Rachel   to do the same with Mel.

Sharing each other's body heat helped some, but Wesley still felt Rachel shiver. Their shoulders already touched, yet he scooted closer, trying to give her some of his heat. He could see the goose bumps up and down the arms of the other three and rubbed his hands vigorously up and down Dusty's arms.

Soon, the children slept. Rachel played with her daughter's hair, braiding it and then combing it out with her fingers. "The blue streaks are gone. Washed out. I'm glad." She looked over at Wesley. "Do you have children, Wesley?"

"Nope. Never been married. Why?" He adjusted his position to find a more comfortable spot for his bottom, being careful not to wake Dusty. He puffed his breath as his side pained and he wished he'd thought to get more Tylenol before hanging the packs out of reach.

"You're really good with them. Dusty and Mel, I mean. Dusty is accepting of most everyone, but not Mel. It takes longer for her."

"She doesn't have much choice. It's accept me or not."

"I know." She leaned her head back against the trunk. "My parents must be really worried by now. We should have been there yesterday, I think. They know I would have called if we were stuck somewhere. I've never *not* called them."

"Are they Christians, Rachel?"

"Yes…"

"Then they have someone stronger to lean on. They're all right."

"I'd rather have someone I can see." She peered at him through the growing darkness.

"I'm only human, Rachel. "Don't place me into too high of a position. Don't ask more of me than I'm able to give." He shrugged. "I'm not God. Chances are I won't make it out of these woods alive."

"And that doesn't bother you?" Rachel's lips twisted, disbelief sang clearly in her voice.

"Some—but I know where I'm going. I personally wouldn't have chosen to end my life this way, but if it's God's will…"

"That's a load of bull." Rachel leaned her chin on Mel's head.

"Shhh!" He placed a hand on her arm. "Listen."

He sat, tense, as their pursuers walked beneath the tree in which they were sitting.

"They can't just disappear," one of them stated.

"Moe's going to be angry."

"You should have killed them yesterday,

instead of just winging that guy."

"Shut up, man! I was just trying to have some fun. Moe didn't say they had to die right away. He'd probably appreciate it if we brought the woman and kids back alive."

"Yeah. A little entertaining diversion. Let's take them alive. The man, too."

"What for? We'll never take him out without him taking out one of us. He's got training, I tell you. I say we kill him and take the others."

Wesley watched the blood drain from Rachel's face as they listened to the men talk. The men spoke about killing and kidnapping as casually as he might speak of the weather. Rachel closed her eyes and pull Mel tighter into her arms. Wesley tightened his grip on her arm as branches rustled.

"Did you hear something?"

"No, man. You're hearing things."

"They must have walked down the creek a ways."

"They can't go far with them kids. That girl don't look very strong. She's a skinny thing."

Wesley continued to listen as the men followed the creek out of range of his hearing. Rachel's breathing quickened and she trembled.

"Rachel." Wesley shook her arm, keeping his grip tight. "Focus on your breathing. Remember what I told you. Breath. In your nose and out your mouth."

She nodded.

"That's right." He prayed, watching her breath, staying focused on her face. Her eyes stayed glued on his as he squinted through the moonlit night. Within seconds, she relaxed. She smiled and leaned back once more against the tree. It surprised him to see how quickly she fell asleep.

He didn't sleep, though. He sat thinking about what Rachel had said. What had happened to turn her away from God? Had she ever known Him? From some of the things her son said, Wesley guessed he knew the Lord, but Rachel and Mel seemed hardened. What had her life been like before it chased her off into the forests of the Ozark? How had her husband died, and what kind of a man had he been? The children didn't talk about him. Rachel seemed sad, rather than bitter. Wesley shook his head.

Amazing, but he found himself wanting to see her smile. Not a smile of sadness, or because it was expected of her, but because she was happy. He hadn't felt himself drawn to a woman in that way for a very long time. When he did finally close his eyes, a vision of a hazel eyed woman swam behind his lids.

8

Rachel woke the next morning to discover her head on Wesley's shoulder and Mel still sitting between her legs. The girl's head crushed Rachel's sternum. She shifted, lifting her daughter's head and positioning it in a more comfortable position.

"Good morning."

Turning her head, Rachel looked into Wesley's smiling face, his eyes crinkling at the corners. "Good morning. Did you sleep at all?"

He shook his head. "A little, but I've gone without sleep before."

"That's what you said about eating." She shifted again, her tailbone aching. "Mel, honey, wake up."

Mel jerked awake. "What?"

"It's time to wake up. You're killing me."

"Sorry, Mom." The girl rubbed the sleep from her eyes and stretched, causing her mother to duck in order to avoid being hit in the head.

"Scoot, Mel."

Dusty yawned and moved out of Wesley's lap. He glanced down at his shirt. "You bled on my shirt."

"Sorry." He glanced down at his side. "You were squashing me pretty good."

Rachel swiveled her body to get a better look. "Why didn't you say something?" She bent, caught a glimpse at the ground, gulped. Swallowing back her fear, she turned and ran her fingers lightly over the wound. "That doesn't look like it's healing very well." She chewed her lower lip. "It's all red."

The wound remained open, oozing a thin trail of blood. She touched the swollen area around it, gently probing. Wesley drew in his breath in a hiss, and she stopped.

"It's fine. Re-bandage it and let's get out of this tree." He stretched, balancing on the tree branches and retrieved the packs.

He sat silently until Rachel had finished, then stood and swung from branch to branch until he looked up at them from the ground.

As her children followed suit, Rachel stared. Her hands ached. It wasn't going to be easy. Her heart flew into her throat as she gauged the distance to the ground. She turned around and hugged the tree trunk, feeling with her foot for the next limb. She slipped, re-scraping her hands, and yelped. Closing her eyes, she shook her head.

"Open your eyes and climb down, Rachel."

"I can't. I'm going to stay here forever. I love this tree."

"Mom, you're holding everyone up. Hurry."

Rachel opened her eyes, turned her head, and peered down into Mel's face. "I can't."

Wesley grasped one of the lower branches and swung himself up. Within seconds, he'd placed his body over Rachel's, one arm on each side of her. "We'll climb down together."

She nodded, relishing the feel of his solidness, and allowed him to coach her down. Her stiff muscles protested each step of the way. With solid ground finally beneath her feet, Rachel stepped away from Wesley. "Thank you, again."

"My pleasure."

Stretching, Rachel felt her vertebrae pop. "Aaah!"

Running a hand through her hair, she frowned. She knew it had sprung into a mess of curls around her head. She'd have given anything for a brush. Why hadn't she stuck one in her purse? She plucked her shirt away from her body. *At least we're no longer covered in mud*. The dunking yesterday had washed them all relatively clean.

Rachel declined the soggy sandwich Wesley held out to her. There wasn't a lot of food left. A few sandwiches and some crackers, a few cookies. She dug through the pack, found the pack of gum from her purse, and popped a piece into her mouth. It would satisfy her for a while. What she wouldn't do for a cup of coffee. Or a toothbrush. Thank God, she wasn't much of a breakfast eater. *Thank God? Ha*! He'd put them here in the first place.

*

Wesley was intrigued by the play of emotions flitting across Rachel's face, ranging from anger to disbelief. Her emotions were clear for anyone to see. His eyes traveled from her face to her hair. He liked the way it curled around her face and, with the dirt gone, he thought her beautiful. A scattering of tiny freckles dotted her nose and cheeks. The only thing marring her skin was the long scratch from her left eye to her chin. He glanced over at Mel. It was easy to see the mother in the young girl. A person just had to look past the shaggy hair and multiple ear piercings.

Standing, he brushed off the seat of his pants. He lifted his arm on his injured side and rotated it in a circle. He winced. Not a good idea. He felt to be sure the gauze was still in place and bent, picking up one of the packs. It was noticeably lighter. "Rachel, let's combine what's in these packs. I'm sure we can leave one of them behind."

She nodded and took the pack from him. She left the jackets, first aid and emergency supplies in one and their rapidly depleting food and water in the other. With a defiant look at Wesley, she slung the heavier pack over her shoulder and handed him the lighter one.

He laughed and accepted it. Reaching over, he tousled Dusty's hair. "Go get your dog and hide the empty pack. The walk is going to be rough for a while, then we'll hit an old logging trail. I'm hoping we can follow it down to the main highway." He watched as Dusty shoved the pack beneath a bush and kicked fallen leaves to provide camouflage.

"Will they be watching it? The road I mean?" It wasn't necessary for Rachel to specify who. They all knew who *they* were.

"They might be. It hasn't been used in a long time though, and I'm counting on that. I'm really hoping I know something on this mountain Moe doesn't."

Wesley hadn't exaggerated the difficulty of the ground they had to cover. The ground was packed hard this close to the top of the mountain, so getting bogged down wasn't a problem. Sharp rocks to climb over and briar patches hindered there progress.

Seeing Rachel close to tears, he waved her to his side. "Let me see your hands."

She stuck them toward him. At sometime, she'd managed to re-wrap them. Stickers poked through the threads of the bandages. Using care, Wesley extracted them, one by one from the dirty gauze. He felt Rachel's eyes on him as he bent over her hands. *Has a man ever taken care of her before? She's as skittish as a white-tail deer every time he touched her.*

When they continued, he took care to hold aside branches and help her over the steeper boulders. He kept an eye on Mel and Dusty. They were like two young goats scampering over the rocks. Good. He couldn't personally help them all over the rough spots.

At one point, they stood on the edge of a steep cliff. The four of them looked down over a patchwork view of farms and fields. With the changing foliage, the green and brown fields contrasted with the red and orange trees providing a view against the blue sky that was breathtaking. Clouds built on the far horizon, lending a touch of grey to the colorful panorama.

Rachel breathed in deeply. "It's beautiful."

"Wow!" Dusty exclaimed.

"You don't see anything like this where we lived." Mel's eyes scanned the horizon.

Wesley eyes lit on each of their faces. He was as pleased with their rapturous expressions as he would have been had he personally painted the view they were seeing. He let them linger for a few minutes before urging them on.

They headed east across the top of the mountain. Trees were sparse this high up and Wesley shivered in his tattered shirt. He kept Rachel and the kids moving forward. As long as they were in the open, they were vulnerable. Clouds continued to build and he kept an eye on the horizon, expecting the rain.

The storm hit an hour later. The deluge swept across the valley, and the group made a dash down the mountain and into the trees. It only took moments before they were all soaked through. Mel screamed as lightening flashed above their heads.

Dusty's eyes lit as he turned to Wesley. "I love storms."

Wesley took Rachel's arm and pulled her along with him. "Storms can be dangerous this high up. The logging camp isn't far. Come on."

Within fifteen minutes, he stood peering through the downpour across an overgrown dirt road toward a two-story log cabin. Wesley held a finger to his lips. When the others nodded, he turned and strode across the road and onto the porch. The sound of the rain drowned out the beat of his boots on the wooden planks. He turned back to the others and motioned them across.

The camp hadn't been used in a while. Windows were boarded shut and the door was locked. He left them standing on the porch and headed to the back. Good—there was one window on the back door that wasn't boarded. He ran back and got the others. Using his elbow, he broke the glass out of the door and helped Dusty climb through. Within seconds, they were inside.

Rachel sneezed.

Wesley's eyes roamed the room. A film of dust covered every surface. A long wooden counter ran along the two walls of the kitchen, broken up with a large stove and refrigerator. A stone fireplace engulfed the west wall and the last wall was covered with boarded windows.

Dusty made a beeline for the refrigerator. He yanked open the door. It was empty.

Opening cupboards, Rachel gave a cry of excitement to find a few canned foods. In a drawer, she located a rusty can opener. She smiled and pulled out several cans of stew and a large pot. She set the pots on the stove and turned the handle. Nothing.

"The gas is off." Wesley sent Mel upstairs to locate blankets. She returned with several dusty, moth-eaten army ones. She tossed them on the floor with a grimace of distaste. The blankets kicked up more dust, causing Rachel to sneeze again.

When Dusty went to start a fire in the fireplace, Wesley stopped him. "Not there." Wesley pulled a handful of debris from the kitchen sink. "Use the sink. The fireplace will alert our pursuers to where we are." He removed the grate from the hearth and set it on top of the sink. "Your stove, Madame."

Rachel smiled and set the pot on the make-shift stove. The four of them sat, wrapped in dusty army green.

"I don't suppose there's a radio?" Rachel stared into the flames of the fire.

Wesley shook his head. "There's hasn't been anything of value here since the loggers moved out a few months ago. They would've taken the radio with them. They leave the blankets and food. I think they rent this place out to groups during the summer."

Rachel got up and stirred the pot. "Almost done. At least we're out of the rain tonight." She sat back, legs stretched out in front of her. She took off her shoes and wiggled her toes. Shivering, she pulled the blanket higher on her shoulders.

Reusing the cans, Wesley dished out the hot stew. Soon after eating, Dusty and Mel curled up on the floor, back to back and soon slept.

"Will they come here tonight?" Rachel leaned her head against the wall.

"I don't think so. If they do know about this place, they'll wait out the storm somewhere. They don't appear to be hunting us in a hurry."

"Why is that?"

Wesley scooted closer to her. "There's really no where for us to go. Not quickly anyway." They sat in silence for a moment. "They will come, though. We'll have to leave before it gets light."

She nodded.

"You're a strong woman, Rachel." His admiration sounded in his voice.

"You've got be kidding." She laughed. "There's nothing strong about me." She bent her knees and, wrapping her arms around them, rested her chin there.

"Sure there is. You've been raising your two children alone. You're on the run for your life with a complete stranger, thinking at times that I might be one of those pursuing you."

Rachel smiled. "I did consider it, but not after they shot you."

Wesley took her hands in his. "You've got torn up hands and I have yet to hear you complain."

"I've complained a lot to myself." She pulled away. "I've been afraid for longer than I can remember." A tear slid down her cheek.

Wesley found himself aching to wipe it away. He stuffed his hands into his armpits. "I'm a good listener."

She turned her head so her cheek rested on her knees instead of her chin. She met his eyes. "It's not very interesting."

"Try me." He pulled his hands free and grabbed a blanket, wrapping it around his shoulders.

"My husband's name is…was Dennis. We were happy for a while, really. Then—nothing seemed to satisfy him. Not me, not his job, not his home." She sighed heavily. "So…he started drinking. Just a little at first. When we moved to the city things got worse. He was away from home more and drank more when he was home. We bought a house and he was all right for a while. Then, when Mel came along he was so excited, and even more so when Dusty was born. Then—that too got boring.

"I'm not positive, but I think there was someone else. He was away so much. He craved more excitement than being married to me could give." She wiped the back of her hand across her face, erasing her tears.

"You haven't been happy in a while, have you Rachel?"

She shrugged and a look of surprise crossed her face. "I was happy when my children were born. It does something to a woman when her husband turns away from her.

135

When you marry, you think everything is perfect and that no matter what anyone says—it'll stay that way."

"How did your husband die?" Wesley stood and went to stir the embers of the fire.

"He drove off a bridge one night. He was drunk."

Wesley resumed his seat next to her. Throwing caution to the wind, he reached forward and brushed Rachel's hair from her face. "Did he drive off on purpose?"

"They weren't able to figure that out."

Wesley studied her face for a moment before asking quietly, "When did you turn away from God, Rachel?"

She took a deep breath. Her eyes flashed in anger. "God…turned…away…from…me." She spit each word.

"God never turns away. He'll be right where you left him when you're ready."

"Good for Him. He'll be waiting for a long time."

"Surely there's *something* good you can give Him credit for."

"My kids." She turned away. "I'm finished talking now, Wesley. I'm really tired. Okay?"

"Sure." He sat there in the light of the fire and watched her back. She appeared so fragile, and he had to restrain himself from reaching for her. He ached to pull her into his arms and hold her. The feeling was foreign to him. He'd spent most of his adult life in the military and, as a result, spent most of his life alone, surrounded by men. Occasionally, he'd visited his parents in Colorado. They were always pleased to see him, but they stayed busy with their retired lives and he never stayed more than a couple of days.

He sighed, checking the fire. Leaning back against the wall, he crossed his arms across his chest beneath the army blanket.

He'd never had a serious relationship with any one woman. Before committing his life to Christ, he'd had many relationships with different women, none lasting more than a few months. He'd been excited about his job with the forest service. He'd looked forward to the solitude. If someone would have told him he'd be running for his life with a woman and her two kids, and finding himself falling for the woman after a couple of days, he would have laughed at them.

He chuckled. When time passed and his eyes burned, Wesley stretched himself on the floor between Rachel and the door. Within seconds, his eyes closed.

He opened them when Dusty crawled over and lay down beside him.

"Hey, buddy. I thought you were asleep."

"I was for a while." Dusty lay on his back and stared above him. "Don't take it personal, Wesley. Mom won't stay mad."

"She won't, huh?"

"Nah. I've been trying to get her to go to church with me for months. She hasn't gone much since Dad died, and not much before that. I think she used to go a lot, when she was a kid."

"She must have really loved your father." Wesley folded his arms behind his head. *That hurts my side. Not a good idea.* He placed them back at his side.

Dusty shook his head. "Maybe once, but I don't think they loved each other much toward the end. I think Mom just took being a wife serious, you know? Everything had to be just right."

"What makes you say that? Did they fight a lot?" He sighed. "Never mind, Dusty. It's none of my business."

"I don't mind. I can tell you like her." The boy turned toward him and smiled. "I think it freaks her out that you take care of her. That you're so nice to her."

"Freaks her out?" Wesley was surprised at how astute Dusty was.

"Yeah. She took care of Dad. I don't remember him ever taking care of her. When he was home, which wasn't often, he usually took me fishing or something. Mom acted like she was happy about it, but I think she would've liked to come along. He never asked her to." Dusty rolled to his back. His voice lowered until Wesley had to strain to hear him. "She takes care of us. Too much sometimes. I don't think me and Mel appreciate her enough." He sighed. "Mom started having anxiety attacks a few months after Dad died."

"Your sister doesn't help much, does she?"

"No. She's been mad at Dad for a long time and takes it out on Mom. Dad never really had much to do with her after I was born." A sad smile spread across his face. "I think that's why she's so weird, you know? The striped hair and earrings. Just trying to get a rise out of him. Trying to get his attention."

"Did it work?"

"Nah. He would just yell at Mom for letting her get away with it. When Mel started high school, I think Mom gave up. She gives up on a lot of things. I try to help her, being the man of the house and all, but she doesn't really let me. She doesn't like to fail."

Wesley laughed. "I figured that out on my own."

"So," Dusty grinned. "Do you?"

"Do I what?"

"Like my mom?"

He grinned back. "Yeah, Dusty. I think I do. It's our secret though, all right?"

Dusty rolled over to his back. "I can keep a secret." The boy was quiet for a moment, then squirmed again. "Wesley?

"Yeah?"

"If we have to be here...doing this...well, I'm glad you're here with us."

Wesley reached through the dark and patted Dusty's shoulder. "No problem, buddy." *But I would have liked meeting all of you under different circumstances.*

He lay there for a while, mulling over the facts Dusty had told. *Forgive me, Lord, I shouldn't have pried, but I want to know everything there is about her.*

A cloud passed over the moon, sending the room into deeper darkness and Wesley rolled over, trying to sleep.

9

Rachel screamed when a hand shook her awake. Her eyes bolted open and she looked up into Wesley's eyes.

"I'm sorry I startled you. It's time to wake up. We've got to get moving." Wesley smiled before heading to the shelves containing canned food.

Tossing her blanket aside, Rachel sat up and rolled her shoulders. She lifted a hand to her hair and groaned. Her curls were plastered to her skull. Real cute. She ran her fingers through it, trying to fluff some life back into the curls.

Her stomach growled and she mentally ran through the list of remaining food. Not enough. She dug through the contents of her purse and pulled out another stick of gum, popping it into her mouth. Hopefully it would fool her stomach for a while. What she wouldn't give for a cup of coffee. She laughed as she remembered she'd wished the same thing yesterday morning.

Wesley held out an opened can of peaches and she shook her head. "Is that the only can that's edible?"

"There's one more. The others are dented or rusty." He offered the can again. "You've got to eat."

She smacked her gum at him. "I'm fine."

"Mom, you always eat…" Mel started to speak and Rachel shushed her. Taking the can from Wesley, she shoved it into her daughter's hands.

Mel used her fingers to pluck one of the slices from the can.

"Melanie, really! I've taught you better manners than that." Rachel scowled.

Licking her fingers, Mel made a face. "It's too sweet and there're crunchy things in it."

"It's probably crystallized." Wesley bent to wake Dusty. "There's no telling how old it is. If it's not moldy, eat. It's all we have. Share with your brother."

Rachel watched her son sit up and grab the can of peaches from Mel.

"Hey!" Mel made to take it back.

"Share, Mel."

"He could've asked for it, Mom." Mel folded her arms across her chest and glowered at her brother.

"Shouldn't we be leaving?" Rachel raised eyebrows at Wesley.

"Let's go." He stuffed the blankets into one of the packs, not bothering to fold them. He hoisted the pack onto his shoulders. "We've combined everything into these two packs. Rachel, you and Mel take turns with that one. Dusty, you take the dog." He looked around the group. "Ready?"

Wesley held the door open for the others to pass through. Once outside, he took the lead again. He led them deeper into the woods.

Fall fell early on top of the mountain and as the trees grew thicker, Rachel shivered. She wished she hadn't have left her jacket in the pack.

Close to noon, Wesley allowed them to stop and rest next to some huckleberry bushes. They ate as many of the berries as they could find. Rachel drank the small amount of water remaining in one of the bottles and filled the bottle with berries. She shrugged when she caught Wesley watching her.

"You gotta take it when you find it." She popped a berry into her mouth.

"That's a healthy attitude. What happened to the panicked woman from yesterday?"

If you only knew. You're the one who

chased her away. "I sent that woman packing." Rachel finished her berries, wiped her hands on her jeans and hoisted up her pack. Waving Wesley forward, she said, "After you, sir."

Wesley's brows drew together. He stared down at her, then shrugged and turned away, resuming his place at the front of the line.

Rachel watched the backs of those in front of her. Wesley's strong back showed through the tattered shirt that blew about him with the breeze, giving her peeks of the gauze beneath.

Mel walked dragging her feet, shoulders slumped, staying as close to Wesley as she could without tripping over his feet. Dusty copied Wesley, stepping where the man stepped, moving aside branches for his mother as Wesley did for Mel, and followed the man's gaze whenever he looked into the trees.

Rachel sighed. Dennis should have put more of an effort into his children. She lowered her head, watching her own feet plod steadily forward. She ran into Dusty as they suddenly stopped. Raising her head, she saw Wesley hold up a hand. He'd halted them on the edge of an old logging road.

"What?" Rachel walked to stand beside him.

"Shhh." Wesley looked both ways.

"It doesn't look as if its been used much." Rachel allowed her own gaze to run over the road. Old tire tracks cut through tall grass and weeds. Saplings tried to gain a foothold in the packed dirt of the tracks. She peered at the trees above them. The wind whispered softly through the leaves, and she smiled.

Wesley gave her a hard look, holding a finger to his lips.

"Sorry," she mouthed. She stepped back, putting her arms around Dusty and Mel. "We have to be quiet." Birds fluttered in the trees above them.

"Rachel!" Wesley's voice was low and harsh. Cold and controlled. "What's wrong with you?"

Tears welled in her eyes and spilled over. "I don't know." Her legs went weak and she crumpled to the ground, putting her hands over her face. "I can't do this. I'm not strong enough. I just want to forget it's happening." She raised her wet face to meet his astonished one. "I thought, maybe if I pretended we were just on a hike...oh, I don't know." She covered her face again. "Take Dusty and Mel. Leave me here."

Wesley pulled her hands from her face. "It *is* happening, Rachel." He tugged on her. "I want you to stand up, right now. I mean it, Rachel. This has gone on long enough. You're putting us all in jeopardy."

"But..."

"There are no buts." He yanked her to her feet. "Get up now or we will leave you."

"You can't talk to her like that." Mel stepped closer to her mother. "She has problems. Emotional problems."

Rachel looked at Mel, startled. "Well...I wouldn't say that I..."

"She certainly does have problems. Move across that road, Rachel Kent." He pushed her forward. "Start walking."

She jerked around to stare at him. "Are you crazy?" she hissed. "I'm a sitting duck out there." Rachel felt the heat rise into her cheeks.

"Then you'd better move fast. Go!" Wesley pointed.

Stomping her foot, Rachel whirled. She stopped at the perimeter of the road and peered both ways. Not seeing anyone, she stepped out...and froze. Her heart pounded so hard, she doubted she would be able to hear the bullet before it slammed into her. She risked a glance over her shoulder at the others.

"Go, woman." Wesley hissed from behind her.

Rachel set her teeth, squared her shoulders, and ran as fast as she could into the trees on the other side. She stopped, panting for breath, feeling each pound of her heart in her ears. Then...she stood upright, anger taking over.

Kicking at the fallen leaves under her

feet, she steamed. How dare he? *No one talks to me that way.* Not anymore. She glared across the road. Wesley looked back at her, grinning. She gasped as he gave Dusty a high five. She glared at him and held her breath, waiting for Mel to join her.

Mel didn't bother to look. The girl sprinted across the dirt road.

Rachel grunted as the force of Mel smashed into her, sending them both to the ground.

"I made it," Mel said, breathless. "Thank you, God."

Rachel looked at Mel in surprise and pushed her daughter off her. *God, huh?* She stood and brushed off the seat of her pants. She noticed leaves in Mel's hair and reached up to remove them. "You should look both ways before crossing the street," she teased. Her eyes hardened again as she waited for Wesley and Dusty cross.

*

"That was awesome," Dusty told Wesley.

He smiled down at the boy. "You liked that, did you?"

"How did you know she would do it? Once you got her mad, I mean?"

"I didn't. I took a chance." Wesley put a hand on the boy's shoulder. "Ready?"

Dusty nodded. "You should probably go

last. Mom still looks really angry."

Wesley laughed and looked to where Rachel waited, hands on her hips. "She sure does, but I'm sure I can take her. Let's cross together."

Taking the boy's elbow in his hand, Wesley kept his eyes on Rachel as they jogged across.

She lit into him as soon as he stepped into the trees. "Nobody, and I mean nobody, talks to me that way."

Wesley looked down at her standing with eyes flashing and curly hair blowing in all directions. *What a spitfire! Well, she's going to need all the fire she possesses to get through this.* "Sorry, Rachel, but you weren't cooperating."

"I've been pulling my weight. You can't say that I haven't."

"You're right. I can't say that, but I can say, and I repeat, we can't keep stopping every time you feel frightened or anxious." He bent, moving his face to within inches of hers. His heart tightened at her frightened look. "You've got to pull yourself together for the sake of your children." He straightened. "Fall apart after we get out of this."

"Why you arrogant, overbearing..."

Her words were cut off and she took pulled back as Wesley took a step toward her. Without speaking, he spun around, winked at

Dusty and once again resumed the lead.

He led them on until dusk, ignoring the whining of Mel and the stony silence of Rachel. Whenever he thought of her earlier outburst, he smiled. He could hear her stomping behind him. *Lord, this woman is something. She's grabbed a hold of my heart and I don't ever want her to let go. Use these circumstances to draw her closer to you.*

Finding them a shelter under some low hanging branches, Wesley dropped his pack. Unzipping it, he withdrew a water bottle and passed it around while Rachel rationed out the berries. *How am I going to feed them, Lord? The few cans of food we have won't last long. I've no weapon and no way of hunting. We can't risk a fire anyway.* He sighed. *Maybe I could set a trap.*

"What are these?"

He looked to where Mel stood a few feet away. She clutched a handful or purple berries.

"Muscadines. Wild grapes. They're delicious. We'll pick as many as we can." Wesley studied the trees around them. "Pecan trees, too. Dusty, help me." He took one of the coats from the other backpack and spread it on the ground. "Search the ground under the leaves. The nuts are probably buried from the wind."

The four of them set to work with a vengeance, loading their pockets and the packs with all the berries and nuts they could find.

For the first time since he'd met them, Wesley saw what seemed like a genuine smile on Mel's face. The worry lines on Rachel's face looked to be easing. He caught her eye and smiled. *Thank you, Lord, for providing.*

He watched as Rachel fussed over her children. She spread one of the threadbare blankets on the ground, handed them their jackets and checked to be sure they zipped themselves up. At one point she caught him watching and turned away, her face red. Wesley smiled and chuckled, finding amusement in her discomfort.

After the children were asleep, Rachel scooted close to Wesley. "Here's a blanket."

He wrapped his arms tight around his chest. "You keep it. It's the last one."

"I've got my jacket." She tossed the blanket in his lap.

Wesley wrapped it around his shoulders. "Thanks."

Rachel sat quiet for a few minutes, before blurting, "How's your side?"

He looked over at her. "It was bleeding a bit earlier, but it's stopped now. Thanks for asking."

"I'm sorry." She hunched down in her coat, her chin disappearing in the collar. "You were right. I was wrong."

"About?" He wasn't going to make this

easy for her.

She glared at him. "About the way I yelled at you. I *am* prone to anxiety attacks. I *do* try to act like nothing is wrong when I'm worried. Sometimes I carry it too far." She sighed. "I don't like this tension between us, Wesley. I don't function well under stress."

"Apology accepted, and you do better under stress than you give yourself credit for." He smiled, keeping his face averted from hers. "I'm sorry, too."

"No, you're not. I know you deliberately provoked me back there." She hugged her knees. "I know you're smiling. You don't have to hide." She sounded annoyed. Wesley heard rustling as if she tried to get comfortable.

"Those men said you had training, do you?"

Wesley closed his eyes for a moment, then opened them and turned to her, his eyes searching hers through the dusk. "Yes. I'm a former Army Green Beret." *And I don't like talking about it.*

"Why are you here now? Why'd you decide to be a forest ranger?"

"I got tired of that life. Being a forest ranger suits me. It's a solitary life."

"You don't get lonely?"

He shrugged. "I didn't think so, until you and the kids showed up."

"What do you mean?"

"I think maybe I've been lonely after all. See, Rachel, the fighting got to me. I didn't want that lifestyle anymore, so I did a complete turn around and hid. I withdrew from everyone I knew, moving from forest to forest. My friend, Saml, he's my boss, was a beret with me." He searched her face. "When you, Dusty and Mel showed up in my cabin, well...to be honest, I was a little annoyed. It didn't take long for me to begin to enjoy the company."

"You can't possibly be saying you're enjoying this!"

He laughed. "No, just the company."

"So, that's how you learned to be so gruff." She sat, flicking the tab on her jacket zipper. "Do you have a plan, Wesley?"

He thought for a moment before answering. "We're going to follow this road. At one time, it led to the main road. I'm hoping Moe hasn't thought of it."

"He wouldn't be very bright if he didn't."

Wesley was surprised at her perception. "You're right. I apologize. I don't have another plan, Rachel. Other than trying to get us out of here alive."

"I like that plan."

Wesley laughed and reached over to take her hand. "So do I."

He felt her flinch and try to pull back. He held on, refusing to let go. Wesley pulled her closer and ran the fingers of his other hand over her palm. Sometime during the day, she'd removed her bandages. He traced the scabs on her wounds, feeling her tremble.

"Don't be afraid of me, Rachel," he told her, his voice soft. "Never be afraid of me." He put his arm around her shoulder and pulled her close, tucking her head under his chin.

Rachel shuddered. "But I am afraid, Wesley. Of everything."

"Talk to me."

She sighed. "I told you my husband Dennis drank, right?" Rachel toyed with the frayed collar of his shirt.

Wesley grunted, embracing the warm feelings she aroused.

"When he started drinking, he became abusive. Not physically, just verbally. I looked forward to the times he'd have to leave on a sales trip. One night he didn't make it home."

"That was one of the times you'd looked forward to him leaving." It wasn't a question. Wesley stated what he felt was fact.

She nodded. "Yes. And now I feel as if his death was my fault. Like I wished for it to happen."

Wesley squeezed her. "It wasn't your fault. No more than this is. Things happen for a purpose, Rachel. It's what you get out of it that's important." She opened her mouth and he placed his hand across her mouth.

Mutt growled low in his throat.

Glancing over to where the children slept, praying they wouldn't move, Wesley froze, ears straining to hear.

There. A twig snapped, then another.

He released Rachel's mouth and leaned forward to peer through the branches covering them.

The night fell silent again. Wesley saw the dog huff and lay its head back onto its paws. "Must have been an animal."

She pulled back and patted the ground beside her. "We'll put our backs against the tree and spread my jacket and the blanket across the front of us. It's too cold for you to sleep with just that thing." She motioned toward the army blanket.

Wesley smiled. He wasn't going to argue against spending another night sharing Rachel's warmth. Being cold was as good an excuse as any other. He scooted back beside her, drawing her close to him. "Good night, Rachel."

10

Rachel opened her eyes feeling the roughness of Wesley's dirty tee-shirt beneath her cheek. He smelled musty from the creek water and perspiration. She breathed deep. Smiling and burrowing deeper, she took another breath. She relished his warmth against the chill of the morning and ran her hand softly across his chest, the worn cotton like silk beneath her fingers.

Closing her eyes again, she reveled in the comfort of his presence. His arms tightened around her, startling her.

Stealing a peek from beneath her lashes, she saw his eyes were still closed. Rachel smiled, then bolted upright. *What am I doing? What if my kids see me?*

Glancing to where Dusty and Mel lay, she sighed, relieved to see they were still sleeping. They didn't move. Two lumps covered with jackets and wrapped in blankets. The army green of their coverings blended them into the shadows.

Rachel rested her head back against the tree trunk and saw a white piece of paper tangled in the branches over her head. She let her blanket fall and reached up, gently pulling it free. As she read, she gasped.

"What?" Wesley's eyes opened.

Narrowing her eyes, Rachel handed him the paper. "I found this." *He woke awfully fast. Was he not asleep?* A flush burned her cheeks. Her eyes searched his face as he read.

He handed the paper back to her without a word and scratched his head.

"Wesley?" Rachel let the paper fall from her fingers.

Crawling from beneath the overhanging branches, Wesley took a few steps and stood rigid, staring into the woods.

Rachel followed him, placing a hand on his arm. "Wesley?" He looked troubled, his face pale beneath his tan. He shivered when she touched him. "Talk to me."

"This could have been avoided so easily."

"I don't understand." She peered into his face. "Where did this paper come from?"

"I'm assuming it was posted at the campsite."

"The campsite! How did it get all the way up here?"

He shrugged. "The wind. Maybe they posted more than one sheet. Who knows?" He took the wadded paper from her and tossed it. Rachel watched the ball of white roll beneath a bush.

Wesley glanced behind them. "Get the kids up. Have them eat some of the grapes and nuts. We've got to be moving."

Rachel nodded and rushed to do as he'd told her. Her heart lodged in her throat and she swallowed repeatedly. *What does the paper mean? What do they mean by the mountain's rightful owner?* She retrieved the paper from where it had blown up against Dusty and stuffed it into her pocket. *I thought I was frightened before. Now we're not just dealing with a nut case, we're dealing with a nutcase on a mission.* She glanced again to where Wesley stood guard. *He looks more worried than he has since we've met him. I think that terrifies me the most.*

Squatting, Rachel gently shook her children awake. "Time to get up."

*

Wesley's stomach plummeted after reading the notice. *If only someone had seen that paper. So much death could have been avoided.* He pounded his thigh. *How many men are following Moe?*

Shoving his hands into the pockets of his jeans, Wesley cringed every time Rachel or

3

one of the children's voices carried to him. *Was Moe close enough to hear? Were his men?*

He sighed. Despite the early morning chill, sweat beaded on his forehead and he felt warm. He wiped his hand across his face. Things were going to get physical, and he dreaded it. Turning to watch Rachel and the children wipe away traces of where they'd slept, his shoulders slumped.

"Rachel, it's time to go."

"We're ready." She'd shouldered one of the backpacks and held the other out to him.

Wesley jerked it from her hands and slung it across his shoulders, then turned to leave. The force of the bullet as it ripped through the canvas, spun him around. "Get away!" he yelled above Melanie's screams. He dove for the bushes as another shot rang out. He caught Rachel's eye as she peered from her hiding place. "Go! I'll catch up." He heard her thrash through the bush and he crawled rapidly away from where the shots were fired from.

His shirt clung to his wet back. *Am I shot? I didn't feel the bullet*. He twisted his arm around to feel his back and withdrew sticky fingers. The liquid was clear. Lifting his fingers to his nose, he smiled. *Thank you, God*. The bullet had punctured the can of peaches as it traveled through the pack. Wesley slid the pack from his shoulders.

He wiggled his finger through the hole.

The bullet had passed through the side of the pack and out the other. His turning to leave had saved his life. Thank God, neither of the children had been standing close to him.

Wesley jerked around as someone touched his shoulder and he body-slammed them to the ground. The person beneath him grunted.

"Rachel?" He frowned down at her. "I told you to go." He grabbed her hand and pulled her to a crouch. "Where's Dusty and Mel?"

She pointed, holding her side.

Wesley rose and sprinted in that direction, staying low and dragging Rachel with him. She panted behind him, whimpers interspersed with her gasps for air.

It wasn't long before Wesley could hear their pursuers crashing through the brush behind them. As soon as he spotted Dusty and Mel, he shoved Rachel ahead of him. "Go! Don't stop. Don't look back."

"Wesley," she pleaded, her eyes huge in her pale face.

"Please, Rachel." He cupped her face. "Go."

Rachel put her hand over his and nodded. Turning, she ran and disappeared into the trees.

Wesley turned to face their attackers. Twigs snapped, and voices drifted to him on the wind, hoarse and whispering. He dropped the pack and scurried into the bushes. He didn't wait long. Two men walked up and stopped beside the pack. He ducked as their eyes scanned the foliage where he hid.

One of them laughed. "Ran like rabbits, didn't they?"

"I swear I hit that yellow-bellied man they got with them. It sure would be more fun if he'd stop and fight."

It's a fight they want, huh? Wesley glanced around.

"He probably crawled off somewhere to die."

Wesley picked up a rock lying next to him and tossed it into the bushes opposite of the two men.

They spun around. "What was that?"

"Go see."

"You go see."

"Fine." The first man held his gun ready and walked toward the sound. The one left behind, backed up, bringing himself closer to Wesley. With a patience born from missions of his former military career, Wesley waited.

When the man was within a couple of feet, he sprang, grabbing him in a headlock.

The man clawed at the arm holding him, raking his fingernails, leaving deep furrows. He gasped, struggling for air. His legs thrashed, kicking up dirt and leaves. The hand holding the rifle lifted, swinging the gun toward Wesley's head.

Ducking, Wesley tightened his forearm against the man's throat until the man lost consciousness. The man fell without a word.

Wesley's hand shot out and grabbed the Remington 22-250 before it hit the ground. He unbuckled the ammunition belt from around the man's waist. Hearing the other man returning, his training came back to him in an unwelcome rush. Wesley spun. In one fluid motion, he knelt, aiming the rifle.

His shot took the man in the chest, killing him instantly. Wesley rose and went to stand over the dead man's body, removing the hunting knife from his belt.

He stared down at the body, his face frozen impassively. Spotting a small pack lying a few feet away, Wesley stooped and rummaged through it, pulling out a water bottle and package of jerky.

Movement behind him caused him to whirl, rising to his feet, knife in hand. The man he rendered unconscious stood ten feet away, a knife in his own hand. His eyes flicked over to his dead comrade before landing on Wesley.

"You killed my brother."

"Then let's keep it in the family." Wesley firmed his jaw, tightening his grip on the knife. Keeping step with each other, the two men shuffled sideways, moving in a circle, warily eyeing the other.

"There's lots more of us, mister. Friends and comrades." The man bent his knees, bending slightly at the waist. "I'm Bruce. Thought you might want to know the name of the man who kills you."

"Okay, Bruce. I'll go through each of you one by one. Your next." Wesley kept his eyes glued to the man's brown ones.

Bruce faked a lunge and laughed. "Should have left when you had the chance, ranger man. We left plenty of notices."

"I never got a notice." Wesley shook his head. Raising his hand, he wiggled his fingers in invitation. "Let's dance."

The man dove, his knife narrowly missing Wesley's mid-drift.

Wesley counteracted the stab with a nerve numbing blow to Bruce's forearm.

Grunting and still maintaining a grip on his knife, the man stumbled backward.

Taking the initiative, Wesley charged forward, ramming his shoulder into the man's chest.

The man's breath left in a huff. He arched his back, sending Wesley tumbling to the ground.

With panther-like quickness the two men were on their feet, once again circling each other like boxers in a ring.

Sweat blurred Wesley's vision. He

swiped an arm across his face.

"You're bleeding, ranger man," his adversary taunted.

Wesley glanced down to see the gauze red with fresh blood. He cocked an eyebrow and waved the other man forward. "Don't worry about me."

With a roar, Bruce dove catching Wesley around the middle and tackling him to the ground. Wesley's knife flew, landing several feet away in the leaves. He rolled from beneath his attacker.

The man rushed him again.

Flexing his knees, Wesley planted both boots in the man's chest and thrust him away. Scrambling through the leaves, he searched for his knife.

Bruce roared again, and Wesley rolled. He grabbed the dead man's pack and jumped to his feet.

Wesley swung the pack, connecting with the man's head. Bruce remained on his feet and charged, tackling Wesley to the ground. Straddling him, Bruce aimed the knife for Wesley's chest.

The knife came within inches, hovering over his chest. Wesley's gaze darted from the knife to his attacker's face. The man grunted, face turning red with the effort to keep the knife moving downward.

Wesley pushed harder. The wound in

his side screamed.. Ignoring the pain, Wesley strained, pushing Bruce's arm back. His hand slipped and Bruce gained another inch. Wesley grunted and gave a final push, tossing the man over. Wesley jumped on top of him.

Inch by slow inch, the knife lowered closer to Bruce's neck. With a roar, Wesley used his remaining strength and drove the knife forward, imbedding it in the other man's chest. Bruce screamed. His cry echoed through the trees. The dying man's eyes were wide as the light flickered from them.

Wesley rolled off the body and lay panting on the forest floor. He let his head fall to the side and scanned the line of trees. When would more come? They'd seen four. His side burned. Rubbing his palm across the gauze he winced. It was covered with blood, dirt and debris from the forest floor.

He stared through the trees into the blue sky above. *Lord, I never wanted to kill again*. The picture of the young South American girl flashed through his mind. A fist grabbed hold of his heart, and squeezed.

He rose to his elbow, lunging to his feet when he heard more crashing through the bushes. Scooping up the rifle, he sprinted in the direction he'd sent Rachel.

11

When the shot rang out, Rachel cried, "Wesley!" She drew her children close to her side and switched her attention to the cliff before them. She stared over the edge. *What do I do now? I can't jump! Wesley, where are you?* Below them ran a swift running river, boiling and rushing over rocks and around boulders. They were trapped. *And where was Wesley?* She spun around to face the trail.

"Mom?" Melanie's voice trembled.

Someone came fast through the trees toward them. Dusty stepped in front of his mother and sister, one hand holding Mutt's leash, a thick stick gripped in the other. "What do we do, Mom?" He stood with legs spread apart.

Rachel glanced back at the raging water. "I don't know, Dusty." She reached over and pushed him behind her.

"They're coming closer!" Mel screamed.

Rachel opened her mouth to scream along with Mel when Wesley burst from the trees. Rachel heard loud curses and yells, along with several gunshots. Wesley held a rifle high above his head.

"Jump!"

Rachel stared at him in terror. She couldn't move. Her legs remained rooted to the spot where she stood.

"Now! They're mad."

Dusty and Mel took one more look toward the trees—and jumped. Rachel remained frozen, her eyes glued on them as they went over.

Wesley tossed the pack over the cliff, scooped Rachel into his arms, and leaped, plummeting them twenty feet to the roiling water below.

Frigid water closed over her head, stealing her breath. Rachel's heart pounded as her lungs screamed for oxygen. The river rapids ripped her from Wesley's arms. Opening her mouth to scream, she gulped water. Her lungs burned. Rachel fought to get to the surface and gulped air into her lungs before submerging again.

The backpack of blankets and jackets weighted her down. Kicking, she twisted to free herself. Her lungs burned, and Rachel panicked. She thrashed and kicked against the rocks as she was pulled past them. When her arm slipped free of the strap, she let the pack float down the river ahead of her.

Without the weight of her pack, she planted her feet on the bottom of the river and lunged upward. Inhaling life saving oxygen, she was dragged under again.

The river carried her bobbing over the surface, tossing her into boulders and knocking the breath from her. After what seemed an eternity, the water calmed, depositing her into a shallow pool.

She came up coughing and sputtering. Rachel struggled to her feet and stumbled toward the bank. She stopped with the water at mid-thigh. Great, gulping sobs shook her body as she watched Wesley pull Dusty and Mel from the water.

Through her tears, her eyes sought Wesley's. He splashed through the water to reach her.

Wesley pulled her into his arms. "It's okay, Rachel. They're okay." He patted her back. "Your children are strong swimmers."

Hiccupping, she blinked the tears away to see Dusty and Mel sitting on the bank watching her, fear on their faces. She pulled away from Wesley and rushed to them, struggling to push her way through the water.

Reaching the bank, she held her arms wide and Dusty and Mel ran to her, their cries mingling with hers. Her eyes met Wesley's over their head. "Thank you."

He plopped down on the ground next to

them. "You're welcome." His breath came in short gasps.

Noticing the uncommon paleness of his skin, Rachel released her children and moved to his side. "Are you all right?"

"I pulled the packs from the river. Do you see them?"

Rachel frowned. "Yes, why?"

"Do you have a needle and thread in either of them?"

"Yes."

Wesley lifted what remained of his shirt, revealing the re-opened flesh wound in his side. "I seem to have caused more damage jumping off that cliff than the bullet did when it grazed me. I banged into a couple of large rocks." He stared in her eyes. "I need you to stitch it up, Rachel."

She shook her head. "Oh, no, Wesley. You can't ask that of me." She scooted backward on her hands.

"Rachel..."

"I can't."

"You can." Wesley sighed. "I can't keep re-opening the wound. I won't be able to keep up my strength going like this. If I could reach it, I'd sew it myself."

Melanie handed her mother the needle and thread. When Rachel looked at her, questioning, Mel gave a sad smile. "You know you're going to do it, Mom. Might as well accept it now and get it over with."

Rachel jerked the needle and thread from Mel's hands. "Fine. If you die of septic poisoning, or whatever it's called, don't come running to me."

Handing her a lighter from his jeans pocket, Wesley laughed. "Okay, I won't. The lighter's waterproof. You can sterilize the needle with it."

Dusty handed Wesley a smooth stick. "It's to bite down on." He grinned. "I saw it in a movie once."

Returning his smile, Wesley nodded. "I don't think it'll hurt more than bashing into that rock did, but thanks." He shook his head, flinging water from his hair. With the back of his hand, he swiped his face.

Rachel held the tip of the needle over the flame of the lighter until the needle turned black. She sniffed, took a deep breath, and carefully guided the thread through the eye of the needle. She knotted it and met Wesley's gaze.

She took another deep breath. "Ready?"

"If you are." Wesley lifted his shirt once more. "Just pull the edges together. Don't worry about doing a neat job. It won't be my only scar."

"I can sew, Wesley." Rachel scowled, bending over the wound. "Just never used this particular skill on skin before." *Human skin is really tough*. She'd expected the needle to slide through easily, yet she had to apply quite a bit of pressure to get it to pierce the skin.

After several stitches, she glanced at Wesley, gauging how he fared.

Beads of moisture glistened on his forehead and lip.

"Are you okay? I swear you'd be sweating blood if it was possible." Rachel poised the needle.

He nodded. "It does hurt a bit, Rachel. It's either sweat, or cry. Which would you prefer? I go with sweat."

She stuck the needle roughly back through the skin and Wesley grunted. Rachel lifted her head and smiled mischievously. "Sorry."

"Uh Huh." He held his bottom lip between his teeth and stared toward the river.

She followed his gaze, and gasped.

On the cliff above the river stood three men with guns staring down at them.

"Can they reach us?" Rachel turned back to her stitching, pulse racing. "I'll hurry." She jabbed the needle through his skin again.

"It looks like they're carrying hunting rifles. Not the fastest, or the most accurate, but someone who was an exceptionally good shot might be able to reach us." He drew in a breath sharply as Rachel tugged on the thread.

"They used automatic weapons at the campground."

"They're playing with us. Ow! They don't want to kill us that fast."

"Sorry."

"Automatic rifles are faster. At the camp they wanted to kill everyone as quickly as possible." He sucked in his breath again. "Slow down, Rachel."

"They know you're wounded. They're the ones who shot you. It doesn't seem like playing to me." She stabbed the needle. "You have got the thickest skin!"

"They want me out of the picture. I took out two of them back there. I think they want you and the kids alive."

Rachel pulled the thread through again. "They want us alive? Why? What did you do?" Her hands stilled and she glanced at him.

"I don't know why. Games, I guess. Maybe hostage. After I sent you on, I hid in the bushes. I lured one away, put one in a headlock, and when the first one returned, I shot and killed him." He sighed. "When the other regained consciousness, we fought. He died. I heard more coming, and since I was outnumbered, I ran after you."

"I thought you were dead," Rachel said, her voice barely above a whisper. "When I heard the gunshots, I thought you had left us."

Wesley reached over and lifted her face

17

to meet his. "No chance, Rachel. No chance."

Rachel sensed she could drown in his blue eyes, and pulled away. She transferred her attention to completing the stitching job she'd done on his side. With shaking hands, she tied the string into knot and bit off the excess with her teeth. Her cheek brushed against his skin and she jerked back as if stung.

Glancing up at the cliff, she noticed the men were gone. "How long until they reach us?"

Wesley pulled his shirt down and shifted, groaning. "Unless they choose the same way we did, it'll take them a couple of days to go around." He tried getting to his feet and fell against the trunk. "Guess the adrenaline wore off."

Rachel placed a hand on his chest. "Stay down. We've got time to rest." She pulled the pack containing their food toward her. Rummaging through it, she came up with the can of peaches. She held up the one with the bullet hole. "That was close."

"Too close. When I felt something wet run down my back, I thought I'd been shot."

Setting the damaged can down, she opened the one she shoved in at the last minute. The can was dented, but not punctured. "The peaches are still good. I know you won't eat them, but at least drink the juice from this can."

"I will if you'll eat something."

"Fine." She grabbed a handful of berries and popped them into her mouth. "Happy?"

He laughed and drained the juice from the peaches. He called Dusty over and handed them the two cans. "Here. Eat up."

Dusty nodded and went to where Mel sat, hands wrapped around her knees.

"That pool is pretty shallow," Wesley noted. "Might be able to catch a fish."

Rachel looked at the water. "With what? My bare hands?"

"Sure. If the water's shallow enough, you and Mel ought to be able to catch something."

She glanced down at her wrinkled clothes. "Well...it won't hurt my clothes. Will you be all right?"

He grinned. "I'll be fine."

"Okay. Mel?"

Shrugging, Mel stood and walked to the water's edge. "I can if you can."

"It's a race. First person to catch one, gets the first bite. Dusty, start the fire."

"Is that all right, Wesley?" the boy asked.

"Sure. They all ready know where we are. Spread the wet blankets and jackets to dry while you're at it."

Rachel and Mel raced into the water, re-soaking themselves. Rachel stopped and stared into the clear water. Although it reached her knees, it appeared to be only a few inches deep.

A shadow caught her eye and she squinted, bringing a fish into focus. She dove for it and lost her footing. She heard Wesley laugh when she came up out of the water. She turned to glare at him.

"Be patient, Rachel. Stay still and the fish will come to you."

"I got one!" Mel lifted a fish above her head. Her hand slipped and it became a game of catch as the fish flopped from one hand to the other. Getting a firmer grip on it, she tossed it on the bank. "I'm eating first."

Mutt went for the flopping fish, barking and growling.

"No, Mutt." Dusty pulled the dog away. "Good job, Mel."

Hearing their conversation filled Rachel with new energy. Spurred on by the promise of cooked fish and a chance to be warm, she concentrated on catching a fish. She squatted in the shallowest section of the pool, peering through the water. Inch by inch she extended her hand in front of her. One fish swam too close and she whipped out her hand, snaring it. She shrieked as her fingers closed around the slippery fish.

"Good job," Wesley encouraged.

Within the hour, Wesley skewered five

fish on sticks and they sat holding them over the fire. The smell of roasting fish wafted up, causing Rachel's stomach to growl. Steam rose from their wet clothes as they all huddled as close to the flames as Rachel deemed safe.

She lifted her stick from the fire. "Hey." She glowered at Wesley. "Why couldn't we have used sharpened sticks to fish with? It would have been a lot easier."

*

Wesley laughed. *Rachel was good for his soul.* "The way the two of you were floundering around, you would have speared your foot, or each other."

"Couldn't we have determined that?" She stood and glared down at him.

"Rachel." He patted the ground beside him. "Sit down. Did you think, even once while concentrating on those fish, about the men chasing us?"

She sat beside him, still holding the uneaten fish. "No."

"Okay, then."

She huffed and handed him one and a half of the fish. "Half for the dog."

He went to return it and she backed away. "Rachel, the children need it more than I do."

"Wesley, you're injured. You've been passing on food for the last couple of days. Just eat the fish." She tore off a chunk of hers,

21

pressing the meat between her fingers to check for bones. "Dusty, Mel, make sure you check for bones. I don't want you choking."

"Mother, please. I'm fifteen. I'm capable of eating fish." Mel ripped into her fish.

Now that the logging road was several feet above their heads, Wesley had no idea where they were. He supposed they could follow the river in the general direction the road took. Where was Moe's camp? Were they closer, or farther away from them?

He studied the two kids. Now that she was cleaned up, Wesley could see how pretty Mel was. The blue stripes were gone from her hair, along with the heavy eye makeup. She closely resembled Rachel, right down to the freckles. The girl sat staring into the flames of the fire, her arms wrapped around her knees. Dusty sat holding the dog, chin resting on Mutt's head. *Two tough kids. They've really pulled through*.

Switching his attention to Rachel, he admired the way the fire illuminated the different highlights in her hair. The sun was disappearing over the mountain and half of Rachel's features were lit, the other half dark. The fire set sparks in her eyes. Her dark lashes cast shadows on her cheeks and there was a piece of fish stuck to the corner of her mouth. Wesley's fingers itched to wipe it away. *I'm falling, aren't I, Lord? I'm falling hard. I never would have thought I'd fall for a woman with two kids, much less a woman who is angry at You.*

12

Rachel stretched her arms above her head, opening her eyes. The morning wind blew crisp and she inhaled deeply, filling her lungs with the fresh air. Wesley groaned, attracting her attention.

Turning her head, her eyes fell on his flushed face. Rachel tossed aside her blanket and reached up, putting a hand on his forehead. Heat radiated into her palm.

"You're burning up." Rachel grabbed the backpacks and rummaged through them looking for her purse. Finding it, she dumped the contents on the ground, looking for her container of pain reliever. The small tin glinted at her through the menagerie of tissues, receipts and other small items.

She snatched the last bottle of water and shook three of the pills into her hand. "Wesley." She shook him. "Take these. You're burning up with fever." Rachel helped him to a sitting position. Taking the discarded blanket, she wrapped it around him.

Wesley tossed the pills into his mouth,

chasing them down with the water. Handing the bottle back, he rolled to the ground, looking at Rachel with glazed eyes.

Lifting the blankets and tee-shirt, Rachel studied the wounded area. It was red and inflamed. No red fingers snaked away, and Rachel's pulse slowed. *Good. No blood poisoning. Yet.* "You're awfully hot, Wesley. I'm sorry I don't have anything stronger than Tylenol."

"Don't worry about it. I'll be fine."

"You're not fine. This wound might be getting infected." Rachel sat back on her knees. "We need something to clean it properly." She gnawed the inside of her mouth. "I don't suppose there's a store nearby?"

Wesley shook his head. "No. The only store's the camp store and that's miles away." He tried to sit up, his arms shaking.

Rachel reached over to assist him.

"There is a ranger station about two miles west of here."

"Will there be a radio there?"

"No. There hasn't been a full-time ranger on duty for years. It's more or less a shelter for stranded hikers. Like us." He gave her a crooked smile, sweat beading on his forehead.

"Can you make it?"

He nodded. "With your help, but it'll be slow."

Rachel crawled over and woke Dusty and Mel, explaining to them about Wesley's fever and where they were going. "There're only a few nuts left for breakfast." She glanced at the river and grimaced. "And river water."

Handing Dusty the pack Wesley usually carried, Rachel helped the wounded man to his feet. She staggered under his weight.

"Sorry." He stepped away and Rachel pulled him back.

With Wesley's weight leaning on her shoulders, they followed the river west. Underbrush grew thick along the bank of the river. Dusty struggled to clear a path for them. He stomped down the weeds and brush where he could, leading them in a zigzag path around obstacles
when he couldn't.

Melanie trudged along behind her brother, keeping her head down.

Legs shaking and threatening to collapse under Wesley's weight, Rachel called a halt. She slid to the ground, taking Wesley with her. Her legs shook and her shoulders ached. Digging the water out of the packs, she offered it once more to Wesley, ignoring his protests.

"River water is fine for me, Rachel."

"Just drink it. I'm too tired to argue with you." She felt his forehead and sighed. "A little cooler, but you're still too hot, Wesley. I'm giving you more Tylenol." *Although it's too early for another dose, but I don't know what else to do.* "It'll be all right, I think."

He frowned at her.

"What?"

"Rachel, I'm not worried about overdosing on Tylenol. I'm going to the river."

"Wait, Wesley." She crashed through the brush after him.

Wesley knelt beside the river and ducked his head. Rising up, he shook, flinging water from his head. "That was cold."

Scooting beside him, Rachel slipped under his arm, slinging it across her shoulder. "Lean on me, Wesley." She pulled against his struggles.

"Let me walk under my own steam," he retorted. "I'm not dead."

She reached up again to feel his forehead. She pulled back in shock as he knocked her hand away. "What...?"

"Look at your children, Rachel," he told her, his voice low. "I need to walk under my own power."

Dusty and Mel watched them. Mel's eyes were red-rimmed from crying. Dusty's chin quivered. Rachel looked at them, then back to Wesley, comprehension dawning on her. Dusty and Mel needed Wesley now as much as they needed Rachel. With either of them gone or disabled, the children would lose hope. Rachel met Wesley's eyes and nodded.

He touched her shoulder. "It's not much farther. I'll make it. It's just like having the flu."

"But people with the flu need bed rest." Tears welled in her eyes.

Wesley chucked her under the chin. "Thanks for worrying, Rachel, but we don't have the luxury of bed rest."

The tower of the ranger station rose forty feet in the air above them. *How will Wesley make it up those stairs? He's wobbling now*. Rachel's neck hurt from looking up.

"You three go first." Wesley put a hand on her shoulder. "I'll follow at my own pace. Once you get up there, check for any supplies we can use."

Rachel studied the old worn stairs, her eyes traveling to the top of the tower which missed shingles. The windows were busted, shrouded with cobwebs. "This has been vacant for a long time, Wesley. There probably won't be anything of value left."

"There'll be something. I told you it served as a shelter for lost hikers. It gets stocked with canned food and water a couple of times a year. Go on."

She sighed and headed up the stairs with Dusty and Mel following. Dusty clutched the dog in his arms.

The stairs shook beneath Rachel's feet and she stopped, gripping the railing. "One at a time. Stay where you are until I reach the top."

Testing each step before putting her full weight on the weathered boards, Rachel reached the top and looked around her. They were once again near the top of the mountain. Trees covered the landscape laid out before her in every shade of red, yellow and orange. She searched the ground, looking for any sign of the men following them. She located the river and let her eyes follow it east. She didn't see anyone.

The door to the tower opened with a squeak as she pushed on it. "Come on up."

She looked around the circular room. Dirt covered the table and chairs, the air heavy with dust. A long wooden counter ran around one wall and a pane of glass covered a case. Another door stood ajar, leading to a small closet.

When Dusty and Mel joined her, she set them to work finding anything that might be of use. Rachel directed her attention to the glass case. Under the glass was an axe, two pocket knives, one machete and a compass. Beneath the case was a cupboard. Opening it, she discovered several jackets and blankets. She pulled out the largest of the jackets and set it aside for Wesley.

She turned and stepped outside, her eyes raking the forest. *Where is he*? "Find anything?"

"I found a first aid kit," Dusty answered.

"Mel's going through the closet."

Rachel stepped inside and took the kit. She almost dropped it when Wesley stumbled into the room and leaned against the wall. Rushing to his side, Rachel helped him into one of the wooden chairs. "Let me see what's in this kit. I'll be right back."

"I'll be here." He closed his eyes, laying his head back.

Dust flew when she plopped the plastic kit onto the table. She popped the latch and peered inside. She found gauze, band-aids, antibacterial soap, ointment, and yes...she held up a bottle of hydrogen peroxide.

"Melanie." Rachel took out the soap, gauze and peroxide. "Did you find any water?"

"Six bottles." Mel stepped from the closet, her face split with a huge grin. "And there's canned food, mostly stew, and a couple bottles of juice."

"Wonderful." Rachel caught the bottle Mel tossed to her. "Cram everything you can into the food pack."

Rachel poured the water over the cake of soap, then bent over Wesley's stitched skin. She couldn't locate a clean rag, so she rubbed the soap between her hands, working up the suds. "This will hurt. I'm sorry." Using her fingers, she scrubbed along the stitches, popping several of them open.

Wesley groaned and pulled back.

"Be still. Stop being a baby." Rachel poured the peroxide over the wound, washing away the soap. She poured three times, then recapped the bottle. "I'm sorry. You're bleeding a little."

"Stop apologizing." Wesley clenched his teeth. "You're doing what you have to." He took a deep breath. "God provided again, Rachel. The abandoned cabin, this tower, and just when we ran out of food, He gave us more."

She snorted. "He's the one who put us here."

"That's not true. You made the decision to stop and camp."

"He allowed it, knowing those men were going to be there, killing everyone." She folded her arms across her chest.

"Yes, He did. He has a reason."

Rachel made a face of disgust. She told him what she'd found in the case. "What do you want me to take?"

"Everything. Give one of the pocket knives to Dusty, the other to Mel. They can carry them in their pockets. Put the axe through the strap in your pack and keep the machete close. Give me the compass. I've also got the gun. If we get separated, at least we're all armed." He closed his eyes.

Rachel's mouth fell open. "I couldn't use that thing on anyone! Do you really expect my children to fight for their life armed with a pocket knife?"

Wesley opened his eyes, staring into Rachel's. "I expect them to do whatever is needed. You couldn't use a weapon on someone if it meant the life of you or one of your children?"

Taken aback, she shook her head. She wasn't sure what she'd expected, but it wasn't this. Coming face to face with someone, knowing she may have to kill them, turned her stomach. She glanced over to where Dusty and Mel shared a can of cold stew with Mutt. She turned back to look at Wesley. She sighed, her breath shaky.

"Yes, I guess I could...if it came to that."

"That's my girl." Wesley took a deep breath and fell asleep.

The rush of pleasure Rachel felt at being called his girl sent a flood of warmth to her face. Even under these circumstances, Wesley had a way of making her feel cherished and worthy. It's been such a long time since she'd felt that way.

She grabbed one of the cans of stew and smiled with gratitude when Dusty handed her a rusty fork. Eyeing the fork warily, she shrugged and dipped it into the can. She smiled again. *I'd rather eat with a rusty fork then not eat.* Eating half the stew, she set the rest on the table for Wesley.

She spread the moth-eaten blankets

from their pack on the floor. "Grab one of the better blankets from the closet and get some rest." She noticed her children watching Wesley. "He'll be all right."

"Are you sure?" Dusty peered into Wesley's face. "He looks awfully pale."

"Yeah." Mel's eyes widened. "Like he's already dead."

"Melanie!"

The girl looked at her mother. "Well, he does."

Rachel caught the smile tweaking the corner of Wesley's mouth. "Dead men don't smile." She placed the can of stew in Wesley's lap. "Here, eat."

*

Hours later, Wesley woke, skin no longer burning from an inner fire. His eyes roamed the room, locating Rachel and the kids sleeping on the floor near him. They'd rolled themselves in jackets and blankets.

Feeling under his shirt, he rubbed his hand lightly over Rachel's stitching. The wound no longer felt warm to the touch, just sore. He breathed a sigh of relief and flexed his arm, testing the pull on his side. Better.

He glanced again at Rachel. She frowned in her sleep. *What was she thinking? Are you getting to her at all, Lord?* Wesley picked up the rifle from where it lay beside him. *Am I going to have to kill again? I hope not.* He sighed, his heart heavy and checked the ammunition in his belt. *There's enough here to last quite a while. Why did they each carry so much ammunition? Is Moe readying an army? Is there the remotest chance of getting Rachel and the kids out of here alive*? The gun rattled against the floor boards as he laid it back down.

Rachel woke and smiled.

"Good afternoon, Rachel."

She yawned and stretched, sitting up. "Afternoon? We slept quite a while. How are you feeling?" She brushed her hair back with her fingers.

"Like a new man." He stood and peered out the door. "There's several hours of daylight left. We should be going. We'll be cornered if they find us here."

"All right." She bent and shook Dusty and Mel. "Come on, you two. Time to go."

Mel whined, shoving her blanket off. "Can't we stay here another night? It feels wonderful to be under a roof." She shoved her hair out of her face. "I'm beginning to hate nature."

"We can't stay here." Wesley kept his gaze trained outside. "I knew this station was here, so chances are good that Moe knows it's here, too."

The girl stuffed the blankets into the pack, donned her jacket, stalking past Wesley. He reached out a hand to stop her, just as she leaned against the railing. "Don't…"

The railing gave way and Mel shrieked. As Wesley lunged toward her, she disappeared.

"Mel! Rachel, Mel's fallen over." Wesley rushed to the side to see Melanie hanging several feet below them. She'd managed to grasp the rail as she went over."

"Hang on." He turned to Dusty. "Did you see any rope while you were searching the room?"

"Yeah, but it looked really old, so I left it."

"Go get it." Wesley lay on his stomach and leaned over, stretching to reach Mel. His arms were too short. He looked up at Rachel, forcing his features to remain calm

She bent over the side, her eyes fixed on Mel. Tears ran down her cheeks, yet she didn't make a sound. She glanced at Wesley, then pulled Dusty close when he joined them.

"I'll get her, Rachel." Wesley held up a hand to receive the rope. It *was* old. The fibers were frayed, with several inches of the rope nearly worn through. He took the rope in both hands and tugged. It would have to do. *Lord, make it strong enough.*

"Melanie, listen to me." The girl screamed and kicked her legs, trying to gain a foothold. "Grab hold of this rope. Stop kicking, Mel!"

Her grip on the rail slipped and she

screamed louder.

"Help me!" Her white face stared up at him. "I'm slipping."

Wesley got to his knees and tied one end of the rope around his waist. The other, he lowered over the side, once again lying on his stomach. He kept his voice low, soothing. "No, you're not. Grab a hold of this rope and I'll pull you up."

Mel shook her head.

"Wrap it around your wrist, Mel." He kept his eyes glued to hers, willing her to follow his instructions.

She hesitated, then reached out. She grasped the rope, winding it around her wrist.

"Now, grab hold of the rope with your other hand."

Letting go, she hung there, spinning. "I'm going to fall!"

"No, you're not." He tightened his grip on the rope.

Mel continued to kick, the rope tightened into Wesley's side, cutting into his waist. "Stop kicking, Mel."

She lifted a terror-stricken face to his. Stretching her free arm, she grabbed the rope.

Wesley smiled down at her and scooted his body backward, inch-by-inch. The veins in his arms rose as he used his strength to hold her weight.

"The rope is loosening," Rachel's voice

was shrill. "It's coming apart. You've got to pull faster."

Raising his head, Wesley saw the fibers being cut where the rope met the wood of the balcony. "I'll have to lower her instead. Mel! I'm going to have to lower you."

"No! Those killers are down here. Don't leave me alone." She kicked again.

Dusty leaned and stared down at her. "They're not here yet, but they will be if you don't stop screaming."

"*You* hang here! See how you like it. My wrist burns. I think it's bleeding, and my shoulder hurts."

"I could hang there longer and quieter than you." Dusty gave Wesley a wink.

"Right," Mel snarled. "Mom, make him stop."

"Dusty…" Rachel warned in a whisper, her eyes still locked on her daughter's face.

"Wait, Rachel. Look." Wesley'd been lowering the girl to the ground as she sparred with her brother. "Dusty distracted her. She's down." He let her fall the last few feet. Standing, he shook the kinks from his arms. He glanced down at his shirt. Scooting across the wooden platform had finished off what was left of the fabric. The only pieces still held together were the arms and upper half. He shrugged out of it and tossed the shirt into the tower.

"We should keep that," Rachel told him.

"For bandages, in case someone gets hurt."

"What?" Wesley whipped his head around and stared at her. "Why are you…"

Rachel's face was white, her eyes wide and rolling back into her head. Wesley reached for her as she toppled over. He wrapped his arms around her and lowered her to the wood. "Rachel." He smoothed the hair back from her face.

"Mom!" Dusty dropped to his knees.

"She just fainted, Dusty. She'll be fine in a minute. Take the packs down to your sister." Wesley cradled Rachel's head in his lap. He continued to smooth her hair as he gazed down at her. Soon, he could hear the kids murmuring below. He assumed Dusty was telling Mel of her mother's collapse.

Rachel's lips were parted, just a bit, and Wesley ached to kiss her. The feeling surprised him, especially under the circumstances. He ran a finger down the curve of her cheek. The skin was cool and smooth beneath his touch. He smiled as her eyes fluttered open.

"Hello."

"I thought she was going to die." A solitary tear rolled down the cheek he'd just caressed.

"She didn't." He glanced over his shoulder. "You can hear her arguing with Dusty—if you listen." Their voices were growing louder. "We should get down there before they kill each other...or alert someone to our presence." He helped Rachel sit up. "You okay?"

She nodded. "I'm sorry for being so weak. I stood there like a fool. I wasn't any help at all." She headed toward the stairs.

Shooting out a hand, Wesley stopped her. "You're not weak, Rachel, and you're definitely not a fool. Fainting was a normal response. I'm glad you waited until she was down."

She gave him a weak smile and pulled free. "Thank you." She walked down the stairs, holding tight to what was left of the railing.

Wesley got to his feet. His muscles protested, eliciting a grown from him. His arms still quivered from the strain of holding Mel and he'd pulled the stitches in his side. Not enough to bleed, just enough to pinch. He shivered and thought of the tattered shirt he'd discarded.

With a shrug, he retrieved the rifle and a tackle box Rachel had overlooked. He spotted the jacket she'd set aside for him, and donned it. With another quick glance to assure himself they weren't leaving anything of value behind, he reached over and closed the door.

13

Rachel squeezed a quarter-size circle of ointment cream into the palm of her hand. Taking Mel's raw wrist, she rubbed the cool antibiotic into the welts. She looked up and smiled when Wesley joined them. Her face heated at the sight of his naked chest and she took a deep shaky breath. Two puckered scars sat high beneath his collar bone. Another longer one, ran from beneath his arm and around his ribcage.

Ducking her head, she went back to her task, concentrating too much on smearing the cream.

"You're rubbing too hard." Mel jerked her hand.

"Sorry." Rachel's eyes flicked to Wesley. "I'll take care of your scrapes next."

"I'm fine. We need to be going. They can't be far behind us."

Rachel glanced into the woods. The trees grew thicker the farther down the mountain they moved. She realized they wouldn't see anyone following until the pursuers were on top of them. She twisted the cap back on the cream, dropped it into her pack, checked to make sure Dusty had the dog, grabbed up the pack despite Wesley's argument, and stood ready. "Well? Ready?"

Wesley returned her grin. "Okay, then. Let's go." He turned, cutting a path with the machete.

"Won't they be able to see our trail?" Dusty asked.

"They know where we are. There's no need for us to make the going any tougher on ourselves than needed."

Her skin crawled. Rachel glanced over her shoulder, feeling eyes watching. She pushed Mel, spurring her on. If they were headed down the mountain, they should reach the road soon. She tried counting how many days they'd been running, and gave up. Life existed in a fog now. Fatigue her constant companion. Her steps dragged.

Wesley stopped, causing Rachel to stumble into Mel's back. "What?"

Holding a finger to his lips, Wesley pointed to Mutt. The hair on the dog's neck bristled and he growled low in his throat.

Whipping her head, Rachel peered into the thick brush around them. Nothing. No sound or movement. She turned back to Wesley.

He stood frozen, one hand on Dusty's shoulder. Mel's eyes were wide and she whimpered. Rachel grasped her daughter's upper-arm, and squeezed.

For several minutes the group stood, silent, waiting. Mutt gave one short, sharp bark and they were spurred to action. As one, the group shot into the bushes, running as fast as the terrain allowed.

Mel tripped over an exposed root, and fell.

Wesley pulled her to her feet, barely breaking stride. He cast a glance to make sure Mel was all right, and released her arm.

Mutt barked again as laughter rang out.

"Where are they?" Rachel scanned the trees. "I can't see anyone."

"I don't know." Wesley shoved aside a low hanging branch.

"Why didn't they shoot? Wait." Rachel clutched her side, doubling over. "I've got a pain."

"Can't stop now." Wesley paused long enough to grab her arm.

"When will we reach the road?" Rachel's lungs burned. She forced her legs to run and took deep breaths against the pain in her side.

"Tomorrow at the earliest." Wesley stopped, glanced around, and veered them off in another direction, still maintaining his death grip on Rachel's arm.

He let them rest in a small clearing.

Rachel watched as he walked a circle around them, staring into the woods, eventually stopping and sitting cross-legged on the ground. He opened the tackle box, and smiled. A smile without warmth as his eyes narrowed.

Rachel moved to peer over his shoulder.

Inside the box were two rolls of fishing line and several packages of assorted size fishing hooks. "You're going fishing?" She looked around them. "Where?"

"You could say I'm going fishing. Everybody up." Wesley closed the tackle box and bounded to his feet. Picking up the machete, he once again led the way through the dense underbrush.

Dusty let go of a branch. It narrowly missed hitting her in the face. Mel ducked and cried out in anger. "Watch it."

"You watch it."

The kids were getting testy and Rachel stepped forward, putting herself between them. "Now is not the time. I know you're stressed and tired. We all are. And we're frightened. We need to pull together—not fight."

Dusty looked up, chastised. "Sorry."

Mel rolled her eyes and quickened her pace.

"Okay. We stop here." Wesley dropped the tackle box. "Everyone grab something to eat and drink. Dusty, come help me when you're finished." Opening the tackle box, Wesley took out a roll of fishing line and began cutting it into long lengths with the knife. "Do you know how to tie hooks?"

Dusty took the line. "Sure. Dad taught me."

"Start tying."

Dusty picked up a hook and knotted it to the end of the line. He moved quickly. Rachel's heart clinched. He'd gone fishing many times with his father. She hoped he'd learned more skills to help him in life than how to tie a fishing line.

When Wesley had cut twenty varying lengths of line, he helped Dusty tie the rest of the hooks.

"What are they for?" Rachel wanted to know.

"Traps." He showed Dusty how to hang them from the tree, several inches apart, down the path they'd made. He then took the axe from Rachel's pack and chopped tree limbs approximately three inches thick. He tossed them to the ground and returned the axe to the pack.

He whittled the sticks into sharp points. Rachel's flesh crawled as he laid nasty looking spear upon spear on the ground. She continued in horrified fascination as Wesley constructed his traps.

Night fell before he finished and Rachel glanced often toward the line of trees. No laughter rang forth. No shots were fired. Mutt lay calm at Dusty's feet. She spun when she couldn't immediately spot Mel. Her daughter lay curled in a blanket, asleep, under a low hanging tree. Rachel released the breath she'd been holding.

She pulled her jacket tighter and shivered against the growing chill of nightfall. Locusts buzzed from the trees--Rachel found the sound hypnotizing. She peered at Wesley. Obviously he wasn't going to start a fire. He looked totally absorbed in what he worked on. His skin prickled with goose bumps. She rose and draped a jacket over his shoulders.

Using his belt and the frayed rope, Wesley latched the spikes onto the limber branch of a large tree. With Dusty's help, he pulled the branch back. He held the limb in place while he instructed the boy to use the belt to secure it.

It was then, Rachel realized what he planned to do. The booby traps he laid weren't lethal, but were intended to slow down, or halt their pursuers. The fish hooks hung at face level. If their pursuers came upon them in the shadows, the hooks would be imbedded in the tender regions of their faces and they could become entangled in the line.

She studied the spikes. They were

placed at a man's thigh level. *Why? What's he doing? These men have tried several times to kill him. Why is Wesley so determined to avoid killing? If he did, and he's shown he's capable, our problems could be over.*

*

Wesley shrugged out of his jacket. The night grew cool, yet he perspired beneath the down coat. *How much time did they have before Moe's men caught up with them?* He glanced often at Mutt, alert for any signal the little dog might give.

Tugging against the tree branch, he bent it into a horseshoe. Whoever tripped the wire would be impaled. He hoped this would delay the men in time for Rachel and the kids to reach the road. He had Dusty help him secure the branch and went to wake Mel.

"We're going now? It's getting dark." Mel's annoyance was clear in every stubborn line of her face. "I'm really tired, Wesley. You act like a drill sergeant or something."

"My traps won't be as effective in the daylight." His eyes scanned the two kids. "I want the two of you to talk. Argue if you want. I want the men following us to realize we're on the move. I want them to know exactly where we are."

Dusty's and Mel's eyes grew wide with comprehension, and they smiled.

Rachel giggled as they argued over their

favorite foods.

Wesley glanced at her. He expected her to be having another anxiety attack. She shrugged, smile in place and returned his gaze.

It was humorous—what Dusty and Mel chose to argue about. Wesley returned Rachel's smile and took possession of the machete.

They hadn't gone far when curses drifted to them on the evening breeze. "They've found the fish hooks." The cursing rose in volume as other voices joined the first. Wesley chuckled.

A shrill scream shattered the night air. Someone had triggered the spikes. The man cried for help. Someone else yelled a threat to kill them all. Wesley shoved Dusty forward. "It's time to run. Those I haven't disabled...will be coming."

Mel whirled to face him. "You've made them angry."

"I've cut them back. I'm buying some time. Don't argue. Just run." He held his hand out to Rachel, who grasped it. Wesley gave it a squeeze and let go.

"What are you doing? Aren't you coming with us?" Rachel's chin quivered.

Wesley stared into her wide eyes. "I'll catch up. I will." He held up the rifle. "I can still detain them, I hope."

"Wesley..." She sniffled.

Reaching over, he wiped away her tears. "Go with Dusty and Mel. I'll catch up. I promise."

His heart skipped a beat as he watched her disappear. "Protect her, God." Turning, he jogged back the way they'd come. When the cursing grew loud, Wesley veered off the path and made his way through the brush to where he'd laid the traps.

There were four men. One sat on the ground, his face in his hands, the apparent victim of the fish hooks. Another man wiped his face with a rag. Small cuts peppered his face. Wesley smiled grimly. Another victim of the hooks. A third man stood impaled on the spikes. They'd gone through his legs above the knees and he screamed as he tried to pull himself free. The fourth man studied the spikes.

The impaled man implored the other to hurry. "I'm dy'n here, man."

"You ain't dying."

"I think I got one of them hooks in my eye." One of the men removed his hands from his face. "Can you tell?"

"I've never met such a group of whiners in my whole life! Yo're soldiers. Act like it."

"That's easy for you to say, Rupert. You ain't hurt."

"I'm going to make you think hurt if you don't shut up!" Rupert kicked the man in the leg. "I'm trying to think. Yo're eyes are fine. Just

9

pricked, that's all. The other one is fine. You only need one anyway." He tossed the man a dirty rag. "Clean up. Yo're bleeding."

With the men occupied, Wesley took the remaining spool of monofilament and entwined it around trees and bushes. The line was invisible in the gloom of dusk and he hoped their pursuers would think he'd laid additional traps when they stumbled upon it.

Rupert stalked back to the man on the spikes. "This is going to hurt." Wrapping his arms around the man's waist, he leaned back, pulling.

The man's screams reverberated through the forest. Birds squawked and took flight from where they'd roosted for the night. "Stop, please!" The branch moved with him, not pulling free.

Rupert stepped back. "Frank, get over here."

The man with minor cuts tossed his rag on the ground and joined Rupert. "Grab a hold there." They each grabbed the tree branch and pushed. The impaled man squeaked and fell to the ground. He curled his body around his legs, and wailed.

"Now what?" Frank asked.

"Leave him. Jack can keep an eye on him." Rupert burst into laughter. "Get it. An eye on him, see'n as how he's only one eye that's working."

"You said it was only pricked," Jack whined. He clapped a hand over his wounded eye.

"And you ain't nothing but a fool." Rupert picked up his rifle. "Frank, go check out the trail. Look for more booby traps."

Frank grumbled and shuffled his feet as he proceeded. "Don't know why I have to be the guinea pig. Don't see Rupert putting himself in harm's way." The twisting line blocking the path stopped him cold. "He's made himself a giant spider web, Rupert. I ain't gonna go thru there. Ain't no tell'n what it'll do to me."

Pushing him aside, Rupert stepped forward to study the tangled web. "I ain't never seen a trap like this."

"Ya think it's one of them army ranger traps?"

Rupert shrugged. "Maybe so. We'll go around." He squinted. "Let's go get that ranger. I aim to kill him myself." He raised his voice. "You hear that, ranger man? I'm going to kill you!"

Wesley grabbed his rifle and set off at a jog after Rachel and the kids. They were easy to track. Rachel hadn't bothered with the machete. Wesley followed the trail of broken twigs and flattened grass.

"There he is!"

Turning, Wesley saw Rupert pointing in his direction.

11

"We're gonna kill you, ranger man!" Rupert lifted his rifle and Wesley dove into the brush. "Get'em, Frank."

"I can't see him." Frank sent several shots into the brush.

Wesley scurried on his belly, digging his knees into the soft ground, propelling forward. *Let their shots miss, Lord.* He gave thanks for the jacket he'd thought to put back on. It provided protection against the sticks and rocks poking at him. Locating a dense growth of bushes, he burrowed in to wait.

The two men stopped next to where he hid. Wesley held his breath, body tensed, knuckles white as he clenched the rifle in his hand.

"Let's go, Rupert," Frank whined. "He ain't here. We lost him. I'm afraid of running into more of his traps."

Rupert stood, rifle ready. "Maybe so. Let's go catch that woman and her kids. It's them Moe wants anyway."

Wesley released his breath and listened to their footsteps fade away. Poking his head from the brush, he looked around to see Rupert and Frank disappear down the trail.

He crawled from his hiding place and headed in the direction Rachel had gone, taking care to stay off the path he'd created earlier. He wanted to be sure it was him surprising Rupert and Frank, and not the other way around.

Lord, please let Rachel and the kids have made some ground. He fought his way through the brush, crawling in some places where the undergrowth was too thick. He prayed he headed in the right direction. The thick trees left little room for him to gauge his direction using the stars. *God, be my navigator.*

Wesley stopped and listened. Nothing. He couldn't possibly have left Rupert and Frank so far behind. Reaching the beaten path, he increased his pace, stopping every so often to check for signs of the two men, or Rachel and the kids. After an hour, seeing signs of neither, he stopped.

He stood in the center of the trail and turned. Besides the normal night time sounds of the forest, he heard nothing. He bent to peer at the trail. Branches were cut, rather than broken, signifying Rachel had passed, using the machete. The leaves and pine needles on the forest floor hid any sign of footprints.

"Wesley."

He spun to see Dusty peering at him from the brush.

"Dusty, what are you doing here? Where's your sister? Where's Rachel?"

"I'm here." Mel's head joined her brother's. "Mom went on ahead to lay a path. She told us to wait for you. She's hoping to lead those men away. She said we weren't moving fast enough."

Wesley set his mouth in a firm line. "What if I hadn't come back?"

"You promised."

He whirled to see Rachel standing behind him. She gave him a shaky smile and let the machete fall to the ground.

Rushing to her, Wesley wrapped his arms around her. "Don't do that again, Rachel. Don't go off on your own. Hear me?" He stepped back and forced her to look at him. "Promise me." He pulled her back to his chest. Heart thudding heavily, he tightened his hold, brushing his cheek across the top of her head.

She nodded. "It's too dark, Wesley." Her voice muffled against his jacket. "I was afraid we'd get lost."

Taking her hand, he led her into the bushes. He motioned for the two kids to join him and he led them deeper into the woods. They stopped to rest in a spot covered with thick pine needles and low hanging branches. Thick brush encircled the area, forming an effective security fence against intruders.

"Try to get some sleep." Wesley slid to the ground, using a tree trunk as a back rest. "Daylight is only a few hours away. We should reach the road before noon."

Dusty curled up with the dog, his sister not far away. Rachel set her pack down and plopped to the ground, hanging her head.

Wesley frowned. Propping his rifle

within easy reach, he squatted next to her. "What?"

She shook her head. "Nothing."

Wesley tilted her face to look at him. "There's something, Rachel. Talk to me."

Raising her eyes, she sighed. "I'm tired of being afraid. I was terrified when you left. Then we heard shots and yelling." She dropped her eyes, letting the tears escape.

"You did fine. I wish you would've kept going, but I understand why you didn't." He pulled her to him, cradling her in his lap. "All I could think of was getting back to you and the kids."

"Really?"

"Yes, really." Her eyelids lowered again as Wesley moved in to kiss her. Her lips were as sweet as he'd imagined. Wesley buried his face in her neck, inhaling her scent. He held her while she fell asleep, his eyes wandering to the still forms of Dusty and Mel.

Several hours later, Rachel woke, still in Wesley's arms. *I can get use to this*. She lifted her head from his chest and gazed at his sleeping face. *He's beautiful. Unshaved and unwashed, he's still beautiful*. She ran her fingers through her own unwashed hair. *I must look a mess. My hair's dirty and...oh no, my breath! I let him kiss me. Do I smell?* She lifted her right arm and sniffed.

Wesley opened his eyes and a lazy smile, beginning at one corner of his mouth, spread across his face. "You smell great."

Rachel returned his smile and pulled back, getting to her feet. "Good morning." She took two steps away.

"Good morning. Come back here." His lids drooped, making Rachel's knees weaken.

Her smile faded when she turned and saw Melanie glaring at her. The girl tossed aside her blanket and shoved it into the pack. She grabbed Dusty's blanket, jerking it from beneath him. Her brother rolled and sat up, head hanging. He stared around him with sleepy eyes.

Rachel dug a juice from the pack and handed it to her daughter. "Mel…"

"Don't bother, *Mother*," she spat. She yanked the bottle from Rachel's grasp. Mel fought with the cap, her movements more frustrated as the lid refused to budge. "Dad's barely dead and you're sitting on another man's lap. *Sleeping* there."

Rachel jerked back as if slapped. "Your father's been dead for two years, Melanie."

"It seems like yesterday to me." She finally got the cap removed and gulped the juice.

Wesley and Dusty shared a bottle of apple juice as they gathered the packs. *And I thought Mel and I were getting along better.* "I'm sorry you don't understand, Mel. When you're older…"

"I understand more than you think. I saw the way he looked at you. I saw the way you looked at him." Mel leaned closer and, with what seemed like evil intent to Rachel, whispered, "I'm not even a virgin anymore. I know plenty. Probably more than you do." With that, she spun and grabbed the dog's leash from her brother's hand.

"I'm walking the dog today. I'm not being a slave anymore. I'm taking the easy job." She stepped away a few feet and glared at Rachel.

Rachel stood rooted, unblinking. Where

had that come from? Mel's statement had come out of the blue, blasting Rachel's heart. She realized her mouth hung open and clamped it closed.

Wesley walked up, putting his hand on her shoulder. "Everything all right?"

She nodded.

"Let's go. The road's only a couple of hours away." Wesley swung the heavier pack across his shoulders.

Still in shock, Mel's words hanging heavy in the air, Rachel picked up the remaining pack. Her steps dragged. Her mind reeled, heart held frozen in an icy grip. *Mel no longer innocent? She had to be lying. She's just trying to get even for some imagined betrayal. Why else would she spit that out? It's ridiculous.* Rachel quickened her steps until she walked in step with Mel.

"You shouldn't tell stories like that," Rachel admonished. "That's not the type of rumor you want spread around."

Mel looked around them, flinging her arms wide. "Rumor? Out here? Who cares? Besides, it's not a rumor. It's fact." She looked at her mother. "Would you like the details? Would you like to know with who?" Mel's eyes shone with a malicious gleam.

"No. Yes. I mean...no." Her steps faltered, allowing Mel to walk ahead. Rachel shook her head. Mel stopped on the trail and

3

turned.

Rachel quickened her stride until she again reached Mel's side. Cheeks burning and chest heaving, she gripped her daughter's arm. "Why would you tell me that out here? Aren't we going through enough? Are you deliberately trying to hurt me? All I did was kiss him, Mel. I don't..."

"Kiss him?! I only saw you sitting on his lap."

Rachel stared, confused by her daughter's reaction. Mel yanked her arm free and stood with her hands on her hips. She'd dropped the leash and Mutt quickly retreated to the safety of Dusty's side. Tears spilled from the young girl's eyes.

"I'm sorry, baby." Rachel put her arms around Mel.

She sniffed and pushed her mother away. "I'm being silly. I'm sorry. I really am. I just miss Daddy so much. I don't want to be here anymore. I want to be at Grandma's and Grandpa's."

Rachel pulled her daughter close again. "I know." Her eyes met Wesley's as he turned toward them. He raised his eyebrows in question.

"We're coming." She kissed Mel's forehead. "Okay?"

Mel nodded. "Just don't throw your relationship with Wesley in my face, okay?"

"My relationship? Mel there isn't…"

"Oh, please."

"You're see-sawing back and forth so quickly, Mel, I can't keep up. One minute you're angry, then you're crying, now you're angry again." Rachel grabbed both Mel's arms and shook her. "Now is not the time to get into this. Those men are still out there. They're following us right this minute. Do you understand that?"

Mel sniffed and wiped away her tears. "Yes."

"Good." Rachel stepped back. "We'll pretend that *other* conversation never happened."

"Mom…"

"We'll pretend. For now." Rachel gave her a stern look. *Oh yes, we'll resume that particular conversation when we're out of danger.* She shifted her pack. Wesley slowed his steps to join her.

Once Mel pulled ahead of them, he said, "I'm sorry if I caused more tension between the two of you."

Rachel glanced up at him. "It wasn't you. I don't really even think it was the fact you kissed me." She sighed and shrugged. "Mel's always been dramatic. She enjoys shocking me. I'm sure you heard our conversation." She laughed. "The bears heard our conversation."

He nodded. "Do you believe her?"

"I didn't at first, but…now, I'm not sure.

I know I don't want to deal with it right now." She looked to where Mel walked. Dusty kept trying to talk to her, but the girl shrugged him off. She shoved aside branches, laughing whenever Dusty had to duck to avoid being slapped in the face.

Rachel sighed again. "She's been very difficult since Dennis died. He didn't pay much attention to her when he was alive. I think deep down, she'd been waiting for him to notice her. To *want* to spend time with her." Her words caught in her throat and she swiped a hand across her face, wiping away the tears. "He had no idea of the damage he caused."

Mel turned once, and glared.

Wesley laughed. "I'll walk ahead—with Dusty." He gave Rachel's hand a squeeze.

"Wait." She squeezed back, not letting go.

"Yes?"

Rachel took a deep breath and squared her shoulders. "Why are you trying so hard not to kill these men?"

"Excuse me?" Wesley's brow creased.

"Why aren't you sitting someplace, ready to shoot them as they come down the path? Why didn't you set your traps to kill, instead of wound?"

Wesley dropped her hand. "I've had enough killing. I told you, that isn't my life anymore."

"You did kill. Recently."

"I didn't want to! It was me or them."

"You won't kill even if it means my life?"

He took a deep breath. "It did mean your life. I'll kill if I have to, Rachel. It's difficult to explain." He stopped talking for a minute. "When I was in the Rangers, I loved my job. Everything about it. I loved the excitement, the adventure...and yes, the killing. I reveled in it. It made me feel powerful." He looked at her and retrieved her hand. "There was a particular mission I was involved in. We stormed a house in South America. The home of a suspected drug dealer. Anyway, we went in, guns blazing."

His breath caught. "When it was over, I found myself looking down at the body of a young girl. She was maybe six years old. She'd been shot. Many times. I don't know whether it was my bullet or one of my buddies. She wasn't the only child killed that day. There were women, too. The house wasn't only the dealer's place of business—it was his home."

Running a hand through his hair, he continued, "The deaths of the women and children got my attention. I requested a leave, and it was granted. I searched for the meaning of life and found God. That's when I gave up my old life and embraced the new. I lost my zeal for killing. It doesn't mean I've lost the skill."

Rachel studied his face, her eyes glued

to his. "So, you believe everything happens for a reason, right?"

He nodded.

"Then why are we here?" Her voice rose. "Why did Dennis die and leave me to raise two children alone? Why is my fifteen-year old daughter having sex?!" She yanked her hand free. "God knows what else she'd in to."

Wesley retrieved her hand, tucking it into the crook of his arm. "Dennis and Melanie made their own choices, Rachel. God gave us free will. He lets us know his wishes, if we care to ask, but it's still up to us to make the right choice. As to why we're here, in these woods, running from killers...I don't know. There is a reason, though."

"Will you still think there's a reason if we don't make it out of here alive?" She yanked her hand from his arm with more force this time. "What if I die out here? Or Dusty...or Mel?" She stomped a head of him. "I have a difficult time believing God would thrust us out here for some crazy purpose of His."

Rachel fumed. First the shock from Mel, now this. Wesley could keep his opinions about God to himself. A lump rose in her throat. Tears stung her eyes and she lowered her head. She didn't want Wesley to see her tears. *Why is this happening? I can't take anymore! You deserted me a long time ago. You could have prevented Dennis from driving off that bridge. I should just stop right here and let those men catch up to me. I'm so tired. Tired of traipsing through the woods. Tired of fighting with Mel, and I'm tired of You.*

I'm here to take your burdens, Daughter.

She glanced around her. *Great. Now, I'm hearing voices.* Rachel increased her steps. She peeked back to see if Wesley watched her. He was, his eyes full of compassion. She glowered and whipped back around. Stalking over to Dusty, she draped an arm around his shoulders.

Looking up, he smiled and patted her hand. "You all right, Mom?"

"Just fine, sweetheart. I'm just fine."

*

Well, Lord, You're pulling her closer. Wesley unzipped his jacket against the rising heat of the day. *And she's running in the opposite direction as fast as she can. I hope I'm around to see it when she realizes You're calling her back to You.*

He smiled as she stalked away from him. Allowing his eyes to roam the woods around them, he listened to the singing of the birds. *Where are Rupert and the others? Why haven't we seen any sign of Moe?* Wesley watched the dog prance at Dusty's side. So far, Mutt has been a good security alarm. The dog hadn't failed once to alert them to pursuers.

"I'm hungry," Mel announced.

"We can stop for a bit. What's left to eat in the packs?"

Rachel peered inside the one she carried. "Two cans of stew. A little nuts and berries."

"Bring it out. We'll eat here." He let his pack drop to the ground.

"I'm sick of cold stew, nuts and berries." Mel pouted, tossing her hair over her shoulder. "I can't even remember what pizza tastes like."

"Or hamburger," her brother added. "I'd love a big plate of pancakes with lots of syrup."

Rachel laughed and played with the waistband of her jeans. "I wanted to lose weight. Hadn't thought of this type of diet before."

Wesley laughed along with them. He tossed the last of the berries in his mouth. He reached for the nuts, and stopped. A motor roared in the distance. Gears squealed as they shifted.

"Be quiet for a minute." He held up his hand. There it is.

"It's the road." Dusty shouted. "That's a car." The boy turned and sprinted into the trees.

"Dusty, wait." Rachel grabbed her pack and bolted after him.

Grabbing up his own pack, Wesley took

off after them. "Dusty. Don't run ahead. I can't see you."

When Wesley burst through the trees, Dusty stood on the edge of an old, pot-holed, asphalt road. The boy spun around to face Wesley, tears in his eyes.

"We made it, Wesley. But the car already passed us." He threw himself into Wesley's arms, and sobbed. Wesley tightened his arms around the boy.

He turned his head to see Mel drop to her knees, her sobs adding to her brother's. Wesley looked down in helplessness at the two kids. He raised his head to meet Rachel's eyes.

She shrugged. "Now what?"

"We follow the road out of here until someone picks us up. With any luck, we'll be sleeping in a bed tonight." He patted Dusty's back before standing the boy away from him. "Ready?"

Dusty wiped his eyes on the sleeve of his jacket, and nodded.

Rachel pulled Mel to her feet. "Come on. We're almost home." She kept her arm around her daughter's waist and turned to Wesley with a smile. "We're ready. Let's get out of here."

The sun was warm walking alongside the road and Wesley wished for a shirt to wear, rather than the jacket. He shrugged. What did it matter? Rachel had already seen him wrapped in nothing but a towel. He shook out of the jacket, leaving modesty behind, and hung the jacket through the straps of the pack.

He listened to the chatter around him. Mel laughed at something Rachel said. Wesley hadn't realized the level of stress the kids had been under until a few minutes ago. His heart ached with the severity of Dusty's sobs. He expected Mel to be emotional, but Dusty was the strong, optimistic one.

His fears surfaced, showing their ugly face. *Will Rachel want to continue a relationship once we're out of here? Am I sure I want to? I've been alone for a long time. Am I ready for a family? A commitment?* Wesley glanced over his shoulder. His eyes caressed Rachel's tousled curls and dirty face. He remembered how she felt in his arms and how sweet her kiss had been. *Yeah. For her, I'm ready. Kids and all.*

He flashed Rachel a smile and was rewarded with one in return. Dusty smiled with her. Mel glared. *She'd require some winning over, but I can be pretty persistant.* Wesley smiled at her anyway.

Stress diminishing upon their arrival at the road, Wesley rotated his shoulders, trying to relinquish the kinks. The sun grew warmer, causing him to squint against the glare of the asphalt. They'd been walking for over an hour and had yet to see any type of vehicle. He didn't want to tell the others the likelihood of them seeing another vehicle on this old road any time soon was slim. It was more likely they'd have to walk for quite a while.

He wiped his forearm across his forehead, wishing for the coolness of the top of the mountain.

"I need to rest." Wesley turned to see Mel plop to the grass on the side of the road.

"I thought you wanted to get out of here?" Rachel squatted next to her.

"I'm thirsty."

"There's only a little left."

Dusty fell to the ground beside them. "If we're almost out of here, can't we share it? I'm thirsty, too."

Rachel looked up at Wesley, shading her eyes with her hand.

"You three go ahead. I'm fine." He dropped the pack on the ground and leaned against it. Inwardly, he yearned to continue down the road.

"I'm sorry." Rachel moved over and sat cross-legged beside him.

"For what?"

"For slowing you down. Without us, you wouldn't be in this fix, much less having to stop so often."

He ran his hand down her arm, feeling the fine layer of grit on her skin. "It's all right, Rachel. If you hadn't of burst into my cabin, I'd still be alone."

13

"And none the wiser for it," she told him, smiling.

"And none the wiser for it." He moved his hand up to caress her cheek. "I wouldn't go back for anything."

The sun hung low in the sky before they spotted the vehicle. Its headlights cut through the descending darkness.

"Wait." Wesley's instincts told them the approaching vehicle wasn't there to save them. "Hide in the bushes until I've determined it's safe."

The others ran forward as if he hadn't spoken. Rachel and the kids jumped up and down, waving their arms. "Of course it's safe," Rachel told him. "We're in the middle of nowhere."

Wesley's feelings of alarm grew closer as the vehicle neared. It was an older make of truck. He could make out the silhouette of men in the tail bed. "Run into the trees!"

Dusty dropped Mutt's leash and turned to Wesley. The dog ran under the nearest bush, barking.

A green 1962 Chevy truck rumbled to a stop next to them. Two men stood up in the bed of the truck and leveled automatic weapons at Wesley. "Stay right where you are."

"Ranger Ward, I presume."

Wesley dropped the machete and raised his hands above his head. He turned to address the speaker. "You must be Moe."

The man sitting behind the wheel of the truck frowned, his lips all but disappearing into the thick wiry beard he sported. Long, grey, unwashed hair brushed the man's shoulders. "I go by General Duane Watkins. You will address me as such."

Rachel gasped as the man opened the door and got out. Wesley allowed his eyes to travel from the man's scuffed, steel-toe boots, back to his face. Moe was huge. An easy three hundred pounds and taller than Wesley's six-foot four by several inches. Wesley squared his shoulders, met Moe's eyes and kept his feet firmly planted.

"You've caused quite a bit of trouble for my boys." Moe's voice was low, sinister.

"They've caused a bit of trouble of their own." Wesley met Moe's muddy brown gaze. He smelled the man's pungent body odor, and wrinkled his nose.

Without warning, Moe doubled his fist and slammed it into Wesley's stomach.

The air left Wesley with a whoosh and he fell to his knees. The punch centered in his stomach, radiating pain through his torso to his back. He heaved, catching his breath, and jerked his head, tossing his hair from his eyes. Staying down and peered at Moe. "Feel better?" He smiled.

The bigger man's foot shot out, catching Wesley in the mouth. He toppled over with a muffled thud. Blood spilled down his chin. The rocks dug into his shoulders, scraping his bare back. He grinned and spit blood from his mouth. "That all you got?"

Rachel screamed and rushed to Wesley's side. "What are you doing?" she hissed. "Don't provoke him."

"Get back, Rachel. Don't worry about me." Wesley wiped his mouth with the back of his hand.

Moe grabbed Rachel's shirt with one hand and flung her away. She hit the ground with a short cry.

Moving to help his mother, Dusty put his skinny arms around her neck, holding tight as one of the men tried to separate them. "No. Leave me alone. Get away from her!"

The man wrapped his arms around the boy's waist, and heaved.

Dusty reached for Rachel. "Mom!"

She lunged for the man holding her struggling son, and faltered. "You? You're the man from the rest-stop. Let him go." She aimed a kick at the man, who laughed and backed away.

Mutt ran growling from the bushes and attached himself to the man's leg.

He yelped and shook his leg, trying to break the dog's hold. Dusty pulled free of the man's grip. The other man yelled and laughed from the truck bed. He raised his rifle and took aim.

Pulling the dog free, Dusty shoved him toward the trees. "Run, Mutt!"

A bullet hit the ground near the boy and dog. Mutt ran, yelping, tail between his legs.

Rachel screamed and tried to put herself between her son and the truck. Moe turned to strike her.

"Don't touch her," Wesley growled. He pushed to his knees, bumping into the man nearest him. Using two hands, the man shoved Wesley back to the ground.

Moe straddled him and bent down until they were face to face. "Heed her advice, ranger man. Don't provoke me. I *will* come out the victor." Grabbing the waistband of Wesley's jeans, he pulled him to his feet. His cold eyes turned to his men. "Get them in the truck."

One of the men jumped from the truck bed and hurried to tie Wesley's hands behind

3

his back. Another did the same to Rachel. They left the children untied, ushering them toward the rear. Another man tossed in the packs, then rammed the barrel of his gun into Wesley's wounded side, prodding him.

Holding his breath against the pain, Wesley shrugged him off. Stepping up onto the bumper, he climbed unassisted into the bed.

He moved to sit next to Rachel and the kids, but one of the men steered him away, jamming him again with the gun barrel. They shoved him next to the cab. Wesley grunted as his chest made contact with the hard metal railing.

Squirming to a sitting position, he stared at Rachel. Her eyes were wide in her pale face. Dusty and Mel sat silent beside her. Tears coursed down the girl's cheeks. Rachel's eyes met Wesley's. He flashed her a crooked smile.

Licking his split lip, he tasted the copper tang of blood. He'd never seen Moe's foot coming. The man was quick. Surprisingly so for someone so large. *I've got to keep his attention focused on me. Not on Rachel and the kids.*

He shifted. The hard bed of the truck bit into his buttocks. A hard kick to his ribcage, sent spasms of pain through Wesley with each breath. Cracked ribs, probably.

The truck left the logging road, forging a path of its own through the woods. A path littered with holes, rocks and fallen trees. By

4

the placement of the emerging stars, Wesley figured they were headed east. Soon the stars were hidden by thick foliage.

Wind whistled through the pine trees and Wesley shivered. The truck was cold on his bare back and he longed for his jacket. It lay amongst the backpacks tossed at the other end of the truck. *What do we do now, Lord? My hands are tied, literally. I'm as good as dead, but what about Rachel and the kids?*

He caught Rachel's attention and she mouthed, "What are we going to do?"

Wesley shrugged. "Wait," he mouthed back.

She nodded, and turned away.

They were bounced and tossed around in the bed of the moving truck. At one point, Wesley fell against one of Moe's men and was shoved roughly away. He caught Moe looking through the rearview mirror of the cab. He smiled and felt an overwhelming urge to wave.

*

After seeing her son almost shot, Rachel feared it was only a matter of time before they were all killed.

Her bruised body ached from being bounced around, and she wished for her hands to be free. She longed to hold her children. They looked so frightened. She met Wesley's gaze and gave him a shaky smile. His lip still bled. Rachel's fingers itched to wipe it clean.

Her hands shook behind her, causing the rope to cut into her wrists. Sweat beaded on her brow. Her breathing escalated and she began to hyperventilate. She looked at Wesley, barely able to make out his features in the deepening darkness.

"Breathe, Rachel." Wesley's voice soothed her.

She nodded and drew in deep breaths, releasing them slowly. She kept her eyes glued to Wesley, using him as her life preserver.

He turned his head and smiled at Moe. *Why does he insist on aggravating that giant of a man? He should know better. He's an ex-Green Beret for goodness sakes.* She frowned across the truck at him. "Stop it."

Wesley shrugged. "What?"

Narrowing her eyes, Rachel shook her head. He knew darn well what she meant! She turned away from him and directed her attention ahead of the truck, paying close attention to her anxiety level.

Soon, darkness fully engulfed them, save for the twin beams from the truck's headlights. She raised her head. Tree branches, covered with scant leaves, blocked out the stars. Fireflies blinked off, disappearing into the grass. Somewhere in the distance, a bull frog bellowed. It reminded her of home. Her breath hitched and she stifled the tears threatening to spill.

*What are you thinking Mom and Dad?
Have you long since called the police?* Rachel
bent her head, wiping away her escaping tears
on her shoulder. *Have they given up searching
for us? Do you think we're dead? I wish I could
let you know where we are.*

She caught the man from the rest-stop
staring at her. He winked. She gave a disgusted
sound in her throat and turned away. The man
swore and made a move toward her. His
comrade shot out a restraining hand, making a
head motion toward the cab. The first man
laughed and stopped, leaving Rachel alone.
"Until later," he whispered. "We have an
appointment, you and I." He waved his finger
from Rachel to himself.

Rachel's heart thudded and she fought
the urge to look at him. A cold sweat broke out
on her forehead. She vowed not to give him the
satisfaction of seeing her fear. She smiled at the
worried look on Mel's face. "It'll be all right,
baby."

Tears flowing down her face, Mel
nodded.

Dusty scooted closer to his mother. "If
he touches you, I'll kill him. I will. I mean it."

"There'll be no need to kill anyone."
Someone kicked her and Rachel cried out. Her
leg throbbed.

"No talking," one of the men ordered.

Wesley spoke up. "Dusty, stay still."

7

"Smart advice, ranger man." The man perched on the side of the truck, his rifle aimed toward Wesley. "That boy makes another move toward me, and I'll shoot him."

"Tough guy. He's just a boy. Stick to someone more your size."

The man sneered. "Like you?"

"Yeah." Wesley's face set in determined lines.

"Please, stop it." Tears flowed anew down Rachel's face. What was Wesley trying to prove? This type of behavior was alien to her. She couldn't recall a time when Dennis had ever felt the need to prove how macho he could be.

She swallowed, hard, and turned again to face ahead. She caught a glimpse of movement in the tall grasses beside the road. The truck's light shone on Mutt's face as he peered at her, struggling to keep up. Rachel's heart melted, and she smiled. Dumb dog.

"Your camp must be on the other side of the mountain." Wesley's voice broke the quiet. "We've been driving for quite a while."

"What's it to you? We'll get there when we get there. It ain't gonna be no party for you when we do."

"Just making conversation."

"Well I don't like it. Moe won't like it neither." The man laughed. "We've got some of your friends back at camp. Do the names Rupert and Frank mean anything to you?"

8

"Yeah. They're old buddies. I can't wait to see them."

Rachel listened, confused, to the banter between the two men. Her fear grew as they neared camp. She wanted to scream for them to stop. Clamp her hands over her ears and shut out their words.

Thunder rumbled overhead, and she groaned. Great. As if she weren't uncomfortable enough. Within minutes the sky opened, dumping rain down on them. With her hands tied, Rachel wasn't able to pull her wet clothing away from her. Her comfort level dropped another notch.

The truck hit a large bump and she found herself in the lap of one of the men. He groped her, cackling.

Bile rose in her throat. She struggled to rise from his lap, only to fall again. He laughed and pulled her close. The man's mouth searched for hers. Rachel squirmed and bit his hand when he was foolish enough to bring it too close to her mouth.

The man yelped and back-handed her, knocking her to the bed.

Rachel scooted across the bed as fast as she could with her hands tied. Her heart hammered in her chest.

The man she'd bit, rose and followed her until the truck hit another rut in the road, and he fell over the side. He picked himself up from the dirt, accompanied by raucous calls from his buddy.

After sprinting to the truck, he leaped onto the bumper, and pulled himself over the side. No one called to the driver to stop. They'd have left the man behind if he hadn't caught up.

He made his way to Rachel's side and pinched her face between his fingers. Holding tight, he pushed his face into hers, drawing his tongue across her lips and up her cheek.

The bile rose in Rachel's throat, choking her. She gagged.

The man laughed and pulled back. Smiling down at Wesley, he resumed his seat, perched on the edge of the truck bed.

Wesley's face remained turned in the man's direction, body stiffened.

A chill ran down Rachel's spine and she flinched, fearful of what Wesley would do. He continued to look in the man's direction, challenging him.

It wasn't long before Rachel's rain soaked hair hugged her face, obscuring her vision. She tossed her head, trying to remove the plastered curls. They wouldn't budge. She stuck out her lower lip and blew. Her hair didn't ruffle. Sighing, Rachel hung her head.

Mel smoothed her mother's hair back into a slick helmet. Rachel shot her a grateful smile. "Thank you."

"You're welcome." She laid her head on

Rachel's shoulder, and shuddered.

Rachel's head bobbed as they continued through the night, her eyelids growing heavy. She'd jerk awake when the truck bounced through another hole or over a fallen tree. Her tailbone screamed in pain and her left arm had fallen asleep. She tried peering through the dark at Wesley. She could barely make out his form. The night grew darker.

Feeling Mel's breath on her ear, Rachel turned.

"Mom?"

"Yes?"

"I'm sorry." Mel sniffed.

"For what?" Rachel pulled her head back, peering at Mel's face.

"For everything. For being such a pain after Dad died. You know." Mel took a deep breath. "I'm sorry I've been such a disappointment to you."

"Oh, honey, you haven't..." A sharp kick to her shin halted her words.

"Leave her alone." Wesley's voice cut through the darkness.

A muffled thud, then Wesley grunted.

"I'm fine, Wesley. Don't worry." She cried out as the butt of one of the guns rapped her hard on the knee.

"No talking." The man kicked her.

"Stop kicking me." Rachel spat. "You treat us like we're prisoners of war."

"You are. Now be quiet."

"Untie my hands, and I'll be quiet."

"You're in no position to bargain."

Rachel smiled and decided to adopt her daughter's earlier attitude. "If you don't untie me, I'll scream."

"Go ahead. See what you get."

Opening her mouth, Rachel let forth a long, shrill shriek. Birds took flight into the night. She found herself thrown to the bed of the truck as it halted abruptly. Before she could decipher she might be in danger, Rachel felt herself lifted from the truck and stood roughly on the ground. *Bad idea*.

Moe towered over her. He lowered his head, putting his face inches away from hers. Rachel cringed from his sour breath. Her stomach churned and she turned her face.

Gripping her cheeks in one giant, meaty paw, he pulled her closer.   Her cheeks stung from the pressure.

What are you trying to pull, little lady? There's no one here to hear you scream? Would you like me to take that purty little girl of yours and hand her over to my men?" His thick tongue snaked out, licking his lips. "They're just itching to have a go at her. Or maybe that's more your style? Maybe you would enjoy entertaining them. They've been without a woman for a long time."

Rachel shook her head. "No. Please."

Her stomach rolled. She trembled, leaning against the truck.

"Would you like me to tell you exactly how my men will use your daughter, or you? How they'll visit you one by one, casting lots to see who goes first?" He grinned, his mouth mere inches from her ear.

Her flesh crawled.

Rachel swooned, her legs buckling beneath her.

Moe gripped her arm, holding her on her feet.

"No." She swallowed, fighting against the rising vomit.

"Then a little cooperation would be appreciated. No screaming. I don't like it." He stepped back. "I don't want to hurt you. You're my guest." He lifted her again, as if she weighed nothing, and dropped her in the bed of the truck. "Heed my warning, girlie."

Her hip struck the metal of the truck bed and she grunted, the air leaving her lungs. Rachel breathed in small, shallow breaths. *Okay, God. Maybe I'm ready to listen. What do you want from me? What do you want me to do?* She heard nothing and closed her eyes in despair.

Rachel lay there, unmoving. Her eyes opened and peered across the bed at the dark shapes of her children. She was against someone's legs. Since they didn't kick her, she

13

assumed it was Wesley. When they nudged her, she pressed back, comforted by his presence, and closed her eyes.

16

The truck shuddered to a halt, waking
Rachel. She sat up and groggily looked around
her. The sun peeked over the top of the
mountain, illuminating a clearing full of pitched
army-issue tents. A fire pit blazed in the direct
center of the camp. A number of men looked
up, seeming to focus on Rachel. Various
weapons lay scattered around their feet. A
couple of skinny dogs ran up, growling and
barking to greet those in the truck.

Mortification swept over Rachel as she
realized she'd fallen asleep. Her cheeks flamed.
How could she sleep under the circumstances?
Were Dusty and Mel all right? She whipped
around, breathing a sigh of relief when she
spied them curled up together, asleep.

"They're fine," Wesley reassured her.

Rachel smiled, lowering her eyes. *How
does he do that? Read my mind?* She lifted her
tied hands, grateful they bound hers in front of
her, and ran her fingers through her hair,
grimacing at the oily feel. She ran her tongue
over her teeth. Ugh!

Moe and his men headed toward the

tents, leaving Rachel and the others in the truck. She looked at Wesley. "Maybe Dusty and Mel can make a run for it." She fought to keep her voice from trembling, her tone hushed.

He shook his head. "Too risky. There must be twelve to fifteen men here. We can't take the chance on one of them shooting."

"You think they'd actually shoot Dusty or Mel?" Rachel's eyes widened.

"Why not?" One corner of his mouth lifted. "You said they killed an entire campground of people. I assume that included children."

Her shoulders slumped. "I'd chosen to forget about that." She remembered the forlorn shoe beneath the swing, its owner no where to be seen. Small footprints disappearing beneath a collapsed tent. She shook her head, forcing the images from her mind.

Two men approached the truck and ordered them out, waving their rifles. Rachel balanced her tied hands on the rail and lifted her right leg, swinging it up and over. Her foot caught, and she stumbled, tripping.

The men laughed as she landed in the dirt, scraping her face against the rocks and pine needles. One of them kicked dry leaves and gravel at her, coating her hair. Her scraped skin burned and tears welled in her eyes. She blinked them away.

Another man stuck his leg out as

Wesley climbed down, tripping him. He landed with a thud beside Rachel.

"You okay?" Wesley asked.

She nodded. "They think it's funny, causing me to fall. They seem to get a perverse pleasure out of torturing us." She climbed to her feet, her battered body protesting, and swiped her hands across her skinned cheek. It stung.

"No." The word issued from Rachel's throat as a croak. As if in slow motion, she watched as Mel struggled with the man trying to subdue her. Her right hand disappeared in the pocket of her jeans and re-emerged wrapped around her pocketknife.

Her abductor laughed, his hands roaming over her young body before he spun her, pulling her back close to his chest.

Mel closed her eyes and sunk the knife into the man's thigh.

His howl of pain rang through the camp. He doubled his fist and backhanded the girl across the side of her head, sending her crashing to the ground. He yanked the knife from his leg and advanced slowly, stopping to stand over the girl.

Rachel's body trembled with fear. Her daughter stared stony faced and wide-eyed into the man's face.

He laughed and folded the knife before stashing it into his own pocket. He stalked over

3

to Dusty and searched the boy's pockets. He sneered when he found the other pocketknife. Turning, he yanked Mel to her feet.

Dusty and Mel were ushered into a tent. They looked back at their mother, tears streaming down their faces. "Where are they taking them?" Her words caught in her throat. She struggled to her feet and took a step, determined to follow.

A man stepped in front of her, gun held at the ready. The other man stepped behind her.

"Moe wants to speak to them alone."

"Why? About what?"

The man shrugged. "About whatever he wants." He placed a booted foot between Wesley's shoulder blades when Wesley attempted to rise. "Stay down, ranger man."

"I'm their mother. Anything he can say to them, he can say to me." Rachel took another step forward.

"Moe wants them alone, and out here, Moe gets what he wants." The man behind her slammed the stock of his gun between Rachel's shoulder blades. She crashed to the ground with a sharp cry. Her breath left her in a rush, sending leaves fluttering in the air around her.

She laid there, the throbbing in her back adding to her woes, with her face buried in the damp autumn leaves. A shudder shook through her and a sob escaped her throat.

"Rachel."

She turned her head to look at Wesley. The compassion on his face was almost her undoing and tears spilled from her eyes.

"Don't give up, Rachel. Whatever happens. Promise me."

She turned her face away. "We're already dead."

"No, you're…"

His words were cut short as the two men hauled him to his feet. They each took one of his arms, not untying his hands, and dragged him away, leaving Rachel in the dirt.

The tears flowed unchecked as she watched them toss Wesley into one of the tents. She continued looking, hoping, praying, to see one of her children emerge from Moe's tent. They didn't.

*

Wesley allowed himself to be dragged, forcing his body to remain limp and heavy. He peered over his shoulder at Rachel's white face before they tossed him inside a tent. *How long until they come to finish me off?*

Struggling to his knees, he worked himself across the floor of the tent until he could see out the flap. Rachel sat, tied by one ankle to a stake in the ground. Her face buried in her untied hands.

Moe exited his tent and went to stand before her. Wesley's body tensed. Rachel looked up, a frightened expression on her face. Wesley couldn't hear what Moe said, but the shattered look on Rachel's face said enough. Her shoulders slumped and she turned her face away, again covering it with her hands.

Wesley worked at the bindings around his wrists until he felt the blood run. The ropes wouldn't budge. The person who'd tied them, knew their knots. *Help them, God! What are you waiting for? Will it take my life for You to do something? I'll give it—gladly, if only You'll free them*.

Dusty and Mel were led from the tent, not being allowed to stop or talk to Rachel. The men ushering them ordered the children to keep their eyes straight ahead.

"Dusty! Mel!" Rachel wailed, lunging forward as far as her tether would allow. "Where are you taking them? Please! Let me talk to them." She fell to her knees. "Please."

The men rushed the children across the clearing into another tent. One man stood guard, feet planted, arms folded across his chest.

"I want my children." Rachel stood and grasped the chain holding her to the stake. Gripping it with both hands she tugged.

Moe stalked to her. "Silence." He raised a fist to strike her.

Rachel cringed.

"I don't care what you do to me. Hit me

if you want. Just let them go. Please." She dropped again to her knees and shuffled toward Moe, her hands folded in front of her. "Please."

"They're valuable to me. They belong to me now. They're spoils of war." His voice rose and carried easily across the clearing to Wesley's ears.

Wesley released the breath he hadn't known he'd been holding. *The children are safe. As long as Moe believes them valuable to him. But what did he want with Rachel?*

Moe said something else and glanced in Wesley's direction.

He shrank back into the tent. One of Moe's men came forward and zipped the lining closed, shutting off his view.

Listening to the sounds of camp, Wesley sat. Footsteps crunched past the tent. Voices murmured in low tones. Once, a thud and Rachel cried out. Everything in him strained to rush to her aid. He sat in the gloom of the tent, shoulders hunched, and prayed.

*

Rachel shrank back when Moe approached her. He unhooked the chain from her ankle and thrust a frying pan into her hands.

"You're our new cook. If you try to run, remember, I have your children. I will shoot either you, or them." He grinned, displaying teeth stained with tobacco juice. "Is it a gamble you're willing to take?"

7

Eye wide, she shook her head. Her voice trembled. "I've never cooked over a fire before."

"Hope you're a fast learner. Supply tent is over there." With that, Moe stalked away, disappearing into his tent.

She stood staring at the pan in her hands. A cast iron skillet. She bit her lip and headed with heavy steps toward the supply tent. Changing her mind, she switched directions and entered Moe's.

"You're not allowed entrance unless I summon you." He sat behind a folding table. Assorted maps and papers were scattered across the battered surface. She took a step backward, but he waved her forward. "I'll let you slide this time."

Glancing around the tent, Rachel's eyes widened as she saw cases marked with things such as guns, ammo, explosives and flares. Flares! *I've got to get them. How? What can I do to get Moe to give me access to his tent? Bring him his dinner? Stage a commotion outside? What do I have to offer?*

Rachel started. Moe stared at her. Swallowing against her rising alarm under his scrutiny, she blurted out, "How long do you plan on keeping us here?"

Moe shrugged. "As long as you prove useful. You can do tasks that will enable my men to be used elsewhere." He leaned back, folding his hands across his paunch. "Basically, how long, depends on you."

Her hand fell, the heavy skillet banging against her leg. "What happened to you? You're a general aren't you? You served our country. How can you do this?"

He bolted to his feet. "I should have been a general. I served my time. I went to war." He paced the tent. "Not general material they told me." Moe waved his arms. "Look around you, my dear. What do you see now? A general? That's right. I am the general, here."

Nodding, she backed toward the tent flap, keeping her eyes focused on the man's enraged face. "What did you say to my children to get them to agree not to speak to me?"

Moe stopped, stared for a moment and fell back into his chair. "I told them I would kill you if they didn't do exactly as they were told. Threats work wonders with children, don't you think?"

Rachel swallowed against the lump in her throat. "And Wesley?"

"Ranger? Why, execution of course. He's a prisoner of war...and he did kill my men."

"It was self-defense." She struggled to keep her voice from trembling. "He could have killed more. At any time. Think about it. He's a trained Green Beret. He could have killed them all."

Moe put his hands together, touching

9

his fingers to his chin. "You may be right. I'll bring it before my men. Let them decide. They may enjoy sporting with him more. Give them a morale booster." He got to his feet. "My men are hungry."

Rachel nodded. "May I fix something for Wesley."

"No."

"Even prisoners of war deserve to eat." Rachel's lip curled.

Moe laughed and waved her away. "Ranger is welcome to whatever is left."

"Thank you." Rachel backed away and hurried to the supply tent. A small gas powered generator enabled Moe to keep a small refrigerator. She located eggs and bacon. Simple enough. Gathering together what she needed, Rachel rushed back outside. Thankfully a fire already burned in the pit.

Her hands trembled as she broke eggs into the skillet. One man, a patch over his eye, glared at her. Rachel's heartbeat accelerated and she stirred the eggs quickly, tossing in slices of bacon.

The men lined up, plates held out. Several grumbled at the burned bacon and over-cooked eggs. Rachel dropped her eyes, knees weak. She worked as fast as she could, shoving full plates back into their hands. She was careful to hold aside a few eggs and bacon to share with Wesley. When the last man retreated from the fire, she leaned back, popping the kinks from her aching spine.

Moe sat hunkered on a sawed log, watching her. Rachel's skin crawled as his gaze raked over her. Summoning all the will power she possessed, she returned his stare. She squared her shoulders and kept her eyes locked on his. Moe nodded and resumed eating.

Rachel still hadn't seen her children. One of the men took a plate to them, not allowing them to come outside. Picking up her own plate, Rachel headed toward Wesley's tent. The man guarding it stepped aside, allowing her entrance.

Squinting against the dim light, Rachel could make out Wesley's form on the far side. She set the plate on the floor and rushed to his side.

"Wesley." She placed a hand on his chest. His hands were tied, yet he bolted up at her voice.

"Rachel."

She wrapped her arms around him. "I'm so glad to see you."

"Are you all right?" His eyes caressed her face.

"I'm fine." She rubbed her hands over his arms and shoulders. "You?"

"Fine."

"I've brought you some food." Rachel retrieved the plate and spooned up some of the eggs. "I don't know how long I have, so I'll have to be quick." She fed him as they talked. "I've talked Moe out of killing you."

"I'm obliged," Wesley mumbled around the spoon.

"Don't thank me yet. He's going to let his men decide your punishment."

Wesley sighed. "I think I'd be better off dead."

"Don't say that. There are flares in Moe's tent. I'm going to try and get to them. If I can set one off..."

"No way." Wesley drew back, shaking his head.

She set the empty plate on the ground. "I have to, Wesley."

"It's too dangerous. Moe will never let you in his tent unsupervised."

She turned her face away.

"Rachel...how do you plan on getting inside? Look at me."

Keeping her face averted, she allowed him to struggle to his feet.

"Rachel?"

Stiffening her back, she stood, her eyes locking on his face. "There's only one way to get inside his tent long enough. I'll have to spend the night."

Wesley shook his head. "No. It's not worth it."

Turning, she walked toward the

entrance. She stopped and put a hand on the flap. Without turning, she said, "Dusty and Mel are worth it. You're worth it. It's all I have to bargain with." *You're worth everything. I love you. You make me strong*. She squared her shoulders and took a deep breath.

"Rachel!" Wesley's pained voice tore at her heart. "Rachel, look at me. It won't make a difference. Please don't do this!"

Without looking back, she pushed aside the tent flap and stepped outside. Rachel choked back the sobs as Wesley continued to cry her name.

*

Wesley dropped to his knees, the impact shooting stabs of pain through his legs. The pain matched the ache in his heart. With tear-filled eyes, he watched Rachel exit the tent. His shoulders shook with suppressed sobs. "No, Rachel." His voice grew hoarse. *God, no. Not that. I'd rather die*. He pulled against the ropes around his hands, frantic. His arm muscles screamed as he strained against his bindings.

Wesley roared as the bone in his left wrist snapped. Pain reeled through him, nauseating him. He cursed as he rolled to the ground, falling on his raw wrists. The eggs and bacon Rachel had fed him rose in his throat, threatening to choke him. His heart lay heavy in his chest.

With her face swimming before him, he focused on all the parts of her he loved. Her hazel eyes. The curly hair his fingers ached to brush through. The lips he desired to kiss again. He shook his head, vowing to hold her again. Wesley's resolve strengthened.

I can do all things through Christ who strengthens me.

So be it, Lord. If this be Your will. If this is what it takes to draw Rachel back to You, I submit. But I will not go down without a fight. I will fight to my last breath. If the apostle Paul could lay down his life for Your people, I will give mine for a beautiful woman and her children.

Drawing upon the skills he'd learned as a Green Beret to ward off thirst, Wesley willed his mind to become vacant. He blocked out the pain in his hand and wrists. Forcing himself, he managed to get into a sitting position. Cross-legged, he sat and stared at the tent opening. Waiting.

As the day wore on, the heat inside the tent stifled him. His mouth was full of cotton and his lips were chapped. Sweat beaded upon his brow and lip. Ran down his chest. Wesley continued to ignore these things and sat still. Anticipation ran through his veins.

17 CHAPTER NAME

Stifling her tears, Rachel approached Moe's tent. She hesitated, unsure of whether to proceed. *I can do this. I can*.

She took a deep breath and called, "Moe? I'd like to come in."

"Come on, then." His voice sounded gruff, harsh.

Knees shaking, Rachel pushed aside the flap. Moe's body odor in the hot tent slapped her in the face. She swallowed hard, taking short breaths through her mouth. *Did the man never bathe?*

He sat behind his table, aluminum cans of beer littering the ground around his feet. His mouth opened and he belched.

Rachel faltered, then strode forward. Her back ramrod straight, hands folded behind her, she blurted, "I've a proposition for you."

Moe raised his thick eyebrows. "I'm all ears."

Rachel willed her voice to remain calm. "I've come to offer myself to you."

"Offer yourself? In what capacity?"

"As a woman." The butterflies in her

1

stomach grew more active, buffeting her insides.

"I couldn't hear you. Speak up, woman." His voice boomed against her eardrums.

"As a woman." She lowered her eyes.

"As *my* woman?"

Rachel's hands shook. She clasped them tighter. What if he refused? "Yes."

Moe laughed, and Rachel weakened. She looked at him beneath lowered lashes. His eyes raked over her. "Well...I've seen cleaner." His eyes returned to her face. "Why?"

"In exchange for Wesley's life." She dropped her eyes again, focusing on the dirt and blades of grass littering the tent floor.

He stared at her silent. Rachel waited interminable minutes. Her resolve faltered.

He laughed again. "It's a deal." Moe rose from his chair and walked an unsteady circle around her.

Rachel stood motionless, not looking.

"You're a bit scrawny. I could have you if I wanted, whether you offered or not. You're no match for my strength. You realize that don't you?"

She nodded.

"Okay. I promise you I will not take the ranger's life." He strode back to his chair, squeezing his bulk into it. The metal groaned beneath him. "I'll call for you at nightfall." He reached for one of the cans and popped the top.

"Is there somewhere I can clean up?"

He looked at her, surprise on his red-veined face. "I'll have one of my men escort you to the creek."

"I'd also like free run of the camp." At his look, she added, "You have my children. Where would I go?"

He laughed louder, his guffaws ringing through the tent. "Point taken." His shoulders continued to shake as he turned back to the map spread before him.

With that, Rachel was dismissed. She turned and rushed from the tent. She ignored the curious looks of Moe's men and bent over near the border of trees. Clutching her stomach, she vomited. With a groan, Rachel collapsed to the ground and buried her face in her hands.

A man approached her a few minutes later. "You want the creek? Come on."

She looked up.

"Let's go, lady. I haven't got all day." He strode off.

Rachel got to her feet, her legs weak, and followed him. He led her several yards into the woods and stopped before a small creek which flowed into a deeper area beneath a rock bluff. The water swirled, murky and dark around the bluff's base. Heavy branches cast the area into shadow.

Rachel turned and glared. "Turn around."

"What for?" He leered at her.

"I'm Moe's woman. Would you like me to tell him you watched me as I bathed?" She stood, hands on her hips. Rachel struggled to appear brave, lifting her chin. She hoped the man couldn't hear her heart beating.

He swore and turned his back on her.

With shaking fingers, Rachel peeled the dirty clothes from her body and stepped into the creek. The icy water took her breath away as she inched her way in. Her legs grew numb before adjusting to the frigid temperature. Diving, she plunged beneath the bluff. She stayed under water until her lungs screamed for air. If only she could take that one breath. That one last breath. The faces of her children and Wesley hovered before her and she rose, gasping to the surface.

She swam to the shallower end of the creek, stopping when the water reached to her shoulders. Taking a deep breath, she submerged and scooped a handful of sand, scrubbing her body until it felt raw. With another handful, Rachel rubbed her scalp, rinsing until her hair was clean.

Back on shore, she reached for her dirty clothes and tossed them into the creek. She rinsed as much of the dirt and odor from them as she could, then donned them.

In the shade of the forest, wearing wet clothes, she shivered and looked forward to the openness of the clearing. "I'm ready."

Without looking back, the man led her back to camp.

She found a log to sit on next to the fire and waited, letting the sun warm her. Her curly hair dried and fluffed around her head. She relished the feeling of being clean again.

When Dusty and Mel were led from their tent, Rachel looked up. She hopped from her seat and ran to them. "Dusty. Mel." She wrapped her arm around them and squeezed with all the strength she had.

Mel struggled free. "We're not supposed to talk to you, Mom. Moe won't like it."

"He won't mind," Rachel said through her tears. "We have an understanding." Her voice broke. "It's so good to see you."

Dusty squeezed back. "It's good to see you, too." He looked around. "Where's Wesley?"

"In that tent. Moe has agreed to leave him alone."

Her son grinned. "I heard Mutt sniffing around our tent and got our guard to allow us to go to the restroom." His voice broke. "I thought Mutt was dead."

Rachel smiled back. "He never could stay far from you, son."

The man assigned to guarding the children ordered them to follow him. Rachel gave them another squeeze. "It's all right. Go with him."

Mel frowned at her. "They let you take a bath? I want one. I can't stand being dirty for another minute." She plucked at her dirty shirt.

Rachel's heart lifted to see the old Mel. "I'll see what I can do." She watched as her children were led away, her heart lighter.

Dusty glanced over his shoulder and waved. Rachel waved back. Stirrings of sadness threatened to well again. She squelched them down.

"Hey, woman! I'm hungry." Moe yelled from his tent. "What are we keeping you around for?"

Sighing, Rachel headed to the supply tent to see what she could find to feed them.

She grabbed several cans of beans and set a pan over the burning fire. Dumping the beans into the pot, Rachel stirred. The men lined up and she plopped ladle after ladle of overcooked beans onto tin plates.

The men grumbled and complained, saying the food was better before she started cooking.

The setting sun cast shadows of apprehension over her. When would Moe send for her? She hoped it was after the other men settled down for the night. She didn't think she could handle them watching her, knowing, as she entered Moe's tent at bedtime.

Spending her time in thought, Rachel devised a plan to confiscate some of the flare guns. How would she get them out of the tent? What if she were caught? Then everything would have been for nothing. She propped her elbows on her knees and rested her chin in her hands. *It's all so hard.*

Rachel waited what seemed an eternity. Moe's men walked past her, into Moe's tent and out again. Into the children's tent and out again. They ignored her, for the most part, and her apprehension grew. She followed the men with her eyes. Her head pounded. Her knuckles hurt from pressing her hands tight together.

No one went into Wesley's tent and Rachel's conscience pricked her. She realized she hadn't taken him any food or water since morning. *I'm sorry, Wesley. I'm not strong enough to see your face, knowing what I'm going to do.* A tear escaped and Rachel swiped it away, angry at herself for being weak. *When will I stop crying? I've been weak my entire life! Is that why my life is so hard? Why do I have to fight for everything?* Her shoulders slumped.

Making a disgusted sound in her throat, Rachel turned away when one of Moe's men glanced her way. She didn't care what they thought of her. No one could be more disgusted with her than she was herself.

7

Her heart pounded when one of the men approached her.

"Moe wants you." The man leered at her before turning to join his comrades.

Rachel's breath escaped her and she bent over, balancing her hands on her knees. *I can do this. I can. Wesley's life is at stake.* She willed herself to stand and walk toward Moe's tent. Her legs shook and her steps dragged, yet she forced herself on. With an unsteady hand, she pushed aside the tent flap and stepped inside.

Moe reclined on a pile of dirty blankets tossed in the corner of the tent. A low burning lantern cast a dusty glow. Rachel's nerve threatened to leave her at the sight of his bare, hairy chest. *I can't do this.* She inhaled sharply and choked as his body odor and liquor fumes seared the lining of her nose.

"Take off your clothes," Moe ordered, his words slurring. "It's light enough for me to see what I'm getting."

Nodding, Rachel unbuttoned her shirt. She blinked against the tears welling in her eyes. She turned her back to the waiting man and laid the shirt carefully over the box marked flares. Taking another deep breath, she unfastened and peeled the now loose-fitting jeans over her hips. She kicked them off and laid them with her shirt. She turned and stood before Moe in her underwear.

"All of it." His eye lids drooped. "And hurry."

Rachel's lips curled into a slow smile when he burped. She fumbled with her bra clasp. *He's drunk. If I stall long enough...maybe.*

He jerked his eyes open.

"Never mind," he told her. "I'll do it. You're too slow." He leered and pulled aside the single blanket covering him, then reached up and blew out the lantern, casting them into darkness.

Her heart skipped a beat as she knelt and crawled beneath the blanket. The alcohol fumes threatened to overwhelm her and bile rose in her throat. The blankets were saturated with his odor.

Moe threw a heavy arm over her and— snored.

She lay stiff next to Moe, being careful not to wake him. After what seemed an eternity, his snores leveled off and she crawled from the blankets, feeling her way to her clothes.

Checking often for signs of Moe waking, she removed two of the flare guns. She donned her clothes and stuffed the guns down the waistband of her jeans, checking to be sure her shirt hung loose enough to hide the bulge they made. Rachel hoped he wouldn't again order her to remove her clothes before she could hide the flares.

9

As she reached to unzip the tent, Moe's voice slurred behind her. "Where are you going? We haven't done anything yet."

Without turning, she answered, "I need to use the restroom. I'll be back."

He snickered. "Enjoy the show, my dear."

She glanced over her shoulder. Nausea rose within her as he sat up. Turning, she rushed outside.

Rachel stopped in her tracks. A pole had been erected next to the fire pit. An iron ring hung from the top of it.

*

Wesley lifted his head when Rupert and Jack entered the tent. His heart beat steady and strong. His body numb. He shrugged off their hands as the two men lifted him to his feet. "I can walk on my own."

"Still the tough guy, huh?" Rupert shoved him.

"You're going to pay for the loss of my eye," Jack told him. "Oh, yeah. You're going to pay."

Without faltering, Wesley strode toward the pole. He closed his eyes, for a second, upon sight of the ring, then turned to face Rupert. "Then let me earn my pay."

Whirling, he head butted Rupert and dealt a hard karate kick to Jack's stomach.

Moe called to someone to halt. "Let

them handle it," he ordered.

Wesley stood, hands still tied behind him, his legs spread slightly. He bounced lightly on the balls of his feet. "Come on. Don't you have anything to give back?"

Rupert roared and charged, bringing Wesley to the ground.

Jack got to his feet, breathing hard, and delivered a swift kick to Wesley's stomach. A crunch, and Wesley groaned. He rolled and forced himself to stand. He spit blood and turned back to face his attackers.

Grinning, he lunged at Jack, plunging into the man with his shoulder. They both went to the ground and Wesley yelled as Jack fell on him, the man's knee connecting with Wesley's thigh.

Another kick, then another, each sending fresh waves of pain through Wesley's body. With his hands tied behind his back, he wasn't able to cover himself, and something snapped. He drew in his breath sharply at the stabbing pain.

Jack rolled to his feet. Reaching over, he grabbed a stick of firewood and crouched over Wesley.

Wesley smiled up at him. "Go ahead, Jack, Use it."

The man grimaced. "Enough of this, Rupert. Let's string him up while there's enough of him left to string!" Jack tossed the wood aside. Together, he and Rupert grabbed an arm and dragged Wesley to the pole.

Wesley drew in a painful breath as they cut loose his bindings and retied his hands over his head, securing him to the iron ring. Hanging his head to the side of the pole, he looked up. His eyes met Rachel's across the clearing.

She stood crying, not turning as Moe moved to her side. The big man put an arm around her shoulders and jerked her close to him.

Keeping his eyes focused on hers, he didn't waver as the first lash of the whip seared across his shoulders. He wanted her face to be the last sight he set eyes on. Another slash ripped across him and he drew in his breath with a hiss. Willing himself not to cry out, he thanked God the children were nowhere in sight.

His flesh tore and the blood ran, soaking the waistband of his jeans. *You endured, Lord. Give me Your strength.*

Rachel cried out, yelling she loved him.

He smiled, his vision blurring. "I love you," he mouthed to her. She covered her mouth with her hands.

"Ain't that sweet." Rupert whipped again, before stepping back and letting Jack have a turn.

Another whip stroke and Wesley sagged against the pole, the pain in his broken wrist and back pulling him down. His sight grew dark, and he blinked. Knowing Rachel watched him, he summoned the strength he had left and, using the pole as leverage, got to his feet. Each movement was agony, stealing his breath.

Jack grabbed him by the hair and slammed his head into the pole, opening the skin above Wesley's right eye. Blood ran into his eyes, obscuring his vision.

He shook his head, clearing his vision, and refocused on Rachel. He held her eyes with his, using her as his life preserver. She smiled at him through her tears and said something he couldn't make out. Another whip lash, then something struck him in the back of his head. His world faded.

*

Rachel whirled. Her heart plummeted to the pit of her stomach. "You promised me." She doubled up her fists and beat Moe's chest. Her hands pounded a rhythm. "You promised me."

He captured her hands in his, and laughed. "I promised you *I* wouldn't kill him, my dear. I never said anything about my men." He shoved her to the ground.

Rachel fell, striking her leg on a rock. Her head bounced off the packed dirt, causing her to see stars.

Moe staggered drunkenly to his tent. His laughter continued, echoing across the camp. "Come see me when you're finished mourning."

Pushing herself to her feet, Rachel pulled the flare guns from her waistband. She held one in each hand and lifted them to the sky. Screaming, she pulled the triggers, watching as the flares burst into the night sky. Sparks rained upon her hands and arms and she relished the brief burning pain. Spent, she fell to her knees.

Sobs wracked her body, and Rachel welcomed the hard ground as she fell prostrate. She ignored the rocks digging into her face. She welcomed the sting of the pine needles. *Okay, God. You win. I can't do this. Help me! I beg You, Lord, save us! I'm Yours. I'll do whatever You ask of me. Jesus, save me.*

Moe rushed from the tent as the flares burst into the sky. Pandemonium ransacked the camp. Jack dropped the whip he held and ran for the truck, leaving Wesley hanging limp from the pole.

From their tent, Dusty and Mel yelled for their mother. The sides of the tent shook as they hit against it, fighting to get it unzipped. Torn between her children, safe in the tent, and the man she loved, Rachel turned to Wesley.

She ran to his side, tugging on the ring hammered into the wood. It wouldn't budge. She scraped at the wood with her hands, driving slivers beneath her nails. Her fingers grew

14

slippery with blood as she broke the finger nails to the quick. Giving up, she wrapped her arms around Wesley. Her wails joined the cursing of the men as they rushed to gather their weapons. Unmindful of Wesley's blood soaking her clothes, Rachel slid to the ground, tears spilling.

Propeller blades thumped overhead, swirling leaves and dirt in a cyclonic motion. Rachel looked up, squinting against the blowing grit. The helicopters must have been close. Their search lights lit up the clearing and she closed her eyes in silent relief.

God, why couldn't they have gotten here sooner?

She rose and placed a kiss on Wesley's lips, then rested her forehead against his.

Taking a deep, shuddering breath, Rachel let go and stepped back, her legs trembling beneath her. The world spun around her. She looked up into the face of a man peering down from the helicopter...and fainted.

18

A rhythmic beeping. A hushed whoosh. The strong smell of disinfect. Muted voices.

Rachel's eyes popped open. Harsh lights glared down on her and she squinted. She bolted up, head swimming and stomach rolling, and fell back. Something pulled on her hand and she looked down at the needle pricking the skin.

The faces of her parents, Bill and Dottie Miller, were the first Rachel's eyes focused on. Her mother gave her a tender smile, causing Rachel to burst into tears. She laid there, tears running down her cheeks and soaking into the hospital pillow.

"It's all right, Sweetheart." Her mother patted the hand without the needle. "You're going to be just fine."

"Dusty? Mel?" Rachel sniffed and hiccupped.

"They're fine, too."

Rachel's father bent and kissed her forehead. "That little dog of Dusty's is okay, too, in case you were wondering. We've taken him and the kids home with us."

1

Glancing again at the IV needle in her hand, Rachel's eyes traveled along the tubing to the IV stand. She squirmed, noting the heart monitor and oxygen regulator. Another needle was taped in the crook of her elbow. "What's wrong with me?"

Bill pulled up a chair for his wife to sit on. "You're suffering from exposure, malnutrition and some contusions. The doctor just wants to keep you here for observation. You're badly dehydrated."

"How long?"

"A day or two."

Rachel nodded. "I want to see my children."

Her father smoothed the hair back from her face. "I'll go get them. Your mother will sit here with you."

"Thank you." Rachel closed her eyes. "I'm so tired, Mom."

She felt her mother pat her hand. "Of course you are. You just lie there. We'll take good care of you." Her mother fussed with the hospital blankets, tucking them around Rachel.

Rachel opened her eyes, visually caressing her Dottie's face.

"We were so worried about you." Dottie's chin quivered. "Oh, not at first. When you were one day late, we figured you just decided to stay at the campground a little longer, but then the days stretched into three, then four, and we called the police." She sniffed.

"In the beginning, the police wouldn't do anything. Then they called and told us about finding all those dead people. They found your car and we thought for sure the three of you were dead. We had to give them pictures." Dottie cried harder. "Then, when they couldn't find your bodies, we had hope again." She reached in the bodice of her dress and pulled out a tissue. She lifted the damp tissue to her eyes. "It was so hard to hold onto our faith."

Rachel reached up and wiped a tear from her mother's cheek. "Don't cry Mom. God brought us through, but it was a long hard road for me to travel." She let her hand fall to her side. Wesley's face flashed through her mind and her heart pained her. "I had to hit bottom, and hit hard, before He had my attention." She gave a short laugh. "Then God answered very quickly."

Dottie smiled through her tears and cupped her daughter's face in her hands. "You've had a long, tough time of it, Honey. You rest now."

Closing her eyes, Rachel smiled as Dottie straightened and blew her nose. Three short, delicate bursts. Listening to the familiar sound, she fell asleep.

Rachel woke later to Mel's crying. She opened her eyes and looked into the red-rimmed ones of her daughter. Turning her head, she spotted Dusty, standing with his arms hanging limp by his side. Tears ran down the boy's face.

Opening her arms as wide as the tubes and wires would allow, she drew her children close to her. "I've missed you two," she whispered, burying her face in Mel's hair. The three sobbed together.

"We'll wait outside," Rachel's father mumbled. He took Dottie by the arm and pulled her along with him.

"We were so afraid," Dusty's voice was muffled in Rachel's shoulder. "When the police took us from our tent, and we saw you lying on that stretcher…"

"We thought for sure you were dead," Mel added.

"I fainted." Rachel held her children back from her. "Let me look at you." She reached over to the bedside table and pulled a tissue from the box. "Here, let me wipe your faces. There's no need to cry anymore. I'm fine. We're fine."

She took her time wiping their faces, savoring the moment, relishing in each freckle on her son's face. Mel scowled and grabbed a dry tissue when Rachel started on her face.

"Did you see Wesley?" Rachel's voice broke. Her hand stilled for a moment, before her eyes moved from Dusty's face to Mel's.

Please, God, let the police have cut him down before taking my children from the tent.

Dusty shook his head. "There was no sign of him, Mom. Do you know where he is?"

Rachel closed her eyes. Her heart sunk. The ache in her chest grew at the thought of Wesley. She shook her head and swallowed past the lump in her throat. The simple act of wiping her children's faces left her drained.

Her parents stepped back into the room and Bill took Dusty and Mel with him to the hospital waiting room.

Rachel scooted to a sitting position. "Mom?"

"Yes, dear?" Dottie hurried to her side.

"Help me up." She pushed against the bed.

A cheery, overweight nurse entered carrying a covered tray. "Lunch time. I hope you're hungry," she sang. She wheeled over the bedside table, placed the tray on it and, with a flourish, removed the lid. "It's chicken Alfredo."

"I'm not really..."

"Sure you are, Sweetie." The nurse unfolded Rachel's napkin, tucked it under her chin, and fluffed the pillows. "Gotta eat to get your strength back. You're nothing but skin and bones. We've got to put the bloom back in those pretty cheeks." The nurse patted Rachel's cheek and left.

Rachel pushed the tray away. "I'm not

hungry."

"Now, Rachel…" her mother began.

"I'm not hungry." Rachel folded her arms across her chest. "I want out of here." Her face fell and she broke into sobs.

"Oh, Honey. I'm sure you'll go home to…"

Rachel waved her away. "I'm sorry. Just leave me alone for a while, okay?"

Leaning over the bed, Dottie hugged her. "Sure thing, Sweetie. I'll be in the waiting room if you need anything."

Nodding, Rachel leaned back against the pillows. Wesley's face swam across her mind and she hiccupped again, trying to stifle her sobs. Her throat hurt from crying. Her eyes burned.

She looked over at the pitcher of water on the table. It was too much of an effort to reach over and grab the handle. She clenched her hands together at her sides. The IV bothered her and her side hurt from being kicked. Rachel's head throbbed.

Remembering her time with Moe, Rachel leaned and vomited over the side of the bed. As dry heaves shook her body, she pressed the nurse call button. The same overly cheerful nurse arrived.

As fast as the woman's bulk allowed, she hurried to Rachel's side. "Now, Honey, what's wrong? You haven't eaten a bite. There shouldn't have been anything in your stomach to throw up." She grabbed the pitcher of water and poured Rachel a glass. "Here, you go. Small sips now."

"I need to use the restroom," Rachel told her in between sobs.

"Are you sure? It'll be painful. You're bruised up. It might be better to use the bed pan."

"I'm sure." The nurse helped Rachel swing her legs over the side of the bed.

"You want me to help you?"

Rachel shook her head.

"All right, then. You go on while I clean this up."

Shuffling her feet, and pulling the IV stand along with her, Rachel made her way to the small restroom.

She placed her hands on the sink and leaned toward the mirror. Haunted eyes stared back. They were bloodshot and swollen. Her cheeks were raw from the constant running of her tears. Rachel turned on the faucet and splashed her face with cold water.

God, help me! What have I done? She slid to the floor.

Rachel shivered on the cold tile floor and wrapped her arms around her knees. The IV pulled on her. Ignoring it, she hid her face in the fold of her arms. *Can I hide myself?* Sobs started anew, and she let the tears flow. *Can I ever forget the look on Wesley's face when I told him what I planned to do? Can I forget the pain I've caused him?*

Rachel's shoulders shook. Her throat spasmed, sending raw pain through her. She gagged and crawled to the toilet.

"Rachel? Honey?" Dottie called through the door. The door knob rattled. "Rachel, open the door. If you don't open this door, I'll get a key and come in after you."

"Leave me alone. I'm fine."

"You're not fine." The knob rattled harder. "That's it, young lady. I'm getting the doctor."

Rachel heard her mother's retreating steps and had the insane urge to laugh. She felt as if she were a teenager home after a long night of partying with her friends. She wiped the back of her hand across her mouth.

It was only a matter of minutes before a key was inserted in the lock and the door swung open. Her doctor and two orderlies entered the small room. The orderlies held her still while the doctor injected a needle into her IV. Rachel grew lethargic, her thoughts fuzzy.

Thank you, God, for modern medicine, was her last conscious thought.

When Rachel awoke, her mother sat, asleep, in the striped salmon colored chair beside the bed. Licking her lips with a thick tongue, Rachel reached for her cup of water.

She took small sips through the bendable straw, the cool water providing relief to her scratchy throat.

Night had fallen, and only a small nightlight glowed next to the door. The shot the doctor gave her, had enabled her to spend several hours not thinking about the past week, and she was grateful. Rachel shifted her weight in the bed, and groaned. Her backside was getting sore.

Dottie opened her eyes and bolted up. "What's wrong?"

"Nothing." Rachel set the cup back on the bedside table. "I was thirsty, that's all. Did Dad take Dusty and Mel home?"

"Yes." Dottie glanced at her watch. "I'm sure they're all sleeping." She switched her gaze to Rachel. "Would you like to tell me what's going on?"

Rachel looked at her mother, surprised. "What?"

Dottie switched on the light next to the bed. "You won't eat. You hardly drink, and you cry all the time." She moved and perched on the side of the bed. "Don't get me wrong, Honey. I know you've been through quite an ordeal, but you're alive and your children are waiting for you. It seems to me as if you've given up. That's not the child I raised. I did not raise a quitter."

"I'll be fine, Mother. I just need a few

days." Rachel plucked at the hospital blanket.

"You don't have a few days, Rachel Anne." Dottie stood and picked up her purse. "You're a mother. You have two obligations waiting at home for you." The older woman looked down at Rachel, lips pressed together in a firm line. She took a deep breath. "I'm going now. I'll be back in a few hours."

Rachel's eyes widened in shock as her mother stormed from the room. She hadn't been lectured like that in years.

I'm sorry, Lord. My heart aches so much. I'm safe here in the hospital. They have things here to help me forget. Her thoughts drifted to her children. Their tear stained faces. *Mom's right. I have two children who need me.*

She took a deep breath and pressed the nurse call button.

An older, more subdued nurse responded. "Yes?"

"I'm hungry now. Do you think you could bring me something to eat?" Rachel focused on Dusty and Mel. Their faces hovered in the front of her mind, reminding her of what she still had to live for.

"I'll be right back." The nurse appeared minutes later with warm chicken noodle soup and apple juice. "If you hold this down, we'll give you a more substantial breakfast."

Rachel nodded, and lifted her spoon.

*

Her parents and children woke her the next morning. Dusty plopped on the bed hard enough to bounce Rachel, and she grimaced. She sat up, forcing herself to smile.

"You two look great," she said.

Mel plopped down opposite her brother. "We have our own rooms."

"You were so worried about that," Rachel laughed. "You were so afraid you'd have to share with your brother."

"Grandma and Grandpa let Mutt sleep with me," Dusty added. "And they said we could wait a week before starting school."

Rachel looked at Mel. "You okay with that? Going to school with hillbillies?"

The girl hung her head, smiling beneath lowered lashes. "They're not so bad."

"She's met a boy from down the road," Dottie informed Rachel.

Rachel raised her eyebrows. "Really?'

"Yeah." Mel blushed. "He's really cute. He's got this curly hair and these dreamy blue eyes and..." She punched Dusty when he made gagging noises. "Stop it, twerp."

Rachel met Dottie's eyes above the kids' heads. She smiled, her heart sad. Life does go on, and so would she. She listened to the sibling bickering, and counted her blessings. Her children were safe beside her. They'd arrived at their destination...battered but alive.

When the doctor came in to take her

vital signs, Bill took the children to the cafeteria with promises to return soon. Rachel's mother took up her usual vigil next to the bed, arms folded across her chest as she waited for the doctor to finish.

The doctor flipped through Rachel's chart. "Looks like you'll be going home tomorrow. I'll give you something to help you sleep. But only a few days worth." He scribbled a phone number on a sheet of paper. "Here's the number to a doctor who can help you through your trauma. I'll be very surprised if you don't have some post traumatic stress."

Rachel took the paper. "Thank you, but I'll be fine."

The doctor smiled. "Just in case."

Once the doctor left, Dottie sat next to her daughter, taking Rachel's hand in hers. "Talk."

Tears welled in Rachel's eyes, and she shook her head. "Oh, Mom."

Dottie gathered her daughter in her arms. "It's going to be okay, Rachel."

Rachel sniffed. "I know. It was horrible. I've never been so frightened, tired and hungry. Those men were ruthless. Wesley was shot and whipped. They..."

"Who's Wesley, Honey?" Dottie rubbed Rachel's back.

"He's the man who helped us. He gave his life for us." Rachel pulled back, meeting her mother's eyes. "I loved him."

A smile broke across Dottie's face. "If you're talking about that handsome ranger…why, sweetie, he's not dead. He's unconscious, but he's alive. A bit battered, sure, but…"

"He's alive?" Rachel's heart pounded. "Where is he?" She grasped the IV tube and pulled it from her hand. She winced. A small trickle of blood ran onto her sheet. "I have to see him." She bolted from the bed.

"Rachel, I don't think…"

"Please."

"He's in the room next door."

Rachel rushed from the room, casting looks in both directions. "Which way?"

"Turn right. And cover yourself!" Dottie called. "Your gown is open down the back."

Gathering the gown together in one hand, Rachel turned. A nurse shot out a hand to stop her and Rachel pushed past.

She stopped and stared into the room. She shook her head at herself, running in a frenzy. Her tears welled, threatening to choke her when she made out Wesley's form on the bed.

The cheery nurse from the day before put an arm around her. "Go on in, Sweetie. It's all right." The compassionate tone in the woman's voice was almost Rachel's undoing and she sagged against the door frame.

13

"Go on," the nurse urged, giving Rachel a gentle push.

Rachel walked into the room, her eyes never leaving the man on the bed. "How is he?" she whispered.

"Well, he's hurt pretty bad. I won't lie to you." The nurse checked Wesley's IV. "He's got several broken ribs, a broken wrist, severe lacerations on his back. Somebody whipped him, you know."

A sob escaped Rachel and she put a hand over her mouth. "I know," she answered, her voice hoarse.

"He also has a concussion," the nurse added. "But the doctor is pretty confident he'll pull through."

"Has he been awake?" Rachel moved to the side of the bed. She stared down at Wesley' beaten face and reached out to tenderly caress the yellow and purple bruises.

"A little—off and on, but he's pretty heavily medicated." The nurse put her arm around Rachel again. "Would you like to stay with him for a while?"

"Can I?"

"Sure you can." The nurse gave her a squeeze. "Just take it easy."

"I will." Rachel reached over and gently picked up Wesley's unbroken hand, tracing the welts with a finger. She held his hand to her face. Turning it over, Rachel placed a kiss in his palm.

Thank you, God. She switched her eyes back to Wesley's face, studying the straight nose and swollen lips. One eye was purple and swollen to the size of a golf ball.

She traced the outline of his split lips with her finger. Tears escaped and rolled down her cheek. She sighed and lifted his hand to her lips again. Wesley's hand tightened around hers and she turned her head to gaze into his open eyes.

19

Wesley smiled and closed his eyes again, drifting back to sleep. Rachel leaned her head forward, careful of the tubes and wires connected to him. She laid her cheek against his chest, grateful for each rise and fall of his breath. She kept her ear there and counted, one, two, three…

The rattle of iron curtain rings attracted her attention. Rachel peered through lowered lashes. Dottie peeked in the room. Without moving her head, Rachel told her, "I'm fine, Mom. I just want to stay here a while. I need to be with him."

"All right."

Dottie's voice sounded hurt and Rachel listened to her retreating footsteps. *I'm sorry, Lord. I can't leave him right now. I don't mean to hurt my mother, but I have to stay here.*

Wesley's breath shuddered and Rachel jerked awake. She wasn't aware she'd fallen asleep. Her eyes searched his face.

"You're heavy," he said, not opening his eyes. "I can't breath."

"I'm sorry." Rachel lifted her head and,

1

reaching up, smoothed his hair. "Can I get you anything?"

"No. Just stay with me."

"Nothing could make me leave."

He smiled and his breathing became smooth again.

As dusk fell, casting the room into shadow, Rachel's doctor entered. He frowned down at her. "Mrs. Kent. We can't have you sitting here through the night. You need to take care of yourself, too."

Rachel shook her head. "I won't leave him."

"I have to insist." The doctor took her hand, forcing her to look at him. "We're taking good care of Mr. Ward. Go back to bed, Mrs. Kent. I'll have the nurse get you if he wakes again. Deal?"

She turned back to Wesley and kissed his forehead. The doctor led her back to her room.

Dottie sat in the chair next to the hospital bed.

"I'm sorry, Mom."

Her mother leapt up and helped Rachel to bed. "I understand, Rachel. I just want to take care of you."

"Then you understand how I feel about leaving Wesley." Rachel sat on the edge of the bed and allowed her mother to swing her legs up.

2

Dottie plumped the pillows and tucked the blankets tight around her. "You haven't eaten in a while. Let me get you something."

Rachel nodded. "I am hungry."

Face flushed, Dottie smiled. "You got it. Coming right up."

Rachel watched her mother rush from the room. She sighed deeply, and leaned back into the pillows. *Thank you, God, for Wesley's life. Thank you for rescuing me, in more ways than one.*

Dottie returned with a nurse who insisted on reconnecting Rachel's IV. "Don't pull this out again, young lady. The IV tower is on wheels. If you must go, take it with you. If we don't get you re-hydrated, you won't be leaving anytime soon."

Another nurse carried in a tray and set it on the swinging bedside table. "I want you to eat all of this." She lifted the lid, revealing vegetable soup, apple juice and Jello.

Rachel frowned. "You said I could have real food."

"That was before you started wandering the halls."

Sighing, Rachel picked up her spoon. She looked up into her mother's tense face. "What?"

"Nothing." Dottie folded her arms across her chest.

"Something." Rachel slurped the soup.

3

Dottie turned and went to stand before the window and bowed her head. She took a deep breath before turning back to face Rachel. "I'm not sure what's wrong with me. I think I'm still afraid I'm going to lose you. The fear hasn't left me yet." A tear slid down her cheek. "Oh, now look. I'm sniveling again." She reached into her bodice and pulled out a folded tissue.

"I'm going to be fine, Mom. Really." Rachel set her spoon down.

"Don't stop eating on my account."

"Come here." Rachel patted the bed beside her.

Dottie sat gingerly on the edge of the bed. "I don't want to hurt you."

"Really, Mom. I'm going to be okay." She searched her mother's face.

"I know." Dottie rubbed her hand. "I'm just being a baby. We haven't seen much of you since Dennis died." She waved her hand as Rachel opened her mouth to protest. "I know, Honey. Things were hard for you and money was tight. What I'm trying to say is…we haven't seen you in so long. Then we thought we'd lost you forever. Now you're here, but you still seem so far away."

Rachel laughed. "Is that all?"

Dottie frowned.

"I'm sorry. I shouldn't laugh. I know I've been preoccupied, but I thought Wesley was dead. I'm still worried about him, but at least I know he's alive." She pulled her mother close for a hug. "Let me finish this soup. The doctor ordered me to go to sleep if I want to visit Wesley later. Why don't you go home? I'll see you tomorrow."

Her mother nodded.

"Bring Dusty and Mel with you. They'll want to see Wesley." *And I need to see them*.

*

When Wesley opened his eyes, it wasn't Rachel he saw sitting next to his bed. Sam slept, hunched over in the hard chair. "Hey, Sam."

"Wesley." The other man's eyes flew open. "I got here as soon as I could. How are you? You look terrible."

Wesley laughed. "I've been better."

"I'm so sorry, Wesley. They told me what happened to you." Sam ran his hands over his balding head. "When I couldn't reach you on the radio the first day, I wasn't too concerned. I tried back later. The third time, well, I got worried."

"How'd you find us?" Wesley struggled to sit up. Sam reached over to push the button that raised the bed. The motor hummed as the bed rose.

"We were in the air, searching the mountain when we saw the flares." Sam released the button. "I looked down into the face of a woman. She saw me, and fainted." Sam laughed. "Haven't really had that reaction

5

before."

"That would be Rachel. Have you met her?"

Sam shook his head. "Not yet. Should I?"

"Yeah, man. You should."

"Like that, huh?"

Wesley nodded, a grin splitting his face. "Exactly like that."

"Man, when I saw you slumped against that pole..." Sam rubbed the palms of his hands on his jeans. "Well..."

Wesley reached over and stilled his friend's hands with his own. "I'll recover, Sam. Thanks for looking for me."

"You would've done the same for me."

"In a heartbeat." Wesley withdrew his hand. "At least Moe is put away now."

"He's closer than you think."

*

Nurses walked, with muted footsteps, back and forth, sending shadows into the room. Rachel stretched, and grimaced when her IV tugged at her. *How long have I been asleep? Has Wesley awakened yet?*

She flung her legs over the side of the bed, pleased to discover her mother had left slippers there for her. She smiled at the huge teddy bear faces staring up at her. Rachel slid her feet into the slippers and grasped the pole of the IV stand. *Bless you, Mom.*

Dottie had also left her a bathrobe, folded and placed across the back of the chair. *At least I won't be flashing people anymore*. Rachel slid one arm into the robe, leaving the other side draped across her shoulders. She didn't want to upset the nurses by disconnecting her IV in order to put the robe on.

It was awkward, but Rachel managed to make her way out of the room and down the hall to Wesley's room.

A few of the nurses looked up as she passed, but none made any move to stop her. Rachel entered Wesley's room, taking care not to rattle the IV tower as she sat in the chair beside his bed. She allowed her eyes to roam over his face.

His mouth twitched, prompting a smile from Rachel. Wesley's lashes cast shadows on his cheeks. *So long for a man. Not fair*. The bruises had increased in color, the swelling subsiding.

She touched her own face, feeling the scabs.

"Hi." Wesley's voice was low and husky.

"Hello, yourself." A grin split Rachel's face. "How are you feeling?"

"Better, now that you're here." Using his elbows, Wesley pushed his torso upright. His arms shook, and he fell back. "Prop the bed would you? I want to see you better."

7

Rachel pushed the button beside the bed and slowly raised the head of his bed. She stopped when he grimaced. "Are they giving you enough pain medication?"

"Plenty." He smiled at her. "I had them lay off the last dose. I wanted to be awake when you came back."

"You remember me coming in?"

He reached out, taking her hand with his uninjured one. "Of course I do." He raised her hand to his mouth and kissed it. "What happened out there, Rachel?"

She looked at him, surprised.

"I know what happened to me," he stressed. "I want to know how the police knew where to find us. I want to hear it from you."

"Oh, that." Rachel tried to pull her hand free, and glanced down at the burn marks on her forearms. Wesley tightened his grip. "I shot up a couple of flare guns."

"You did? Well." He closed his eyes. "You managed to get them. I wondered."

Rachel swallowed past the lump in her throat. "When I saw you hanging there, I thought you were dead. I started screaming and firing the guns. I told God I'd had enough. I couldn't do it anymore without His help. The next thing I knew there were helicopters and...I fainted."

Wesley laughed. "When help arrives, you faint. That's pretty funny."

"I guess." She turned her head away from him. A small tear escaped and slid down her cheek. She tried to wipe it away before he saw.

"Look at me, Rachel."

Oh, God. I remember the last time he asked me to look at him. I remember what I'd just finished telling him I was going to do. Rachel turned her head and fixed her teary eyes on Wesley's face.

"It doesn't matter." He gave her hand a jerk. "I mean it. I understand why you felt you had to do it."

She closed her eyes, and nodded.

"Rachel." He tugged her hand again, causing her eyes to open. "Did you mean it when you said you love me?"

"With all my heart."

"I meant it, too. It wasn't that I said it because I thought I was going to die. I meant it. The rest is history. It's forgotten." Tears escaped, sliding down his cheeks and Rachel wiped them away, using the hem of her robe.

"Nothing happened, Wesley."

"What?" His eyes grew wide.

"Moe was drunk. He fell asleep. I…"

His laughter interrupted her, shoulders shaking hard enough to shake the bed.

"What's so funny?" Rachel yanked her hand free of his and stood.

He snorted. "Moe fell asleep." He

grabbed his side. "Ow! It hurts to laugh."

"Then stop laughing." She stomped her foot.

"Rachel, you do beat all." Wesley fought to keep his lips from twitching.

"I ought to beat you myself." She grabbed her IV tower, and turned to leave.

Wesley held out a hand to stop her. "Don't go. I'm sorry. Sit down." He snorted again and Rachel glared at him. "Please. It's just...oh, I don't know. Maybe it's the medication. Maybe it's that I'm so...relieved."

She sighed and resumed her seat, keeping her lips pressed firmly together.

"If nothing happened between you and Moe, why are you having such a hard time looking at me?" He reached over and cupped her cheek.

Rachel looked down at her lap. "Because I intended for something to happen." She looked up. "I fully intended to go through with it." She broke into sobs and covered her face with her hands.

"But you didn't have to." Wesley stopped laughing and reached for her. "God intervened. He kept you from doing something that would have damaged you so horribly."

"I know He did." She sniffed. "But I'm still ashamed."

"I thought you said I was worth it," Wesley teased. *Thank you, God.*

"I said that out loud?" Rachel smiled at him through her tears. "I thought you were—until you laughed at me."

"Sounds to me as if you've made your peace with God."

"There's no other way the police could have gotten there so quickly. It could only have been the answer to my prayer. I'd fallen as far as I could." She wiped her face on the sleeve of her robe. "I know I have a long way to go before my relationship with Him is totally repaired, but I'm going to work on it."

"I'm glad to hear it." He crooked his finger. "Come here."

Rachel rose and bent to kiss him.

"I love you," he whispered. "You're good for me."

"Entertaining, you mean." She climbed onto the bed beside him and caressed his face. "Do you think there's enough chaperonage here in the hospital for me to lie beside you for a while?"

"How wanton, Rachel. You shock me." Wesley hugged her to him. "Hurry and kiss me before they run you out of my room."

Rachel giggled and lay on the outside of his blankets, tucking her robe securely around her. She buried her face in his shoulder, folding her body so she wouldn't bump him. She listened as his breathing slowed. She realized he'd fallen asleep. Rachel pulled back enough to watch him. *I do love him so.*

When she felt herself growing drowsy, she kissed his cheek and slid from the bed. Smiling, and warm inside, Rachel made her way back to her room.

*

Rachel opened her eyes to see her doctor standing at the foot of her bed.

"Good morning," he greeted. "Are you up to going home today?"

She glanced toward the door of her room. Her parents and children stood beaming in at her. She nodded. "I'm ready."

The doctor slid his pen into the pocket of his jacket. "I'll be back with your release papers. The nurse will be right in to unhook you from your IV and take the catheter out of your arm. We've drawn all the blood we're going to."

"Thank you." Rachel smiled at her family.

Her father handed her a small overnight bag. "The police had your car and the U-Haul towed to the house yesterday. We've unpacked everything and moved you into your old room. Your furniture is piled in the shed."

"Thanks, Dad." Rachel took the bag and set it at the foot of the bed. "Once I'm up and unhooked, I want you to meet Wesley."

"I already have," Bill beamed. "I wanted to shake the hand of the man who saved my baby girl. I met him this morning, right before coming in here."

Dusty pounced on the bed. "Mel and I went, too. Grandpa had to distract the nurses, cause Wesley's not allowed to have kids visit him. He looks awful! He's all beat up and bruised."

Rachel laughed. "He's going to be fine. Nothing that won't heal." She glanced at her father. "I want him to come home with us when he's released. Is that all right?" She peered at Dottie.

Her parents looked at each other, then back at Rachel. "That'll be fine, Dear," Dottie answered. "We'll be glad to have him."

Mel remained silent as the others talked and Rachel turned a concerned look on her. "Mel? Are you all right?"

The girl sniffed. "Wesley looked really bad, Mom. He's like that because of us. We got him involved when we went into his cabin. I've been so mean to him." Her sniffs turned into sobs.

Rachel made her way to her daughter's side, and wrapped her arms around Mel. "He chose to do it for us. He doesn't regret a bit of it."

The girl leaned her forehead against Rachel's chest. "If you say so."

"I say so. Have you spoken with him?"

"She wouldn't," Dusty interrupted. "She just looked in the room and turned around."

13

Rachel released Mel and grabbed her IV tower. "Let's go. Let's go talk to Wesley."

"No." Mel pulled back. "I can't."

"Yes, you can."

Once again dragging the tower, Rachel headed down the hall toward Wesley's room. She peeked through the doorway, surprised to see a police officer and man in jeans standing there.

"Wait a minute," she told her daughter.

Rachel walked into the room and turned a questioning look on the two men.

"Mrs. Kent," one of them acknowledged.

"Is everything all right?"

The officer noticed Mel hovering in the door. "Maybe we should close the door."

"Go back to my room," Rachel told her. "Tell my parents I'll be there in a minute." She closed the door and turned to Wesley. "Wesley?"

"Sit down, please. There's something we need to tell you."

Rachel looked at the men in the room, her heartbeat accelerating. The man in plain clothes motioned toward the chair.

"Mrs. Kent, we've rounded up what we know to be the Righteous Survivalist Group responsible for the killing of the people at the KOA campgrounds."

Rachel glanced at Wesley, then back to

the officer. "Yes?"

"Duane Watkins, aka Moe, was wounded. When we captured him, he told us there were others. Others who are prepared to avenge him."

Rachel gripped the arms of the chair, glad for its solid support. "Avenge him?"

"That's what he said." The plain clothes man stepped forward. "It could just be talk, Mrs. Kent, but it's better to proceed with caution."

"Should I be scared?"

"Rachel," Wesley spoke from the bed. "This is my friend, Sam."

"You're the one from the chopper."

"Yes, ma'am."

"Should I be scared, Sam?"

The police officer wiped sweat from his brow. "Did you have your car registration in the glove compartment of your car?"

"Yes." Rachel's hands began to tremble and she tightened them further. Her knuckles turned white.

The officer sighed. "It's missing. Along with the rental certificate from the U-Haul. Did you list your parent's address on it by chance? Bill and Dottie Miller?"

"Of course I did. I had to give them the address of where I'd be staying." Rachel let go of the chair and crossed her arms in front of her. She hit the IV, pushing the needle further into her hand. She drew in a painful breath and unfolded her arms.

"They know where we are, Wesley." She raised wide eyes to his.

Wesley held her gaze. "It appears so."

"They'll be coming for us, won't they?" Rachel's voice rose. "Won't they?"

"I don't know. Maybe. Probably."

Sam stepped to the side of Wesley's bed. "I've got to go, Ward. Keep me posted. We'll see if we can't hunt down Moe's buddies."

Wesley grasped his friend's hand. "Take care of yourself."

"I will." Sam turned to Rachel. "Ma'am." Rachel nodded.

The police officer stepped forward and put a reassuring hand on Rachel's shoulder. "We'll provide police protection, Mrs. Kent. As long as we think necessary."

"Do my parents know?"

The office shook his head. "Not yet. We were headed to your room next." The officer took a deep breath. "There is one more thing we need to ask of you."

"What?"

"Moe carried no identification on him. We need you to provide a positive ID."

She shook her head. "I can't."

Wesley shifted in his bed. "I can't do it, Rachel. I can't leave this bed. You'll have to do it."

Rachel stood. "I need to tell my parents. I need to be there with Dusty and Mel when they find out." She turned toward the door, and stopped. "What about Wesley? I go home today. Are you going to post a guard outside his room?"

"It's all taken care of, Mrs. Kent."

Rachel nodded. "Where is he? Where's Moe?"

The officer took another deep breath, clearly hesitant to answer her question. "The next floor up."

"Here?" Rachel spun around. "He's here in *this* hospital?" Fear made her legs tremble. She leaned on the IV tower. *When will it end, Lord? How much more?*

20

Rachel paused in the doorway of her hospital room and glanced at her waiting family. She moved stiffly, her legs wooden. Biting her bottom lip, she wondered how to begin. Should she tell her parents about Moe in private? Was it something the kids really needed to know? She shook her head, and pushed open the door.

"Oh, you're back." A nurse bustled in behind Rachel, prolonging the need for her to share the news. "Have a seat on the bed, Mrs. Kent, and we'll get all these lines unhooked. Bet you're ready to go home."

The nurse chattered as she worked.

Dottie's stare over the nurse's head, caused Rachel to turn away, avoiding her mother's eyes. The woman had always been discerning where Rachel was concerned.

"Later." Rachel mouthed. Dottie raised her eyebrows.

When the nurse finished, Rachel grabbed the overnight bag and headed to the restroom. She pulled out a pair of jeans and a cotton shirt from the bag, shaking out as many of the wrinkles as she could. Her hands shook, fumbling over the buttons. She ran her fingers through her hair, taming the curls. Her bruises had begun to fade, coloring her face a dirty yellow and blue. Rachel wished for makeup, and sighed. She'd stalled long enough.

She stepped out of the

restroom to a crowd. Two police officers now joined her parents.

"Mel," Rachel said. "Could you and Dusty run down to the cafeteria and get me a soda?"

"Now?" Mel frowned.

"What are the police here for?" Dusty asked looking from them to his mother.

Rachel shooed them from the room. "I'll fill you in later."

"But..." Mel protested.

"Later." Rachel closed the door behind them. She leaned her head against the door for a moment. *Moe!* She yanked it open. "Mel. Dusty. Stay here. By the door. Don't wander off."

"But you said..."

"I know what I said. I've changed my mind." Rachel closed the door again, and turned to her parents. "Mom, Dad, there's something you need to know."

"Are you in trouble?" Bill asked, arms folded across his chest.

Rachel smiled. "No, Dad. I'm not in trouble."

"Mr. and Mrs. Miller, I'm Officer McHale and this is Officer Porter. We need your daughter to come with us and make a positive identification on the man who kidnapped her."

"You want her to go now?" Dottie's mouth fell open. She snapped it closed. "She's just getting out of the hospital."

"Mom," Rachel interrupted. "The man is upstairs."

"He's here?" Her mother turned to Bill. "Do something?"

"What would you have me do?"

Dottie plopped heavily in the chair. "I don't know. Something. You're her father."

She wrung her hands in her lap. "Are you up to this, Rachel?"

Rachel nodded. "I have to be."

"Okay, then." The older woman stood. "I'll go with you. Bill, stay here with the children."

"Now, Honey. It should really be..."

"I'll go!." She narrowed her eyes.

Throwing his hands in the air, Bill slumped in the chair his wife had just vacated. "Fine."

"Really. I can do this myself," Rachel told them.

Dottie shook her head. "It's best I go with you."

"Dad..."

"Let her go, sweetie. There's no use arguing with her when she's in one of her moods."

Officer Porter interrupted. "Actually, she'll be going to the station. It's fine if she goes tomorrow, or the next day. Whenever Moe is released. We'll do a lineup, and Moe is in no condition right now to do anything."

"Thank, God." Dottie clapped a hand to her chest. "A few days sounds so much better."

The two officers looked at each other. McHale shook his head, frowning. "Okay. We'll be going. Here's my card." He handed the white business card to Rachel. "Let me know if I can do anything."

Knees buckling, Rachel plopped on the edge of the bed, rubbing the bridge of her nose between her index finger and thumb. Pressing her lips together, she planted her hands on her thighs, and pushed to her feet. "I'm going after Dusty and Mel." She glanced at her parents. "I'll be right back."

Pushing the button to the elevator, she glanced back

over her shoulder to see Dottie watching her from the room doorway. Rachel gave her mother a quick smile and stepped forward.

As the elevator ascended, so did Rachel's anxiety. Her breathing quickened and she wrapped her arms tight around her middle. *One, two, three...* She held a trembling hand in front of her.

She leaned back against the elevator wall as the doors opened and stared into the white tiled hall. From somewhere to her right was a steady electronic beep. *Help me, Lord*.

The hall appeared longer than it actually was. Rachel kept her eyes focused on the barred window at the far end. The term "green mile" came to mind and she shook her head to clear it.

Scanning the names posted beside each door she

continued. Her sneakered feet slapped the floor, echoing through the corridor. Moe's room loomed at the farthest end. A police officer, looking bored, stood posted in front of the closed door.

Rachel paused and looked around the nurse's station. Two nurses sat talking and drinking from Styrofoam cups. Walking past them, Rachel stared straight ahead, acting as if she belonged there.

"Excuse me, officer, but Officers McHale and Porter want you downstairs in Rachel Kent's room."

"Why?" The officer looked down at her, a look of puzzlement on his face.

Rachel shrugged. "I'm not sure. I'm, uh, I'm Rachel's sister." *God forgive me for lying.* "They asked whether I would mind sending you down to them. I...I think they have some new information."

"Why didn't they use the radio? I can't leave my post on your say-so, ma'am." The officer glanced at Moe's room, then back to Rachel. "Who did you say you were?"

She hesitated, clearing her throat. "What's wrong with him?"

"I'm not at liberty…" They both turned as a woman cried for help at the end of the hall.

The officer turned. "Don't stay up here, ma'am. Don't go into that room. You need to leave." He kept one hand on the butt of the gun at his hip and sprinted toward the cry.

"I won't." Rachel watched as the nurses ran to follow the police officer.

Taking a quick look around, she opened the door to Moe's room and ducked inside. The light was dim and the room contained a single bed. A monitor beeped. Moe lay with his eyes closed. Heart thudding, Rachel gasped and took a step back.

Moe's eyes opened and locked with Rachel's. A thin smile spread beneath his beard. "Come to finish what you started, Missy?" His voice rasped across the room.

Taking another step back, Rachel bumped against the solid wall which turned out to be her mother. She jumped when Dottie touched her shoulder.

"It's him," Rachel whispered. "That's Moe."

"They didn't shoot him enough times," the older woman muttered behind her. "He's still breathing."

Startled, Rachel turned, eyes widening at her mother's comment.

"What?"

"What are you doing here?" Rachel hissed.

"I could ask you the same thing."

Rachel watched in horrified fascination as her mother strode to Moe's bedside.

The big man turned his head to look up at the woman.

"You, mister, are a fiend! The things I would say to you if it wasn't against the good Lord's will."

Moe laughed. "Don't let that stop you."

"I'm a lady." Dottie stiffened her back. "And I don't use the words necessary to tell you what I think of you."

Moe turned back to Rachel. "I see where you get your fire from."

"Don't speak to her," the older woman hissed. "Don't ever speak to, or lay eyes on my daughter again."

The man's eyes flicked from Rachel to Dottie. "I plan on doing a lot more than talking

11

lady." He lunged for Rachel, held back by the handcuffs keeping him chained to the bed.

Rachel screamed and turned when hands clapped her shoulders.

"Let's go." Officer McHale took her by the shoulders and steered her toward the open door. "You shouldn't be here. Mrs. Miller, you, too. Come with me."

Sticking her nose in the air and stiffening her spine, Dottie preceded Rachel and the officer into the hall.

Officer McHale glowered down at the two women. Officer Porter, and the young officer assigned to guard Moe's room, stood glaring at them from a few feet away.

"What kind of game are you playing, Mrs. Kent?" Officer McHale's brows lowered. "You are jeopardizing our investigation by being up here.

You'll be lucky if Moe doesn't press charges of harassment against you."

"But you said I needed to..."

The officer folded his arms across his chest. "You know full well you were supposed to wait until Moe is released. What were you hoping to gain?"

"I..."

"Did you stage the disturbance down the hall?"

"No, I didn't." Rachel was flustered. Her face flamed. "I did lie to the officer, and I'm sorry about that, but..."

"No, buts, Mrs. Kent. Let's go." He motioned his head toward the elevator. "You first. Your doctor released you. Go home." The officer stepped aside and waited for Dottie to join her daughter. Unsmiling, the man nodded and stepped back, allowing the elevator doors to close.

Dottie pulled a tissue from her purse and wiped her mouth. "I've never met a more disagreeable man than Moe in my entire life. It leaves a bad taste in my mouth just to say his name."

Staring wide-eyed at her mother, Rachel burst into laughter. "I can't believe you." She snorted. "I was terrified out of my mind. We just got chewed out by Officer McHale, right after you walked up to Moe and threatened him. You've got nerves of steel." She held her hands out in front of her. "My hands are shaking."

The hand holding the tissue halted halfway to Dottie's pocket book. "I didn't threaten him, dear."

"What do you call it?"

After replacing the tissue, Dottie snapped her purse closed. Holding it in both hands, she very primly stated, "It was a promise."

Amazing how easily Mom removed my fear. She almost makes me feel like a child again. Rachel gave another small laugh. "You must be the bravest woman I know."

"The man was chained to the bed, Rachel. What was there to be afraid of?"

"I don't know. Maybe the fact he's a crazed lunatic?"

"Isn't that a bit redundant? Crazed and lunatic in the same sentence?" Dottie smiled as Rachel shook her head. "Besides, you were frightened enough for the both of us. I had to break the tension somehow."

Rachel flung an arm around her mother's shoulders. "I love you, Mom. Have I told you?"

"Not lately." The older woman squeezed back. "Let's go get the kids."

The elevator doors opened and Rachel stepped

back and forth, trying to get out
of the way of one of the most
obese women she'd ever seen.
The woman looked easily way
over the three hundred pound
mark.

Dressed in a faded,
flowered dress and garish green
flip-flops with plastic flowers,
the woman clashed with the
muted burgundy of the elevator
walls. Her breath escaped her in
wheezing gasps. She frowned
when she saw Rachel, her
mouth all but disappearing into
the folds of flesh making up her
face.

"Excuse me." Rachel
hopped out of her way. The
woman barreled past, bumping
into Dottie. She muttered, out
of breath, and pushed the
button to continue the elevator
to the lobby.

The elevator was
crowded with the three of
them. The heavy woman's body
odor washed over them,

assaulting Rachel's senses.

Dottie retrieved her tissue from her purse and held it over her nose, breathing through her mouth. The tissue fluttered up and down. The heavy woman stared straight ahead as if the other two women weren't there.

The elevator stopped. Rachel and Dottie squeezed past, rushing to exit.

Stopping a few feet down the hall, Rachel turned. The heavy woman held the elevator doors open, staring after them. Rachel sent her a nervous smile before heading to where her father and children waited.

"What a rude woman," her mother commented.

Glancing back again, Rachel noted the elevators were closed and the woman had disappeared through the front doors of the hospital. "Yes, she really seemed to be in a hurry to get out of here." She shrugged and called to her father. "Let's go. I want to stop by Wesley's room before we leave."

"You just came down," Mel complained.

"I want you to come with me." Rachel set her lips in a firm line.

The return ride in the elevator was quiet except for an occasional huff from Mel, and slurps through a straw from Dusty. Rachel breathed a sigh of relief once they'd returned to Wesley's floor.

She poked her head into his room. Wesley held the phone receiver to his ear while a nurse took his blood pressure. Rachel waved and blew him a kiss. "I'll see you tomorrow."

Wesley hung up the phone. "You can't leave me with an air kiss, Rachel. I want the real thing."

"Flirt." She went to

stand beside the bed. "I don't want to be in the nurse's way."

"I was just leaving." The nurse picked up the tray of medical supplies and left, squeezing past Bill and Dottie.

Wesley took a hold of Rachel's arm, pulling her close. "That was Officer McHale on the phone. He told me you paid Moe a visit."

She chewed her lip for a second. "Yes."

He pulled her even closer. He whispered, his breath tickling her ear. "You shouldn't have done that. You're not allowed up there."

"The police already lectured me." Rachel laughed. "Mom gave Moe a talking to when he said something crude."

"She did?" Wesley glanced over to where her mother waited in the doorway. "I can't wait to get to know your mother better."

Rachel turned her head, and kissed him. "There'll be plenty of time. You'll be out of here in a few days and you're coming to stay with us. You'll still need recovery time, and Mom and Dad have plenty of room."

"I'd like nothing better."

The look in his eyes, melted Rachel's insides and she bent to kiss him again.

*

Rachel got out of the car and stood still, taking in the sight of her childhood home. Her parents' house sat on three acres of lush green property. Tall maple trees shaded the house. A porch, complete with a swing, ran the full length of the front and down one side of the two-story white clapboard house. Off to the right, a magnolia tree, still sporting a few blossoms held an old tire swing.

"I love this place," she declared.

Her father joined her, Rachel's overnight bag in one hand. "It's been mighty quiet since you moved out. It's wonderful to have young voices in the old place again."

She let her eyes wander over the property. "You've cut down some of the trees in back."

"It obstructed too much of the view of the mountains. There's still a lot of underbrush to get rid of, though."

"Any new neighbors?"

Bill shook his head. "The Williams' moved out shortly after you did. Their place is pretty run down and in need of repair. Can't seem to find any renters. The old Fuller place is vacant, too. It's been kept up pretty well. Their kids still come by once in a while. Stay a few nights now and then." He shrugged. "Basically, it's just me and the old lady on this road now."

"Old?" Dottie punched his arm. "Speak for yourself. Y'all come in and I'll fix up some dinner."

"I'll be in shortly." Rachel motioned for Dusty and Mel to join her. She put an arm around each of them. "Who said you can never go back home?"

Mel leaned her head on her mother's shoulder. "I like it here. It's peaceful."

"You're not bored?"

The young girl shook her head. "After last week, quiet is what I want."

"Grandma and Grandpa said the bus will stop right there by the mailbox on Monday to pick us up," Dusty explained. "That's if you have time to register us for school before then."

Realizing the importance of them regaining

appearances of a normal life, Rachel glanced down at her son. "I'll make time."

"Good. I'm ready to go to school."

"Now, Mel, where's this boy I've been hearing about? Grandpa said he was the boy next door. There isn't anyone next door." She led her children to the porch swing and the three sat, swinging their legs.

Mel blushed, ducking her head. "To them it's next door. He lives down the road. Says so, anyway. I haven't been there."

"How'd you meet him?"

Dusty spoke up. "He was riding his bike and Mel waved at him."

"Oh, really?" Rachel put her arms across the back of the swing, one behind each of her children. She pulled them close, placing a kiss on top of each of their heads. Using her foot, she pushed, keeping the swing in motion.

"Should I go help Grandma?" Mel asked. "I've been setting the table for her."

"In a minute. I just want to hold the two of you a little longer. My arms have felt pretty empty lately."

Dusty sighed, and pulled back. "What were the police doing at the hospital today?"

She thought for a moment and decided honesty was the best thing. "They want me to identify Moe."

"Is he dead?" Mel shot up, eagerness on her face.

"No, he's not dead. He is wounded, though."

"I wish he were dead." Mel's eyes focused on something across the yard.

"Apparently, so does your grandmother." At Mel's questioning look, she added, "Never mind."

"Will you be scared to see him again?"

Rachel turned to face her son.

"Yes. Very much so." She smiled, remembering her mother's words to the man. She tightened her arms around her children. "Sit with me. Watch the sun go down over the mountain."

"We've seen it, Mom. First hand." Mel blew her breath out in a huff.

"See it again. In a new perspective." Rachel took a deep breath, filling her lungs with the crisp autumn air. She leaned her head back, and closed her eyes. *It's so good to be home.*

21

Three days later, Rachel helped Wesley up the porch steps, against his protests that he could do it himself. Keeping herself positioned beneath his shoulder, she supported his weight and grinned up at him. "I'm so glad you're here."

He returned her smile, giving her a squeeze. "I'm glad to be here."

Bill hurried and took hold of Wesley's other arm. He placed it around his shoulder, calling for Dottie to open the front door.

"I'm here, I'm here." The screen door squeaked, and Dottie winced.

"I've got to fix that one of these days," Bill commented. "Watch your step, Wesley. Don't want to pick you up off the ground."

"Give me a couple of days, and I'll fix the door for you."

Dottie looked shocked. "You're our guest. You can't be fixing things like a screen door." She scowled at her husband. "Just because someone around here procrastinates."

Letting the door slam shut behind them, Dottie hurried to the sofa and gathered together several of the throw pillows. She was careful to prop them behind Wesley as Bill helped lower him.

Rachel stood back as her parents fussed over the man she loved. She gloried in the feeling. She hadn't been worried about how her parents would receive him, after all, he'd almost given his life for their daughter and grandchildren. It was more how they would react to a man living in the same house as their unmarried daughter.

She glanced over at Mel. Her daughter's face could have been carved in stone. The girl stared, unblinking. Dusty stood beside his sister, grinning from ear to ear. His face shone with pleasure.

Mel looked at her mother and turned, exiting the room.

Shrugging, Rachel switched her attention back to Wesley. Mel would deal with the situation on her terms and in her own time.

"Let me get you a nice tall glass of tea," Dottie offered.

"Hope you like it sweet," Rachel told Wesley. "Mom's tea is more like having tea with your sugar."

"I would love a glass," Wesley replied, smiling up at the woman fussing over him.

The older woman beamed and bustled away.

Wesley grimaced and tried to shift

positions.

"Do you need a painkiller?" Rachel asked.

He shook his head. "No, it's just the scabs pulling on my back. I'll be fine." He reached back and removed one of the pillows. "And one too many pillows." He reached up and grabbed Rachel by the hand, pulling her onto his lap.

"Will your mother be shocked?" He nuzzled her neck.

She shrieked and tried to pull away. "She might." Rachel looked up to see her mother smiling from the doorway.

"I think it's lovely. I like seeing my daughter happy again." She held a tray loaded down with glasses of amber liquid.

"I plan on keeping her that way." Wesley took one of the glasses and lifted it to his mouth.

"Good." Dottie set the tray on the coffee table and stood, looking down at him. "I'm a very good judge of character, Mr. Ward, and I like you. Did the first time I saw you. But I must warn you...I'm like a bear defending her cub when it comes to Rachel. No hanky-panky beneath this roof."

Wesley choked on the tea, dribbling it down his chin. He raised wide eyes to Rachel.

She laughed and wiped his chin. "Don't worry, Mother. Wesley's always been a perfect gentleman."

"Good." The older woman nodded and left them alone.

"You said you wanted to know my mother better," Rachel told him. "Well, there she is."

Wesley shook his head. "Is she always like this?"

"Always." She gave him a quick kiss, and stood. "You get some rest. I'll be back later. I need to take Dusty and Mel to the school. Will you be all right?"

He nodded and set his glass on the table. He sat back and laid his head against the sofa cushions. "Just fine. I'm really feeling good, Rachel." He twirled the hand with the cast. "And lucky for me, it's my left wrist I broke. Don't worry about me."

"I can't help it." She smiled over her shoulder at him. "I love you."

*

Wesley smiled back and watched her walk from the room. *How am I going to tell her, Lord? She's so happy now. I probably shouldn't let her leave. Not with the latest news. Protect her, please. Keep your angels around her and the kids.* He sighed. *I'm going to have to pull the rug out from under her feet. I thank you that Rachel and her family aren't big television watchers. They won't have seen it on the news.*

Mel watched him from the archway

leading into the living room. "Mel? I thought you were going to register for school."

The girl chewed on the inside of her cheek. "Mom's getting ready."

"Still mad at me?"

Mel looked surprised. "For what?"

"Loving your mother." He kept his eyes locked on the girl.

"Do you love her?"

"With all my heart." Wesley watched the play of emotions flit across Mel's face. Doubt, fear...and something else. "What is it, Mel?"

She looked down at her hands. "At least you're not like Daddy. You don't look like him or act like him."

"That's probably a good thing, don't you think?"

"I guess." Mel raised her eyes.

"I'm here for the long term. I don't want to take your dad's place. I'm perfectly satisfied with being your friend. Deal?"

Mel nodded. "I'll try."

"That's all I can ask."

Rachel entered the room and interrupted them, putting a hand on her daughter's arm. "Ready?"

"Ready." Mel gave Wesley another glance, and a hint of smile.

Wesley got to his feet, pushing up from the sofa with his hands. The wounds on his back pulled, and he drew in a sharp breath. Keeping a hand firm against the wrappings around his ribcage, he walked to the window and watched as Rachel backed the car out of the driveway.

"Should you be up?" Bill walked up to stand next to him.

"I've had enough lying around."

"I don't make a good patient myself." Bill hesitated, shoving his hands into the pockets of his work pants. "What's bothering you?"

Wesley turned his head to study the older man. "How did you know?"

"Saw it in your eyes." He motioned his head toward the sofa. "Let's sit down."

Nodding, Wesley resumed his seat on the sofa.

Bill took a seat across from him. "You having second thoughts?"

"About what?" *Were both of Rachel's parents this blunt?*

"About Rachel."

"No." Wesley leaned forward, balancing his elbows on his knees. He took a deep breath. "The police came to my room this morning, right before I was released. Seems sometime before dawn, someone helped Moe escape from the hospital. Shot the nurses and the guard."

"Really! And no one heard anything?" Bill rubbed his chin.

"Whoever did it, knew the hospital. Knew the shift change. They used a silencer. When the relief nurses came on duty, they discovered the bodies, and Moe gone. The timing couldn't have been better. After med rounds and before breakfast." Wesley looked into Bill's eyes.

"Wasn't Moe severely wounded?"

"He'd been shot a couple of times, but no major organs were hit. With help, he could've walked out." Wesley sat straighter. "I don't know how to tell Rachel."

The older man nodded. "That is a tough one. Let me think on it. I'll get back to you later."

"Just flat out tell her." Dottie walked up behind her husband's chair.

"Is there anything in this house you miss, woman?" Bill swiveled in the rocker to face her.

"Not much." She folded her arms across her chest. "Just tell her, Mr. Ward. My daughter's strong."

"Wesley, please."

"Okay, Wesley then. Just tell her. I think my daughter has proven by now that she's tougher than she looks." Dottie folded her hands across her middle. "She's weepy, but that doesn't make her weak. Just emotional. She'll be very upset if she finds out you're keeping something from her."

*

Rachel drove the car into the school parking lot, choosing a spot near the front entry door. She turned to look at the small, red brick buildings. A new gymnasium had been built since she'd graduated. The school also sported a new electric sign, announcing an upcoming football game.

"It's small," Mel pointed out.

"There were ninety-two in my graduating class," Rachel told her.

"That's all?" The girl plopped back against the seat. "Everyone's going to know me."

"Nothing wrong with that." Rachel turned off the ignition and unhooked her seatbelt. "Unless it's bad stuff. Let's go, you two." She grabbed her purse and the folder containing her children's academic records.

"Look, Mel." Dusty drew their attention to a boy standing on the sidewalk. "Isn't that your friend?"

"Bobby Joe!" Mel slid from the car, slamming the door. "Hey!"

The boy's eyes shifted from the girl to Rachel, then back to Mel. "Hey to you."

"Mom, this is Bobby Joe."

Rachel extended her hand. "It's nice to meet you...Bobby Joe."

He looked at her offered hand for a moment before shaking it. He raised cold blue eyes to Rachel's face, not smiling, and she flinched. "Ma'am."

"Isn't his accent cute?" Mel beamed at him.

Without taking her eyes from his, Rachel answered, "The cutest."

"What are you doing here?" Mel grabbed the boy's arm.

"Registering, same as you."

Mel turned to her mother. "Bobby Joe's new to the neighborhood, too."

Rachel frowned at the way her daughter pressed against the boy's arm. "That's great." *Yep, we've got to have that talk*. She turned to Dusty. "Ready?"

"You bet!" Her son ran ahead of her and opened the double glass doors.

The dim lighting of the office caused Rachel to squint after the glare of the sun outside. Two women sat behind the counter, smiling up at her.

"New students?" One of them asked.

"Just these two are mine." Rachel inclined her head toward Dusty and Mel. She handed the woman their records. "They'd like to start on Monday."

"That shouldn't be a problem." She handed the records to the other woman and transferred her attention to Bobby Joe. "Are your parents here?"

"No, ma'am. My daddy's dead and my

mama's at work."

"Doesn't he have the cutest accent?" Mel whispered. "I could listen to him talk all day."

"You've already mentioned his accent. Settle down." Rachel closed her eyes and breathed in slow breaths. She re-opened them and waited, eyes on Mel and the boy, until the receptionist handed back her children's shot records and birth certificates.

"I'm sorry," the woman told Bobby Joe. "You'll have to return with your mother. You can't register yourself."

Something cold flashed in the boy's eyes before he squeezed Mel's hand. "Catch ya later."

"See you, Monday." Mel waved and turned to her mother. "I told you he was cute."

"Yes, you did." Rachel turned back to the secretary. "Here's where we're staying. At least temporarily."

The registration took less than half an hour. Soon, Rachel had them headed back toward home. Her thoughts drifted as she drove, focusing mainly on her daughter. *The way Mel hung on that boy, I'm going to have to bring up the little bombshell she dropped on me in the woods*. She sighed. *I was actually thinking about forgetting about it*.

Her parents and Wesley sat in the living room when Rachel arrived home. When all three heads swiveled in her direction, it was obvious they were waiting for her. Wesley reclined on the sofa. Her father sat in the easy chair with Dottie perched on the arm beside him. All three of them looked up when she and the children entered.

"What? Has something happened? Should I send the kids out of the room?"

Wesley shook his head. "No, they should hear this. It concerns them, too." He patted the sofa next to him. "Sit down, Rachel."

She motioned for the kids to sit on the floor. Lowering herself slowly to the sofa, she raised anxious eyes to Wesley's face. "Must be serious if it calls for a family meeting." Her joke fell short.

Taking her hand in his, Wesley stroked it, sending shivers down her spine. He sighed. "Early this morning, someone broke Moe out of the hospital, killing two nurses and wounding another. The officer guarding Moe's room was also shot and killed."

"What...how?" She looked around at the faces in the room.

"That's all we know." Her father rose and paced the room. "Officer McHale informed Wesley this morning. They'll have increased police protection here by nightfall."

"What about Dusty and Mel at school?" Rachel pulled her hand free.

"They won't be able to go until Moe is

11

back in custody."

Mel bolted from the room and pounded up the stairs. A door slammed. Dusty raised a tear-streaked face to his mother.

Rachel hugged him to her. "I'm so sorry, honey."

"It's all right. They'll catch him."

She rested her chin on his head. "I'm sure they will." She met Wesley's gaze, giving her son a gentle nudge. "Go on in the kitchen. Fix yourself a sandwich."

He nodded, leaving the adults alone.

Wesley stood and Rachel stepped into his arms, relishing the feeling of safety. "When is it going to end?" she sniffed.

He shrugged. "I don't know. But it will end. Someday."

Tears coursed down her cheeks. "That's not good enough. Not nearly good enough." She stepped back and looked at her parents. "Moe knows where we are. Now my parents are involved."

"I told you the police should've shot to kill," Dottie stated.

Rachel laughed. "I'm serious, Mom."

"So am I." The woman arched an eyebrow at her daughter. "There's nothing we can do about it now. We might as well accept the fact. Bill, go get your gun."

Her husband moved to do her bidding and stopped when Wesley placed a hand on his arm. "I've got one you can use, Wesley. I've a couple of old hunting rifles, but they still shoot straight." He pulled free. "I'll be back in a minute."

Wesley scratched the stubble on his chin. "Rachel, your parents can't run off half-cocked thinking they can catch Moe themselves."

"They're not. They will protect their home and family, though. If you can stop them...go for it." She turned.

"Rachel, wait."

She stopped, looking at him. "My Dad won't spare their life if they come after us."

Wesley's brows drew together. "You blame me for this, don't you? You blame me because I didn't take care of Moe's men. Admit it."

She shrugged.

"I could have killed them all. Or just about. I was trained for it. I could have gone straight for Moe and put you and the kids in more danger by leaving you alone. Think about it." He scowled down at her. "When we did get to Moe's camp, I was tied. Remember? I was tied up, chained to a pole and beaten. If you can think of another way I could've killed Moe without you or one of the children being killed right along with him...tell me. Right now."

Rachel flinched from the anger on his face. "I'm sorry. You're right."

He scoffed and turned away from her. She reached out a hand, grasping his arm. "I'm not blaming you. Not really." Her words stuck in her throat. "I'm scared."

He spun around and grabbed her to him. Rachel's breath squeezed from her as he tightened his hold. "So am I. I'm terrified of losing you, but we'll get through this. I promise." *Help us, God*.

They pulled apart at a knock on the front door. Mutt, unnoticed until now, streaked past them, barking shrilly.

"I'll get it," Wesley ordered as Dottie walked past him. He peered through the curtained window before opening the door to Officers McHale and Porter. "Officers."

"Mr. Ward." They stepped into the house, ignoring the dog which ran in and out between their legs.

Dottie hurried to close the door after them and peered through the curtains. "Coast is clear," she stated.

The officers glanced at each other without expression, then turned to the others. "You need to keep everyone away from the windows."

"Mom," Rachel warned. "Behave yourself."

Her mother looked offended. "I was only trying to help."

"Where are the children?" Officer

McHale asked.

"They're upstairs. We've told them about Moe's escape."

The officer nodded. "The other day, during your little escapade in the hospital, did you notice anyone else on Moe's floor? Someone who looked as if they didn't belong there?"

"No, but…"

Porter opened a manila folder he carried and handed Rachel a composite photo. "Ever seen this woman?"

She perused the photo and handed it to Wesley. "Yes."

Her mother interrupted. "The elevator stopped a couple of floors down and a very, large, very smelly woman got on. She rode to the lobby with us. She breathed heavily, like she'd been running."

Rachel handed the photo back to the officer. "This is the woman who got on the elevator with us."

Porter slid the photo back into the folder.

"That is Mrs. Watkins," McHale told them. "Moe's mother."

"His mother!" Dottie's hand flew to her throat. "We rode the elevator with a murderer's mother. I declare!"

"Mother," Rachel warned. "Stop interrupting."

"We believe this woman was on the fifth floor, studying the area. We believe," McHale's eyes fixed on Rachel, "that she was the woman who cried for help, luring the guard away from Moe's room. Thus enabling you to go in."

"Why? I'd never seen her before that day." Rachel moved to Wesley's side.

"You aren't insinuating my daughter is associated with that…that woman!" Dottie's cheeks flamed red.

Bill entered the room, leaning the rifles against the wall, and placed a restraining hand on her arm. "Settle down. The officer isn't insinuating any such thing." His head turned. "Are you?"

McHale shook his head. "Just checking. Didn't think so. We believe it to be a coincidence. We also believe she went back this morning and freed her son."

Leg's collapsing, Rachel plopped onto the sofa. A whoosh of air flew from the cushion. "And killed several people in the process."

"Yes, ma'am. She is an extremely dangerous woman." The officer looked around the room. "No one leaves this house without an escort. Porter and I will be on watch tonight. Tomorrow, another shift will come on. Please inform us if you see anyone around your property who should not be here."

Rising, Bill extended his hand to the

officers. "Thank you, gentlemen. We'll take care."

McHale glanced toward the rifles as he walked out of the room. "Going hunting?" He stared at Bill.

The older man straightened his shoulders. "No, sir. Just cleaning my guns."

Expressionless, the officer nodded. "Thought so."

22

The morning sun made its appearance, peeking through the window sheers when Rachel parted them and stared out at the white van parked in front of the house. *Nothing like subtlety. They might as well mark "Police" on the van in big red letters*. She let her eyes travel the length of the road, from the mailbox to the house. Nothing moved.

Wesley came up behind her and wrapped his arms around her waist. "You shouldn't be standing by the window."

She shrugged and leaned back against his chest. His solidness was reassuring, comforting. "Why is the van sitting there in plain sight? I mean, wouldn't they be more effective out of sight?"

"They're out there as a deterrent. They want to keep Moe away while they search for him." Wesley stepped back, pulling Rachel with him. She turned in his arms. Standing on her toes, she kissed him.

"Wouldn't it be better if he came to us?"

"You really want to take that chance?"

"No, but we're prisoners in our own home." She slid out of his grasp.

"Only for a time."

"When I prayed to God at Moe's camp, and the

helicopters came, I thought everything was going to be fine." She sat on the sofa and looked up at him. "I thought once I turned my life over to God, He would make life easy."

"He never promised to make life easy." Wesley kneeled before her, taking her hands in his. "He only promises to walk with you through it."

She sighed, and slouched down into the overstuffed cushions. "I suppose."

The phone's shrill ringing broke into Rachel's brooding.

Mel bounded down the stairs and barreled through the door. "I'll get it," she sang. She snatched the phone from its cradle, lifting the receiver to her ear. "Hello?"

Rachel watched as her daughter's face fell and the girl hung up the phone.

"Who was it?"

"No one." Mel slouched down beside her mother. "There wasn't anyone there."

"Were you expecting someone?" Rachel teased, bumping her daughter playfully with her shoulder.

The phone rang again and the girl bolted from the sofa. "Hello?" She frowned and hung up the phone, then plopped back next to her mother. "Someone laughed and hung up."

The phone rang again.

"I'll get it." Wesley crossed the room in three long strides and picked up the receiver.

"Who is it?" Rachel mouthed.

He shrugged. "Nothing. It's quiet."

He'd no sooner hung up the phone before it rang again.

"My turn." Rachel snatched the phone from its cradle and banged the receiver several times against the end table. With a smug look, she hung it up.

"What in the world?" Dottie poked her head into the room.

The phone rang again and Rachel grabbed it. "What?! You sick perverted fre…"

"Mrs. Kent?"

Rachel grimaced, embarrassed. "Yes?"

The voice on the other end cleared its throat. "It's Officer McHale. Is everything all right? Did someone drop the phone?"

"Oh. Uh…no. I banged it."

"Excuse me?"

Rachel let herself fall into the recliner. "Someone has been prank calling and hanging up. I thought they were doing it again."

"I see." McHale paused. "I was just checking in. Is the van still out front?"

She carried the phone to the window and peered out. "Yes. I thought you were out there."

"I had to leave. We've got some officers outside. They can handle surveillance."

"Okay." *Rookies. Great.* Rachel turned from the window.

"We'll check in with you several times a day," the officer explained. "If you need anything, please don't hesitate to call me. Don't go outside. Flash the porch lights if you need the officers in the van."

3

"All right. Thank you." She hung up the phone and turned to the others. "That was Officer McHale's ear I banged the phone into."

"Why would you do that? I taught you better manners." Dottie withdrew back into the kitchen.

Rachel's eyes connected with Wesley's amused ones. She shrugged. "Nothing like going back to live with your parents, is there?"

Mel rolled her eyes and flounced out of the room. Her brother entered with a checkerboard, followed by Bill. Rachel sat back on the sofa and propped her feet on the coffee table.

Sitting next to her, Wesley rested his arm along the back of the sofa. "It's hard settling back down after the week we had, isn't it?"

She nodded. "Unimaginably so. I wouldn't want to repeat that particular adventure though." She watched her father and son set up the checkerboard on a fold out table. "Who do you think was calling?"

Looking at her, Wesley said, "You know who called."

"Can we trace the call?"

He shook his head. "They haven't been staying on the phone long enough."

Rachel sighed. "So now it's time for games."

"Looks that way." He pulled her closer to him. "Look at it this way. We know Moe is still around, so the police will have a better chance of catching him."

Bill looked up from the checkerboard. "Don't worry, honey. My guns are primed and ready. He shows his face around here and I'll shoot first and ask

4

questions later."

Smiling up at Wesley, Rachel then turned to her father. "I hope it doesn't come to that."

"Just so you know."

"Rachel," her mother called from the kitchen. "Help me out here, would you?"

"Coming." Rachel patted Wesley's knee as she got up. She headed toward the kitchen to see her mother struggling to light the pilot light on the stove. "What do you need me to help you with? It only takes one person to light the stove."

"I know, but…" the pilot lit with a whoosh and Dottie jumped back, fanning her apron. She glanced down at the black hole burned into the bright yellow fabric.

"Mom!" Rachel grabbed her arm. "Are you all right?"

"I'm fine." She untied the apron and tossed it in the garbage can. "That was my favorite apron." She fiddled with the knobs on the stove. "Darn stove's been acting funny all day. One minute there's no gas…the next minute, well, you saw."

Rachel nodded. "Maybe we should just have cereal."

Her mother shook her head. "You know I hardly ever serve cold cereal. Your father likes a hot breakfast when the weather turns cool."

"Maybe just this once?"

"No. The pilot's lit now. Still can't figure out why it went out. Hand me the bacon from the fridge, will you?"

Rachel opened the fridge and handed her mother the pound of bacon. She glanced up as the floor creaked over her head. *That's funny. Mel's the only one upstairs and her room's on the other side.* She shrugged. *Dad must be up there*. She turned to see her mother looking at the ceiling above them.

The older woman shrugged, and turned back to the stove.

A loud thump startled Rachel. She dropped the carton of juice she held and looked over in time to see Wesley take the stairs two at a time. She grabbed a handful of napkins and tossed them over the spilled juice, then ran after him.

She reached the top of the stairs in time to see Wesley dart into her parent's room, and Mel screamed. Rachel peered around Wesley at her daughter, who sat on her grandparent's bed, the phone to her ear.

"Who are you talking to?" Rachel stepped into the room, hands on her hips.

"I have to go," Mel said into the phone. She hung up the phone and glared at her mother. "Wesley scared me."

"Who was on the phone, Mel?"

"Bobby Joe."

"How many people have you given this number out to?" Wesley asked.

"No one. I called him," she answered flippantly. "Is that okay with you?"

"Mel," Rachel warned. "Are you sure you haven't given this number out to anyone?"

"Who would I give it to? I don't know anyone

but Bobby Joe."

"We heard a thump," Wesley interrupted.

The girl looked at the bedside table. "I knocked a book off the table. It was an accident."

Wesley's eyebrows rose and he looked at Rachel. "I'll see you back downstairs."

Frowning down at her daughter, Rachel shook her head. "Next time you get on the phone, let us know first."

"I feel like I'm in prison," Mel wailed. "It's so boring here. We can't go to school. We can't go outside. Now I can't even talk on the phone to Bobby Joe."

"Just let us know. Or here's a unique concept— ask." Rachel turned to go back downstairs. "Come help with breakfast," she tossed over her shoulder.

Dottie was on her hands and knees, finishing the cleaning up of the juice when Rachel and Mel entered the kitchen.

"I would've cleaned that up," Rachel admonished.

Dottie rose, wiping her hands on the clean apron she wore. "Everything all right?"

Rachel nodded. "Mel was using the phone in your room."

"That's all right. Call the boys in, won't you?" Dottie asked Mel. "We're ready to eat."

Throwing her mother a smug look, the girl spun on her heels and flounced out of the room.

Mel sulked through breakfast, answering questions directed to her in monosyllables. She shoveled the eggs into her mouth, hardly pausing for

7

breath. When she'd cleared her plate, the girl scraped back her chair and rushed up stairs.

Rachel shrugged when Wesley threw her a questioning look. He raised his eyebrows and redirected his attention to the food in front of him.

Her daughter stayed upstairs while Rachel helped Dottie clean up after breakfast. Occasionally, Rachel would glance at the ceiling above them, listening for sounds of movement in the room over her head. Things remained quiet.

As she reached up to put the last plate into the cupboard, Mutt raced across the linoleum floor. His nails scratched against the surface and the little dog growled. Rachel looked with wide eyes toward the back door. "Mom," she whispered. "Look at Mutt."

The dog dug at the door, his growls growing more fierce.

"There's someone out there," Dottie noted. She slowly reached around Rachel and set the latch on the door. "Go get your father."

Rachel tossed the dishtowel on the kitchen table and hurried into the front room. "There's someone out back. Mutt is digging at the door and growling."

Wesley grabbed his pistol from the drawer of the desk he'd hidden it in and led the way into the kitchen. Bill followed, his hand clenched around a rifle.

Rachel put a restraining arm around her son and held him a few feet back from the men.

Standing with her hands on her hips, Dottie announced, "Bill, you two had better not have those guns down where the children can get to them."

"Dottie, hush." Bill slowly parted the checked curtains on the kitchen door window.

"I don't play with guns, Grandma," Dusty explained. "I'm twelve. I know better."

"I don't like it."

Bill threw her a warning glance. "Dottie, be quiet."

"Can you see anything?" Rachel asked, tightening her hold on Dusty.

"Nothing." Her father stepped back from the door.

Over their heads, the floor boards creaked. Wesley held a finger to his lips. "Listen."

Sure enough, Rachel could hear two distinct footsteps in the room above them. "Stay," she ordered Dusty.

Not heeding Wesley's warning to stay in the kitchen, Rachel whirled and followed him up the stairs. She stopped Wesley with a hand on his arm. "Let me," she whispered. She pressed her ear to the door to her parents room.

Mel giggled.

Rachel tried the door handle and found it locked. She pounded on the door. "Melanie, open this door. Right now!"

She heard scuffling and whispered words before the door cracked open. Rachel pushed her way inside, Wesley and her father close behind her.

Mel stood in the center of the room, shirt rumpled and crooked. She hurriedly smoothed it down, covering her mid-rift. "What?" she asked, wide-eyed. "Can't I have any privacy in this house?" She plopped on the bed.

"Who were you talking to?" Rachel stood over her daughter, glaring.

"Nobody."

Rachel stooped and lifted the bed ruffle. Blue eyes, beneath shaggy dark hair, peered back at her. "Come on out, Bobby Joe."

The boy crawled from beneath the bed and dusted off his jeans.

Wesley stuffed his pistol into the waistband of his pants. "How did you get in here?" He walked to the open window.

"I climbed the tree," Bobby Joe answered, his voice belligerent.

Mel smiled at him. "He came to rescue me. Bobby Joe said you have no right to keep me prisoner here."

Rachel exploded. "It's for your own protection! I can't believe you went behind our backs and let this...this boy in here. Have you no sense of morality? No scruples? Did you think you wouldn't be discovered?"

Her daughter glared back and folded her arms across her chest. "We weren't doing anything wrong."

Eyeing the rumpled bedspread, Rachel flung an arm in that direction. "What about this? Nothing wrong? Sneaking him into your grandparents' bedroom was wrong enough!" She spun and paced the room.

Wesley took the boy by the arm. "I'll take him

downstairs and hand him over to our friends in the van. They can take him home."

"Thank you," Rachel said, before turning back to her daughter. "Go to your own room and stay there." She held the door open and watched as Mel crossed the hall and slammed her bedroom door. Taking a deep breath, Rachel headed downstairs to talk to Dottie.

Bill ruffled Dusty's hair once Rachel finished explaining and claimed they had a rematch in checkers to continue. Once they'd left, Rachel pulled out a kitchen chair and sat down, leaning her arms on the table.

"I don't know what to do with her," she admitted to her mother. "She's been nothing but a trial since Dennis died."

"She needs your understanding right now, more than ever." Dottie patted her shoulder as she walked by. She went to the cupboard and withdrew two coffee mugs, placing one in front of Rachel. "Things are tough at that age. She wants to go out and be with her friends. Instead, she's cooped up here with us."

Rachel raised troubled eyes. "She has to. It's not safe out there. Not until Moe is found."

Dottie poured coffee into Rachel's cup, then into her own. "You know that and I know that. Mel, at fifteen, doesn't."

"She should. Dusty does." Rachel stirred in a teaspoon of sugar, watching the swirling motion of her spoon.

"Dusty's different." Dottie sat down across from her daughter. "He's always been easier."

11

"That's for sure." Rachel sighed. "She blurted out once, while we were in the woods, that she isn't a virgin anymore." A tear escaped her cheek and she raised a hand to brush it away. "I didn't know how to handle that particular outburst. I chose to shove it aside until a better time."

Her mother nodded. "These things happen. Mel is accountable for her own actions, honey."

"I know, but…"

Wesley re-entered the kitchen, interrupting them. "Bobby Joe has been sent on his way home. I gave him a lecture about sneaking into a young girl's bedroom, but I don't think it made much difference."

Rachel stood. "Thank you. Would you like a cup of coffee?"

He took a chair next to the one Rachel had vacated and turned it around. He straddled it, folding his arms across the back. "Yes, thank you. I wonder how he got through the yard without the police seeing him?"

"Easy," Dottie explained. "The woods are thick on the border of our yard. Bill has been cutting things back, but the underbrush alone is thick enough. You could walk through it and be at the house before anyone saw you."

"I don't like that," Wesley stated. "I should've thought of it. McHale needs to know about Bobby Joe gaining access to the house so easily." He accepted the cup of hot coffee from Rachel and smiled his thanks. He frowned. "Where were the police? They must have *someone* stationed in the back."

"I agree," Rachel said, resuming her seat. "This

time it was Bobby Joe. Next time it could be Moe."

Her father and son joined them.

"Couldn't you lay some more of those booby traps?" Dusty asked.

Wesley laughed. "Not in the city limits. I don't think our police friends would appreciate it if they, or a neighbor, stumbled onto them."

The boy's shoulders slumped. "I guess not."

Rachel smiled at her son. "It was a good idea, Dusty. Mutt's a pretty good warning system though. He'll keep watch for us."

23

Wesley stood before the bathroom mirror, twisting his body to look over his shoulder. The slashes from the whipping he'd received were scabbed over, leaving dark criss-crossed lines. He winced as he turned wrong, pulling on his damaged ribs. He poked gingerly at his side. Besides a small amount of pain, things appeared to be mending well.

"That looks really bad."

He spun around in surprise to see Dusty standing in the doorway.

"It must've hurt a lot."

Wesley nodded. "I thought I locked the door." He picked up his gun from beside the sink and stuck it safely into the waistband of his pants.

The boy shook his head. "All I did was push it open."

Grabbing a tee-shirt he'd draped over the towel rack, Wesley donned it, speaking through the fabric as he pulled it over his head. "Yeah, it hurt quite a bit." His head poked through the neck.

"I think Mom thought you were dead." Dusty looked up at him. "She was really sad in the hospital."

Wesley laughed. "I thought I was dead, too." The knowledge of Rachel's grief over his supposed death warmed his heart, even as he felt guilty he'd caused her even a moment of pain. He slipped his feet into gym shoes.

"What will you do if you ever see them again?" Dusty sat on the closed toilet lid.

Stalling by filling his hand with shaving cream, Wesley thought. He lathered his face. "I'd like to think I'd do the right thing."

"What's that?"

"Let the police handle them." He picked up the razor and shaved in long strokes.

Dusty was silent for a moment. He took a deep breath, then quietly asked, "What would you *like* to do?"

Wesley halted his shaving and turned his head to look at the boy. He smiled through the shaving cream. "Beat the snot out of every one of them."

The boy laughed. "That's what mom would want you to do."

"But it's not what God would want me to do." Wesley resumed shaving.

"I guess not. Mom's never been too worried about what God wants, until lately." The boy squirmed. "Oh, hey, Mom."

Rachel leaned against the doorjamb. "Hey yourself." She playfully punched her son in the arm and smiled at Wesley. "You two are right. I would like every one of them beat to a bloody pulp, but I'm practicing forgiveness today."

Leaning forward, Wesley kissed her, leaving shaving cream smeared around Rachel's mouth. "I'm proud of you."

She grabbed a nearby towel and wiped the cream from her face. "Thank you." She handed him the towel as her eyes traveled over his face. "Your bruises are almost gone."

"I'll be pretty again in no time." He wiped his face and popped the towel at her. "Almost as pretty as you."

Rachel shrieked and ran down the hall with Wesley in close pursuit.

"Get her Wesley." Dusty ran after them. "Let her have it."

Wesley grabbed her around the waist, pulling her to him. He looked down at her flushed face and shining eyes, then lowered his face to kiss her.

The smoke detector went off shrilly over their heads. Dusty clapped his hands to his ears.

Stepping out of his embrace, Rachel yelled down the stairs. "Mom! You all right?"

Wesley frowned at the interruption and rubbed the back of his neck.

Dottie poked her head out of the kitchen. "I'm fine. I don't know why they're going off. I'm not cooking anything."

"I replaced all the batteries last week," Bill explained, joining his wife.

"Where are the alarms?" Wesley asked, still scowling. *Guess I'd better get used to interruptions. I'm sure a ready-made family has plenty of them.*

"The kitchen, the hall, and the upstairs hall," Dottie explained, wiping her hands on a dish towel.

3

Rachel screamed and whirled as someone pounded on the front door.

"Police! Everyone okay in there?"

Wesley gave Rachel the okay to open the front door. He took the stepstool Bill offered him and pulled down the face plate of the alarm over their heads. Everything appeared fine.

As Rachel spoke with the officer at the door, Wesley headed to the next alarm. As he reached to remove the face plate on the last smoke detector, he smelled the smoke.

He looked around, searching. Over his head was a latch. Smoke seeped around the attic door. Wesley reached up and pulled down the ladder. Withdrawing the pistol from the waistband of his pants, he crept up into the darkness.

The ladder shuddered and he glanced down to see Bill following. Wesley held a finger to his lips and the other man nodded. *Not that anyone can hear us over that shrieking.*

He poked his head through the attic opening, expecting an ambush. Nothing.

The darkness was thick and heavy, making it next to impossible to see anything. The smoke was stronger and Wesley pulled himself up the ladder and stood, hunching beneath the peaked roof. He stifled a cough. He didn't want to alert any possible intruders to his precise location.

"Can you see anything?" Bill whispered, his mouth close to Wesley's ear.

"Not yet." He peered through the gloom. There.

Beneath the attic window. An orange glare. "Get the fire extinguisher. There's a fire up here."

Bill disappeared and Wesley stuck his pistol back into his waistband. Trying to avoid getting too close to the now shooting flames, he searched the attic trying to locate the cause of the fire.

Within seconds, Bill had rejoined him and extinguished the fire, the white powder creating a fog.

"Here it is." Wesley bent over an aluminum arrow. He reached down to retrieve it and burned his fingers. Shaking his hand, he glanced around the attic, looking for something to use to pick up the arrow. An old trunk nestled beneath the window, the antique wood now scorched black on one corner.

He slammed back the lid, grabbed the first article of clothing he touched and bent to retrieve the arrow. Lifting it, he sniffed and wrinkled his nose against the sweet scent of gasoline. Walking over to the window, he peered out. "How long has this window been broken?"

"First I've known of it."

Glass crunched beneath their feet. "They must have shot the arrow through the window at the time the alarms went off," Wesley explained. "We wouldn't have heard the glass breaking over the alarms." He clapped Bill on the shoulder. "Let's go check out that last alarm. There's something fishy going on here."

Mel stood at the bottom of the ladder, concern evident on her face. "What's going on? Is there a fire?"

"Go downstairs with the others," her grandfather ordered. "We'll be done in a minute.

There's nothing to be worried about."

"But…"

"Go on now."

Wesley removed the alarm face plate and withdrew the battery. He handed it to Bill. "Look. It's different from the other ones."

Bill studied the battery in his hand, gingerly placing his tongue on the end. "It's dead. I don't use this brand." He shrugged. "What does it mean?"

"It means someone has been in your house."

"When?"

"I don't know. Maybe when you were at the hospital." Wesley disconnected the wires and replaced the face plate. "Let's go back to the others."

Rachel stood in the foyer with two police officers when Wesley and her father joined her. She looked up, a question in her eyes.

"Call McHale," Wesley told her. "Then everyone gather in the living room. We'll explain what we've discovered."

One of the officers spoke up. "We've already called McHale. He's on his way. Should be here in five minutes.

Once gathered, the group stared at Wesley who still held the arrow in his hand. He glanced around the room to see Rachel perched on the arm of the sofa next to her children. Her eyes were wide in her pale face. Her parents took the armchair. Bill's arm lay protectively across his wife's shoulders.

The doorbell rang and Wesley hurried to answer, peering through the curtains first. McHale stood there and Wesley stepped back to let the officer proceed him to the living room.

"Heard y'all had a fire," McHale stated.

Wesley picked up the arrow and handed it to the officer. "Someone shot a fire arrow through the attic window. They used the smoke detectors to cover up the noise. Sometime within the last few days, someone came into the Miller home and replaced a new battery with an old one. Then they waited for their opportunity."

"Why?" Dottie stiffened.

McHale frowned. "They're playing games, Mrs. Miller. Dangerous games." He looked at Wesley. "It bothers me that someone can so easily gain access to this house." He turned to his officers. "Isn't one of you patrolling the back?"

"Yes, sir. Randomly."

Rachel shot to her feet. "If they want us, why don't they come and get us?" She stalked to the front door and yanked it open. "You hear me? Come on! We're waiting!"

One of the officers jerked her back and slammed the door. "Please don't do that." Still holding her arm, he led her back to the sofa.

She tugged her arm free and sat back on the arm of the sofa.

Wesley cocked his head, frowning. "That was foolish, Rachel. You know what type of people we're dealing with."

"You're acting like Mel." Dottie folded her arms across her chest.

Mel opened her mouth to say something, then snapped it shut when her mother glared at her.

McHale shook his head. "We don't always know why people do what they do. People like Moe...well, we just don't know. Haven't dealt with his type in this town before." He turned to Bill. "I suggest you keep your shutters closed to prevent something like this from happening again."

The older man nodded. "I'll do it right now. Dusty, you can help me. I'll close the shutters from the outside and you latch them from in here."

McHale sent an officer to stand guard, then turned his attention back to Wesley. "The FBI is flying in. They'll be taking over jurisdiction. Be here by tonight. In the meantime, we'll keep guards posted around the house. There's at least an acre of yard between the woods and the house and a lot of bushes between here and there. We'll have to keep a sharper eye."

"You should have thought of that," Dottie said, pursing her lips. "Your men are out front. Occasionally, one of them strolls around to the back. How else did you think Moe would get in? They wouldn't walk through the front door."

"Point taken, Mrs. Miller." McHale shook Wesley's hand. "We'll take better care."

Wesley smiled and nodded. "I sleep down here on the sofa. I keep my pistol with me wherever I go. You hear gunfire, you come running."

The officer laughed. "You bet I will."

Once the officers left, Wesley turned to Rachel,

fixing a stern gaze on her.

Dottie stood. "Come on, Mel. Let's go into the kitchen. These two need a moment of privacy." She tossed her a daughter a condemning look before leaving.

Rachel watched them go, and licked her lips. Taking a deep breath, she turned to Wesley.

He took a seat across from her. "What did you think you were doing? Do you realize you could've been killed when you opened that door?"

She looked down at her folded hands. "I wasn't thinking."

"That's right. You weren't thinking." Wesley took her hands in his. "My heart stopped when you jerked open the door. We've gone through too much for me to lose you now."

Tears filled her eyes. "I know. A fine thank you it would have been."

"Thank you?"

"For almost giving your life for mine."

He pulled her close and hugged her—hard. "I'd do it again, Rachel. I'd take every whip stroke again, if it would guarantee your and the children's safety."

She sniffed against his chest. "I know you would. I'm sorry."

"Forgiven." He tilted her face up to his. "Forgotten."

"I don't deserve you." She smiled at him through her tears.

The phone range and Rachel jumped. She giggled. "Let someone else get it."

Mel yelled as she ran for the phone.

Several minutes later, the phone rang again.

Rachel's shoulders slumped. "Not again. I don't guess we can unplug the phone?"

"I'll see what I can do." Wesley kissed her forehead and picked up the extension in the living room. He kept his eyes on Rachel as he spoke. Smiling, he hung up the phone.

"McHale's bringing us a cell phone." He held the phone out to Rachel. "Would you like the honors?"

She laughed and pulled the cord from the wall.

*

Rachel could have kicked herself for her stupidity. *How could I have let my anger jeopardize everyone? What is wrong with me?*

She glanced around the kitchen table at the faces she loved. Her father's sun-creased face, her mother's round cheerful one, the young, fresh looks of her children, and the solid, handsome features of Wesley. He caught her looking, and winked. She gave him a small smile and looked back to her plate.

Once a timid woman, these bursts of anger surprised her. When Dennis had ranted and raved, she'd withdrawn into her protective shell until the storm passed.

She sighed, staring at the food on her plate. Rachel spread the eggs around with her fork. Scratching against the shuttered window drew her attention.

The wind blew harder outside. She could hear it whistle through the shutters. In the other room a shutter blew open, banging against the wall. Mel screamed and jumped from her chair.

"I'll get it," Bill announced.

He returned within minutes, face drawn into a frown. "Heck of a storm brewing out there. Dottie, maybe you should get the candles. We'll probably lose electricity." He shook his head. "I feel sorry for the officers sitting in that van. It was shaking to beat all when I looked outside."

Lightening cracked outside, followed by a boom of thunder. Mel pushed her chair closer to her mother.

Dottie bustled to the cupboard over the sink and pulled down a box of candles. "Bill, maybe you should turn on the weather."

He nodded and headed into the living room. The others followed and huddled together, eyes on the television.

Dottie set a candle on the coffee table. "It's too late in the year for twisters, right Bill?"

"Normally. That wind is blowing something fierce, though."

Rachel watched as her father walked the perimeter of the room, checking the shutters. He opened one and peeked out. "Van is still out front."

"Where did you expect it to go?" Dottie asked, peering over his shoulder.

He shrugged. "Nowhere."

"Weather just says thunderstorm warning with high winds," Wesley noted, putting an arm around Rachel's shoulders.

Another thundering crash and the electricity

11

went out, plunging them into darkness. Rachel could hear her mother stumble around. Soon, she had lit a candle.

"Now, isn't this cozy?" Dottie looked around the group. "Anyone up for ghost stories?"

Rachel laughed, full of sarcasm. "We're living something worse than scary stories."

"But you are living," Dottie reprimanded her. "I just thought we could focus on something other than the storm."

Rachel turned to speak to Wesley and halted when she saw his face. His features were rigid, jaw set firmly. "What?"

"Shhh. I hear something."

"The storm?"

Wesley got to his feet. "No, something else." He put his hand on his pistol. He tossed the cell phone to Rachel. "Call McHale."

She missed the phone in the dim light and felt around the sofa cushions until she found it. Crouching, she held the phone closer to the candle's flames and punched the speed dial number.

Her father reached for the rifle he kept propped against the wall.

"There's no service," she told Wesley. "Must be the storm." She slid the phone into the pocket of her jeans.

Wesley opened the front shutter and looked back, his eyes wide. "Everyone down the hall and out the back door," he barked. "Now!"

Rachel shoved Dusty and Mel in front of her.

Suddenly the white van plowed through the front of the house, showering them all with glass. Plaster and splintered wood rained down upon their heads.

She glanced over her shoulder to see two armed men struggle against the debris to open the van doors.

Wesley yanked open the back door and ushered them all into the driving rain.

"This way!" Bill yelled above the wind. "Follow me!"

The dense foliage along the tree line cut down on some of the wind and rain, but they were all soaked by the time they reached the woods.

Mel yelled and waved her arms as they ran. Rachel threw her a concerned look. Her daughter's face twisted with tension. The wind roared too loud for her to make out what Mel was saying, but she was sure it wasn't pleasant.

Dusty tripped and fell. Wesley grabbed the boy's elbow, pulling him to his feet. He whispered something in Dusty's ear, and prodded him forward.

At the edge of another clearing, Bill stopped them. In the yard stood a run-down clapboard house. He stepped cautiously out of the trees and walked toward the house. A red light shone bright, then dimmed and Rachel reached out, grabbing the tail of his shirt.

When he turned to look at her, she pointed. Bill's eyes grew wide and he ducked back with the others. "This house is supposed to be vacant."

13

"Well, it's not now," Wesley said. "Someone is smoking in there."

"What now?" Rachel asked.

"We go to the Fuller place," her father told her. "It's a mile in the other direction."

"Wait, Bill." Wesley's hand shot out. "Let me take a look first."

Rachel held her breath as Wesley skulked across the yard and peered in the window. The wind continued blowing strong and several times she saw him stagger as a burst blew against him.

"It's that kid," Wesley told them when he came back. "Bobby Joe."

Mel took a step around him. "He'll help us. We can hide at his place."

Wesley held her back. "No. We don't want to involve him." He turned to the others. "From what I could see, the kid took shelter from the storm and decided to have a smoke. I could look some more, but I think it's better if we get moving. Rachel, do you have the cell phone?"

She nodded and handed it to him.

He dialed McHale's number, and frowned. "Still no signal." He handed it back to her.

Bill nodded grimly, and herded them in the opposite direction.

Shoulders slumping, Rachel followed. This trek through the woods seemed eerily familiar to the nightmarish past week. She wrapped her arms around her, warding off the bone seeking chill of the evening, and lifted her eyes to focus on the rounded shoulders of

14

her father.

24

Rachel shivered, wet, cold and afraid. The downpour had quit and the wind kept her shirt plastered to her body. Her jeans felt as if they weighed fifty pounds and chaffed her thighs. Lightning continued to crack over their heads and her scalp tingled from the electricity.

Her father halted them at the edge of his yard. The lights from the van illuminated the house and two men walked through the rooms. A flashlight beam swept across an upstairs window. A voice caught on the wind and carried through the night to Rachel's ears.

Her children crowded close on each side of her and Rachel put her arms around them, sharing and receiving what warmth there was.

"I can't believe this is happening to us again," Mel cried.

Putting her hand over the girl's mouth, Rachel whispered, "We'll be all right. Grandpa and Wesley will make sure of it. We're not alone."

"God is with us," Dottie reminded them.

Rachel turned to her mother with a smile. "Yes, He is."

Bill tapped her shoulder and Rachel turned to follow her father as he led them away from the house.

1

They continued to battle the wind and rain as they trudged through the forest. Rachel's foot sank ankle deep into the dank leaves beneath her. She grimaced and pulled her foot free.

Lightning flashed close overhead. The night brightened around them and Rachel ducked as thunder boomed.

Dusty squeezed her hand.

Thirty minutes later, they came across the other house. The woods crowded close around the little grey farmhouse, and Rachel ducked again when lightning struck nearby. She swore she smelled burning wood.

Wesley looked in windows and tried doors. When the next boom of thunder exploded over their heads, he slammed his elbow through the window in the kitchen door. Reaching through, he turned the latch. He then stepped aside to usher the others through.

Darkness shrouded the house. Lightning flickered, casting dancing shadows through the boards covering the front windows.

"Did anyone happen to grab candles?" Rachel whispered.

Dottie spoke up. "I have two stuck in my apron pockets. No matches, though."

Rachel shuffled forward, hitting her foot on a table leg. She yelped and hopped, holding her foot. Something brushed past her, and she screamed. "There're rats in here!"

"I'm not staying." Mel turned to run outside.

Wesley grabbed the girl's arm, holding her still.

"It's Mutt!" Dusty yelled. "Not rats. Mutt followed us."

"Give me one of those candles," Bill ordered, his voice slicing through the darkness. "Can't see a thing in here. We'll have to search for matches."

Rachel felt her way around the kitchen, shuffling her hands through kitchen drawers. Her heartbeat erratically and she flinched each time her fingers brushed across something soft. *If I touch a real mouse, I'm leaving. I don't care if Moe is out there*.

Most of the drawers were empty, but one still contained a few odds and ends. "Here's a book of matches!"

Her father grabbed them from her hand. "There's a few here." He struck the match and held it to the wick of the candle. The sharp odor of sulphur filled the room and Rachel sneezed.

Within seconds a bright flame burned. Rachel's spirits lifted with the light. Bill held the candle high, illuminating the room.

Dust cloths covered most of the furniture and Wesley whipped them off, handing each of them one of the dusty cloths.

The dust tickled her nose and Rachel's eyes watered, then she sneezed again and wrapped the cloth around her, snuggling into the warmth it provided. A sofa and a loveseat provided the group with a soft place to wait out the storm. Rachel snuggled next to Wesley, her children on her other side.

Wesley wrapped his arm around her shoulders. "Better?"

"Absolutely." She smiled up at him. Hiding from pursuers, in the dark, with Wesley's arms protecting her was becoming too common place. Rachel sighed deeply. *God, will we ever be back to a normal life?*

The phone in her pocket rang, startling her. She sat up, causing dust to fly into the air and fished out the phone. "Hello? Hello?" She looked at the screen. "The call failed."

"The only person who has this number is McHale," Wesley stated. "At least we know he's trying to contact us."

"What do you think happened to the officers in the van?" Dusty's voice was muffled, soft.

Rachel shook her head as Wesley looked down at her. "Lie," she whispered. He nodded.

"I think Moe's men stole the van and crashed it into the house, hoping to corner us in there."

The boy frowned. "Yes, but they had to do something with the officers. They wouldn't have just handed the van keys to them."

"They killed them," Mel hissed. "What do you think happened to them? They kill everybody."

Rachel sent her daughter a sharp look. "That's enough. There's no reason to be cruel." She turned to Dusty. "Any number of things could've happened. Let's not speculate."

Dottie sniffed from across the room.

"Mom?"

"They destroyed our house." Dottie's voice shook. "You were raised in that house."

"I'm sorry, Mom."

"It's not your fault." Dottie sniffed again. "It is just a house after all, but I sure did like it."

"I can rebuild it," Bill told her. "Don't fret."

The wind whistled through the broken window, eerie like a badly filmed movie. Shivers ran up and down Rachel's spine. Her breath caught as the thunder and lightning diminished. She snuggled tighter into Wesley's embrace.

The old house sported a tin roof. As the rain poured harder, the drops made a drumming beat against the metal panels. Conversation became almost impossible and Rachel's eyelids grew heavy.

*

Mutt growled low in his throat.

Wesley bolted to his feet, almost dumping Rachel, who dozed, on the floor.

"Huh?" Rachel sat up, dazed.

"Hold the dog, Dusty." Wesley ran through the kitchen and yanked the door open. Shooting an arm out, he pulled a struggling Bobby Joe into the house. "What are you doing out there?"

"I...I saw a light and came to investigate." The boy looked at the floor and shuffled his feet.

"There's no way you saw a light; unless you were looking for one." Wesley spun the boy around and shoved him toward the living room. "Look who I caught peeping."

Bobby Joe whirled, a switchblade in his hand. He swiped at Wesley, catching the knife in the man's shirt, ripping it.

Wesley lunged closer, grasping the boy's wrist.

He applied increasing pressure until the boy yelped and dropped the knife.

Mel jumped from her seat. "Bobby Joe!"

"Sit down, Mel," Wesley ordered. At her belligerent look, he barked, "Now!"

The girl's eyes widened and filled with tears as she plopped next to her mother.

Grabbing one of the kitchen chairs, Wesley sat it in front of the others. With a firm hand, he shoved Bobby Joe into the seat.

"Hey!" The boy scowled, attempting to rise. Wesley shoved him back down. "What is this? An interrogation?"

"That's exactly what it is." Wesley stood in front of the chair, feet planted shoulder width apart, arms crossed.

Bobby Joe scowled. The flame of the candle darkened the boy's eyes, reflecting the light. For several seconds Wesley stared down, maintaining eye contact until the boy looked away.

"I'm not telling you anything!" Bobby Joe spit on the floor.

Taking hold of the boy's chin, Wesley squeezed. "Oh, I think you will." Without turning, he ordered, "Bill, lock that door, will you? Have Dusty help you pile the table and chairs in front of it." He continued to squeeze until his fingers dented the boy's cheeks, pushing between his teeth.

"What's going on?" Mel cried. "Bobby Joe? Mom, make Wesley stop. He's hurting him."

Wesley turned and noting the tears on the girl's

face, eased pressure.

Rachel put her arms around her daughter, drawing her close. "I think Bobby Joe has been following us. Am I right?"

"That's what I think." Wesley bent closer, his face inches from the boys. "It's time for you to answer some questions."

The boy pulled out of Wesley's grasp, and shrugged. "Whatever. You guys are all dead anyway."

"Who are you?"

"Bobby Joe *Watkins*."

"What's your relation to Duane? You might know him as Moe."

A slow smile spread across the boy's face. "He's my father."

Mel gasped, putting her hands over her face.

The rain pounded harder and Wesley raised his voice. "Why are you following us? How did you know where to find us?"

Bobby Joe held his hands up. "Whoa. Slow down. One at a time, dude." He laughed. "My dad called and told me y'all escaped. Said to go scouting around. I did. End of story."

Patting the boy's pockets, Wesley located a cell phone. "When's he calling again?"

Bobby Joe folded his hands behind his head and leaned back in the chair. "I'm supposed to call him. Should have about five minutes ago." He grinned.

"What happens if you don't?"

"He comes looking for me."

Wesley nodded and tossed the cell phone to

Bill. He withdrew the pistol from his waistband and handed it to Rachel. "Guard him."

Her hand shook as she took the gun. She nodded and aimed the weapon at the boy.

Bobby's Joe's infuriating smirk intensified her nervousness and she shifted the gun to one hand, wiping her free one down the front of her blouse.

Wesley took Bill by the arm and led him into a dark corner of the room to talk.

*

Mel walked past Rachel, wiping her face on the sleeve of her shirt. Drawing her foot back, she kicked forward, planting her foot in Bobby Joe's chest. The chair fell back with a crash.

Bobby Joe lay on the floor, legs in the air, and gasped for breath. He reminded Rachel of a fish, stranded without water.

Striding forward, Mel landed another hard kick in Bobby Joe's ribs. "You used me! I thought you really liked me."

Rachel shot out her hand to stop the girl before she could kick again. "Mel, stop."

Her daughter jerked free of her grasp and flounced next to her grandmother. Dottie opened her arms and Mel buried her face in the older woman's bosom, sobbing loudly.

"Get up," Rachel ordered Bobby Joe. "Get up or I'll shoot you like the dog you are."

He got to his hands and knees, then squatted before her. "Shoot," he sneered. "I dare you."

Rachel's hand shook. "I will shoot you. I will."

Her hand continued to tremble and she raised her other hand to steady it.

"You're terrified," the boy taunted, rising slowly to his feet. "You don't have the guts to pull that trigger." He took a small step backward.

Her finger tightened on the trigger. "Stop moving!"

Wesley came up behind her and took the gun from her hands. "I've got it."

Breathing a sigh of relief, Rachel relinquished her hold, knees unsteady. She leaned against the back of the sofa. "I could've done it."

"I know." Wesley patted her shoulder.

Mutt tore past them, barking furiously toward the door. Rachel spun.

"He's here." Bobby Joe laughed with glee. "Y'all are gonna get it now!"

Wesley put his hands on Rachel's shoulders, forcing her to look at him. "I'll be back for you."

"What?" Her mouth hung open. "What do you mean? You can't leave us!"

"I have to go. I'll be back for you. I'll find you." He pulled her close, cradling her head to his chest. "If they catch me, they'll kill me. I don't think they'll kill you women or the children. Not for a while. You're worthy hostages." He set her back from him, staring into her eyes. "I've got to let McHale know where we are. I can reach him the fastest."

"Your ribs...your wrist...you aren't..."

"Sweetheart, please."

Rachel's heart thudded in her chest. Sobs rose

threatening to choke her. "You don't know they won't kill us. You don't know where we'll be."

"You go with him, Bill." Dottie stood, chin lifted.

"I won't leave you."

Dottie reached up and caressed her husband's face. "Wesley's right. They'll kill him, and you along with him. Take Bobby Joe with you. He'll give you security. Moe won't kill us while you hold his son."

Rachel watched in dismay as her father nodded. "You're both going?" Her shoulders slumped. Hot tears burned tracks down her cheek.

"I'll be back for you. I promise." Wesley grabbed her to him one more time. "I love you." He kissed her, then turned.

Her lips tingled from his kiss and Rachel rubbed a finger along them.

Bobby Joe rushed past, kicking Mutt out of the way. In his haste, he pushed aside chairs to reach the back door.

Grabbing hold of the boy's arm, Bill dragged him to Wesley. "Got us a hostage. My wife thinks he might come in handy."

"Definitely." Wesley grinned.

"Please." Rachel grabbed his arm. "I can't do this again. We'll all go. We'll go somewhere he can't find us. Please."

Wesley tilted her face up to his and brushed his lips across hers. "I love you."

"I love you." Tears spilled down her cheeks as her father kissed her mother goodbye. One more hug from Wesley and she stood alone, her heart a stone in her chest.

He sprinted toward the front of the house, dragging a struggling Bobby Joe.

Bill tossed one last glance at Dottie, then Rachel, and followed the other man.

Feeling more alone than she'd ever felt, Rachel grabbed her children to her, and turned to face the kitchen.

The backdoor crashed open sending the table skidding across the room. Moe entered with a single armed man.

From the front room came sounds of boards being ripped from the walls and tossed onto the floor. Rachel tensed and gripped her daughter's arm. "Scream, Mel. As loud as you can." *Why can't it rain now?*

Mel screamed, whipping her head back and forth, and despite their circumstances, Rachel caught herself smiling at the dramatics.

"Where's my boy?" Moe roared.

"He ain't here," Dottie told him, stepping forward.

The big man towered over the woman, his face red. Rachel watched in fascination as the veins in his neck bulged. He shoved Dottie out of the way and went to stand before Rachel. "Where is he?"

The man's spittle sprayed her face and she turned her face away. She swallowed against the bile rising into her throat.

"I asked you a question." He backhanded Rachel across the face. The force of the slap burned her skin and knocked her to the floor. "Now get up and answer me."

"Stop hitting her!" Dusty stood before them, his hands doubled into fists at his sides. "Touch her again and I'll kill you. Your son went with Wesley and my grandpa."

Moe laughed and turned to his partner. "Gather them up. Take them with us. I think maybe we'll be making a trade."

25

"Where are we going?" Involuntary shivers snaked down Rachel's spine. "Where are you taking us?" They'd been walking for an hour, through the increasing wind and occasional downpours of rain. She stopped and looked back, receiving a jab in the ribs for her trouble. She shook the man off. "We have a right to know."

"I got me a place." Moe withdrew a handkerchief from the breast pocket of his overalls, and mopped his brow. Rachel peered closer. Moe's face shone through the light of the lantern. Was that sweat, or rain, dripping from his face onto the plaid shirt he wore?

"Feeling poorly?" Rachel asked, her words dripped with sarcasm.

Moe's accomplice jabbed her again, forcing her to turn around.

"I hope you drop dead," Rachel tossed over her shoulder.

"Rachel!" her mother admonished.

"What? He's our enemy."

"The Lord tells us to love our enemies." Dottie put a hand to her chest and leaned against a tree. "This fast pace is too much for me. I've got to rest." She

1

panted, her chest rising and falling beneath the apron she still wore.

Rachel turned to Moe. "My mother needs to rest. She can't keep up this pace in this temperature. The air's too cold for her lungs."

"No time."

"Dead hostages won't make a good trade." Rachel stood before him, hands on her hips. "Besides, you look like you could use a rest."

Moe wiped his brow again. He glanced to where another man joined them. The two men stood awaiting orders. They shifted their weight from foot to foot, their breath leaving vapors on the night air. "Take a break," Moe ordered.

Rachel helped her mother slide to the ground. They sat with their backs against a fallen log. Rachel gathered her mother and children close to share their body warmth. Moe hadn't allowed them to bring the furniture throws and Rachel shivered hard enough for her ribs to ache.

The wind and rain finally stopped and it was the time of the night that was the blackest. The hours right before dawn. Besides the lantern one of Moe's men held, the woods were dark, and silent. Rachel listened, hoping to hear sounds of Wesley following them. She shook her head. He was too good for them to know whether he was there or not. She looked at her daughter. Mel's features were pale and hard to discern.

"I loved Bobby Joe," Mel wailed.

"Hush, Mel," Rachel scolded. "You saw him what...two, three times? We've got bigger things to

2

worry about. There's no time for your melodramatics." She took a deep breath as her daughter sobbed. "I'm sorry, Mel. I don't mean to sound heartless."

She scanned the surrounding trees looking for landmarks. Autumn leaves fell around them. Ghosts riding on the breeze. One particular mountain peak drew her attention. Its ragged shadow towered above the smaller hills.

Rachel grabbed her mother's arm and pulled her close. "I know where we're going," she whispered excitedly. "You know that old mine you and Dad told me didn't exist? It does. I found it when I was a kid. I think that's where Moe is taking us. Do you think Dad knows where it is?"

"Of course he does," Dottie replied, lifting the hem of her apron to wipe her face and neck. "We knew where it was all along. We just didn't want you playing near it. It's ancient and falling down. I'm glad to hear you obeyed us."

Rachel gave her mother a quick squeeze. "It's the perfect hiding place. You'd walk right past it if you didn't know it was there." She straightened, a frown on her face. "How did Moe find it?"

Mel jerked.

Rachel looked at her daughter. "Mel?"

The girl slumped, blinking back tears. She looked at Moe's men and leaned closer to Rachel. "I told Bobby Joe about it. He told me he took some beer from his Dad and wanted a place to hide it. I remembered you telling us where the old mine was." She started to cry. "This is all my fault."

Dottie laughed, the sound loud in the stillness of the wood. "Mel doesn't obey any better than you did."

Moe's head jerked in their direction and he mumbled something they couldn't hear.

Rachel rolled her eyes. "I hope Dad remembers it."

"He will. He doesn't forget anything." Using her hands to push herself up, Dottie stood. "Let's get that man back on his feet. The sooner we get there, the sooner your father and Wesley can rescue us."

Rachel glanced at their captor. He sat near the lantern, hunched over his rifle. She could see the light bouncing off the sweat beaded on his brow. He definitely didn't look good.

Rachel held up her hand for Dusty to grab and help her to her feet. "How are you holding up?" she asked him.

"I'm fine." He shrugged. "Kinda par for the course isn't it? I mean, this is getting to be old."

Rachel laughed and ruffled his hair. "Yeah. It is getting old." She peered into her son's face. "Are you scared?"

Dusty shook his head. "No. Wesley'll save us. God had us run into him for a reason."

Rachel kissed his forehead. "Yes, he will and yes, He did."

Moe struggled to his feet, using his rifle as a walking stick. *Maybe it'll go off and he'll shoot himself.* Rachel shook off her feelings of remorse for her thoughts. She sighed and quickened her pace until she stood beside her mother and children.

As if he could read her mind, Moe scowled at her. With effort, he stood straighter, keeping his eyes on her. Rachel smiled.

The walk wasn't much farther, just difficult. Rachel kept a hand on her mother's arm as they climbed up the mountain behind her parent's house. The rain left the rock loose and the ground muddy. The trail was slick with wet leaves and they slid several times, sometimes losing more ground than they gained.

Mel gave a small shriek and slid several feet. Moe's men laughed and one of them reached out to grab her, wrapping his arm around her waist. Rachel watched as her daughter yanked an arm free and pounded the man's head with her fist.

He laughed and released her.

The girl sent the man a withering glance. *If only looks really could kill.*

As they neared the mine, one of Moe's men gave a Bob White bird call. Someone answered with the same.

More gun prods in the back and Rachel and the others found themselves ducking and entering the first cavern of the mine.

Moe's mother stood several feet past the entrance, a lantern burning in her hand. Her bulk seemed even larger than Rachel remembered. The lantern cast a giant shadow of her figure on the rocky mine wall.

"Where's Bobby Joe?" Moe's mother asked outright.

Moe collapsed onto a pile of wood. "Her man's got him." He tossed his head at Rachel. "I brought them along for a trade."

Moe's mother leaned over him. "Fool," she spat. "You were probably followed here. What's wrong with you anyway?" She sniffed. "You're sweating and you smell foul."

"You took me from the hospital, Momma. I'm hurt'n," Moe whined. "Anyway, I thought you wanted them to find us."

"Maybe I do. Maybe I do." The woman cackled. "It's going to be an interesting day. Oh, Lordy, yes!"

Rachel watched mother and son bicker, her eyes wide. This whimpering man was not the Moe from the mountain. It was clear to her where the power laid. The amazing authority of the woman towering over him seemed to drown any strength Moe had. Rachel shrank back when Moe's mother turned her wrath in her direction.

The large woman stalked toward her, lantern swinging. "That man of yours better not lay a finger on my grandson," she warned. "He'd better not have one scratch on him. You hear?"

Rachel nodded. "Wesley wouldn't hurt him. Unlike your son, he doesn't harm children."

The woman slapped her, causing Rachel's head to whip back. She winced as her skull collided with a wooden pillar. Her head throbbed and stars danced before her eyes. "Don't speak unless I give you leave to speak." The woman glanced at Dusty and Mel. "One hair harmed on that boy's head and I'll take one of yours. It won't be pleasant. I believe in an eye for an eye."

Dottie stepped forward, eyes blazing. "You'll not touch one of these children."

Moe's mother spit at her feet. "And who'll stop me? A bitty thing like you? Hah!" She turned away. "Tie them up over there." She motioned one of the men into the corner. "Just tie their hands. They ain't gonna go anywhere's."

The woman lit a cigar, then pulled up a barrel to sit on. Her thighs and hips hung over the top, like bread that had risen too high. She sat and watched as the men tied up Rachel and the others. "Might as well introduce myself. Name's Mabel. Course y'all can call me Mrs. Watkins. Don't want to be too friendly. You'll be dead in less than twenty-four hours." She sent a smoke ring into the air. "Hey, Moe, how long you figure until that ranger man finds us?"

"I don't know, Ma. Daylight I guess."

"He armed?"

"Yes'm. Gots a pistol."

Mabel blew another ring. "Guess he'll probably bring the police, too." She shrugged. "Oh, well. Ain't no way around it. I ain't averse to a shoot-out."

Moe struggled to breathe. He lay limp across the corded wood. The man kept his hand on his chest and his wheezing carried across the mine shaft to where Rachel sat. "He doesn't look very well," she told Mabel. "He needs a doctor."

"I mind my own, girlie." Mabel blew out another puff of smoke. "Moe, pick up that whiskey bottle and take it to bed. You'll feel better in a couple of hours. Take an extra blanket with you. Your clothes are wet. I'm going to need you. Can't have you dying on me." She squinted through the smoke at Rachel. "That's a purty little girl you got there. My Bobby Joe has taken a fancy to her, so he says."

Rachel sat up straighter. "He can't have her."

"I reckon we can take what we want." Mabel stood and bent over Rachel, blowing smoke in her face.

Rachel turned her head, holding her breath.

"Moe's taken a fancy to you," Mabel whispered hoarsely. "Don't see it myself, but I'll let him have a go, before I kill you. He's been a widower for quite some time. He told me what you promised back at his camp. A shame y'all got interrupted." She laughed, the sound like tumbling rocks in a grinder. "Oh, yeah. It'll be a fun time once I get my Bobby Joe back. We might even keep your girl around for a while, depending on Bobby Joe, of course."

"Of course," Rachel muttered.

She stared at Mabel's back as the woman walked to the other side of the dug-out room. *I thought Moe was the crazy one. I was wrong.* Rachel pulled against the rope binding her. *Lord, please let Dad remember the back way in. Let him and Wesley have the element of surprise.*

Rachel noticed her mother's head droop. "Go to sleep, Mom," she whispered. "Lean against me. I'll stay awake."

Dottie shook her head. "Wouldn't be right."

"What's wrong with it? I'll wake you if I need to.

8

Wesley won't be here for a few hours anyway." She glanced at Dusty and Mel. "They're sleeping. You'll be stronger with some rest."

"Okay, but it doesn't seem right for me to sleep when our life is at stake." Dottie scooted until her back was against Rachel's. "Promise to wake me if anything happens."

Rachel heard her yawn, and smiled. "I promise you'll be awake."

She leaned her head back against her mother and stared at Mabel. The woman lumbered around the mine shaft, gathering together supplies to cook something. She kicked at one of the men who had fallen asleep.

The man mumbled and drew his legs up closer to himself. Mabel kicked him again and ordered him to go outside and relieve the man out there. The man stood, muttering curses as he shuffled out the door.

Mabel puffed like a train as she bustled around, her breath coming and going in gasps. For a woman of such large size, she moved quickly. A few minutes and a pot hung over the fire.

Rachel looked around until she located Moe. He laid curled up in a corner. The snores emanating from him bounced off the mine walls. He clutched an empty whiskey bottle in his hand. Rachel smiled. At least that's one less worry for Wesley when he finally arrived. Her eyes roamed the perimeter of the shaft.

A busted cart lay in pieces next to the rusty track. She tried to focus down the laid track, but the darkness was too thick. Rachel was concerned, knowing that was the only way Wesley could get the drop on Moe and his mother. She prayed for a diversion when the time came.

Mabel finished what she'd been preparing and settled herself back on the barrel, spooning what looked like congealed beans into her mouth. She talked around the beans. "Guess you knew about this place, didn't you?"

Rachel averted her eyes. The woman's eating habits repulsed her.

"Guess you also know about the back way in." Beans fell onto the woman's heavy bosom. "There ain't no back way in anymore." The woman threw her head back and laughed, beans falling from the corners of her mouth. "Seems there's been a cave-in. We didn't do it. Was already caved in when we got here."

"How did you find it?"

"My son is one heck of a hunter, missy. He can find about anything." Mabel wiped her mouth on her arm. "It's a pity I got to kill you. Been a long time since I've had womanly company."

Rachel rolled her eyes.

"Still think they'll come for you?" Mabel spooned in another mouthful of beans.

"I know they will."

"Well, that's good." Mabel patted Rachel's cheek. "I'd hate for you to be disappointed." She placed her hands on her knees and got to her feet, letting the pan slide to the ground. "A person shouldn't be disappointed before they die."

"Stop talking about killing me and just do it!"

Mabel laughed. "Moe told me you were feisty. Can't kill you now. Gotta use you as bait." She walked away laughing.

The woman is insane. Rachel shook her head. *Completely out of her mind. She's much more frightening than Moe. She went in so many directions during a conversation, it was impossible to keep up with her.*

Dottie "humphed" as Rachel's head bumped her. Rachel raised her head. The possibility of a cave-in in the room caused her heart rate to accelerate, and she focused on her breathing in order to relax. The mine was old, but this part looked sturdy enough.

Huge wooden beams criss-crossed, holding back the earth. Rachel breathed deep, smelling the moist, dank dirt. She'd loved the smell as a child. This had been her special place once.

Pebbles rolled down the wall facing her and Rachel leaned forward. She raised her eyes to the low ceiling, scanning frantically for falling dirt. Dust fell, but nothing bigger than a pebble.

"Scared, are ya?" Mabel somehow lowered herself to the ground and lit another cigar. "Don't worry. It ain't gonna fall down on us. Not tonight anyway." She took a large drag off the cigar. "Ain't nothing better than a smoke when contemplating on something, is there?"

"I wouldn't know," Rachel answered. "I don't smoke."

"Pity." Mabel crawled over to Rachel and thrust the cigar into her mouth. "Try it. Might as well try

11

something new before you die."

Rachel choked on the acrid smoke. She turned her head, spitting the cigar out. Mabel gasped and backhanded her. "Don't waste a good cigar. That's a sin."

She picked it up from the dirt and placed it back between her own lips. "Well...at least you tried it. Now, when somebody asks, you can say you had one."

Rachel narrowed her eyes. "Stop hitting me!" *Why does everyone feel compelled to slap me?*

The heavy woman leaned forward, locking her eyes on Rachel's. "And what are you going to do about it?" She heaved herself to her feet and went to stare down at her son.

"That woman's loonier than a fruit bat," Dottie whispered from behind Rachel.

"If people don't stop hitting me, they're going to knock my head right off my shoulders!" She took a deep breath to steady herself. "I'm sorry I woke you."

Dottie scooted around next to Rachel. "You woke me up when you moved forward."

"I thought the sky was falling."

Dottie looked above them. "I don't see anything. That woman is stinking this place up with that foul cigar." She peered at Rachel. "How'd it taste?"

"Mother!"

"Just asking."

"I didn't really taste it. I took one puff and choked." Rachel smiled. "I think the thought of it having been in Mabel's mouth grossed me out more than the cigar did."

Dottie leaned against her. "Good. Wouldn't want you to start smoking."

"I've got a plan in mind," Rachel told her mother. "Whatever I tell you to do, do it. No questions asked. Can you do that?"

Dottie looked over at her. "I'll do whatever you say, Rachel. Is it going to be dangerous?"

"Very." Rachel set her lips in a firm line. "Pray hard tonight."

26

The darkness in the mine thinned as the morning light invaded the small cavern. Rachel's arms cramped from being tied behind her back. She flexed her fingers, urging the blood flow back into her hands. Eyes gritty from lack of sleep, she swallowed against her thirst.

Mabel kicked Moe awake, attracting Rachel's attention.

"Get up, you lazy oaf," Mabel bellowed.

Moe grunted and curled tighter into a ball. His mother kicked him again. "Take your men outside and scout around."

Moe sat up, his cheeks flushed above his beard. "I've got a fever. I think I'm infected."

"With laziness." Mabel picked up the empty whiskey bottle and hurled it at him. The bottle struck the man on the shoulder, rolling to the ground. "If you've got a fever, the cold air will do you good. We need warning when that ranger gets here."

Dusty woke and yawned. "I'm thirsty," he told Rachel, smacking his lips.

"Me, too." Mel shook her head, flinging her hair from her eyes.

"Hey!" Dottie called. "Do you think we could have a drink over here?"

Mabel whirled. "You're in no position to make demands, old woman."

"Old woman?" Dottie sputtered. "Why, you..."

"Please," Rachel implored. "They're only children. We've been here for hours."

"Next thing, y'all will want to go to the restroom." Mabel picked up an old rusty knife lying next to the woodpile.

"Well, since you mention it," Dottie said with a smile.

"Hold still. Wouldn't want to cut you when you're trussed up like a turkey." The woman sawed through the rope with the dull knife. "That wouldn't be fair."

Cut us? Rachel shook her head, bewildered. *Mabel doesn't make any sense. One minute she talks about killing them, the next she wants to prevent us harm.* Rachel shrugged and waited for her ropes to be cut.

"There ain't nowhere for ya to run," Mabel told them. "Just go down the shaft aways. I don't want to be smelling nothing."

Rachel, her breath catching with excitement, glanced at her mother. This was going to be easier than she'd thought. Her hands trembled with excitement and she shoved them into the pocket of her jeans. Too nervous to keep them there, she pulled them free. Trying to appear nonchalant, she put an arm around her children and steered them around debris and into the shaft.

The further they walked, the darker it became.

The pale light from the lantern left behind with Mabel stretched their shadows ahead of them. It wasn't far before they stumbled across the cave-in. Rachel heard squeaking and looked up. The ceiling above them was blanketed with bats. Some slept, while others twitched and flapped their wings. She shuddered.

She held a finger to her lips. "Don't make any loud noises," She transferred her attention back to the obstacle before them. "We need to find a way through this pile of rocks before Mabel gets suspicious."

The group split up, venturing out as far as the light from the lantern let them. Rachel swept her eyes from floor to ceiling. The bats moved restlessly above her head.

Mabel's voice echoed through the shaft. "What's taking y'all so long?"

"Almost finished," Rachel yelled back. She heard a rock tumble against another. The bats overhead squealed in protest. "Hurry, she's coming."

Rachel felt along the pile of dirt and debris. The damp earth smelled of mold and sour vegetation. She fought against a sneeze and buried her nose in the crook of her arm.

"Here," Dusty told them. "I've found a way through."

He pointed to a small opening in the pile of wood, dirt and rocks. Rachel peered through and saw daylight. The opening appeared to be maybe two feet in diameter. She looked down at her bosom and shook her head. *Not for me, but Dusty and Mel will fit.*

"It *is* a way out!" she exclaimed. "Hurry, Dusty.

You first."

Dusty wriggled through the hole like an eel. "Come on, Mel, it's easy."

Mel climbed halfway through the hole and got stuck. "My hips won't fit," she cried. She squirmed harder, bringing down a cascade of dirt and pebbles.

"Stop squirming, Mel. You're going to bring the whole thing down on us."

Thundering footsteps signaled Mabel's approach. Rachel's breathing quickened. Her heart beat hard against her ribs.

"She's coming!" Rachel put her shoulder against her daughter's rear, and pushed. "Help me, Mel. Use your arms to pull your way through. Dusty pull from your end!"

"It's hurting me, Mom! I'm getting scraped up."

"I'm sorry, honey. Better scraped than dead." Rachel gave one more mighty shove, and Mel fell through, landing at Dusty's feet. Rachel whirled to see the light from Mabel's lantern. "Go, Mom."

"I'll never fit through there. Mel had a tough time and she's half my size." Dottie put her hands on Rachel's shoulders. "You go. I'll be fine."

"Don't be ridiculous," Rachel hissed. A bullet whizzed past her head.

"Run, kids! Get out of here!" She looked up to see Mabel brandishing a pistol. The woman staggered as if drunk.

Mabel raised her hand again and took aim. Rachel shoved Dottie to the ground as another shot rang out.

Rachel had a moment of searing pain--then nothing as her head made contact with a rock.

*

Running, leaving Rachel behind, had been the hardest thing Wesley had ever done. Hiding in the brush outside the mine, restraining a struggling Bobby Joe, when every fiber of his being wanted to rush inside and rescue Rachel, was the second hardest thing.

Where was Rachel? Was she all right? Wesley fought to keep his mind focused on her rescue—not worry. "Please, God. Keep her safe.'

His heart skipped a beat as a shot rang out. Throwing himself over the boy, he drug Bobby Joe to the ground. He laid there, his body sheltering the boy. Bobby Joe struggled beneath him.

"Stop it," he hissed to the boy. "I'm not going to hurt you. I don't want you to get caught in the cross-fire if shooting starts." Wesley raised his head, his eyes scanning the mine entrance.

Moe and the two men standing guard, bolted. With curses, they disappeared inside.

Wesley glanced at Bill. "Ready?"

"Ready as I'll ever be." The older man tightened his grip on the rifle he carried.

Pulling his gun from his waistband, Wesley took a firm hold on the gagged young man next to him.

Bobby Joe grunted and pulled back.

"What are you fighting for?" Bill gave the boy a shove. "I thought you wanted to go to your dad."

Bobby Joe shook his head, mumbling.

Bill stood, staring down at him. "If you think I'm

going to take that gag off you, you are sadly mistaken. Hold back all you want, but I will *not* make it easier for you to yell for help."

"Come on." Wesley waved them forward, not lessening his grip. He shoved the boy down behind a fallen water trough while he and Bill took up positions on each side of the mine entrance. Bobby Joe crawled into the nearest brush.

Wesley took a step toward him. He changed his mind. The boy was tied and gagged. Where would he go?

He heard Moe yelling and a woman cursing. Sidling up to the entrance, he peered inside. Where was Rachel? He couldn't see her or the kids.

"Where's Dottie?" Bill looked frightened. "I don't see her or the others."

Wesley shrugged. He moved to take a step forward, then froze. He watched in horrified fascination as a heavy-set woman slammed Moe against one of the wooden pillars. She kept her face inches from his while she screamed.

"Go down that shaft and get them!"

"Why? You said you shot her? Why should I take the chance of getting suffocated under tons of rock, just for a dead woman? This mine is unstable. You said so yourself. Now with you shooting...the whole thing could come down on top of my head."

The woman slammed him back again. "Cause I said so. That's why."

Moe bent down and picked up a whiskey bottle. He clutched it to his chest. "Let me have the lantern."

"I'll let you have it." She grabbed the whiskey bottle from Moe's hands and tossed it into the fire. With a cackle, she spun and fled down the mine shaft.

Wesley dove back into the brush, dragging Bill with him as the bottle exploded, sending flames chasing out the entrance of the mine and down the shaft. Wesley listened in dismay as the ground shuddered. With a mighty roar, the earth gave way and the roof of the mine fell.

"Rachel!" Wesley rushed to the entrance, choking on the dust. He held his shirt over his mouth and nose, trying to get closer. He ran the length of the opening, searching for a way inside. The mine was sealed.

He turned to see a stricken Bill standing a few feet from him. The man stood frozen, the rifle forgotten on the ground at his feet.

"Dottie?" the older man whispered.

Wesley took Bill by the shoulders and shook him. "Bill! Listen to me. Is there another way in?"

"What?"

"Another way in." Wesley shook him again. "To the mine. Is there?"

"Yeah. There used to be. I don't know if it's still there. It's on the far side of the mine. About a mile from here."

Wesley clapped him on the shoulder. "Let's go." He turned to get Bobby Joe, and stopped in his tracks.

The boy lay partially buried under debris. The bush he'd chosen to hide behind buried beneath a mound of dirt and rock. A large boulder had struck the

7

boy in the head. Wesley laid a finger on the boy's neck, praying for evidence of life.

"Is he dead?"

Wesley nodded. *Help him, Lord. Have mercy. He's only a boy.*

As he straightened, Wesley turned to see McHale and other officers rushing up the hill toward them.

"What happened?" McHale leaned over, balancing his hands on his knees. He gasped for breath.

Wesley explained about the explosion and cave-in. "Bill told me about another entrance. We've got to go. Rachel and the others may still be alive." *Please, God. Let them be alive. Mabel shot her? Which her? Please, not Rachel. Let me have heard wrong.*

The officer nodded and ordered one of the other officers to care for the dead boy. "We'll take the jeep. It'll be faster." He peered up at the taller man. "I told you to wait, Wesley."

Wesley locked eyes with the officer. "I know. I couldn't."

McHale shook his head. "Let's go."

"I'll drive." Wesley held his hands out for the keys.

Frowning, McHale tossed him the keys and switched directions. He spoke into his walkie-talkie, informing the other officers of where they headed.

Bill sat in the back seat, quietly giving directions.

"She's going to be fine, Bill." Wesley glanced in the rearview mirror. "Dottie's okay."

"I have to believe that."

As they rounded the curve of the mountain, Wesley hit the brakes hard, causing the jeep to skid sideways.

Mel and Dusty ran toward them, waving their arms and yelling. Wesley jumped from the jeep, Bill right behind him.

The two children were covered in dirt, and Mel's shirt was torn down one side, revealing a raw scrape in her skin. Bill gathered them to his chest. "Where's your mother? Your grandmother?"

Tears ran down Mel's cheeks, leaving tracks in the dirt. She gasped, speaking fast. "Mom made us crawl through this hole. It wasn't big enough for them." Sobs shook her body. "That woman shot her, Grandpa! She shot Mom. Dusty and I saw her do it. We saw through the hole." She buried her face in his chest. "Mom pushed Grandma out of the way and got shot."

Dusty sniffed. "That's all we know. Then the rest of the mine came down. We barely got out."

Their grandfather held them at arm's length, smoothing the hair from their faces. "Thank God the two of you are okay."

Wesley took Dusty by the arm. "Are you sure, Dusty? Are you sure your mother was shot?"

"Yes. We saw her." Tears poured down his face.

"Can you take us to the place you escaped from?" His breath caught in his throat. His voice shook. "We need to hurry."

The boy nodded. "Sure. It's not far from here."

Wesley ushered the children into the jeep.

What will I do if Rachel's dead? He shook his head. *I've got to concentrate. Rachel's and Dottie's lives may depend on it.* He took a deep shuddering breath. *She won't be dead. She can't be. I've just found her, Lord. Please don't take her away from me.*

McHale slid behind the wheel. Wesley climbed in front with Bill climbing into the back. The older man sat with his arms around his grandchildren. He held them close and prayed, his voice sending a soothing peace over Wesley's soul.

The short drive to the back entrance of the mine seemed to take hours, when in actuality it took minutes. Wesley leapt from the jeep before McHale brought the rig to a complete stop.

His heart dropped as he ran a few yards into the mine. The shaft was completely blocked. The hole the children escaped from--gone.

"Dottie! Dottie!" Bill sprinted past Wesley and dug at the mound of dirt and rocks with his hands.

Wesley turned, yelling to McHale. "Get help up here! Now! We need men and shovels! Lots of them!"

The officer took one look and turned, running toward the jeep. He returned within moments with a shovel and pickaxe.

Wesley grabbed the tools from his hands and tossed the shovel to Bill. Using all his power, he swung the pick axe. The contact of steel against rock sent shudders up his arms and into his shoulders. He worked to loosen the dirt, while Bill shoveled.

"Stay back," he ordered Dusty and Mel. "It might collapse further. Stay by the jeep."

"I want to help," Dusty begged. "Please."

Wesley glanced over his shoulder. Concern for Rachel caused him to be harsher than he intended. He took a breath to steady himself. "I mean it, Dusty. Take your sister and get out of here."

Mel tugged on Dusty's arm. "Come on. We'll wait for Mom outside."

Sweat poured down Wesley's forehead, burning his eyes and obscuring his vision. He wiped his arm across his face. His eyes met Bill's.

The older man's hands were shaking as he shoveled the dirt. Tears fell from the older man's eyes.

"They're all right, Bill," Wesley told him. "We'll reach them in time. I know it."

Bill nodded and continued to shovel.

Wesley felt like crying himself. His heart kept time with each swing of the axe. *God, please*, he prayed. *I love her. She's the woman I've been looking for my entire life. For the first time in a long time, I feel alive again.*

He choked back his sobs and swung the axe faster.

The dust rose as Bill flung the dirt behind them and soon both men were choking. Dust clogged Wesley's throat. "Get some water, Bill. I'll keep working."

Bill shook his head. "No. You go."

"Grandpa?" Both men turned to see Mel standing in the entrance. "I've brought water."

Wesley gave Bill a sad smile and took a drink from the bottle the girl handed him. God never failed to give them what they needed. *Lord, I need Rachel. Please give her to me*. He handed the water to Bill.

The older man started singing "Amazing Grace" as they shoveled and sobs rose in Wesley's throat.

He glanced behind them. *Where is our help?*

27

Rachel opened her eyes to utter darkness. For a split second, she panicked, thinking she'd gone blind. She tried sitting and fell back with a groan. She'd been shot. The details came rushing back to her.

"Mom?" Rachel's voice felt weak to her ears. She cleared her throat. "Mom!"

She heard movement to her right. "I'm here, Rachel. Thank God you're okay." Dottie took Rachel in her arms, feeling her face with her fingers. "I thought you were dead."

"What happened? Where's Dusty and Mel?"

"They got out." Dottie began to cry. "You saved them, Rachel. You shoved them through that hole, then you saved me." Her mother sniffed, rocking Rachel in her arms. "You pushed me out of the way when Mabel shot."

"Mom, stop. Please." Rachel took a shuddering breath. "You're hurting me." Her head spun and the rocking motion made her nauseous.

Dottie stopped and lowered Rachel's head to her lap. "Where were you shot?"

She felt along her side. "Under my right ribcage. I think the bullet went all the way through. I can't see though. I know my eyes are open, but I can't see anything. Not even shapes."

"That's because it's dark. Real dark." Dottie smoothed Rachel's hair from her face. "I heard an explosion then the roof caved in. We're trapped."

"How long have we been here?"

"I don't know. It seems forever, but it could be only a few hours."

"Are we alone in here?"

"I think so. I haven't heard anything," Rachel felt her mother shiver. "It's so dark, I haven't explored very much. I thought I might have heard a rat a few minutes before you woke up. There was something scratching."

"Help me sit up," Rachel told her. "Then maybe you could crawl around and see if you can find anything to help us."

"Okay." Dottie sounded reluctant. "But you know how I feel about rats."

"I know." Rachel leaned her head back against the dirt wall. *Thank you, Lord that Dusty and Mel got out safely. Please don't have let Wesley, or Dad, have been in this mine when it caved in.* She took a deep breath and held up a hand. The dark was so thick, she couldn't see her hand.

Dottie shrieked.

"What?" Rachel exclaimed. She lifted her head fast enough to make her dizzy.

"I touched something fuzzy."

"Well…what is it?"

"Oh, my." Dottie's words came back as a hoarse whisper. "It's someone's head."

"Is it still attached to the body?"

"Yes. I think it's Mabel."

"Is she dead?"

"I think so. Oh, goody!" Dottie gasped. "I don't mean goody that Mabel's dead."

Rachel laughed at her mother's childish enthusiasm.

"I found a lantern. It still has oil in it." Rachel heard the oil slosh.

"I've got matches in my pocket. I got them from the vacant house." Rachel shifted, digging her hand into her pocket. The effort sent stabs of pain through her, making her gasp.

"Throw them to me."

"Mom."

"Just kidding. I'll come get them." Her mother scuffled across the dirt floor.

Dottie's hand closed over hers and she took the matches. Within seconds, she had the lantern lit. Rachel smiled. *Amazing how just a little light makes things seem better*.

Her mother set the lantern near her. "Let me look at you." She lifted Rachel's shirt, commenting on what she saw.

The bullet had gone through, exiting through the fleshy part of Rachel's back, below her ribcage. The shot had flung Rachel to the ground, landing her on her back. Lying there, Rachel's blood had soaked into the loose dirt. The mud now plastered her shirt to her skin and slowed her bleeding.

"So," Rachel asked. "Will I live?"

Her mother stared into her face. "Yes. But if you start bleeding again…well, Rachel I don't know. We need to get out of here." Dottie stood, holding the lantern high above her head.

Rachel lay still. She was cold and crossed her arms across her chest to help still her shivering. The shaking hurt. *Lord, it never really occurred to me I might not make it out of here.* A tear escaped and rolled down her cheek. *I'm thankful I turned back to you before it was too late. What about Dusty and Mel? Wesley? To find him now and not have the opportunity to love him? That hurts as much as this hole in my side.*

She turned her head and studied the area they were trapped in. Beams lay propped and staggered above them, holding back the earth. The way they'd come was obliterated. A solid wall. The wall behind her, the one Dusty and Mel had escaped through, was also closed off. Rachel sighed. "It doesn't look good, Mom."

"There's always hope as long as a person draws breath." Dottie placed her free hand on her hip. "Your father will find us. He won't give up until he does. Wesley doesn't seem like a quitter either."

Rachel studied her mother. She stood in her housedress and apron, brandishing the lantern like a weapon. Her gray hair hung in strands around her face. Her arms were covered in dirt. To Rachel, she'd never looked more beautiful.

Dottie swung the lanterns light to the opposite side of their cave. She put her hand over to mouth to stifle a scream. Rats crawled over Mabel's body. "Git! Shoo!" She stomped her feet at the rodents.

4

Several rats looked up, their eyes glowing red. Dottie bent and picked up a chunk of wood. Raising her arm over her head, she threw it into the center of the rats, sending them squealing and running for cover.

Bile rose into Rachel's throat and she shivered. She hated rats. "Set the lantern in the center. Hopefully that'll keep the rats away from us."

Dottie shook the lantern. "There's not a lot of oil left, Rachel. What if we set some of this wood on fire?"

Rachel shook her head. "The fire would use up our oxygen."

Dottie set the lantern on the ground. "Then I'd better start digging. Maybe I can at least dig a hole to get air in here."

"What are you going to dig with?'

"My hands. They're the best tool I've got. But, I'm hoping to find a good piece of wood."

Rachel scooted out of her mother's way. "Be careful. I don't know how sturdy this roof is." She sighed and groaned. Taking a deep breath hurt her side. "I wish I could help."

"I'll do what I can. I know your father is looking for us. He'll find us before long." Dottie rolled a boulder to the floor.

Rachel watched as her mother took handful after handful of dirt and tossed it into the corner.

The flame on the lantern flickered. Rachel stared in horror as the flame grew smaller. "The lantern's burning out."

Dottie turned. "I don't want to wait in the dark,

Rachel. Not with those rats."

"I don't either. Let's take the chance with a fire. There's got to be a hole here somewhere. The rats come and go. We just have to find it." *I don't want to die in here. Not in the dark with rats.*

Dottie set to work piling small pieces of wood in the center of the floor. She poured what little oil remained in the lamp over the kindling and struck a match. The flame started small and grew larger. Dottie sat back on her haunches. "Well, we've got fire." She looked at Rachel. "How are you feeling?"

"Fine. A little warm, but okay. I think I'm getting a fever" Rachel closed her eyes. "Rest, Mom. That wall isn't going anywhere."

Dottie sighed. "I'm not making much progress, am I?"

Keeping her eyes closed, Rachel shrugged. "We'll just have to wait."

*

The men McHale contacted arrived to help Wesley and took over the digging. The officer ordered Wesley and Bill to take a break back at the jeep. Wesley shook his head.

McHale stood firm. "Those two children need to know things are going to be okay." He held up a hand when Bill opened his mouth to speak. "I mean it. Take thirty minutes. Have some lunch and reassure your grandchildren. There's three men in there digging. They can handle it."

"Five men can dig faster."

"Wesley," McHale warned. "I will arrest you for

obstruction of justice if you don't follow my orders. There's coffee and sandwiches at the jeep." With those words, he took the shovel from Bill's hand and the axe from Wesley's. "See you two in thirty minutes."

Wesley clenched his fists at his side. He shrugged off the hand Bill put on his shoulder. He took a step toward McHale, who turned back to face him. At the challenging look on the officer's face, Wesley spun on his heel and stalked outside.

He placed a hand against the mine entrance and leaned against it, his head hanging. Wesley hadn't let anger overtake him to the point of violence since his military days. It scared him. The arm holding him up shook. Sobs wracked his body as he stood there.

Bill stood next to him and laid an arm around the younger man's shoulder. "Don't lose faith, Wesley."

Wesley wiped his forearm across his face. "I should be in there digging for her, Bill. Not taking a break like some weak fool."

"You aren't weak. You're an incredibly strong man. McHale's right. You need rest. I'm surprised you've gone this long, with healing ribs and a broken wrist." Bill hesitated. "The children are watching. Stand up."

Wesley squared his shoulders and turned. Mel and Dusty stood with their arms around each other. The fear on their faces wrenched his heart.

"You found her." Mel stated without expression. "She's dead." Tears rolled down her face.

Wesley held out his arms and the girl launched herself into them. "No, we didn't find her."

"Then why are you crying?" Dusty wanted to know. Bill gathered his grandson close to him.

"I just had a weak moment. I'm fine now." He looked at Bill. "There's food waiting for us."

Wesley took the coffee and sandwich the officer handed him and glanced at his watch. He would eat, but not for a minute longer than the thirty McHale told him to take. He might be selfish, but he wanted to be the one to find Rachel. He wanted to be the one to carry her out of the mine. He wadded up the wrapper from the sandwich and threw it into the back of the jeep. He guzzled down the last of his coffee, and stood. A bark drew his attention.

Mutt ran to them, tail wagging. Burrs and twigs stuck up from his hair.

"Mutt!" Dusty grabbed Mutt and buried his face in the dog's fur. His eyes shone with tears when he looked up at Wesley. "Mutt can help you dig."

Wesley held out his arms and the boy handed him the dog, stepping back. "Mutt will find Mom. He can sniff her out."

"I'm going back," Wesley stated. Bill nodded and shoved the last bite of his sandwich into his mouth.

The older man looked at his grandchildren. "You go ahead, Wesley. I'm going to stay here a while longer." Mel smiled.

"I'll bring her back," Wesley promised. "I'll bring Dottie to you."

Nodding, his eyes shining with unshed tears, Bill answered, "I know you will."

McHale handed the axe back to Wesley on his

return. "We've made some progress," he told him. "The only thing is, we don't know how thick is this barricade. We could be almost there, or we could be feet away. There could be no room at all. You know this, don't you?"

Wesley nodded, his eyes intent on the officer's face. "I know. But I choose to believe they're not buried."

"You have to prepare for..."

He whirled and shouted. "They're not dead! Stop saying that!"

McHale's face set in hard lines. "Wesley Ward. You're an ex-Green Beret. You know what the odds are." The officer sighed. "I'm not asking you to give up. Just to be prepared."

Wesley turned and swung the axe. "I know, McHale. Would you behave differently if things were reversed? If the woman you loved was behind that mound of dirt?"

McHale shook his head and turned, heading back to the jeep.

Since he'd received his salvation two years before, Wesley'd never had his faith tested to this extreme. He was faltering and knew it. *To be honest, it's the faltering faith making me angry.*

The axe struck rock, sending shock vibrations up his arms and into his shoulders.

Mutt ran back and forth along the barrier, sniffing. At one point, he quit and began digging. One of the workers set his shovel in the dirt next to Mutt and heaved away great shovels full of dirt.

"I think I'm through," someone shouted. Mutt barked.

Wesley spun around as a woman's scream echoed through the mine.

"Rachel!" he cried.

*

Rachel woke to see Dottie leaning against the wall of the cave, her mouth open in sleep. Her body hurt and the wound burned. Rachel licked her dry lips. "I'm so thirsty," she whispered.

The fire burned down, its glow not quite reaching all four walls. Rachel stretched her hand until she grabbed some of the smaller pieces of fallen timber. She tossed them onto the fire, sending sparks like fireflies into the darkness above her.

Movement across from her drew her attention. She heard a muffled curse, a squeal and a soft thud. Peering through the gloom, Rachel could make out Mabel's form rising from the ground. Rats fell or were plucked and thrown off her. Rachel stared in disbelief.

"I thought maybe she was dead after all," Dottie whispered, her voice hoarse with horror. "Save us, God. She's a demon."

"Apparently she wasn't dead." Rachel's eyes widened more as Mabel advanced upon them and she scooted closer against the dirt and rock behind her.

The explosion had burned the flesh black on the right side of Mabel's body. Her hair was singed and missing in places, leaving raw red pieces of scalp showing. The dress the woman wore was melted to half of her body, torn and stained with blood on the other half.

Mabel picked up a small log and advanced toward Rachel and Dottie, the left side of her mouth drawn up into a grimace.

Rachel screamed, still not able to accept what was walking toward her.

Her mother crawled to put herself in front of her daughter and stood in defiance and protectiveness.

"Rachel!"

"Wesley?!" Rachel whipped her head around, searching. "Where are you?"

"We're coming through."

She located his hand poking through a hole several feet down from her. "Hurry, Wesley. She's coming!"

Mabel came slowly, dragging a leg behind her.

Dottie picked up the empty lantern and threw it. It struck Mabel in the forehead, causing her to stumble. Dottie looked around them and found another log. She yelled to Wesley. "Better dig faster, son! This woman is big, mean and nasty. And she looks really mad."

Rachel felt she was in the middle of a nightmare. The fact Mabel was alive and walking was too unbelievable. She closed her eyes and opened them again. The woman still advanced toward her.

Using the rock wall to support her, Rachel struggled to her feet. "What do you want?"

"To kill you."

"Why? Why is it so important to you that I'm dead?"

Mabel raised her arm. "Because of you, my entire family is gone. Buried beneath this mountain. You should be to."

Dottie gagged, holding her apron over her nose. The smell of burnt flesh overpowered her and Rachel breathed through her mouth.

"They're almost through," Dottie told her.

Rachel looked to see the hole widened. *I've got to stall her. Just a few more minutes.*

Mabel's arm rose higher and gunshots rang out.

Rachel watched in horrified fascination as the woman seemed to dance, twisting and turning with each shot that pounded into her body.

When she finally fell, Rachel allowed herself to slide to the floor.

"Rachel. Rachel. Look at me." She glanced wearily to where Wesley's head, shoulders and one arm hung through the hole. In his hand, he brandished a pistol. "Just a few minutes more, Baby. Just a few minutes more."

She nodded and closed her eyes.

"Rachel, keep watching me."

She opened her eyes.

Wesley squirmed through the hole, landing on the ground with a muffled thud. He ordered the others to continue digging and rushed to Rachel's side. Pulling her into his arms, he covered her face with kisses. "I was so afraid. So afraid."

Dottie knelt next to him. "She's been shot. The mud stopped the bleeding, but she needs to get out of here." She glanced back. "Where's Bill?"

"He stayed with the children."

Dottie nodded. "That's good. I'm sure they're frightened."

Wesley placed Rachel back on the ground and lifted her shirt. The area around the wound was clear. No pus or drainage. No spreading red lines. *Thank you, God*. He felt the pulse in her neck. Low, but steady. He smiled up at Dottie. "She's going to be fine."

McHale appeared at his side. "Let me have her." He held out his arms. "Just until you get through the hole. I'll give her back."

Wesley handed her to the other man, his eyes not leaving her face. He crawled through the hole and held his arms out for Rachel.

He held her close to his chest. Rachel murmured and nestled her head into the hollow of his shoulder.

As he exited the mine with Rachel in his arms, Mel and Dusty broke into tears. Mel collapsed to her knees and buried her face in her hands. Dusty grabbed Wesley's arm.

"Is she dead?" His voice broke.

"Dottie!" Bill gathered his wife into his arms. He pulled his wife to him in a fierce hug. "Oh, Dottie. I thought I'd lost you."

Dottie caressed his face. "It'll take more than a maniac to separate us," she told him. "We battle not against powers of this earth. Only God could separate my love from you." She stood on tiptoe and kissed him.

Wesley looked down into Dusty's face. "She's not dead. Just sleeping."

Two men in black suits rushed into the mine. One of them removed his sunglasses. "FBI." He flashed a badge. "Who's in charge here?"

Dottie glanced at McHale, who shrugged, and laughed.

Tightening his grip around Rachel, Wesley stalked past the agents, the others following him. "About time," he muttered.

Rachel's eyelids fluttered.

"Mom?"

"I'm fine, Dusty."

They all turned to Rachel. She smiled at her parents and each of her children, then lifted her face to gaze into Wesley's eyes. She wrapped her arms around his neck. "I've never been better."

The End

ABOUT THE AUTHOR

Multi-published and Best-Selling author Cynthia Hickey had three cozy mysteries and two novellas published through Barbour Publishing. Her first mystery, Fudge-Laced Felonies, won first place in the inspirational category of the Great Expectations contest in 2007. Her third cozy, Chocolate-Covered Crime, received a four-star review from Romantic Times. All three cozies have been re-released as ebooks through the MacGregor Literary Agency, along with a new cozy series, all of which stay in the top 50 of Amazon's ebooks for their genre. She has several historical romances releasing in 2013 and 2014 through Harlequin's Heartsong Presents. She is active on FB, twitter, and Goodreads. She lives in Arizona with her husband, one of their seven children, two dogs and two cats. She has five grandchildren who keep her busy and tell everyone they know that "Nana is a writer". Visit her website at www.cynthiahickey.com

Made in the USA
Lexington, KY
26 October 2014